Praise for Debra Webb

Deeper Than the Dead

"Expertly plotted and whip smart, *Deeper Than the Dead* is an exceedingly clever crime thriller filled with secrets, betrayals, and complex characters. Webb manages to hit that sweet spot between family drama and police procedural. This one is sure to be a hit in the crime-thriller genre. A wild and massively entertaining ride."

—Christina McDonald, *USA Today* bestselling author

The Last Lie Told

"A complex case fraught with angst and danger ends with surprising revelations."

—*Kirkus Reviews*

"Debra Webb writes the kind of thrillers I love to read. Sure, there is a murder or more. Yes, there's a twisted mystery to be solved. Once again, in *The Last Lie Told*, her characters are fully rendered and reveal themselves authentically as her novel unfolds and careens to its stunning conclusion. *The Last Lie Told* is her best yet. Webb is the queen of smart suspense."

—Gregg Olsen, #1 *New York Times* bestselling author

Can't Go Back

"A complex, exciting mystery."

—*Kirkus Reviews*

"Police procedural fans will be sorry to see the last of Kerri and Luke."

—*Publishers Weekly*

"Threats, violence, and a dramatic climax . . . good for procedural readers."

—*Library Journal*

Gone Too Far

"An intriguing, fast-paced combination of police procedural and thriller."

—*Kirkus Reviews*

"Those who like a lot of family drama in their police procedurals will be satisfied."

—*Publishers Weekly*

Trust No One

"*Trust No One* is Debra Webb at her finest. Political intrigue and dark family secrets will keep readers feverishly turning pages to uncover all the twists in this stunning thriller."

—Melinda Leigh, #1 *Wall Street Journal* bestselling author of *Cross Her Heart*

"A wild, twisting crime thriller filled with secrets, betrayals, and complex characters that will keep you up until you reach the last darkly satisfying page. A five-star beginning to Debra Webb's explosive series!"

—Allison Brennan, *New York Times* bestselling author

"Debra Webb once again delivers with *Trust No One*, a twisty and gritty page-turning procedural with a cast of complex characters and a compelling cop heroine in Detective Kerri Devlin. I look forward to seeing more of Detectives Devlin and Falco."

—Loreth Anne White, *Washington Post* bestselling author of *In the Deep*

"*Trust No One* is a gritty and exciting ride. Webb skillfully weaves together a mystery filled with twists and turns. I was riveted as each layer of the past peeled away, revealing dark secrets. An intriguing cast of complicated characters, led by the compelling Detective Kerri Devlin, had me holding my breath until the last page."

—Brianna Labuskes, *Washington Post* bestselling author of *Girls of Glass*

"Debra Webb's name says it all."

—Karen Rose, *New York Times* bestselling author

SECRETS YOU CAN'T KEEP

OTHER TITLES BY DEBRA WEBB

Vera Boyett

Deeper Than the Dead

Closer Than You Know

Finley O'Sullivan

The Last Lie Told

The Nature of Secrets

All the Little Truths

Devlin & Falco

Trust No One

Gone Too Far

Can't Go Back

SECRETS YOU CAN'T KEEP

DEBRA WEBB

Published by Thomas & Mercer, Seattle

www.apub.com

EU product safety contact:
Amazon Media EU S. à r.l.
38, avenue John F. Kennedy, L-1855 Luxembourg
amazonpublishing-gpsr@amazon.com

ISBN-13: 9781662533556 (paperback)
ISBN-13: 9781662533549 (digital)

Cover design by Shasti O'Leary Soudant
Cover image: © Magdalena Wasiczek / ArcAngel Images

Printed in the United States of America

To all my sweet grandchildren, who make life extra special!

Three may keep a secret, if two of them are dead.
—Benjamin Franklin, *Poor Richard's Almanack*

1

Tuesday, September 2
Wilton Residence
Giles Hollow Road
Fayetteville, Tennessee, 9:15 a.m.

Valeri Erwin waited on the broad, two-story porch, the doorbell she'd rung for the third time still echoing through the house. She checked her cell again. It was well past nine. Where was everyone?

She walked to the west end of the porch and glanced at the detached garage. All four doors were closed. At least one would be open if there was no one home.

Strange.

With a big breath, she walked back to the door and decided to use her key. Though she had been the owner's personal assistant for many years, she still wasn't a fan of entering the house like this. Not since Alicia, the second wife, came along, anyway. Generally if the door was locked, the housekeeper hurried to greet Valeri—overly apologetic for having forgotten to unlock it in anticipation of her arrival. The twenty-thousand-square-foot mansion sat on hundreds of acres, every inch of which was security fenced with only one entrance, which was gated and required an access code. There were cameras and all manner of security equipment at the gate and around the main house. Not to mention there were guns. Guns the owner and most members of staff knew how to use. It wasn't like there was a safety issue. And still this happened on occasion.

Valeri heaved a sigh of impatience, but then she remembered the household staff had taken the rest of this week off. With the summer events over now that Labor Day had come and gone, all but Valeri were taking much-needed vacations.

She never took days off, much less vacations. Whatever would Thomas do without her?

The instant she unlocked the door and opened it, the alarm warned she had only a set number of seconds to disarm it. Frowning, she hurried to the keypad and entered the code. The heels of her shoes clicked on the shiny marble floor.

Was no one out of bed yet?

Unlikely.

Obviously there was no one at all here. Either that, or Thomas and Alicia were still in bed with massive hangovers from their weekend party.

This time Valeri practically gagged. *Not nice, Val.* But the truth was, Thomas Wilton was a very good man. This latest fiasco of a marriage (only six months old at this point) had turned him into an absentminded party boy, as if he were still in college rather than barreling toward fifty. Men could be so stupid—even one as utterly brilliant as Thomas Wilton.

Breathe. Be patient. You were here long before her, you'll be here long after she's gone.

After a walk-through of the first floor, Valeri had no choice but to go upstairs. The idea of finding her employer and Alicia in bed was less than appealing, but what else could she do? Thomas had a very important Zoom meeting in just over half an hour. There was no time to wait and see if he'd stumble out of bed on his own. Besides, after five years working for him, she shouldn't have been embarrassed by anything at all. She had seen him naked during his grief period after his first wife's death two years ago. She had celebrated with him when his professional life hit new, unparalleled heights just last year. She knew this man inside out. As for Alicia, the entire staff knew most every part of her—at least on the outside. She drifted around the house and the pool mostly naked much of the time. The woman lacked anything even remotely resembling modesty or manners.

Frustrated and a little angry now, Valeri tromped up the elegant staircase that wound above the grand entry hall. Who needed a house this huge? Only an eccentric billionaire who'd created and subsequently sold to the US government the most significant air defense system the world had ever seen. No wonder he'd retired eight years ago at forty-one. He had more money than he could spend in a couple of hundred lifetimes, and still it poured in. That was the other thing happening later this fall—the boss's fiftieth birthday.

Alicia would expect Valeri to plan and orchestrate every detail while she took the credit.

Valeri paused at the double doors that led into the primary suite. Deep breath. She gave a firm knock, then opened the doors without waiting for a response. The expansive, luxuriously decorated and furnished room was . . . *vacant*. Her anticipation seeped out of her like the air from a punctured balloon.

"What the devil is going on?" Valeri grumbled.

She left the room, putting through a call to Thomas's cell once more as she moved from room to room over the entire floor and found no one. The call went to voicemail. This was beyond ridiculous. Time was running out. Her frustration and anger funneled into urgency.

Downstairs, she hurried out the back door and to where the utility terrain vehicles were stored. Sure enough, the one Thomas used was not there. The two had to be at the cabin still. He'd said that he and Alicia would be spending the weekend there. Which meant—Valeri smirked as she climbed into a UTV—they planned to drink excessively and party wildly. Thomas always went to the cabin he'd had built deep in the woods on his five-hundred-acre property to be a bad boy. Not that he had done so often. Not since emerging from the grief period, anyway.

Valeri shook her head, her fingers tightening on the steering wheel as she navigated her way through the woods. No matter that the leaves hadn't actually started to turn and the temps were still hovering in the nineties on most days, a hint of fall was already in the air.

The drive to the cabin was a good fifteen minutes along narrow trails that cut through the thick woods. The fact that this land was untouched—never cleared, farmed, or used for pasture—was one of the reasons Thomas had chosen it eight years ago when he returned to Tennessee—after showing them how it was done in DC, he always said. The privacy this property allowed while only a fairly short drive from town was exactly what he'd wanted.

A glimpse of the cabin came into view, and Valeri braced for what was coming. Thomas was a consummate businessman. He could not tolerate incompetence or tardiness. She couldn't help thinking that perhaps something had happened to cause him to be running behind this morning. But then why hadn't he called her to reschedule his meeting? Or answered her calls?

Valeri's nerves were jangling by the time she parked next to Thomas's UTV and climbed out. It was possible he and Alicia had fought. Alicia was untrustworthy, in Valeri's opinion. When he realized exactly what she'd been up to, he would send her packing. But Valeri wasn't going to be the one to tell him—though she did drop hints. He would find out soon enough. Alicia wouldn't be able to cover her tracks for long.

Maybe Alicia's time had run out this very weekend.

The happy thought dissolved as she climbed out of the UTV. It was way too quiet. She shivered as she made her way along the rock path to the wraparound deck that skirted the enormous cabin.

As Valeri took the steps, she noticed that the front door stood slightly ajar . . . only five or six inches, but the sight sent fear prickling down the back of her neck. Thomas was generally very careful about security out here. No matter that the entire property was fenced and gated, with lots of security measures, there were no cameras in this section.

Valeri started to call out to him, but something—some guttural instinct—held her mute. She eased across the porch. Her right hand came to rest on the rough-hewn door, and she paused. A sound . . . heavy breathing and a lapping sound whispered across her senses. Oh God. Were they . . . having sex or . . . ?

Holding her breath, she pushed the door inward. The first thing she saw was a coyote standing next to the sofa. Its predatory gaze locked with hers. There was something . . . red maybe . . . on the fur around its mouth.

It moved. A sudden lunge of scraggly fur. Valeri fell back two steps, and the animal rushed past her, instantly disappearing into the woods.

"Oh my God." She pressed a hand to her chest, fought to slow her racing heart. She shook herself. "Okay, that was bizarre." She steadied herself and grabbed back her courage, then she stepped forward once more, pushed fully beyond the door.

The place smelled of . . . coppery metal and something . . . something that made her stomach twist. She moved deeper into the large room, around the end of the sofa where the coyote had been standing, and that was when she saw the body.

A scream slipped past her lips. Her heart shot into her throat.

Naked, lying face down on the floor next to the sofa. *Male,* she thought. A wail bloomed in her chest. But the hair was wrong, and there was no tattoo. *Not Thomas.* Relief allowed her to breathe once more. The man's right arm was mangled. She realized this was what she'd heard. The coyote had been licking and gnawing on the man's arm. What the hell had happened here?

"Thomas!"

The name burst from her trembling lips, the sound weak and shaky. Valeri's gaze stumbled onto bloody footprints. Careful not to step in the blood, Valeri followed those prints into the kitchen area, where more blood was pooled and splattered around a woman—brown hair, young, maybe mid- to late twenties. She lay naked on the clay-tile floor, her sightless gaze fixed on the ceiling. *Not Alicia.* Regret momentarily flowed through Valeri.

Dead . . . these people were *dead.*

"Thomas?" Oh God! Valeri started to run. She checked the small office and powder room, then rushed upstairs. Every room was empty.

Where the hell was Thomas?

She hurried back downstairs and across the great room to the French doors leading onto the rear deck. Her lungs gasped for air untainted by the smell of death. That was when she saw him. In the hot tub. Floating face down in a pool of bloody water. It was him . . . She recognized the phoenix tattoo across his shoulder blades.

Valeri's knees nearly buckled. She steadied herself and stumbled to him. Her heart thudded so hard, she couldn't catch her breath . . . She wanted to scream but couldn't. She tugged at his body to lift him from the water, but he was so heavy, and it was too late. Thomas was dead.

Fury blasted through her, chasing away the other feelings. What the hell had happened here? And where the hell was that parasitic bitch, Alicia?

Then she spotted her. Her naked body draped along the stairs leading down to the grassy area between the cabin and the dense woods. She was dead too.

Valeri looked away, her gaze settling once more on the hot tub and her beloved boss. A howl of agony swelled in her throat.

Tears spilled from her eyes. How on earth had this happened?

She dropped to her knees. Thomas was dead. The misery pushed its way from her throat with a fierceness that stole every ounce of strength from her body.

Dear God, what was she supposed to do now? For long minutes she sobbed like a child. Her heart threatened to burst . . . her stomach heaved. Her dream . . . all she had worked for . . . it was gone.

When she could manage, she swiped at her cheeks, attempted to calm herself without much success. *Focus.* She had to call someone. She needed help. The police. She should call the police. Of course. Yes. She nodded frantically, the movement somehow prompting her to search her pockets for her cell. The police . . . She needed the police because . . .

They were all dead. She looked around. *Murdered.*

2

Wilton Cabin
Giles Hollow Road, 10:30 a.m.

"Sheriff, please. I need to leave."

Sheriff Gray Benton, Bent to his friends, turned toward the office doorway where Valeri Erwin stood. She stared at him, her face pale, dark eyes pleading for the requested reprieve. As soon as he'd arrived, he'd sequestered her to the small office—the one downstairs room in the cabin that appeared untouched—and had a quick look around before making the necessary calls. Then he'd asked her a few preliminary questions, but there was a hell of a lot more he needed to know. Whatever had happened here, this was one hell of a clusterfuck.

Erwin shook her head, more tears streaming down her cheeks. Her body rocked with sobs. "I . . . I . . . please, just let me get out of here. I can't bear it any longer."

"The medical examiner is on the way, and there's not a whole lot we can do until she does her thing. I have more questions." He understood how difficult this was, but it was necessary. "Unfortunately those questions are best asked after I have the preliminary information only the ME can provide."

Erwin wanted to get as far away from the scene as possible. She was clearly devastated by her boss's death. There were four dead—all homicides—and the whole place smelled of coagulating blood, stale cigarettes, and booze. Whatever went down here, it was preceded by one hell of a rowdy party. Not exactly the norm for the address.

Thomas Wilton, the property owner, was face down in the hot tub. His wife lay on the steps a few yards away. There was an unidentified male on the floor not much more than twenty feet from where Bent stood right now. Along with an unidentified female, naked and also deceased, on the other side of the room, lying on the floor in front of the fridge. In addition to all the blood and booze, there was evidence of drug use. This was a total shit show, and he needed to somehow piece together what the hell had happened. Sadly there wasn't another soul around anywhere on the property . . . except Valeri Erwin, who'd only arrived at this cabin just under an hour ago.

She scrubbed at her face. "Can I at least sit on the porch." She shuddered. "The smell in here is . . ." Another shiver shook her small frame. Barely over five feet tall and maybe a hundred pounds, she looked like a kid, with her dark hair hanging like a curtain around her face.

Bent nodded. "The porch is fine, but do not leave. Got it?"

Her arms wrapped tightly around her, she nodded her understanding. "Got it."

He watched her exit the front door and confirmed that she'd settled into a rocking chair. She dropped her head into her hands and, judging by the way her shoulders shook, started to cry again. Bent didn't really know the woman, but he was aware that she worked for Thomas Wilton. He'd seen her around town now and then. Her name had come up as a witness to a disagreement between two tenants in the rental on the corner of Washington and Franklin. She lived there as well. The last he'd heard, Wilton had bought the place for her so she could kick out the offending tenants.

Bent hadn't read too much into it at the time. Good help was hard to find, and the guy was rich. Or maybe there was something more going on between the boss and his assistant. Hadn't really mattered until now.

Now everything mattered.

He removed his hat and plowed his fingers through his hair as he gazed across the massive living space of what had to be the biggest damned cabin he'd ever seen. Now he had four dead, including the owner, and the owner's personal assistant was the one to find them. He glanced out the window at her once more, settled his hat back into place. If he was lucky, Erwin would have some idea of how this began. These kinds of murders didn't just happen. There would be some sort of buildup, however seemingly insignificant, and then a trigger point.

No indications of a burglary. The door was unlocked and ajar when she arrived, according to Erwin. She swore she didn't touch one thing other than the door and Wilton's head and left arm. At first she'd been so stunned by the coyote and all the bodies and blood, the reality that everyone was dead hadn't sunk in. She had tried to lift Wilton from the water, but then she'd realized it was too late. Most anyone stumbling into a scene like this would have reacted the same.

Bent braced his hands on his hips and surveyed the room at large once more. Upon first look it appeared the party had taken a bad turn. Victim number one, the unidentified male on the floor near the couch, had been stabbed multiple times. Defense wounds on the right arm and left hand. According to Erwin, the coyote had been inside when she arrived, which explained the additional damage to the vic's injured arm.

Bloody footprints, from bare feet, led from the dead man to victim two, the unidentified female, on the floor near the fridge, who had been stabbed as well. Two wounds in the abdomen, one nick in the neck, which, judging by the amount of blood spewed onto the refrigerator and the floor, most likely penetrated the artery just enough to make one hell of a mess.

Those same footprints made a path to the set of French doors that led to the rear deck. Outside, victim three, the owner of the property, Thomas Wilton, floated in the hot tub. His wounds appeared far more defensive in nature. From what Bent could see without removing the body from the water—which he could not do until the ME had a look—there was one stab wound in the middle of his back as well as random injuries scattered over his arms. There were probably others Bent could not see right now. Wilton didn't appear the type to go down easy.

Victim four, the wife, had fallen face down on the steps of the deck, hitting her head. The reddish stains on her bare feet as well as the size told him the tracks in the blood were hers. No visible knife wounds like the others. Odd considering the consistent MO up until that point. Based on the positioning of her body, she was obviously attempting to flee the danger. She was the only one whose body had not gone into full rigor, which suggested the head injury had not been immediately fatal. The fact that her head was turned to the right, showing off the damage to her forehead, also indicated she had survived long enough to at least move her head.

The question was, Did she just happen upon the victims and their killer, or was she the one wielding the knife and fell when she ran? So far there was no sign of a knife or any other weapon. Could be in the hot tub with Wilton.

Bent estimated the attack had occurred late Monday evening, maybe fifteen or so hours ago. The murder weapon for three of the vics appeared to be a knife from the block on the kitchen counter. The perp may have disposed of the knife or taken it with them. Two deputies would be searching the cabin and grounds around it. It hadn't rained for days, so there was little chance of finding tire or footprints.

The fact that all involved in the deadly event were naked suggested a sex party. Bent had spotted residue that he suspected was cocaine, as well as a bowl containing weed and rolling paper. There was no shortage of alcohol. With all the bowls of snacks and charcuterie offerings scattered over tables and counters, it was a miracle there hadn't been more scavengers inside when Erwin arrived.

Wilton had no criminal record or even a parking ticket, for that matter. There had never been a call about trouble at his property. But the man had a lot of wooded acres around him and no close neighbors, so any past disturbances may have gone unnoticed.

Bent surveyed the large great room once more, his attention resting lastly on Erwin beyond the front window. She had been employed by Wilton for long enough to know the man's more personal history. Bent had a good many more questions for her.

"Sheriff!" Deputy Olson shouted.

Bent turned and started toward the wide-open French doors on the far side of the large room. "You done?" he called back to the deputy videoing the exterior part of the crime scene.

"You need to come out here, Sheriff."

He hoped another vic hadn't been discovered. Four was more than enough. Deputy Will Conover and his forensic team, meaning Conover and one other deputy, were headed this way, but Bent had wanted a video done before any intrusion. A thorough search inside and out wouldn't be started until the video was completed.

Crouched next to the female victim on the steps, Olson glanced up as Bent approached. "I'm done, yeah. But while I had the camera focused on her"—he stared down at the woman again—"I thought I saw her chest rise ever so slightly." He nodded to Alicia Wilton. "It's hard to catch, but I'm pretty sure she's still breathing. Pulse is even harder to find, but I think I felt it."

Bent got down on one knee next to Alicia Wilton. "You sure?"

Olson nodded. "Think so." He shook his head then. "I swear she wasn't breathing, and there was no pulse the first time I checked."

Bent checked her carotid pulse. Damned faint . . . almost imperceptible. But it was there. Anticipation seared through him. "Get a paramedic here ASAP."

"Calling now," Olson said.

Bent would like to move her off the steps. She couldn't be comfortable, but he didn't dare. There might be injuries he couldn't see. There was no blood or visible damage anywhere but to her forehead. Still, that didn't mean something inside wasn't broken or damaged in some way, and since she was in no imminent danger right where she lay, he opted not to take the risk. But he could get something to cover her body.

"Hastings," Bent called out. He watched Alicia Wilton's body, saw a slight tremor. She was definitely alive, but not by much.

Deputy Shana Hastings, who, like several others, stood by to begin the search, appeared at his side. "Yes, sir?"

"Check for a linen closet, and find a clean sheet or blanket to cover Mrs. Wilton."

"Will do, Sheriff."

Bent's attention rested on the woman in front of him once more. If she survived, he had a witness. That would damned sure make his life a hell of a lot easier. He glanced toward those open French doors just as Deputies Conover and Shepherd came through the front door.

Where the hell was that medical examiner? She was a doctor; she could help Alicia Wilton until the paramedics arrived.

Hastings returned with a sheet, and they draped it over the woman's body. "Find out what's keeping the ME and how far out EMS is."

Hastings made the calls.

One thing was certain: Bent wanted Vee on this one. Vera Boyett was the best when it came to reading a scene. And if his one barely alive victim survived, Vee would know how to question her to get the full story. Bent counted on Vee as the department's own personal profiler. The woman was that good. A smile tugged at his lips. Her coming back last year was the best thing that had happened to him since he was just a kid. He surveyed the carnage around him. Other than the rare situation like this one, his life was pretty damned perfect now.

Dr. Jenny Collins burst through the front door. "Sheriff!"

"Out here," he called back. From the deck he had a clear view through those French doors all the way to the front. He watched the ME's progress as she noted each body she encountered. A pause at the hot tub and then she made her way to where he waited.

Collins frowned. "You have a live one?"

"We didn't think so at first," he admitted. "Her pulse is faint, but it's there."

"EMS is five minutes out," Hastings said as she tucked her cell away.

Bent sent her a nod and turned his attention back to the ME.

"Let me have a look." Collins got down on one knee on the other side of the victim.

"This is the property owner's wife, Alicia Wilton," Bent explained. "Husband's the one in the hot tub."

Collins leaned down and checked the right eye for a reaction to light. "Well"—she sat back—"my specialty is the dead, but I'll do what I can until someone else gets here to take over."

"Thanks." Bent stood and headed back into the house. He greatly appreciated anything Collins could do for the sole survivor of this nightmare. His attention shifted back to finding and collecting evidence. That was the one thing he could do for all the victims.

"Sheriff!"

He turned back to the ME with a questioning look.

"I think you might be looking for this."

He moved back to where Collins knelt next to Alicia Wilton. Collins pointed to a large, bloody, stainless steel knife lying on the step next to Wilton.

"It was under her."

Bent shouted for Conover, then turned back to the ME. "Looks like you found our murder weapon."

3

Boyett Farm
Good Hollow Road, 11:00 a.m.

Vera Boyett tapped the necessary key to send the email. She pushed back her chair and stood, then stretched. She'd been at this for hours, and her body felt stiff. More coffee and a long walk were what she needed now.

Like that was going to happen. She'd finished the report on her findings for the Moore County Sheriff's Office. But she had an additional one to finish up for Franklin County. With another elongating stretch, she padded out of the library that had been her mother's favorite room in this big old farmhouse. Vera had decided the room would be her office. She liked the windows that looked out over the front lawn, where the many shrubs and flower beds her mother had planted decades ago still bloomed in their season. A set of French doors allowed her to shut herself away from the rest of the house.

She grunted at the idea of just how unnecessary that was these days. There wasn't anyone to shut herself away from, unless she counted Bent. A smile tugged at her lips. And he was rarely here in the daytime. Both her sisters, Eve and Luna, were living with their respective partners. Luna and Jerome had gotten married back in January, built their new home and were expecting their first child in a mere six weeks. The idea that Vera was going to be an aunt still made her feel a little giddy. She wasn't at all sure what the position entailed, but she was up for whatever Luna and that baby needed.

She walked into the kitchen and studied the leftover coffee in the pot. She made a face and decided to brew more. Her single-serve coffee maker had died, and she had opted to go back with a plain, old-fashioned brew type. At moments like this she regretted that decision. It would be so easy to pop a pod in and prepare just one cup.

She rinsed the carafe and added enough water for two cups. The mug Bent had used this morning sat on the counter. She smiled. Though he didn't stay here every night—he had his own place and the horses to see after—he stayed often. Sometimes she stayed with him at his place. At some point they were going to have to figure out the details of their relationship, like where they were going to live—*if* they were going to live together—but there was no hurry. Why change a routine that was working just fine?

After pouring the water into the reservoir and preparing the basket, she set the machine to brew. Deciding to make Fayetteville her home again had been a big decision. One she did not regret in any way. Not one little bit did she miss the busy streets of Memphis. Or the insanity of the caseload as deputy chief of Special Operations with the department there. Nope. Not at all. Her sisters were here. They were settled and happy, and Vera wanted the same. Maybe relationship decisions were harder to make when you were older. She was forty now. However difficult to take such a scary leap, the time had come, and she recognized it. Or maybe she just didn't want to be the only Boyett sister who wasn't in a committed relationship.

Vera was ready for her life to be a bit more settled now and moving forward. The time felt right. Basically the only real question that remained was the choice as to where they were going from here. The house hopping wasn't something she wanted to do forever, but it was not such a big deal.

Or perhaps she was in a bigger hurry than she realized to settle into something permanent beyond what roof was over her head. Eric Jones, her dear friend and former colleague back in Memphis, had gotten married. In truth the run-in with the serial killer known as the Messenger last spring had put her in a bit of a tailspin emotionally. She supposed a near-death experience could do that sort of thing.

Her cell sounded off before she could go any further down that path or fill her mug. She retraced her steps back to her office and picked up her cell. *Luna.* Vera's first thought was that maybe she had gone into labor, but it was too early for that, wasn't it? Her sister had more than a month to go. But things happened. Babies came early all the time, she reminded herself.

Worry twisted through her as she accepted the call. "Hey, Luna. Everything okay?"

If she was completely honest with herself, worry was her first reaction to a ringing phone or an unexpected knock on the door these days. It was the curse of the Boyett sisters. Every unexpected call came with loads of troubling scenarios attached. After what the three of them had been through, it was actually a miracle total panic attacks didn't accompany every single unexpected event. Vera reminded herself to breathe. It was just a phone call, not a disaster notification.

Probably. Maybe.

"Vee, you have to come to my house right now."

Okay, so this could very well be in the ballpark of a disaster. On the bright side, hopefully not a catastrophic-level one.

"What's going on, Lu?" Vera braced for whatever was coming. Couldn't be that bad. Luna was the good sister. She never did bad things or managed to find herself in trouble.

"Please, Vee, just come right now. Hurry!"

The call ended. Vera stared at the screen. Okay. There was no denying the very likely possibility now. Some sort of disaster, for sure.

Vera rushed up the stairs, untying her robe as she went. That was the other thing about working from home: She didn't have to get dressed for the day unless she wanted to. Evidently, she should have this day. Just her luck.

She ripped off the robe and nightshirt and quickly dragged on jeans, a bra, and a black tee. When in a hurry, you could never go wrong with a black tee. She grabbed her sneakers and tugged them on, hopping on one foot at a time as she made her way toward the stairs.

At the front door she grabbed her keys and shoulder bag, and she was gone.

Andrews Farm
Boonshill Road, 11:30 a.m.

A frown creased Vera's forehead as she parked next to Luna's mother-in-law's sedan. Luna hadn't mentioned having company. Vera shut off the engine and grabbed her bag. She looped the strap over her shoulder as she got out. Jackie Andrews was not exactly one of her favorite people. Vera couldn't shake the idea that the woman thought her son was too good for Luna. The very notion thoroughly pissed Vera off. But she didn't get to choose her little sister's husband or his family. Was the mother-in-law the reason for the urgency Vera had heard in Luna's voice? She had never uttered a negative word about Jackie, but there was always a certain tension in her tone whenever Luna spoke of the annoying woman.

Then again, Vera and Eve had both decided that being pregnant had made their little sister more persnickety than usual. And that was saying something.

Be nice, Vee.

As Vera climbed the steps of the new—designed to look old—farmhouse, Luna rushed out onto the porch. Her face was pale, her eyes red, and if possible, her protruding belly looked bigger than it had on Sunday, when she and Jerome had held their first annual Labor Day barbecue in their new home. Dear old Jackie had been in rare form. Not a single aspect of Luna's preparations had met the "mother-in-law test." Vera mentally rolled her eyes. Life was just too short for that nonsense.

Vera pushed all else aside and smiled. "Hey, Luna, what's—"

"You have to help me, Vee." Luna grabbed Vera by the arm and pulled her toward the door.

A quick study of her sister's face told Vera this was bad. Really bad. Luna's movements almost appeared robotic. Stilted and distressed. Her facial expression was a sort of blank beyond the paleness of her skin. Vera had never seen her like this. Not even when their father died. Had she and Jackie quarreled? More likely Jackie had spewed her venom, and Luna had taken it like a repentant dog. Anger stirred in Vera. If that turned out to be the case, she would tell the older woman what's what. She had no business upsetting Luna, considering she was only weeks from delivering the first grandchild.

Not that Jackie Andrews ever thought of anyone else. At least not in Vera's limited knowledge of and experience with the overbearing woman.

Luna pushed the door open with those same stiff movements. Vera couldn't help staring at her as they crossed the threshold into the front center hall. What in the world had happened to upset her so? She wore a pair of faded denim overalls with a white tee. A couple of old paint stains told Vera her little sister was working on the nursery.

"Luna." Vera pulled her sister to a stop and searched her face again. "What in the world is going on? Where's Jackie? Has she done something that upset you?"

Luna only stared at Vera as if she'd lapsed into a coma. Vera glanced around, opened her mouth to call out to the other woman, then froze, her fingers clenching on her sister's arms harder than she'd intended. Luna didn't seem to notice.

"Holy shit." Vera let go of Luna, her arms falling to her sides.

Jackie Andrews lay at the bottom of the staircase. Her chin was braced against the shiny hardwood floor, face forward, her eyes open and staring in their direction as if analyzing and judging every word exchanged. Her arms were draped alongside her body, her left leg twisted awkwardly beneath the right.

Vera rushed to the woman, crouched down and felt for a pulse. Nothing. Jackie's skin was still warm, but it didn't take a medical examiner to recognize she had likely sustained a serious cervical fracture. *A broken neck.* Probably one or both of the top vertebrae, which may have left her unable to breathe without assistance. A bit of blood in her hair suggested a head injury that very well could have rendered her unconscious as well, ensuring no cry for help.

Vera glanced at her sister, who still hovered near the door. "What happened?"

Luna blinked repeatedly as if she'd just awakened from a deep sleep. "I don't know." She abruptly closed the door, evidently only then realizing it was still open. She stepped deeper into the entry hall but didn't come close to where Vera and the dead woman were.

Cold, black fear funneled inside Vera as she pushed to her feet. *Wait, wait, wait.* Her sister's "I don't know" response could not be right. "How did this happen, Luna?"

Luna gave the vaguest shake of her head. "I don't know. I found her this way when I came back from the hardware store."

It wasn't until then that Vera noticed the gallon of paint lying on its side on the floor. Thankfully the lid hadn't popped off and spilled the contents all over the place.

"So you walked in and found her this way." That was certainly a viable scenario. "Who did you call?"

More blinking from Luna. "You. I called you."

Vera fought against a wave of dismay and an even broader expanse of fear. "I mean, did you call for help?"

Luna nodded, her head bobbing too fast. "Yes. I called you."

Vera held on to her patience as she closed the distance between them. "I'm asking if you called 911."

The blank expression on Luna's face turned to confusion. "Why would I do that? She was dead."

Well there was that. "Luna." She took her sister by the arms once more and turned her so they faced each other with hardly more than a dozen inches between them. "Jackie is dead, yes. But you should have called someone."

Another rapid set of eye blinks. "I did," she said, her voice rising with frustration or desperation. Maybe a combination of both. "I called *you*."

Vera drew in a steadying breath. At least one of them had to remain calm and to think logically. "Okay." She ushered Luna into the living room and the nearest chair. "You stay right here, and I'll call Bent."

Luna opened her mouth, let it close, then opened it again. "Should I call Jerome?"

Vera almost choked on a bubble of sound that lodged in her throat but somehow managed to hold it back. "Let's hold off for a minute. First I need to call Bent and then I'll get an ambulance out here, okay?"

Luna's face puckered into a frown. "Jerome will be so upset. He loves his mother."

Concern building like a tsunami at her sister's continued robotic reactions, Vera patted Luna's arm. Shock, no doubt. "Don't worry. We'll figure this out."

She stepped back into the hall and studied the scene once more. Other than the dropped gallon of paint, all appeared tidy and organized. Luna's home was always that way. She was almost obsessive about keeping things around her in perfect order and certainly always spotless.

Vera inspected Jackie's body more closely. Tested her fingers for rigidity. Fingers were still soft and pliable. The facial muscles were as well. Without doubt she'd been dead less than two hours. No indication of rigor mortis.

Bracing, Vera made the call to Bent and headed to the kitchen as she waited for him to answer. No need for Luna to overhear the mountain of anxiety that would unquestionably affect her voice. Jackie's purse sat on the counter next to the sink. Her cell phone right next to it. Vera wished she had a pair of latex gloves, and she would check the call and text logs. Since she did not and there were none under the sink, she ignored the impulse.

"Hey." Bent's voice finally came on the line. "I was just about to call you."

Her situation couldn't wait for an explanation of his. Vera spilled it. "I'm at Luna's. Her mother-in-law, Jackie, has fallen down the stairs. I think her neck is broken." Vera let go a big breath. "She's dead, Bent."

"EMS on the way?"

Vera bit her lip and told him the worst part in all this. "No. Luna didn't call anyone else. Just me."

The moment of silence that followed was no surprise and confirmed exactly how incredibly wrong her sister's decision had been.

"Is Luna okay?" he asked.

"Yeah, I think so. She's maybe in shock. She says she went to the hardware store for paint, and when she came back she found Jackie this way."

"And she called you instead of 911 or Jerome."

"Yeah." Vera hated the doubt in her voice. "She recognized Jackie was dead and thought calling me was the right thing to do."

Bent hesitated a moment as if uncertain what to do. "I'm at a crime scene, but I'll make the call and have EMS head your way. They'll confirm the situation and have a look at Luna. Keep her calm, and find out as much about what happened as possible before anyone else is involved. I'll be there as soon as I can."

"Got it." Vera hesitated, a frown needling across her brow. "What kind of crime scene?" The ramifications of what he'd just said suddenly filtered through the haze of worry and fear shrouding her brain.

"We've got three dead and one in serious condition out at Thomas Wilton's cabin."

"What happened?" Vera rubbed at her forehead with the back of her free hand as she wandered back into the entry hall. Apparently this day was only going to get worse. Three dead? Not the usual crime scene for Bent's jurisdiction. Certainly not at such a prestigious location. Wilton was like a multibillionaire. Then again, rich people weren't above murder. They just didn't generally take a hands-on approach.

"Don't know anything for certain. That's why I was about to call you."

As horrible as a triple homicide sounded, Vera would gladly trade the scene she had walked in on with the one he was working. There was something to be said for impersonal homicide cases.

Her gaze settled on the dead woman at the bottom of the stairs. Not that she was suggesting Jackie's death was murder. But there was no way to pretend it didn't appear suspicious, given it happened in her new daughter-in-law's home—the daughter-in-law she disliked and often openly criticized. The one who didn't call 911. The only other person in the house.

Maybe Vera had seen too many crime scenes and automatically jumped to the worst possible scenario, but she had a bad, bad feeling about this.

4

Andrews Farm
Boonshill Road, Noon

Vera sat down on the coffee table facing her sister. "Luna, EMS is on the way. They'll have a look and confirm what we already know. Then they'll take her body. It's standard protocol."

Luna stared at Vera, no blinking this time. "What do we do next?"

"Before Bent gets here to take your statement, let's go over all that happened. You've had quite a shock, and we need to ensure you have everything straight in your mind."

"Why is Bent coming?" Her big, dark eyes searched Vera's.

Vera moistened her lips, buying time. She wanted to couch this in a way that wouldn't make her sister feel like a suspect. The trouble was, she would be a suspect in the eyes of some, and there was no way around it. Gossip in small towns could be hurtful, and there was always plenty of it when something just a little off or slightly peculiar such as this happened. And the icing on the cake: Luna was—had been—a Boyett. Some in this town would always see the Boyett sisters as suspicious under any circumstances.

"Were you here when Jackie arrived?"

After staring at her hands a moment, Luna nodded. "I planned to finish decorating the nursery today."

Vera worked up a smile. "I remember you saying so on Sunday." Luna and Jerome were so excited about the baby. They all were. This should have been a calm, happy time for the couple.

"Jackie called me early this morning." Luna sighed. "She wanted to help."

"How early?" Vera really, really needed her to focus on the details. Precise details.

"About seven, I guess." Luna shrugged. "I didn't look at the time. Anyway, she said she was coming over to help me with the wallpaper and that she would be here about eight."

Vera didn't ask if Luna had invited the woman. She already knew the answer. No way. Jackie was too damned bossy and thought everything should be her way or no way. She had been a thorn in Luna's side since the wedding plans began. The ornery woman had brought Luna to tears more than once. Holding back the spurt of anger that accompanied the thought, Vera focused on what had to be done. This could turn into a real nightmare. She had to protect Luna. The best way to do that was to ensure there was nothing to pick at when it came to her story of this morning's events.

"What time did she arrive?"

"At eight, just like she said." Luna placed her hands protectively on her bulging belly. "I remember because the grandfather clock in the hall was counting off the hour when she came in."

The clock had been Jerome's great-grandfather's. It was the first piece of furniture brought into this house. By Jackie and her husband, of course, with the story that it had traveled all the way from England with his ancestors. Vera suspected the woman simply no longer wanted the unattractive family heirloom.

"What did the two of you do when she first arrived?" Vera had to stop drifting off track.

"We finished the wallpaper. But when I opened the can of trim paint to do the touch-ups, it was almost empty. What little was left was too thick. I couldn't even stir it. I had to go to the hardware store for more."

"Jackie didn't want to go with you?" Obviously not but she needed Luna to say the words the same way she would have to say them to Bent when he arrived. And to Jerome and anyone else who asked. The idea that anyone would ever think this was anything other than a tragic accident was ridiculous. But Vera was a bit on the paranoid side. Her line of work—her own personal history—made her that way.

"No." Luna inhaled a big breath. "I don't want to say negative things about her." Her voice trembled.

"Just tell the truth," Vera urged. She hoped like hell the truth would be the right story. She scolded herself for the thought, but in Vera's experience it was best to prepare for the worst.

"She likes spying on us." Her hands twisted together. "I've caught her snooping in our mail. Prowling through drawers. I knew that was why she didn't offer to go for me. She's—was like that." Luna drew in a ragged breath. "I asked her to go for me, but she said she'd rather I just go, so I did."

Not surprising at all. "So you left for paint, and she stayed. About what time was that?"

Fear made an appearance in Luna's eyes. "I . . . I don't know. I never noticed."

Forgetfulness was common during the final trimester of pregnancy. "Do you have the receipt for the paint? It's probably date stamped."

Luna nodded. "It's in my handbag. In the kitchen."

When she would have struggled to her feet, Vera shot up. "I'll get it."

"Thanks." Luna eased back into her chair.

Vera couldn't help glancing at the woman lying at the bottom of the stairs as she passed through the hall. She'd had a serious health scare not that long ago. Cancer. The prognosis had been dire. Lost all her hair during treatment. But somehow she had survived. Even had her hair back in time for her son's wedding. It was really tough luck, dying this way after surviving the horrific disease.

Luna's kitchen was at the back of the house. The entry hall cut the front of the first floor in half. A huge living room was left of the center hall, with an equally large dining room to the right, then the two were joined by a kitchen that sprawled across the back with French doors opening out to the massive backyard. The center hall cut right through the middle, bypassed a powder room under the staircase, and flowed to an end in the kitchen. All the bedrooms, five as well as three bathrooms, were upstairs. Luna wanted to be on the same floor with her future children.

Her bag hung on a hook at the drop zone next to a side door that led into the garage. Vera unzipped it, and the neatly folded receipt was on top of everything else. Sure enough there was the time stamp: 9:45 a.m. Vera's stomach dropped to her feet. That would have put Luna back here by about 10:15 or 10:20 unless she made another stop. An hour or more before she called Vera.

Back in the living room, she resumed her seat on the coffee table. "Okay, so the receipt says 9:45."

"What?" Luna made a "that can't be right" face. "That might be what time I left for the store, but it sure isn't the time I paid for the paint. It took us at least an hour and a half to do all the wallpapering."

"Luna, are you sure you didn't stop anywhere else?"

She shook her head vigorously side to side. "There has to be an error with the receipt. We can call Mr. Potter. He's the one who waited on me."

"We can do that, yes. For now, let's not worry about the receipt, okay?" Vera folded it and tucked it into the pocket of her jeans. She didn't want to think about how this receipt made the situation look. An issue for another time, she decided. If the timing came up.

Confusion joined the other emotions rushing around in Luna's eyes. "I was not here when this happened, Vee. Jackie was just fine when I left for the hardware store. She said she would put the nursery furniture back into place while I was gone. We'd had to move things around to hang the wallpaper. I came back well over an hour or hour and a half later, and she was like that." She flung a hand toward the hall. Her lips trembled.

Vera squeezed her sister's hand. "When you came home, you parked in the garage, right?"

Luna nodded, the movement jerky. "I walked in, hung up my purse, and headed to the nursery. I made it to the entry hall and saw her lying there. I guess that's when I dropped the paint. I ran to her . . . It was obvious she was dead. All I could think to do was to call you. But I . . . I had to find my phone."

Vera stilled. "Where was your phone?"

"I was so upset when I left to get the paint, I guess I laid it on the bench by the door when I was putting on my shoes and then I forgot to pick it up again."

Which meant there was no way to trace her movements via her cell phone. Damn.

"So you went to the hardware store without your phone."

Luna nodded. Her eyes filled with tears once more. "I didn't even notice." She swiped at her cheeks. "I need to call Jerome. Oh God, and his father. They're both going to be devastated."

As heartless as it sounded, Vera did not want to notify anyone in the Andrews family until Bent was here. "Let's just wait until Bent arrives."

Luna tucked the dark hair that had come loose from her ponytail behind her ear. She looked so different from Vera and Eve. They had the blond hair and blue eyes of their mother while Luna had the dark hair and eyes of her mother, their stepmother. Usually her hair was immaculately styled. She dressed like a housewife from a '50s television series—always perfectly coordinated, stylish, and modest. But then she was a librarian; what did Vera expect?

Except for today. Today she looked completely out of sorts.

A knock on the front door had Vera on her feet. "I'll get it."

She glanced at the dead woman and hurried to the door. Before opening it, she checked the viewfinder to ensure it was Bent. The cowboy hat and that handsome profile almost made her smile. Almost.

She pulled the door open and nearly wilted with relief. "She's over there." She gestured to the stairs. "Luna's in the living room."

Bent removed his hat as he crossed the threshold. He placed it on the side table. "EMS is a couple minutes out. I didn't ask the ME to come. She can examine the body at the morgue."

As unsettling as the situation was, Vera felt greatly relieved Bent had been able to make himself available right away. She wasn't sure how this would shake down if anyone else wrote it up. Vera needed some time to ensure any discrepancies were resolved—like that receipt. Bent would give her that time. He would realize Luna could never do this. That was a given. The very idea was ludicrous. Vera just wanted to ensure that absolutely nothing gave anyone even the slightest doubt.

Bent studied the body. Snapped a few pics. Vera should have done that. She didn't take offense when he checked for a pulse.

"No rigor in the face yet," Vera pointed out.

Bent stood. "Has Jerome or his father been called?"

Vera shook her head. "I wanted to wait until you were here."

"Understandable. I'll talk to Luna. See if she wants me to make that call."

"Thanks. I'll get her some water."

Bent headed for the living room, Vera made her way back to the kitchen. She took a glass from the cupboard and filled it under the tap. Then she walked around and ensured nothing was out of place. All looked exactly as it had on Sunday, sans all the food and hosting decor. Luna had outdone herself for the family get-together, inviting both sides. There had been at least thirty people. Mostly from the Andrews clan since Vera, Eve, and Luna were it as far as the Boyett family went. Their father had died last year after an extended and deep lapse into dementia. Vera and Eve's mother had died of cancer more than twenty years ago. A few months later, their father had married Luna's mother—a long and "not so pretty" story—and she'd died on the bathroom floor after trying to drown Luna at nine months of age.

Not even going there.

Now here they were with Luna's mother-in-law dead at the bottom of the stairs.

Jesus Christ, this was going to be a nightmare on the gossip grapevine, if nowhere else. Anything related to the Boyett sisters was always a hot topic.

When Vera finally returned to the living room, she passed Luna the glass and settled on the sofa next to her. Bent sat in the chair to Luna's right. He wore his usual jeans and a Lincoln County Sheriff's Department shirt. And cowboy boots, of course. The man never went anywhere without his hat and boots. Her heart reacted to his steady bearing.

"And you're certain about the time you returned?" Bent's voice was gentle. Vera greatly appreciated his ability to be kind. Not something she would have expected from the wild younger version she had known. But then he'd had reason to be angry and hard back then. Life had been difficult for Gray Benton as a kid.

Looking back, she recognized that even then he was a good, kind person beneath all the swagger. At least to those who deserved the effort.

"As best I can recall," Luna confessed. "I can't remember looking at the time at any point this morning other than when Jackie arrived."

Vera hated, hated this for her sister. It was a true nightmare.

Bent braced his elbows on his knees, leaned forward. "Luna, I don't like asking these questions, but it's necessary. Anytime there is an unattended death—a situation where someone dies alone with no witnesses or easily discernible cause—it's necessary to confirm as many details as possible just so there are no lingering questions."

She swiped at a tear that had traced a path down her cheek. "I understand."

"Did you and Jackie have any problems? Any recent disagreements that were perhaps witnessed by other people?"

"Bent," Vera spoke up before Luna could answer, "do you think that's really necessary?"

"It's all right." Luna held up her hands. "I understand that he needs to ask. I know how some people will talk when they hear what's happened. Yes," she said to Bent. "It's well known that Jackie and I don't always agree on things. We've had plenty of . . . *moments* in front of other people. You know—knew Jackie. She wasn't one to hold back—audience or not."

"Can you describe the moments you mean for me?" Bent watched her carefully.

Vera knew the tactic. He was looking for the lie. As much as she did not like this and wanted to protect her little sister, it was crucial to a thorough investigation. And this was an unaccompanied death investigation.

"We disagreed about the baby's name. The color of the nursery. What I cook for dinner. What I wear. Take your pick." Luna hugged herself. "I can't do anything to please her. Jerome tells me I'm overreacting, but I'm not blind or deaf. She does not—did not—like me. But I was always respectful. I never spoke disrespectfully to her in any of those situations."

Thank God. Vera had sensed things weren't so good between Luna and Jackie, but she had no idea it was this bad. Why had Jerome not intervened? Surely he wasn't that blind.

"Lu, I'm so sorry." Vera reached out and squeezed her hand.

More tears trickled from her little sister's eyes. "I really need to call Jerome," she said again.

Bent checked his cell. Since he only stared at the screen, Vera assumed he'd received a text message.

"EMS is here." Bent stood. "I'll bring them in and get this done." He looked to Luna. "You're right. Now would be a good time to call Jerome. I can make that call if you like."

Luna shook her head. "It should be me."

Vera wasn't so sure there would ever be a good time for Luna to tell her husband that his mother had fallen to her death in their new house. But outside a miracle resurrection, there was no way around it.

5

Andrews Farm
Boonshill Road, 1:00 p.m.

Vera sat with Luna in the living room while the paramedic and his partner did their job. He would once again confirm that Jackie was indeed deceased and then they would load up the body and head to the morgue. There was no reason to wait for the medical examiner to inspect the body at the scene since there were no discernible suspicious circumstances surrounding her death.

Except that Luna had called Vera instead of EMS to begin with. Vera pushed the thought away. Didn't mean anything. Her little sister was not herself. She was seven and a half months pregnant and prone to absentmindedness and emotional displays. Vera could only imagine how terrified she had felt when she walked into her home and found Jackie.

The poor woman had fallen down the stairs. After all, she was in her mid-fifties and slightly overweight, carrying the bulk of said weight in her midsection. Accidents happened. Losing her balance and then being unable to catch herself was a reasonable scenario. It was possible she'd had some sort of medical event and had fallen. A stroke, a heart attack. There were all sorts of feasible explanations an autopsy could very well confirm.

Thankfully by the time Jerome arrived, they had loaded the body onto the gurney. He didn't have to see his mother lying at the bottom of the stairs with her face jutting forward as if she were a bearskin rug with the head still attached.

Jesus. Vera really had to get those thoughts and images out of her head.

Big, tall, muscled Jerome stopped at the gurney and stared down at his mother. He leaned down and hugged her, his face against her chest, and his shoulders started to shake. Vera felt terrible for all the bad thoughts she had entertained since arriving. No matter how Jackie had treated Luna, she was the man's mother.

He straightened, squared his shoulders and gave the waiting paramedic a nod, then Jerome turned to the living room. Vera held a sobbing Luna against her chest. The crying had started anew when Jerome entered the house.

Vera managed a nod in greeting.

He gave an answering nod, then knelt in front of Luna. "You okay, baby?"

Luna launched herself into her husband's arms, giving Vera the chance to slip away.

She escaped to the entry hall, allowing the two some privacy. Vera stood at the door and watched as the gurney was loaded into the ambulance. Once the EMS folks had driven away, she closed the door and walked to the kitchen in search of Bent. Not in the kitchen. She moved back into the hall and spotted him at the top of the stairs. Stepping carefully as if the body were still draped there, Vera headed up to where he waited.

For a moment she only watched while he surveyed the landing and inspected the railing. She wanted to ask if he had noticed something that didn't fit but couldn't bring herself to do so. Instead, she studied the carpet for a potential loose spot that may have created a trip hazard. The downstairs was hardwood, but upstairs was carpet with tile in the bathrooms.

"That must be where her head hit the wall."

Bent spoke so quietly, Vera barely heard him. Her gaze followed his gesture toward the wall about midway down the staircase. A slight indentation was obvious from this angle with the way the light from the chandelier rained down on it.

They started down the stairs, pausing at the indentation for Bent to take a closer look. The treads of the staircase were not carpeted, so Vera looked for any sign of blood. No blood visible, but there was a crack in one of the spindles a few steps above the indented area on the wall.

Vera glanced up to the landing, then to the spot on the wall and finally back up to the cracked spindle. It was possible the spindle had been damaged during installation and no one ever noticed. She almost snorted at the idea. That would never have happened. Luna would have noticed. Vera resisted the urge to run her fingers over the blemish.

Her mind played out the scenario necessary to create both the indention in the drywall on one side and the cracked spindle on the other. Jackie would have had to hit the spindle and then bounced in the other direction, damaging the wall, before plummeting the final distance to the floor below.

The way she landed, head facing forward and on her chin, seemed more logical with the bounce effect. It also indicated a good amount of momentum. As if the woman had been running when she pitched forward . . . *or* was pushed. Vera's gut twisted with the thought.

The bottom line was that a body didn't accidentally fall with that level of momentum unless there was a good, solid thrust of some sort behind it.

Vera kicked the idea out of her head and kept her mouth shut about the spindle. Who could say how long it had been that way? A mover may have caused the damage while bringing furniture up the stairs. A painter may have nearly fallen.

"Vee."

She jumped, turned to Bent, who stood a step below her now. "Yes?" She hoped like hell he didn't see the cloud of doubt in her eyes. She blinked a couple of times just in case.

"We should talk to Luna and Jerome and get out of their way."

"We should. Yes." She pushed a faint smile into place to hide the concerns that were piling up faster than flies on a corpse.

In the living room Luna and Jerome sat on the sofa, holding each other and sobbing. Vera wished there was some way she could help, but there was nothing. Losing a mother was heartbreaking—even if she was a know-it-all, unkind . . . *Enough, Vee.*

"Luna," Bent said, "Jerome, we'll get out of your way."

Jerome cleared his throat. "I should . . . should call my father." He let out a big breath. "I don't even know what to say to him."

"I can go tell him in person," Bent offered. "Drive him over here, if you'd like."

Vera's heart lightened just a little. Bent truly was a good sheriff and a really good man. He cared about the people in this county. She was so grateful she had found her way back to him—no matter the bizarre circumstances. Bizarre seemed to be an ongoing theme in the story of her life—of her sisters' lives as well.

"I should tell him. I can drive over there." Jerome extracted himself from Luna and stood. "But thank you, anyway."

Luna started to lever herself up. Jerome gave her a hand. "I'll go with you." She swiped the fresh dampness from her cheeks.

A cell phone chirped a rapid-fire staccato. Vera recognized the sound as Jerome's ringtone. She hoped his father hadn't already heard the news some other way. He fished his phone from his hip pocket and made a face at the identity of the caller.

He glanced at Luna. "It's Dad." He stepped away and took the call.

Vera reached out and squeezed her sister's hand. "Sweetie, you call me if you need anything at all."

Luna managed a jerky nod. "Thanks, Vee." She drew in a deep breath and worked up a trembling smile as she turned to Bent. "I appreciate you coming, Bent."

"I'll be right there," Jerome said, his frantic tone drawing their collective attention to him. His gaze shot to Luna's. "That was the hospital calling from Dad's phone. He's had a heart attack. It's bad. We need to get over there."

Good grief. What else? "Go," Vera urged. "Bent and I will lock up here."

When Luna and Jerome were gone, Vera turned to Bent. "I'll trade you all this for your murder scene."

He chuckled. "You might change your mind after you see it."

She glanced around the entry hall with its clean, crisp painted walls and shiny wood floor. "There's nothing else we can do here. I might as well go have a look."

"I would sure appreciate it."

Vera grinned. "Don't appreciate it too much until after you see the bill I'll be sending the county."

While Bent checked the side door in the kitchen, Vera took a pic of the spindle and then the wall indentation. The idea that something wasn't right wouldn't let go, but she wasn't saying it out loud. She righted the can of paint Luna had dropped when she came inside and found Jackie.

Hopefully that scenario was what actually happened.

Vera shook off any other concept. There was no way Luna hurt anyone. Not once in her whole life had she ever been a bully or one to fuss or fight. In the back of her mind, Vera couldn't help thinking that maybe some errant gene Luna had inherited from her mother had suddenly surfaced.

No way. Luna was nothing like Sheree.

Why the hell was she even thinking about that woman? Sheree was dead and buried. And that long-ago secret as to what really happened to her had come out and shaken things up for a while. They had all, including Luna, moved on.

Vera was immensely grateful that Luna had forgiven her and Eve after they'd stuffed her dead mother into that cave on the farm all those years ago. And then kept it a secret for more than two decades. What kind of sisters did that?

No use rehashing the past.

Damn. Vera suddenly realized that she needed to call Eve. As a mortician at one of the top funeral homes in the area, she would not be happy if Jackie Andrews's body showed up on her mortuary table without advance warning.

As Vera and Bent exited the house, she called Eve and filled her in. She didn't mention her worries about what may have happened at the top of those stairs. Eve would agree that it wasn't likely.

No way.

Vera cringed. Hopefully.

6

Wilton Cabin
Giles Hollow Road, 3:00 p.m.

A stop at the hospital before going to the Wilton cabin had given Vera a chance to check in with Luna about her father-in-law while Bent followed up on Alicia Wilton's condition. The sole survivor from the cabin murders was being airlifted to Nashville's Vanderbilt Hospital. Unfortunately, Mr. Andrews's heart attack had been a major event, and he was being airlifted as well to Nashville's Saint Thomas Hospital. Jerome would be heading in that same direction to be with his father, at least until the man had stabilized.

Luna would be staying behind. The added stress of hanging around a hospital waiting room wouldn't be a good thing, Jerome had insisted. Vera had promised him she would stop by later to check on Luna. Between her and Eve, Luna would be well taken care of. Jerome appeared to appreciate Vera saying so. It was difficult to tell how Luna felt. That was the part that currently worried Vera the most.

Luna wasn't the type to avoid conversation. But whatever she was thinking amid this crisis, she didn't want to talk about it. Maybe Eve could prompt her to share her feelings. Vera shook her head. She should know better than to hope for that. The only people Eve enjoyed conversing with were dead ones. Maybe all the really good morticians did.

Vera was immensely grateful their quick stop at the hospital was pulled off without a hitch. She and Bent were able to slip in and then out through a rear maintenance exit, avoiding the cluster of reporters in the main lobby. It was rarely so easy to steer clear of encounters with the news media, particularly with a high-profile victim like Thomas Wilton. Word of his murder would be the talk of the town already.

From there they left Vera's SUV at Bent's office and drove to the Wilton property. Vera struggled to keep her mind off Luna's nightmare and on the homicide case as Bent briefed her on his interview with Valeri Erwin, which unfortunately provided little insight into the murders.

By the time they were through the main gate and deep in the woods at the crime scene, Vera was more than ready to dive into the investigation.

Frankly, this—Vera surveyed the cabin as she and Bent climbed the steps to the front porch—was a much-needed break from the sister situation.

She waited while Bent unsealed the cabin's front door. The forensics folks had done their work, and the bodies had been moved to the morgue. Dr. Jenny Collins would be a busy lady for a few days. Collins was from Franklin County. She had moved here specifically to take the position of medical examiner. The mayor had appointed her, and no one in the legislative body dissented. She was newly forty, a few months younger than Vera, and single. The best Vera could tell, the woman had her eyes set on Bent.

But Vera wasn't jealous. *Right, keep telling yourself that.*

She kicked the notion out of her head as she followed Bent inside. "Have you notified next of kin?"

The odor of death instantly smacked her in the face, filled her lungs and made her want to gag. You just never got used to that smell.

"No one to notify as far as we know." He flipped on the overhead lights. "Wilton's parents are deceased. No siblings or other extended family that we are aware of. As for the wife, Alicia, Deputy Hastings is trying to track down any family she may have."

"Hopefully Mrs. Wilton will wake up and give you all the information you need." *Like what the hell happened here.* Vera tried to sound optimistic since the wife, though in a coma, was in stable enough condition to be transferred to Vanderbilt Hospital. That was something. Assuming the killer was still nearby, the news would no doubt make him—or her—damned nervous.

"We should be so lucky," Bent agreed. "Unfortunately there are no cameras here at the cabin, but the upside is there's only one entrance onto the property, and that's back at the main house where there are cameras. Olson is there right now, reviewing the footage. A couple of other deputies are conducting a walk-through just in case whoever did this"—he gestured to the room at large—"went there before or after."

"The killer may have been looking for something more than money or jewelry if robbery was the intent."

"There's a hell of a lot to choose from at the main house. Not so much here," Bent allowed, then he walked toward the sofa, where a pool of blood had dried like long-forgotten, spilled spaghetti. "The first victim was here."

"Stabbed?" Vera studied the positioning relative to the nearest egress.

"Three times in the chest. He had defense wounds on his right forearm and left hand." Bent's gaze rested on hers. "A coyote, according to Erwin, was chewing on his arm when she arrived. The door was ajar, and when she opened it, the animal took one look at her and vamoosed."

Vera shuddered. "Is that normal behavior for coyotes?"

"Generally"—Bent pushed his trademark cowboy hat up his forehead—"they avoid interaction with humans. But they will dine on a carcass, human or otherwise, if the opportunity presents itself. With the door open and no one stirring about, it was an opportunity for a fresh meal."

Vera learned something new every day, no matter that she'd grown up here—on a farm, no less. "Have you identified the other victims yet?" Bent had told her that everyone in the place had been naked. No ID handy generally went along with being naked.

"We found a wallet with a driver's license in a drawer in one of the bedrooms. The photo is a match to the male. Seth Parson from New Orleans. Nothing on the female yet. No cell phones for anyone who was here."

"Maybe there was a rule of no phones for this party. They could be locked in a safe somewhere." People often had rules when having private parties of this nature. Based on what Vera had heard so far, this one certainly had all the earmarks of a *very* private party. She followed Bent and the bloody footprints into the kitchen area, where another pool of blood as well as significant arterial spray warned that the second victim had fallen there. "Looks like someone hit an artery."

Bent tapped his abdomen. "There were two stab wounds mid-torso and lots of defense wounds on both arms and hands. Final strike was a jab at the shoulder. I think the pullback on that one is how the nick to the neck happened. Just deep enough to open up that artery."

Vera turned back to the living room area. She visually measured the room at large. Anticipation of a puzzle, and this was definitely a puzzle, tingled along her nerve endings. "Whoever did this was prepared. Walked right in without warning and went to work. No prolonged struggles. No chase." She studied the footprints. "Bare feet. Are you thinking the killer left these tracks?"

"The tracks lead to the fourth victim, the wife, and the knife was found under her, so on first look it would appear she was the killer. But I have a hard time seeing her overtaking all these victims—especially the males—without more of a struggle, or at least injuries to herself." He shrugged. "I suppose the vics could have been inebriated beyond the ability to react. But I'm far from convinced." Bent gestured to the bloodstains near the fridge. "The unidentified female may have been less so than the rest, which allowed her to put up a better fight."

"So, the killer"—Vera did a slow one-eighty turn—"likely entered the cabin—the door was probably unlocked—or came from upstairs and walked right up to where Parson stood at or sat on the sofa." Vera shifted her attention back to Bent. "Once Parson was down, the killer headed toward the kitchen area. My guess is that about that same time, the second victim entered the kitchen from wherever—presumably the deck—and the two intersected in front of the refrigerator." Vera looked to the French doors that led out to the deck. "I'm assuming the unidentified female came from outside since the final two vics—if the wife is a vic and not the perp—were outside, right?"

"Right." Bent started in that direction. Vera followed as he explained, "Wilton was in the hot tub. Stab wound in the back. Defensive wounds on his arms. When he was lifted from the tub, there were other wounds. Two more stab wounds to the chest—one of which was likely the fatal strike. Right hand was sliced along the palm, so he attempted to stop his attacker but wasn't fast enough. Judging by his build, I don't think strength was the problem. Especially if someone smaller, like his wife, was the one wielding the knife. For me, the only way that scenario makes sense is if she was in the hot tub with him. I can't see her putting him in after—unless she had help."

"He may have been too inebriated to put up a proper fight. Alcohol or whatever drug they were partying with." Vera had seen the man in town a few times, and Bent was right. He had a very athletic build. "Any idea as to why the wife may have wanted her husband and their guests dead?"

Bent shook his head. "Not yet. The only thing we have is the fact that the knife was under her body as if she had been holding it when she ran."

"She's lucky she didn't stab herself as she went down."

"True. She was on the steps there." He indicated the stairs leading down to the yard. "Her pulse was so weak, we thought she was dead too, but she somehow managed to hang on. If Erwin hadn't come by today, she wouldn't have lasted another day."

"But she wasn't stabbed, and she had the knife—assuming it wasn't planted under her to mislead the investigation." Whatever the case, the wife was the one variable among the victims.

Bent nodded. "She hit her head on the edge of a step when she fell—hard enough, it seems, to put her life in jeopardy. When the ME was examining her—before turning her over—she discovered the knife. With the knife close by, and since she wasn't stabbed, it's reasonable that she is our prime suspect for now."

Vera surveyed the yard and the woods that lay beyond. "There's always the possibility the killer wanted the wife to look guilty."

"Agreed." Bent led the way back into the house and secured the French doors. "We can hope the killer injured him- or herself with all that stabbing. If so, maybe we'll get lucky and pick up some DNA that will give us a firm direction."

That would only be useful if said killer was the wife or someone in a database, but no need to say as much. Bent knew the deal. Like anyone investigating a murder case, he could hope.

"You're interviewing Erwin again when we finish here?" Based on the woman's statement from that morning, she hadn't appeared to know much beyond the fact that the Wiltons were spending the holiday weekend at the cabin with friends, and the boss hadn't shown up this morning for a scheduled meeting.

"*We* are interviewing her," he corrected. "I'm sure you'd like to get back to Luna, but I could use your insights on every aspect of this one."

Vera held up her hands. "No problem. Eve will take care of Luna until I can get there."

"I appreciate it."

Vera smiled. "Anytime." She decided not to mention that she really was grateful for the distraction, as tragic as it was. Besides, she enjoyed working with Bent.

Right now he looked tired. Murders didn't happen often in his jurisdiction, and to have three—potentially four—at once was deeply troubling for the county's top cop. He was a good sheriff, and Vera was always happy to pitch in. Since leaving her career at the Memphis Police Department and coming back to her hometown, she had found a comfortable place as an adviser and analyst to law enforcement agencies in this as well as the surrounding counties. Over the past year she had built a damned good reputation, if she did say so herself. It was actually going better than she'd hoped. As some would say, it appeared to be her true calling—even when things hit too close to home.

But then, that was the way of things in a small town. Everyone knew everyone else, and most were related by blood or marriage in one way or another, even if several times removed.

"I'll make a walk-through before we go and take some pics." Later she would use those pics to follow up on her thoughts about the case.

"Sounds good." He hitched a thumb toward the French doors. "I think I'll take another walk along the tree line. Make some calls."

Vera hesitated. "You said Erwin didn't notice anything missing."

"Right. She found the bodies and pretty much lost it. After the vics were removed, she and I did a walk-through. She didn't notice anything missing except cell phones." He frowned. "And there was no purse or ID for the deceased female."

"Thanks." Vera headed deeper into the house, and Bent headed out back.

He knew she had her own way just as he had his. She preferred to look at a crime scene as a whole—not just the bodies or the murder weapons. It helped to take note of the way the victim or victims, in this case, lived. Equally important was getting the feel of the scene. Everything from the decor to cleaning habits. It all mattered.

Vera explored the house while Bent did his thing. She wandered through the main living area. The great room some would call the combined kitchen and living/dining area. Beyond where the vics were discovered, the place was cleaner than she would have expected after a weekend of partying. There was a small office and a powder room on the first level just beyond the stairs. Upstairs were the bedrooms. The primary bedroom extended over half the second level's floor space.

There was an en suite. Again, all was spotless. There were a few changes of clothes in the closet, intimate essentials in the drawers, and toiletries in the bathroom. The only money or jewelry lying around was, presumably, the husband's Rolex and his cash-filled wallet on the dresser. No weapons or notes or anything at all that appeared out of place or unusual. Not even a dust bunny under the bed. Just one lone sock. The only indication the room had actually been used for anything other than storage was the unmade bed.

She moved on to the second bedroom. Also clean. She dragged a finger across the wood dresser. Not a speck of dust. Nothing in the closet or drawers. Bed didn't appear to have been slept in.

The final bedroom was another story. Clothes littered the floor. Skimpy lingerie as well as shorts and tanks. A bikini. A few underthings were tossed into drawers. A couple of shirts and blouses as well as jeans hung in the closet. A pair of running shoes—women's—lay on the floor next to the bed. Flip-flops, larger, so probably the man's, were in the bathroom. Discarded towels were scattered on the tile floor. A razor on the sink as well as a few cosmetics. As Bent said, if the woman had brought a purse, there was no sign of it anywhere in the house.

Vera did her due diligence. She checked under the bed and most any other hiding place and found nothing. When she would have left the room, she decided to check the bed more thoroughly. With the tips of her fingers, she drew back the sheet. Nothing but a couple of pubic hairs. She checked under one pillow and then the other.

Something fell from one of the pillowcases. Vera leaned down, studied it. White powder in a neat little packet. Cocaine, she suspected. No surprise. She'd seen the residue on the coffee table downstairs.

Since she didn't have gloves or an evidence bag, she would leave that for Bent or Conover.

Back downstairs, she found Bent on the front porch.

"Find anything?" he asked.

She nodded. "I did. In the guest room where Parson and his potential girlfriend were staying, there's a packet of what looks like cocaine in one of the pillowcases. I didn't touch it, but that may have been one of the drugs of choice this weekend."

"I'll have Conover have a second look just in case he missed anything else."

Vera winced. "Maybe say you found it." She preferred staying on the good side of the deputies, particularly Conover. In her experience it was never helpful to get on a cop's bad side.

"I can do that." He hitched his head toward the door. "You done?"

"For now. I'm anxious to meet Valeri Erwin and hear firsthand what she has to say."

While Bent locked up and resealed the scene, Vera headed for his truck. Whatever happened in this cabin—she turned back to study it as she opened the passenger side door—it had started well before Wilton and his guests arrived.

What Vera needed next was motive. Then the rest would fall into place.

The drive back to the main house seemed strange, considering there was no one else anywhere on the hundreds of acres surrounding them. All the official vehicles were gone at this point. Bodies removed, the scene processed. Conover would be back for a second sweep later today or tomorrow. No employees except Erwin had come to the property at all today. No other family—evidently there was none. No vehicles moving about. No lawn work or housework. Nothing. Leaving a vast property silent except for the breeze and the birds.

It was almost unnerving.

But that deafening silence abruptly shattered as they drove through the main gate, exiting the property.

A sporty sedan waited, parked crossways in the road, blocking their path. A man, arms folded over his chest, leaned against the driver's side door.

"What the hell?" Bent muttered.

Vera squinted to identify the interloper. *Nolan Baker.*

Irritation instantly flamed. "What's he doing here?" Dumb question. He was here for the story.

Bent sent her a look. "He showed up this morning with a handful of other reporters but left for the hospital when the bodies were removed." Bent shoved the gearshift into Park. "He must have heard you and I were headed back this way."

Vera rolled her eyes. "I'm not talking to him."

"I'll take care of him." Bent climbed out of the truck and headed for the younger man.

Nolan Baker, son of Vera's nemesis back in high school, cared about only one thing: himself. Well, himself and catching that big break, but ultimately those were one and the same. Sadly for him, that had not happened as of yet. He was still writing for his small-town newspaper. Nothing wrong with that unless your mother was Elizabeth Bogus Baker (also known as Boggie back in high school). The woman expected the moon and sun out of her son, just like she'd expected her high school football star husband to end up in the NFL. Didn't happen.

Sucked to be so dependent upon other people's success for your happiness.

Nolan had inherited his mother's arrogance and doggedness. Made him a good reporter, she supposed. But it did absolutely nothing for his personality.

She clenched her teeth as she watched Bent instruct Baker to leave. He would, of course. But he would be back . . . over and over again until he got the story.

Especially now. Thomas Wilton was a big deal. The story would go national, for sure. It was just the sort of mystery that reporters would do anything to capture. Three dead. One in a coma. The motive unclear. Money, sex, drugs.

Vera was confident about one thing. This was no sudden, random act. The kills went down far too easily with hardly any resistance, which meant one of two things: Either the victims knew their killer, or this was a well-planned execution that no one saw coming.

7

Erwin Residence
Washington Street, 4:15 p.m.

Vera tried again to kick off this round. "Ms. Erwin—"

"Remind me again why you're asking me questions." Erwin looked from Vera to Bent and back. "I've seen you in the newspaper, but I didn't know you worked with Sheriff Benton."

Vera reached way down deep for her patience. The woman had been using every tactic available to avoid diving into this interview. First with Bent and now with Vera. Erwin had begun her evasion tactics by asking a dozen questions of her own. Then, like now, she interrupted each time Bent or Vera began.

"I'm a crime analyst. Sheriff Benton asked me to have a look at the case." She produced a smile even a dead man would recognize as fake. "Now, let's get started, shall we?"

"Do I need a lawyer?" Again, the younger woman looked from Vera to Bent, but this time her attention remained on the sheriff. "I mean, I feel like the two of you are sort of ganging up on me."

Now she was just plain old being uncooperative. Where was the emotional wreck Bent had told Vera about? The woman who couldn't stop crying?

"You are welcome to call your attorney," Vera said. "We can wait."

"How about I step outside? I have some calls to make." Bent gave Erwin a nod and walked out of the room.

Vera barely suppressed a smile at his strategy. It was easy to guess, particularly considering the way Erwin's face fell, that she had not intended for Bent to be the one to go. Well, Vera squared her shoulders. Erwin would just have to get over it.

The uncooperative witness shifted her startled attention back to Vera, who readied her pen once more to jot notes onto her pad. For the most part the pad and pen were props used when needed to increase tension in the interviewee. "Now, where were we? Oh yes, how did you come to be acquainted with Mr. Wilton?"

In most cases, it was advantageous to start at the actual beginning. Since Alicia Wilton might not survive her injuries, for now this woman was the only firsthand perspective they had to learn one damned thing about the people involved in this mess. Erwin was young. Maybe twenty-eight or nine. She dressed casually but well. Black linen slacks and a billowy, cream-colored blouse with a large collar. Her dark-brown hair was stick straight, as were her bangs. She was petite and quite pretty. Though her personality so far was less than appealing.

"Just over five years ago, I moved from Nashville to Fayetteville," she finally began. "I wasn't sure finding a job would be possible." She shrugged. "I started my search in Huntsville. Most people commute there for the better jobs."

This was true. Huntsville was where the high-tech jobs were, for sure. Basically any sort of work you might look for could be found in the Rocket City.

"Why Fayetteville? Do you have family here?" It wasn't like the area was a go-to place for new college grads searching for their first jobs, or anyone else for that matter. It was a really nice town with lots of friendly folks, but the job market was woefully limited.

"A friend I attended Lipscomb with talked me into it. We were roommates."

Vera would very much like to speak with this friend. "What is your friend's name, and does she still live in the area?"

Erwin shook her head. "Nola Childers. She died right after graduation. She was my best friend." Tears made an appearance. "It was a really terrible time."

"I imagine so." After scribbling a few notes to pique Erwin's curiosity, Vera moved to the next question. It was actually a repeat of the first, but Erwin appeared to prefer taking the long way around to answer. "Is that when you met Thomas Wilton?"

A frown furrowed the other woman's face. "I actually heard about the position at my friend's wake."

Not surprising. It was a southern tradition to gather at a family's home with truckloads of food to pay respects after the loss of a loved one. Conversations often lapsed into the latest news and/or gossip. One more push for the answer to her original question. "Is this where you met Wilton?"

"We didn't officially meet there." Erwin smiled, but it didn't reach her eyes. "I mean, he was there with his first wife—Lena, the one who died. It wasn't until a few days later that I went to his home and applied for the position I have now."

Vera knew little to nothing about Thomas Wilton. Obviously she had heard the name and the scuttlebutt about his big inventions and mega mansion. "You've worked on his staff for five years then?"

"Yes."

Another jotted note. "Can you describe your duties as his personal assistant?"

Erwin heaved a sigh. "I've already gone over this with the sheriff. Do we really have to do it again?" She shuddered visibly. "I just want to be alone. I have a great deal of planning to do."

"Planning?"

"There's the funeral." Erwin turned her hands up. "The dozens of meetings I have to cancel. Business associates I have to notify. The sheer magnitude of what needs to be done is overwhelming."

Vera nodded her understanding. "I'll hurry this along as quickly as possible." She readied her pen. "Your duties were?"

Resignation settled into Erwin's features. "I did the usual clerical and administrative type duties as well as coordination of his social activities with his business appointments. I accompanied him on business trips when needed, and I took care of personal errands more often than not." She stared at Vera then, a question on her face. "Is there anything else you'd like to know?"

"Are you aware of anyone who may have wanted to harm Thomas Wilton or his wife?"

Erwin made a face and shook her head adamantly. "As I told Sheriff Benton, no. Absolutely not."

"Anyone he had angered over a business deal or a personal decision?"

"No." A resolute shake of her head. "Thomas had no enemies."

Vera studied Erwin's face carefully. Her expression and her answers clearly showed she admired and respected Thomas Wilton. Now to see if she felt the same way about his new wife. The subject required a careful approach. Just because the murder weapon was near the wife didn't make her the murderer. They needed some sort of perspective into the Wilton marriage.

"What about Mrs. Wilton? How were things between her and her husband?"

Erwin's expression closed as tightly as a vault at Fort Knox. "I haven't known Alicia very long. She shares very little information of any kind with me."

So, she didn't like the new wife. She could have good reason, or she could simply be jealous. "But you have an opinion of her?" Vera pressed. "You see her every day. Perform tasks for her, I'm sure."

A vague shrug. "She's okay, I guess."

"Mr. Wilton's first wife died . . ." Vera opted for a different course. "Two years ago?"

"Yes. It was a very sad time. Thomas was devastated. Then six months ago he met Alicia on a business trip to Vegas, and two weeks later they were married."

Interesting. For eighteen months, Erwin had had the man to herself. Sharing with the new wife may have caused some friction.

"How did his first wife die?"

"A fall from her horse caused a brain injury. She thought she was fine, and twenty-four hours later she was dead." Erwin hugged herself as if the memory chilled her. "It was so unexpected and so horrible. She was only forty-three and a well-trained equestrian. A renowned dressage rider. It was awful. Just awful. Thomas was so upset, he got rid of all the horses. Even the one she loved so much. He said he couldn't bear to look at them. We all felt so bad for him."

"I imagine so." Vera slipped back a page in her notepad. "I'm sure you were all equally happy for him when he found a new wife."

Something like anger filled Erwin's eyes before she could blink it away. "Alicia is *nothing* like Lena."

Vera left that to simmer for a bit. "You have no idea who the other couple at the cabin was? We've identified the male victim as Seth Parson. But we still have nothing on the female."

Erwin stared for a long moment, as if she hadn't understood the question. "I don't—didn't know either of them."

The pause and the sudden blank expression said otherwise. "Did Mr. Wilton make a habit of inviting strangers to his most private sanctuary?"

Erwin chewed her lip, stared at her hands. "I think Alicia knew the man. I had seen her talking to him before. In town."

Now they were getting somewhere. "When and where did you see her with him?"

More stalling. Erwin studied her cuticles. Chewed her lip some more. "I saw them in town once at that Mexican place on the square. They were having lunch. When Alicia saw me, she got all hyper, telling me how he was an old friend from her days in New Orleans and how he was just passing through on his way back home."

"Did she ever mention him again?"

Erwin shook her head. "But I saw them once outside that gas station on the corner of Highway 64 and Wilson Parkway. It looked to me like they were arguing."

"When was this?" A new anticipation seared through Vera's veins.

"Last Thursday. I remember because I was out running errands and picking up beer for their big weekend party. When I saw Alicia there, I wondered why she didn't pick it up herself. They sell beer at that gas station."

"But you'd never seen the other woman before?" Vera needed something on her.

Another shake of her head. "No. Sorry."

"Did you have reason to believe Alicia was having an affair?"

Another long pause, then a shrug. "I can't say for sure, but she and Thomas had been, I don't know, kind of at odds a lot lately."

"Arguing? Shouting? Throwing things? Or giving each other the silent treatment?" Specific details mattered in a homicide investigation. Vera needed a better grasp on the Wiltons' relationship. Difficult to get when half the couple was dead and the other was in a coma.

"Just a lot of tension. I could feel it. Thomas preferred keeping his private life private, so there was no yelling or anything like that."

"Did you and Alicia have any disagreements?" Vera couldn't ignore the possibility. Erwin was a reasonably attractive young woman who revered her boss. The new woman in his life may not have sat well with her. Or vice versa. Wilton had bought Erwin this house—a historic home on Washington Street. The place had years ago been renovated into four apartments, but it was all Erwin's to use or rent out now, thanks to the generosity of her boss. A new wife might be suspicious of such generosity.

Erwin moved her head firmly side to side. "I am beneath her concern. The only time she noticed my existence was when she wanted me to do her a favor."

"What sort of favors?"

"Taking packages to the post office. Picking up her dry cleaning."

Few rich people had the time or inclination to bother with the mundane. Mailing packages fit neatly into that category.

"Did you ever notice where the packages were going?" Vera inquired. This might be nothing, but it was an avenue that needed to be explored. Wilton's most recent personal merger was his marriage to Alicia. Anything Alicia knew or did was relevant.

"New Orleans." Erwin looked startled. "I didn't connect that she told me the man was from New Orleans until you asked just now. Do you think that means something?"

"It's possible. That's why we ask so many questions." Vera backed up to a previous question. "You're certain Mr. Wilton had no business issues? No problems at all that may have prompted something of this nature? I'm confident there is a great deal of cutthroat activity in the defense industry."

Erwin squared her shoulders and lifted her chin in obvious defiance of the notion. "I am fully aware of all his business dealings, and I am positive there was no trouble at all. Thomas was a consummate businessman, and everyone liked him."

Which left only one glaring option—if that was the case. His new wife's past. Maybe a jealous lover from that past. Like Seth Parson. "There will be a search of all Wilton's property, his home, vehicles, basically everything for any little thing that might provide insight into what happened. Would you be willing to cooperate with that search?"

Erwin no doubt knew where all the safes were hidden, as well as the combinations.

"Of course. Anything I can do to help." She shook her head, her shoulders sagging and her expression wilting. "I still can't believe he's dead. It just makes no sense. Thomas had no enemies. Unless . . ."

Vera stared at Erwin expectantly. "Unless what?"

Another of those vague shrugs. "I mean, if Alicia was having an affair . . . her lover would be an enemy, right?"

Oh yes, this woman did not like the new wife.

"Could be," Vera agreed. "Well, we'll get out of your way now so you can take some time to pull your plans together. The sheriff and I will meet you at the Wilton home in the morning at eight to start the search. Does that sound doable?"

"Sure. Okay." Erwin stood. Glanced around before meeting Vera's gaze once more. "Do you think I'm in danger? I mean, I don't have a security system or anything."

Vera studied her a moment. "Do you have reason to believe you are? I mean, if this wasn't about his business dealings, then . . ."

Erwin waved her hands as if dismissing the idea. "You're right. I'm being silly." She frowned at Vera. "Sometimes I have a tendency to overreact."

"I'm sure it's the shock of all that's happened." Most folks were rattled when a neighbor or colleague was murdered. "See you in the morning."

Erwin nodded. She followed Vera to the door.

Vera hesitated there. "We didn't notice a vehicle belonging to Seth Parson at the Wilton house."

Erwin frowned. "Oh, wait, I know. I had to stop by the house early Friday morning to send that final agenda for the Zoom meeting we were supposed to have today. While I was there, I heard Thomas telling Alicia that he would pick her friends up at their hotel and bring them to the house."

"Do you know where they were staying?" There could be useful information or items at their hotel.

Erwin shrugged. "No clue."

Vera thanked her again and left. Erwin was understandably shaken by her boss's death. She had been holding back to a degree until Vera pushed harder. And still Erwin's vague and somewhat reluctant answers made one thing very clear: Vera needed more on Valeri Erwin and Alicia Wilton before she could get a sense of the relationship between the two women and the man who was the apparent axis of their respective orbits.

When Vera reached the sidewalk, Bent was leaning against his truck.

"Did you learn anything useful?"

"Maybe. Seth Parson was someone from Alicia Wilton's past. Erwin had seen them together, and Alicia tried to gloss it over. Also, things between Alicia and her husband had been tense lately, according to Erwin. And Alicia had her mailing packages to New Orleans. She doesn't remember the addressee, but considering Parson was from New Orleans, that could be relevant."

"Did she know where Seth and the woman were staying or if they had just arrived in town?"

"They had been here for a bit, I think. She remembered seeing Alicia at lunch with Parson. But she didn't know where he was staying or anything about the vehicle he was driving. She did hear Wilton on Friday morning telling Alicia that he would pick them up at their hotel."

Bent straightened away from his truck. "Then I need to find that hotel."

"Won't be difficult as long as they were staying in town and not in Huntsville." Fayetteville didn't have that many options.

"I was thinking," he said as he scrubbed a hand over his jaw, "if Alicia wanted to end her marriage and walk away with more than a tidy settlement, she might try offing her old man. But who was she running from? I mean, why run after murdering three people—unless someone was after you?"

"I'd go with Seth Parson." Vera laughed a dry sound. "Except he's dead too. Since we have no idea who the other female victim was, it's hard to conclude anything about her—beyond the fact that she was deceased at the time as well."

"There's one thing we can be sure about."

Vera searched his face for a clue. "What's that?"

"Someone wanted at least one of the four dead and made it a point to ensure no one was left to tell the tale."

"No question about that." Vera glanced up at the windows of Erwin's apartment that overlooked the street. "How sad to have everything and still not be able to trust others or to even protect yourself."

"Yeah. Money can't always buy the thing that matters the most." Bent touched her arm. "I should look into where Parson was staying. You can join in the fun."

Her SUV was at his office. She might as well.

The sudden clang of the ringtone she'd chosen for her cell made her jump. "God, I need to change that ringtone." She dug around in her bag until she found the source of the annoying noise. She frowned at her sister Eve's name and face flashing on the screen. She almost groaned at the possibility that Luna may actually have gone into labor after all the stress she'd been through today. Or the possibility that Jerome's father had died.

Jesus, this day needed to get better. At least a little bit.

"Hey, Eve, what's up?"

"You need to get over here," she said, her voice a near whisper.

Vera frowned. "What's going on?"

"That woman—Geneva, Jackie's sister—is here, and she's ranting about how she knows Luna had something to do with Jackie's fall down the stairs. She's acting crazy."

Damn. "I'll be right there."

"Maybe you should bring Bent with you. This is bad, Vee. Really bad."

"Just take care of Luna. I'll be right there."

Vera looked to Bent. "We have to go to Luna's first. Geneva whatever-her-name-is has shown up at her house, making accusations that Luna was involved in Jackie's fall." Vera didn't even want to consider how this day could get any worse.

He reached for the passenger door to open it for her. "Let's go."

"Thanks." She appreciated him coming. They needed all the backup they could get. This was evidently going to get ugly.

8

Andrews Farm
Boonshill Road, 5:50 p.m.

Bent parked beside Eve's little sedan. Vera stared at the sporty SUV Geneva Fanning drove. Vera remembered it from Sunday. Judging by the scene playing out on the front porch, she was extra thankful Bent had come along. Eve and Geneva, arms waving, appeared to be in a shouting match.

Vera exited the truck before Bent could reach her door and headed for the steps, Bent right behind her.

"What seems to be the problem, ladies?" Bent asked as they reached the porch.

"She"—Eve stabbed a finger at the older woman—"showed up here and got Luna all upset. I've asked her to leave, but she refuses."

Eve wasn't into anger. She was generally the calm one who tried her level best to stay out of family drama. The fact that she was visibly pissed off said loads about Geneva's behavior.

Geneva was Jackie's younger sister and—not to speak ill of the dead—the one who'd gotten all the looks. According to Eve, by the time Geneva was twenty, she had won every beauty pageant in the state. Vera mentally rolled her eyes. And dear old Jackie got all the bossiness and judgmentality. Vera knew little about the sisters other than what Eve had told her. Luna rarely talked about Jerome's family. With good reason, it seemed.

"Sheriff, I'm glad you're here." Geneva turned her attention to Bent. "You need to listen to what I'm saying." The woman was literally vibrating with fury. "I know what my sister said in her text messages to me just this morning—right before that . . . that Boyett girl murdered her."

Vera clamped her jaw shut to prevent herself from defending her sister. It was best to let Bent handle this. The woman had clearly lost her mind. To ensure her sister didn't launch a rebuttal either, Vera pulled Eve close. "Go inside and make sure Luna is okay."

Eve nodded and sent Geneva one last blistering look before disappearing into the house. Vera took a breath and turned back to the ridiculous situation at hand. Unlike Jackie, who'd preferred to dress comfortably and didn't bother with makeup, Geneva outfitted herself as if she were headed to a meeting with the mayor himself. Her makeup and hair were meticulously done. No gray in sight and not one wrinkle. Frankly Vera didn't see how she accomplished the latter without the assistance of BOTOX. Also unlike Jackie, Geneva maintained her figure, also according to Eve, as if her life depended on it. Vera had to hand it to her, she looked damned good for a woman on the back side of fifty.

"See for yourself." Geneva thrust her cell phone at Bent.

Bent accepted the woman's phone and scanned the messages.

Geneva glanced at Vera with suspicion in her eyes. "Jackie has been having trouble with Luna since she and Jerome got married. We were all worried about the situation, and now look, Jackie is dead." Her lips tightened with the fury vibrating in her words.

Vera held her own anger in check. "When you say *we*, Mrs. Fanning, who do you mean?"

"Jackie, her husband, me, and my husband." The way she glowered at Vera as she answered warned that the question had only made her angrier.

"Jerome has never mentioned any trouble." Vera hoped like hell he hadn't. Luna surely would have revealed an issue at that level.

Geneva huffed a breath. "Of course he hasn't. He does all in his power to make her happy." She shook her head. "But I'll bet he changes his mind now. Your sister killed his mama, and there is no way he's going to forgive that." She pointed a finger at Vera. "You Boyett sisters should all be in jail. You killed Luna's mother. And what about all those other bodies found in that cave on your farm? Jackie said that girl would be the death of her."

Before Vera could launch a rebuttal, Bent stepped in. "Mrs. Fanning, I don't see anything here that suggests Mrs. Andrews was concerned for her safety. I reviewed those same text messages on her phone earlier today." He passed the phone back to the older woman. "What I do see is a woman who wasn't happy with another's choices."

"You would see it that way," Geneva snarled. "I guess I'll just have to call another law enforcement agency if you refuse to properly investigate what I am telling you was a murder!"

Vera thought of the time stamp on the receipt from the hardware store. A lump swelled in her throat. No way. The time stamp had to be a mistake.

Bent held up his hands. "Mrs. Fanning, you've made an accusation, and I have an obligation to look into it. Rest assured we will investigate the situation. For now, I believe everyone involved would be best served if you go home and let us do what needs to be done. Under the circumstances, you need to stay clear of Luna and her home." When the woman would have argued, he added, "Anything you do could interfere with the investigation."

This appeared to appease her. "Very well then. I'll go home and inform my husband that you are taking this seriously."

Of course she would. Her husband was on the county council. She would throw that bit of leverage into the mix. Vera despised that sort of attempt at intimidation. Well, the woman was wasting her time. Bent would not be intimidated or blackmailed or pushed around. Frankly Vera didn't see how the man kept his cool.

"You keep me posted on Mr. Andrews's condition," Bent called after her as she stormed away.

Fanning gave him a nod as she climbed into her SUV. Vera said nothing until the woman was flying along the driveway, headed for the road.

"I cannot believe she would do this. No one who knows Luna would believe such an absurd accusation." Vera glanced at the front door, dreading even the idea of Luna going through a ridiculous investigation like this.

"You're right." Bent rested his hands on his lean hips. "But I have to look into it, or it'll only get worse."

Vera understood. "I'll let you explain that to Luna. She'll take it better coming from you."

Bent chuckled. "Thanks."

They found Eve and Luna in the kitchen. Vera was glad her little sister had been far enough away not to overhear what was happening on the porch. She walked straight up to her and hugged her.

"I'm so sorry this is happening." Vera drew back and gave Luna a sad smile.

"That woman is out of her mind." Eve looked to Bent. "Can you make her stop throwing those unfounded accusations around?"

"It's a free county," he reminded Eve. "Luna could sue for defamation. But, in my opinion, the best way to handle the situation is for me to prove her claims are baseless."

Luna turned to Bent. "I understand she's upset, but this is preposterous. As much as I wished Jackie would stay out of my marriage, I would never have wished her harm, much less harmed her myself." Luna sighed. "No matter how much the hateful woman deserved it."

Vera groaned. "Never say that out loud again. Ever."

Luna wilted against the island. "You know what I mean. I couldn't do anything to make her happy."

"She was a crazy bitch," Eve grumbled. "That's the problem."

Vera held up her hands. "You don't say anything like that out loud again either, okay?" Eve reluctantly nodded. "First." Vera turned to Luna. "How is Jerome's father?"

"The same. He's in and out of consciousness but hasn't been able to speak yet. Anything he tries to say is gobbledygook. They're planning surgery in the morning. They want his vitals a little more stable first."

Damn. "I'm sorry to hear that, Lu. Poor Jerome."

Bent leaned against the counter next to the sink. "Luna, let's go through what happened this morning one more time. Then I want you to make a list for me of all the inappropriate things Jackie did since you and Jerome married. The things she said. Also make a list of any arguments you and she have had. Anything you said to anyone else about Jackie that could come back to haunt you. You can pass all that along to Vera when you've finished."

Luna shook her head. "I have never said anything about her to anyone. I know better."

"She hasn't," Vera pitched in. "Luna doesn't do that. She's barely mentioned anything to us."

"That's good. It'll work to your benefit." Bent glanced from Luna to Vera and back. "You need to find a way to tell Jerome about this before Geneva does."

Luna drew in a big breath, her hands bracing her belly. "I will."

This was enough. "When Bent is through with his questions, I'm taking you to the farm." Vera didn't want her sister staying here alone. "Just until Jerome is back."

When Luna would have argued, Vera went on. "You have to protect yourself, Lu. If Geneva shows up and you're here alone, she can say anything about how you react, and it'll be her word against yours. You don't need to be alone. And if she catches you alone, take your cell phone out immediately and start recording."

"I need to finish the nursery." Luna looked ready to cry, and Vera didn't blame her. This was insane.

"Eve and I will help you finish. But you can't be alone right now."

"Suri's out of town for a conference." Eve shrugged. "I can stay here with you at night and help with the nursery. You'll be at the library most days." She looked to Vera. "Vee will have her hands full helping Bent with this."

Vera was surprised at Eve's initiative and, at the same time, tremendously grateful. She did need to focus on clearing up this mess, and there was the triple homicide investigation. She held her breath as she waited for Luna to make her decision.

Luna nodded. "Okay. Let's do that." She turned to Vera. "I can come to the farm when Eve goes to work on my days off from the library."

"That sounds like a really good option." Vera was grateful Luna hadn't put up a fuss. Being alone right now was too risky on more than one level.

"You two are going to be busy." Eve looked from Vera to Bent. "I just heard about the murders at the Wilton place."

Luna looked surprised. "Who was murdered?"

"Thomas Wilton," Bent answered, "and two visitors we're assuming he or his wife invited for the weekend. Alicia, his wife, survived, but she's in critical condition."

"What about Valeri?" Luna asked. "Is she okay?"

"You know Valeri Erwin?" Vera shouldn't have been surprised. Luna had been the library director for a while now. She knew anyone and everyone who ever checked out a book at the local library.

"I do. She came to the library a few times." She frowned. "I haven't seen her in a while, though."

"Maybe you can tell us more about Valeri while we're here." Vera needed a better grasp on the woman.

"I don't know that much." Luna eased onto a stool. "She picked up two or three books on a few occasions. She was always friendly."

"Has she ever come to the library with a friend?"

Luna appeared to think about that one for a moment. "Not that I've seen."

"What genre does she read?" Bent leaned against the counter next to the sink.

Bent was quite the reader himself, Vera had learned. Westerns. True crime and even a few romance novels had made their way onto his bookshelves at home. She loved the idea of Bent reading a romance.

"Mysteries or something on that order, I think. I'll check tomorrow to be sure." Luna sighed. "I'm sorry, but I think I need to lie down. I am utterly exhausted."

"Come on." Eve offered her hand. "Let's get you propped up on the sofa, and I'll start dinner."

"One other thing," Bent said. "If Jackie's handbag and phone are still here, I need to take them in."

Luna pointed to the countertop behind him. "They're right where she left them. I didn't want to touch them. I intended to have Jerome take care of getting them to Leonard when he was home."

"You were smart," Bent assured her.

Vera gave her sisters a hug and reassured them while Bent rounded up an evidence bag for Jackie's things. Then she and Bent headed out.

Outside, he hesitated at the hood of his truck. "I have to finish up a few things at the office." He held up his phone. "Just got a text from Conover. The wife's prints were on the knife."

Vera raised her eyebrows at the news. "Looks like Alicia stays in that number-one-suspect spot for now."

"Looks like." He opened her door for her. "Your place or mine tonight?"

And there it was, the million-dollar question.

"I'm coming to your place." She slid into the passenger seat. "I'll even start dinner."

He grinned. "I should invite you to a crime scene every day."

A smile tugged at Vera's lips. It really was time to make a decision about the future. The idea had butterflies taking flight in her belly. Made her feel a little off balance. She had long assumed she was too old and too jaded to get excited by a potential step toward a more permanent relationship. She'd been wrong, apparently.

Then again, maybe she should wait until they got through this investigation and straightened out the business about Jackie's death. It was best to make the really big decisions with a clear head and from a place of calm.

Vera almost laughed out loud.

When had her life ever been calm?

9

Benton Ranch
Old Molino Road, 8:15 p.m.

Vera sipped her water. The steaks had been perfect because Bent prepared them. But the salad was a little wilted. She should have stopped at the store on her way here rather than just poking around in the fridge. Fresher greens would have been nice. A rich red wine would have helped. But Bent wasn't much of a wine drinker—not much of a drinker at all since his younger days.

She might have thought to stop at the store if she hadn't decided to check out Seth Parson's room at the Best Western with Bent. She'd needed the distraction from what happened at Luna's house. Anyway, the two of them, as well as Conover, had gone through the room Parson had rented two weeks ago, according to the manager. They found a few clothes and not another damned thing. Parson's car turned out to be a 1977 Pontiac Firebird Trans Am in near-mint condition. It still sat in the parking lot. Other than a few receipts from gas stations and fast-food stops, they discovered nothing useful to the case inside the vehicle either. There was the usual info about the vehicle and the registration documents but not one thing related to Alicia Wilton or the woman with him, other than a pair of well-worn high heels.

Vera stood, grabbed Bent's plate and her own. "I could use a whiskey, how about you?"

He got up as well and reached for the salad bowls, stacked them together and gathered the silverware. "Sounds like you have something on your mind." He shot her a look underscored with an empathetic smile. "You were a little quiet during dinner."

Bent was very, very good at reading her. Maybe a little too good. "It would be weird if I didn't after the whole Jackie thing." She settled the plates next to the sink, then one by one scraped their dinner remains into the trash. Vera shook her head. "This is not good, Bent. The kind of thing that can leave a fissure in a relationship—one that might never truly heal."

Bent dumped the wilted lettuce from their bowls. "Jerome is a smart guy, and he loves Luna. I can't see him believing his aunt's accusations."

Vera braced herself and said what she recognized needed to be said. "But what if there's some truth to her story."

He placed the bowls on top of the plates in the sink and leaned a hip against the counter. "Are you saying Luna admitted to pushing her mother-in-law down the stairs?"

Vera scowled. "She told me exactly what she told you." Except he didn't know about the time stamp on the hardware store receipt. Tomorrow, for sure, Vera had to check into that issue. Worry and fear swelled in her chest. Had to be a mistake.

But what if it wasn't?

"You think she's holding something back?" He elbowed her out of the way. "You pour the whiskey. I'll load the dishwasher."

She didn't argue. "Let's have that drink and then we'll talk." The chances of her sleeping tonight if she didn't have at least one were next to none.

While Bent rinsed the dishes and put them in the dishwasher, she poured healthy shots of Gentleman Jack into two glasses. By the time he joined her on the sofa, she was already making headway on hers.

Bent picked up his glass and sipped the whiskey. He didn't say a word, just watched her with those assessing blue eyes. Her own eyes were blue but not like Bent's. His were that incredible blue of the sky on a clear, sunny day. The color that everyone noticed. And those amazing eyes were set in a face even more handsome now than when they were so damned young and so crazy in love. That he wore his hair longer, the way he did back then, and still looked amazing—maybe more so even—made her entire being feel lighter somehow.

"You trying to start something besides a conversation?"

His deep voice rumbled through her, and she would love nothing more than to absolutely start something. But that would only be putting off the inevitable.

"We both know," she said pointedly, "the way her head hit the wall, and that broken spindle tells a story of its own. The woman didn't just fall down the stairs."

There, she'd said it. That part, anyway.

"I can't argue the assessment." He took a swallow of Gentleman Jack. Licked his lips as if savoring the taste.

Vera could hardly shift her attention away from those lips. Damn, this man made her want him so easily. "The drive from Luna's house to town and back is maybe twenty-five minutes. Add to that the time to select the paint, have it shaken, and then to pay for it. I'm guessing she was gone an hour and fifteen minutes or so. Maybe a little longer if she took her time to avoid going back to face Jackie any sooner than necessary."

"You think someone else stopped by while Luna was out?"

It didn't help that he sounded skeptical. "It is possible," she argued. "If we're looking at potential scenarios, that could be one."

"You're right." He swept a wisp of hair from her cheek with his fingertips, making her shiver. "Are you thinking the husband?"

Vera forced her full focus on the conversation rather than the man who she just noticed smelled so damned good. Hard to ignore with them seated hip to hip. He'd worn that same subtle, earthy aftershave for as long as she had known him. The scent made her restless.

"Why not? Statistics show it's more often the spouse than another family member or a stranger. Maybe that's why he had a heart attack?"

Hope dared to sprout. "They may have argued. He pushed her—whether by accident or on purpose. Then he rushed home and had a heart attack."

Vera tightened her fingers around her glass, had another sip.

Bent did the same. "Has Luna mentioned trouble between Jerome's parents?"

"No, but she wouldn't." Vera shrugged. "Eve and I tell each other everything, but Luna's much more private. I'll ask her. In light of what's happened, she should tell me whatever she knows."

"Any news on the father-in-law?"

"If he remains stable, they'll do the surgery he needs in the morning." Vera opened the last text she'd received from Luna. "Still in and out of consciousness. Vitals are fairly stable. Jerome is staying at the hospital until his father is out of surgery and stable." She met his gaze once more. "Sounds guardedly optimistic."

"Certainly could be worse." Bent finished off his whiskey. He set his glass aside and turned toward her, reaching again for a strand of hair. "What about other theories?"

A shiver rushed over her skin as his fingers trailed along her neck. "I get the feeling you're not really in the mood to discuss scenarios." She was rapidly losing the mood for conversation as well.

"As true as that is"—he grinned—"I agree we should consider all options when and if we find solid evidence to believe the woman was pushed."

Vera's gaze narrowed, and that warm feeling vanished as the meaning behind his words penetrated her weary brain. "You asked the ME to have a look at the body, didn't you?"

He shrugged. "After Fanning's theatrics, I figured we should cover that base. So yeah. I did."

Vera couldn't deny it was a good move. "I actually intended to suggest as much."

"That's because you're good at your job." He glanced at her lips, then sighed. "Any new thoughts on Erwin and the triple homicide we have hanging over our heads?"

"The jury's still out on Erwin." Vera placed her empty glass next to his. "I'll do some digging. See if her past really looks as unremarkable as she would have us believe. We need more on Alicia and who she was before she became Mrs. Wilton. Finding out who Seth Parson was to her might give us something on Alicia as well as the unidentified female vic. We also need to know what Alicia was set to inherit if her husband died."

"You have your work cut out for you." Bent teased another lock of her hair with his fingers. "I'll have Hastings assist you with that, if you'd like."

"Let me do the background digging. Hastings can focus on the present and local sources."

"All right." Bent nodded. "We'll concentrate our efforts on that and whatever Conover can give us from the scene. By the way, I sent Deputy Lenora Pinckard to Vanderbilt to keep watch on Alicia Wilton just in case the killer isn't finished. The Davidson County sheriff is providing a deputy to rotate twelve-hour shifts with her. I wanted one of ours close by for the duration."

"If she wakes up and can tell us what happened, that would be optimal." But Vera and Bent both understood that was not likely. With the kind of head trauma the woman had sustained, she might not remember anything. The best they could hope for was one or more fragmented pieces of the puzzle.

"We can always hope," he agreed.

A knock on the door yanked their collective attention from the case. "You expecting company?" Vera hoped like hell it wasn't more trouble. Luna or Eve would have called if there was any news from Jerome. But this was a fairly large county; homicides might not happen often, but there were other crimes that required the sheriff's attention.

"I wasn't, but it looks like it found me anyway." Bent got up and walked to the door.

Vera picked up their glasses and took them to the kitchen sink while Bent handled his visitor.

"Dr. Collins, come in."

Collins? Vera poked her head beyond the cased opening that separated the kitchen from the living room. When did the ME start making house calls without a dead body to examine? Vera lifted an eyebrow. Maybe because the body she wanted to examine was very much alive and belonged to Bent.

Collins stepped in, all smiles and looking surprisingly fresh for a woman who'd just spent the better part of the day with murder victims. "Sheriff, I hope I'm not disturbing you."

"Jenny, how are you this evening?" Vera walked to the sofa and sat down.

"Vera, I'm glad you're here."

Vera would just bet she was. *Not.*

"Have a seat," Bent suggested to the ME, looking for all the world like he might fake a call to get the hell out of there.

"Thank you." Collins settled on the sofa with Vera, which ensured Bent had to take a chair. Oh, that was a slick move.

Vera waited. Bent did the same. Collins looked from Vera to Bent.

"You mentioned that you were glad I'm here." Vera couldn't tolerate the anticipation a moment longer.

Collins nodded. "Right." She inhaled a deep breath as if she'd only then remembered why she'd come at all. "I had a look at Jackie Andrews's body as you suggested."

This she directed to Bent. Vera told herself he'd only done this because Geneva Fanning had put up such a fuss. He'd said as much. And Vera had mentioned being worried about how it would look that Luna hadn't called for EMS before calling her. His decision made total sense.

Still, at this precise moment with Collins looking all secretive, Vera didn't like it one little bit.

"And?" Bent prompted.

"I can't say conclusively of course," Collins admitted, "but based on your photographs and what I found in my examination, she may have hit the spindle and then the wall during her fall down the stairs. Her injuries appear consistent with that scenario."

Vera's breath stalled deep in her lungs. This was stacking up toward something she did not want to hear.

"Beyond the head trauma and cervical fractures," Collins went on, "there was a fairly deep abrasion—a scratch—on her right forearm that moved from the elbow toward the wrist as if she'd been trying to pull away from someone's grasp, or perhaps someone was holding on to her arm when she fell. There was a tibial fracture to the left leg. The type of fracture consistent with perhaps hitting something stationary that stops your momentum. I can say without doubt that hitting the wall was likely the cause of the head trauma. The awkward landing certainly created the cervical fractures."

"What you're concluding," Vera spoke up, needing to confirm what the ME appeared to be taking the long way around to say, "is that in light of the injuries she sustained, this was no typical trip and fall."

Collins nodded. "I'm quite confident this was no accidental fall. Not unless the woman was running toward the stairs and"—she shrugged—"leaped down them for reasons we can't fathom. Bottom line, the momentum required is consistent with a hard shove. The scratch on her right arm almost certainly confirms she was not alone when she fell."

And there it was. The worst possible news outside a straight-up confession from Luna.

But that simply could not be.

"What's your estimation regarding time of death?" Bent showed no reaction to this news, which Vera greatly appreciated. The fewer folks who recognized this was unsettling, the better.

The truth was, the fewer folks in a small town who knew anything even remotely unpleasant about you, the better. No one could use against you what they didn't know. Then again, some just made stuff up.

"Between ten and elevenish. Most likely closer to ten unless the house was set to a serious chill." With that, Collins stood. "Well, I won't take up any more of your time. I felt sure you wanted to hear this in person and not by phone."

Bent was on his feet next. "You're right." He thrust out his hand. "Thank you, Dr. Collins. I appreciate your quick work. I know you have your hands full at the moment."

And she did. Vera stared at their clasped hands. The woman hadn't let go of his hand yet.

Vera blinked the ridiculous thought away and shot to her feet. She produced a smile that felt as stiff as she imagined it looked. "Thanks, Jenny."

Collins flashed her a smile before turning back to the sheriff. "I'm assuming this information stays between the three of us until we have additional facts."

Vera should've been grateful the new ME appeared to want to be a team player, but trust never came that easy for her.

"I find that's the best course of action in most situations," Bent confirmed.

"Mum's the word then."

Bent saw her to the door. When he'd closed it, he leaned against it and eyed Vera. "We have a problem."

"A big problem." Vera walked toward him, worry expanding inside her so fast that the air trapped in her lungs, and it was just going to stay stuck deep in her chest along with the scream she wanted to expel.

When she stopped in front of him, he reached for her hand, cradled it in both of his. Warmth spread instantly through her, allowing her to breathe again.

"We both know," he offered quietly, "Luna would never do something like this without one hell of a good reason."

"No reason will be enough for her husband or for the woman's family." Vera knew exactly how that would go.

Bent nodded. "You need to talk to her, Vee. Make sure she was at the hardware store until right before she called you."

The fact that they hadn't checked Luna for any indications of an altercation loomed like a dark cloud in the back of Vera's head. If she'd scratched Jackie, there could have been genetic material under her nails. Just another detail that would come back to haunt them if this turned into a murder investigation.

Vera resisted the urge to shake her head. This just couldn't be right.

"I'll confirm the timeline." What else could she do?

"I'll keep Fanning calm until we have everything we can find to support what we both know."

Vera wasn't sure there would ever be enough ways to properly show her appreciation to this man.

Like a light bulb turning on, Vera abruptly understood the one thing she could do. Determination flowed through her, steadying her frazzled nerves. She could find the person who actually pushed Jackie down those stairs because it absolutely could not have been Luna.

10

Wednesday, September 3
Boyett Farm
Good Hollow Road, 8:00 a.m.

"What do you mean, she's gone to Nashville?" Vera stopped pouring coffee into her mug to glare at the screen of her cell.

Eve heaved a big breath into the phone. "She wanted to be there with Jerome during his father's surgery. She left half an hour ago."

Vera shoved the carafe back into the coffee maker. "Why didn't you call me? I could have gone with her." Even the idea had her mentally groaning. She had not one but two cases to deal with. Luna taking off on her own right now was not another worry Vera needed.

"She's a grown woman, Vee," Eve argued. "You're being ridiculous. She's not a child, and being pregnant does not make her disabled."

Vera resisted the nearly overwhelming urge to roll her eyes. She hated doing that, but everybody around her was constantly doing or saying dumb shit, and it made her head want to explode. "Eve." The fact that her name came out unnaturally calm should have had her sister worried. Vera did not feel even in the region of calm. "I am aware that Luna is fully capable of driving anywhere she likes, BUT my concern is that Geneva Fucking Fanning will be there and cause a scene, which will NOT be good for our little sister's mental well-being."

She started to pace the room as the worry expanded like a balloon being overfilled.

"Oh," Eve chirped.

Vera stopped in the middle of her kitchen and held her tongue until another wave of fury had passed. "You see my point then."

"I really don't think that will be a problem. Jerome would never allow his aunt to be mean to his pregnant wife. I'm certain of it."

"I hope you're right." Vera struggled to regain a bit of actual calm. "He does love her. We can both see that, but his mother just died, and his aunt is accusing Luna of being responsible."

"And his father had a heart attack," Eve put in. "I think he's going to be more concerned with his father and Luna than anything Geneva says."

Vera sagged against the counter. "I guess you're right."

"Oh my God, we had to go through all that just for you to see that I'm right?"

"Don't push it." Vera decided she didn't need another cup of coffee and poured it down the drain. "I have a million calls to make, and I may have to take a trip to Nashville myself, so I should let you go."

"She'll be fine," Eve repeated. "Luna promised she would text us when she arrived, and she would keep us posted on how things go. So don't go checking up on her. Old Geneva will really go over the edge if you show up."

Vera's mouth gaped. "Why? I didn't push her sister down the stairs." That was the way of things, though. Vera was always the one everyone gossiped about. Everything the Boyett sisters did ultimately landed on her shoulders.

Now she did roll her eyes. She would always be the outsider for daring to leave, staying gone so long and then having the audacity to come back.

"You know how it is, Vee. Don't let it get to you. Look at it this way: As long as they're talking about you, they're letting someone else rest."

Vera smiled. Their mother always said that. "Yeah, yeah. And, just so you know, if I go to Nashville, it's about the Wilton case. Speaking of which, I need to get to it. I'll check in with you later."

"Hey," Eve said before Vera could disconnect.

"What?"

"Just don't go getting yourself in a bad spot. You have a habit of drawing a big-ass target on your back when you dive into an investigation."

Her sister had a point. "It's the only way to find the whole story. When the killer reacts, you know you're getting close."

"That's what worries me. Talk to you later."

The call ended, but Vera didn't move for a bit. The fact was that the only way to flush out a killer was to get as close as possible. She knew that better than anyone. Most homicide detectives would agree.

Vera headed to her office. She'd left Bent in his bed at five this morning. She'd awakened early and hadn't been able to go back to sleep, so she'd come here to work. She'd spent an hour online looking for anything she could find on Valeri Erwin and any relatives she might have in her hometown of Knoxville and the surrounding area. Since she'd found very little, Vera had called her old friend Eric in Memphis PD. Eric Jones was the best at what he did. It wasn't enough to call him a senior crime analyst. He was far more than simply that, but it was his official job title. With his connections and database access at Memphis PD, as well as with the FBI, he could find just about anything. Hopefully he would be calling her back soon.

Next up, Vera decided as she settled at her desk, was to find any available information on Nola Childers. Although Erwin's roommate might have nothing to do with anything, she was at least partially responsible for Erwin landing in Fayetteville. Hopefully Childers had friends or family who would remember Valeri from the time period the two were at Lipscomb together. She also needed whatever she could find on Seth Parson and the mystery woman who were from New Orleans. Was Seth the addressee on the packages Erwin had mailed for Alicia? Or some relative of Alicia's?

Bent would be at the Wilton mansion by now, executing the search warrant. If they were lucky, he would find something useful to the investigation. There were only two reasons for the sort of murders carried out at that cabin: love or money.

The love part was better defined as jealousy or obsession. To Vera that was the more likely scenario based on what she knew at this stage. A competitor, whether slighted by some deal or envious of some business arrangement, would have likely been more direct and concise about the murders. These kills spoke of passion far more so than mere anger or revenge over some business deal.

She reminded herself to visit the hardware store and check on that time stamp at some point today. Not that she was in a hurry. The truth was, for now, she could assume it was a mistake. Once she had confirmation—if it wasn't—there was no unringing that bell.

Blocking the entire concept from her brain, she focused on the calls she needed to make. Finding information on most anyone was fairly easy online if you knew where to look. Particularly if social media was involved, and it generally was. From there, tracking down a phone number wasn't a problem. When it was, she just called Eric. She and Eric had been good friends and colleagues for most of Vera's fifteen-year career at Memphis PD. They'd briefly shared a more intimate relationship but had found they were better as friends. Mostly because Vera had spent the larger half of her life in love with Gray Benton.

A smile tugged at her lips. She supposed that had to be a sign. The two of them were meant to be together. The memories from Luna's wedding had her thinking about wedding dresses and . . .

Vera shut down that line of thinking and got on with her phone calls. Maybe she would make a few calls to see what she could find out about Seth Parson before digging deeper into Erwin. Finding anyone connected to Parson and the still-unidentified female vic could very well be far more relevant to how the two ended up dead.

An hour later Vera hadn't found anyone available for questioning, but hopefully at least one or two of those she'd reached out to would call her back. Whenever she left a message in a situation like this, she tried to make it seem as if a return call would be in their best interest. No one ever wanted to think, even for a moment, that they could be in trouble with the law. It was kind of like the scam calls claiming to be from the IRS. Few people wanted to ignore the possibility they might be on an IRS call list.

Eric had gotten back to her almost immediately with a name. Seth Parson had a brother, one Larry Parson. The brother had been in prison for second degree robbery until four months ago. The phone number Eric gave her may or may not have been up to date, but she'd left a message. If she was lucky, she would hear back.

The echo of the doorbell had Vera getting up. She tucked her cell into her hip pocket, stretched and headed into the hall. Maybe Bent had news, though she imagined he would call since executing a warrant at a property as large as the Wilton place would take all day—at least.

She checked out a side window and was surprised to find Valeri Erwin at her door. Wasn't she supposed to be with Bent? How strange and, frankly, inappropriate that she would show up here. But—Vera smiled in triumph—the move spoke loudly and clearly about one thing: Erwin was concerned about her past being dug up. Unless, of course, she had some big revelation to make. That was about as likely as snow in September in southern Tennessee.

Vera disarmed the security system and opened the door. "Ms. Erwin, did we have an appointment? I thought you'd still be at the Wilton home with Sheriff Benton."

"No, I'm sorry. We don't have an appointment, and the sheriff said I could leave." Erwin wore a sad face. "I just couldn't be at the house any longer while they . . ." She closed her eyes and shook her head. "It makes it all too real."

Vera thought about saying, *Like the three dead bodies didn't?* Instead, she offered, "Would you like to come in? We can have coffee."

"Yes. Please."

Erwin stepped inside, and Vera closed the door behind her. "They won't leave too much of a mess. But it's important that they make sure there isn't anything they missed in the house that might help them find the person or persons responsible for this tragedy."

"I understand, but it's still sad." She followed Vera to the kitchen.

Just maybe the woman would let something slip over coffee. Vera could always hope.

"I'm sure—" Vera was suddenly propelled forward. Her cheek hit the cool floor as pain shattered in the back of her skull.

She tried to force her eyes open. Not happening. A scream echoed in her ears. Hers? Erwin's?

Soft . . . almost soundless footsteps. Was someone else in the house? Vera ordered her body to move . . . her eyes to open. But nothing happened. The pounding in her chest . . . the rush of blood through her veins made it hard to breathe. But it was the ache in her head that overwhelmed all else. Bent's face kept flashing through her mind. She needed to get to him . . . to move.

Get up! Get up!

There were other sounds . . . muffled . . . far away. If only she could open her eyes. *Get up! Get up!*

Her mind went blank.

Vera opened her eyes slowly. Pain splintered her skull, and she squeezed them closed once more. Something was wrong. An explosion of remembered pain flashed in her brain. Falling forward. Face smacking the floor.

She forced her eyes open once more. Ignored the resulting pain. She needed to get up. Slowly but surely, she pulled her arms toward her shoulders and flattened her palms on the cool hardwood. With effort she pushed herself up onto all fours. The room spun, and she swayed. Her stomach pitched, so she closed her eyes again.

Slow, deep breath. She opened her eyes again and dared to sit up on her knees. The island was close enough for her to grab on to the counter's edge. She levered herself to a standing position. It took a moment for the room to stop spinning. Coffee. She and Erwin had been coming into the kitchen for coffee.

Where was Erwin?

Fear arced through her as she moved her body so that she could look around the room. It hurt too much to move her head. Erwin lay on the floor at the kitchen door, her upper body still in the hall.

Vera staggered over to her, dropped to her knees. Erwin lay on her back. The blood on one side of her forehead was accompanied by a sizable lump. Vera touched her throat. Pulse was steady. Thank God.

Erwin stirred. Her eyes opened. She blinked.

"Are you all right?" Vera scanned the length of her. Saw no other indication of injury.

Erwin moistened her lips. "What happened?" She raised up onto her elbows. Grimaced.

"I'm not sure." Vera surveyed the entry hall. The front door stood open.

"Wait." Erwin scooted up into a sitting position now. She held her head with her hands. "Something flew at you. Like a baseball bat. I swung around, and there was a man . . . He'd hit you with the bat or whatever it was. I tried to run away, but then he hit me." She touched her forehead.

Vera's pulse jogged into a faster rhythm. Her head throbbed. She felt nausea roiling in her stomach. "Did you get a good look at him?"

Erwin blinked, nodded, then made a pained face. "He wore a ski mask."

"I need to call Bent." Vera winced at the pain that roared in her head just from talking. She tried to think.

Wait. Could their attacker still be here?

Vera got to her feet and half walked, half staggered into the hall. The front door stood wide open. Her heart fluttering wildly, she hurriedly stumbled toward it, shut and locked it. When she turned around, Erwin had made her way into the hall. She cradled her head, her expression still pained.

She could be hurt worse than it appeared. "You need me to call an ambulance?"

"No." Erwin dropped her hands to her sides. "I think I just need to sit down."

Fighting another wave of nausea herself, Vera ushered her to the bench near the stairs. "Just wait here. I need to have a look around."

"You don't think he's still here, do you?" Erwin's eyes were huge with fear.

"I think we'd know it by now if he was." They were making too much noise for an intruder not to hear.

Moving slowly since her balance still left something to be desired, Vera headed toward the kitchen to ensure the back door was locked, but the mess in her office snagged her attention. Someone had ransacked the room. She moved in that direction. Her desk drawers had been pulled out. A few bookshelves had been emptied. Family photo albums had been flung like damaged butterflies onto the floor. How the hell long had she been out? Surely not long enough for this. She closed her eyes and gave herself a moment, then opened them once more. The room was still in disarray.

"Son of a . . ." The notes she had made during her research this morning were scattered here and there, but at least most appeared to be in one piece. She considered picking them up, but the ache in her head said bending over was not going to be a good thing. Better to wait until later.

Vera returned to the bench and sat down next to Erwin. She tugged out her cell to call Bent. Once that was done, she intended to learn the real reason this woman had shown up at her door.

11

Wilton Residence
Giles Hollow Road, 10:30 a.m.

The rest of the Wilton household staff had appeared as scheduled a couple of hours after Bent's deputies began the search of the main house. He'd sequestered the threesome to the main living room since that area was done.

At this point, with the downstairs complete, he'd sent two of his deputies upstairs and the other two outside to get started on the many outbuildings. Nothing of consequence had been found, which wasn't entirely unexpected. With what Bent had learned from his many calls to Wilton's business associates and attorneys this morning, it looked more and more like these murders had nothing to do with Wilton's business and everything to do with his personal life. Possibly Wilton suspected his wife of an affair, perhaps with Parson. Or Wilton's wife wanted to get rid of her wealthy husband, and things had gone way wrong. Either way, when a crime of passion or greed was planned to the degree he suspected this one was, care was generally taken to ensure nothing was left to tell the tale. Luckily for law enforcement folks, few killers ever managed to cover all potential telling details.

The only way to find those little missed pieces was to question anyone and everyone close to the victims. Bent started with the gardener, one Jose Martinez.

"Have a seat, Mr. Martinez." Bent gestured to one of the two chairs in front of the desk in Thomas Wilton's home office.

Martinez was in the neighborhood of forty, looked fit. His chambray shirt and jeans suggested he chose comfort over anything else. The leather ankle boots said the same.

"When was the last time you were here, Mr. Martinez?"

"I was here on Thursday. I cut the grass. Took care of the shrubs. Once it was all done, I left for the weekend. Mr. Wilton wanted everything good shape and the staff gone by dark on Thursday."

The man's voice was deep, heavily accented. His demeanor proved straightforward. There was a sadness in his eyes. He had liked his employer.

"Mr. Wilton gave these orders personally?"

Martinez nodded. "Yes."

"And you were to return to work when?"

"Next Monday."

"How long have you worked for Wilton?"

"Since he built the place eight years ago."

"Would you say the two of you were friends?" Considering the timeframe, that was a distinct possibility.

"Yes. We friends for sure." Martinez nodded again. "Mr. Wilton was a fair boss."

Bent had heard nothing less about Wilton's business dealings. "Do you know of any reason anyone might want to harm him or his wife?"

A firm shake of his head this time. "No way. Mr. Wilton had no enemies. He never have trouble. Never."

Having an employee of eight years think so highly of him spoke well of Wilton, for sure. "What about his wife?"

Martinez exhaled a big breath. "His first wife was good woman. Saint, you would say. This one different. She's mean. Snob, you would call her."

"How so?" Innuendos were well and good, but Bent needed facts and specifics.

"I did not trust her." His head was wagging from side to side again. "She tell me a task she want done in yard, then if her husband didn't like, she'd swear I misunderstood her. She did same thing to the others. Just ask them. They tell you. She lied all the time."

Bent's cell vibrated deep in his pocket. "Excuse me a moment." With a triple homicide and the business with Vera's sister Luna, he couldn't afford to ignore a single call. *Vera.* "I have to get this." He gestured to Martinez with his phone. "Give me a minute."

The man nodded, and Bent stepped into the hall outside the office. "Hey."

"Someone came in the house and attacked me. Erwin too."

When he would have demanded more details, Vera tacked on, "I'm fine. It's not a big deal. I didn't want to bother you, but since Erwin was involved, I knew I had to."

What the hell? Worry ignited in his gut. "I'll be right there."

Bent rushed upstairs and found Hastings. "I need you to continue with the interviews of the household staff. I'll be back as soon as I can."

"Will do, Sheriff."

He was out the door and on the road within the next minute. The idea that Vera was always the one the bad guys went after wasn't lost on him. Most likely because she wasn't one to play by the rules. She always stuck her neck out too far. Pushed the envelope. Took the bigger risk.

He had to get it through her head that his heart couldn't take her continued indifference to her safety.

Lincoln Medical Center
Medical Center Boulevard, 1:00 p.m.

A serious concussion.

After hearing what happened, Bent wasn't surprised Vera had a Grade 3 concussion. The attacker had used something—a baseball bat, Erwin believed—to wallop Vera in the back of the head.

Fury tightened his gut. Made him want to tear something apart. He'd sent Conover to the farm to search for anything the attacker may have left behind—prints, the baseball bat, any damned thing. Two other deputies had interviewed the neighbors. No one had seen anything. Not surprising since the area was one farm after the other with tens if not hundreds of acres between the houses. Not a single one of those neighbors had video doorbells. So that aspect was a bust, but he'd had to be sure. The deputies had done a thorough search around the house and yard and come up empty handed. The chances of finding any evidence were about nil.

"This is really bad timing," Vera grumbled, drawing his full attention back to her as she gathered her things to leave the exam room. She stared at Bent in frustration. "It's the last thing I need right now. I can't drive for at least twenty-four hours. And only then if my symptoms have subsided. This sucks."

Bent got exactly what she was saying. This was his fault, in her opinion. He shouldn't have insisted that she and Erwin come to the ER and then she wouldn't have the diagnosis along with the doctor's instructions. Well tough. If she didn't want him to take care of her, she shouldn't have called him. Not that he would ever say as much. He was lucky she had called. Vera Mae Boyett had been known to ignore this sort of thing and to not call for help. He was grateful she had, because she had not been okay. He had taken one look at her and known she was hurt far worse than she would admit.

"It sucks, I know." He doubted his understanding mattered or made her feel better, but he had to try. "I sent Conover and a couple of deputies over to your house."

She shot him a look that said the idea was a colossal waste of time. "God, I hate this. There are way too many things I need to be doing."

"You'll be fine," he assured her. "All you need is rest and a little time."

The way she glared at him spoke loudly and clearly as to what she thought of that counsel.

"I'm going to the Wilton house with you to finish those interviews." When he would have argued, she gave him the side-eye. "Don't even go there."

"Whatever you say." He put on his hat and opened the door.

"I don't know what you expected to find at my house. If the man wore a ski mask, he probably wore gloves."

Bent had anticipated she would say as much. "Yeah, most likely. But it doesn't hurt to check. Not all criminals are that smart."

"Assuming it wasn't Erwin," Vera said in an aside, her tone nothing short of furious, as they exited the double doors into the lobby. "She barely had a scratch, as it turns out, and she was right behind me. She probably had some heavy object in her purse and swung it at me."

The doctor confirmed Erwin had absorbed a blow to the forehead, but the injury wasn't a concussion and only required a butterfly strip. Still, she claimed to have lost consciousness, which, in Bent's opinion, was highly unlikely.

"You think she did this just to get a look at your notes?" Made the most sense, he supposed. He glanced down the corridor, spotted the woman in question waiting at the nurses' station.

"You're damn straight I think it's a possibility. Especially after that load of irrelevant crap she used as an excuse for dropping by. She only wanted to see what I had found out. I wasn't unconscious long enough for anything other than someone—most likely her—to shuffle through my stuff and toss things around. Ten minutes, maybe." Vera wore a smile for the benefit of the woman now rushing across the lobby toward them, but her tone told Bent she was anything but glad to see her. "Just wait. You'll see what I mean. The real question is, Why? Maybe she was working with Alicia. Or maybe she is our murderer, and she wanted us to believe it was Alicia."

Bent grunted. "Maybe."

"I'm so glad you're okay." Erwin rested her hands against her cheeks in a show of dismay. "The nurse said you have a really bad concussion. This is just terrible."

"I'll be fine," Vera said tightly.

"Are you sure? You really look—"

"Ms. Erwin," Bent interrupted as he ushered Vera toward the exit. "Deputy Houser is waiting in the ER drop-off lane to take you to your car. I'm sure you'll want to get home after the morning you've had."

Erwin blinked. "Thank you. Yes. I am overwhelmed and exhausted." She suddenly looked the part, when the moment before she'd been over-the-top exuberant. "And my head, it really hurts."

Outside, Erwin waved as the deputy drove her away. Vera scowled as she climbed into Bent's truck and fastened her seat belt. "That woman is in this up to her eyeballs."

Bent started the engine. "Is that your anger talking or your professional opinion?"

"Right now"—Vera shoved on her sunglasses—"they are one and the same."

Bent would wager the Wilton case was mostly solved already. Vera's instincts were always on the money—even after a severe blow to the head. He glanced at her profile, fear mingling with his worry now.

How in the world would he ever protect her from herself?

12

Wilton Residence
Giles Hollow Road, 1:40 p.m.

Vera was astounded at the very idea that Bent had for one second been naive enough to believe she would go home and rest. He should've known better.

She might stay seated on the leather settee in Thomas Wilton's home office, but she would be a part of these interviews if she had to be propped up with the Sherpa-covered throw pillows the decorator had deemed a perfect complement to the room. Bent had finally recognized he was fighting a losing battle and relented—as long as she drank the water and ate the chips he had insisted on picking up after they left the hospital. She had no idea what purpose he thought the chips served, and she didn't care. As long as he agreed to her terms.

Once they'd reached a compromise—mostly on his part—he'd given her a folder containing his latest notes and background info on Wilton's household employees to review while he checked in with his team of deputies to see how the search here was going. The ones he had sent to her house had found nada, of course.

As for the Wilton home, the interior of the house was done, and all were focused on the grounds now. By the time Bent returned to the elegant office with the next staff member to be questioned, Vera had devoured the chips and drunk most of the bottle of water. She had to admit that the combination of salt and water was helping with the nausea and the weakness. She might even thank him for the suggestion.

Later, of course.

Today a whole slew of reporters had been waiting outside the gate to the property. No surprise, Nolan Baker had been front and center. Vera was pretty sure he'd taken a photo of her as she and Bent rolled past. The man was relentless. It was a miracle he hadn't shown up outside her house already.

"This is Helen Carter."

Vera snapped to attention as Bent gestured for the woman he'd introduced to have a seat. Carter took the chair on the left of the desk.

"Vera Boyett is my associate," he explained as he settled into the chair on the right. "She'll be assisting with the investigation."

Vera looked from Bent to Carter. "Thank you for agreeing to speak with us, Ms. Carter."

Even with the full head of gray hair, Carter looked to be no older than mid-forties. But the background info sheet Bent had provided stated she was fifty-nine. Maybe it was the trim figure or her manner of dress, but she looked great. She was a widow and had been in charge of the kitchen in the Wilton home since it was built.

"I'm happy to help any way I can." Carter studied Vera as she said this. "I've worked for Mr. Wilton since he moved to Fayetteville. He was an excellent employer and a fine man. We're all devastated by this tragedy."

"You knew his first wife then." The statement was Bent's way of leading into queries about his second wife. A strategy Vera employed regularly.

Since his second wife was the latest big change in Wilton's life and the only survivor of the weekend killing spree, she would be the subject of close scrutiny. Based on Erwin's statements alone, Alicia Wilton was a definite suspect. Not to mention finding the murder weapon under her.

Carter shifted her attention to Bent. "Of course. A lovely woman. Really lovely. Nothing like . . ." She cleared her throat as if she'd caught herself before saying too much.

"Ms. Carter." Bent removed his hat and placed it on the desk. "If there is anything about Alicia Wilton that will help with this investigation, I hope you'll share the information with us." He glanced at Vera before meeting the other woman's gaze once more. "Mr. Wilton was brutally murdered. We need to find the person or persons responsible. I'm not suggesting Mrs. Wilton had anything to do with what happened, but it's important that we look into all potential avenues."

"Alicia," Carter began, "is not a nice person. I can't say that she is capable of murder." She shrugged. "But . . ." She paused to swipe at the tears that had slipped past her lashes. "But she is hateful and self-centered. No one on staff has been excluded from her insensitivity. She treats us like lower-class citizens. She never asks for anything. She demands everything."

"Did you or one of the other members ever speak to Mr. Wilton about this?" Vera hoped the answer would be yes. She had no tolerance whatsoever for those who treated anyone as if they were lesser humans.

Carter lifted her chin. "I did. Yes. He apologized and said that he would speak with her."

"Did anything change?" Bent glanced at Vera as he asked the follow-up.

Vera knew what he was thinking—it probably hadn't changed one thing. The power Alicia held over her new husband was likely not related to her less-than-award-winning personality.

"Actually"—Carter shook her head—"it made things worse. Alicia became more careful about her digs. She even warned me that if I said anything to him again, she would see that I paid dearly. So I let it go. I love my work. I didn't want to get fired because she wanted to be—excuse my French—a total bitch."

"Did you ever see any behavior or overhear any conversations that suggested to you Alicia was hiding things or activities from

Mr. Wilton?" At this point Vera didn't see any reason to beat around the bush. This woman was in the house every day, all day long. She surely heard many things.

"If you're asking," Carter said pointedly, "if she was fooling around behind his back, I'd say yes. She was always having these little private chats. If any one of us happened to pass the open door of wherever she was, she'd slam it shut. She was very secretive."

Bent considered this news for a moment before moving on to his next question. "Do you know if Mr. Wilton became aware of whatever Alicia may have been doing behind his back?"

Vera imagined the answer would be yes, considering the tension Erwin had mentioned. Surely others in the household were aware of the discontent.

"I can't be certain," Carter admitted. "I suspected he knew. There was a sort of odd distance between them in recent weeks." She looked from Bent to Vera. "And I noticed the way he blew her off. You know like when she'd try to kiss his cheek, and he'd turn away. Or take his hand, and he'd move out of reach. He was not happy about something. You couldn't help but notice the signs of trouble."

Vera's instincts sharpened. One witness's statement prompted curiosity in an investigation, but when a second witness confirmed the same, the game changed. The accusations were far more likely to be fact than innuendo.

"Did any of the other members of staff notice?" Vera asked.

"We all did. Ask Renata, the housekeeper. Since she's really quiet and rarely speaks anything other than Spanish, Alicia talked more openly in front of her. Renata told me Mrs. Wilton was up to something."

"When was this?" Bent's shift in posture announced that his own interest in the scenario had spiked.

"Early last week. Then we all . . ." Carter's breath caught, and she swiped at the tears overflowing now. "I'm sorry, Sheriff."

"No need to apologize. Take your time."

When she'd regathered her composure, she began again. "We all talked—the three of us, I mean. Renata, Jose, and me. It was after I heard about the murders, I went to their house. We all agreed that we should have realized something bad was coming."

"Renata and Jose are together?" Vera shifted to the next page in the folder of info Bent had given her. The two employees had different last names. Renata Hernandez and Jose Martinez.

"They aren't married, but they are together. They rent a house from me. It was my mother's. A few months ago they were having difficulty finding a place, and the house was just sitting there empty since my mother passed."

Vera nodded her understanding. The arrangement was obviously beneficial to all involved.

"Beyond giving them the news about Mr. Wilton, what else did you talk about?" Bent asked.

Carter drew in a deep breath. "As I said, all of us felt we should have seen something like this coming. We made the decision that we weren't saying anything unless we were questioned and had no choice. Mr. Wilton is dead. It sounded as if Alicia would probably die, too, so what was the point of allowing his name to be dragged through the mud? He wouldn't want his private business to become public gossip."

Vera could, on some level, see her point. From all appearances, these people had great respect and admiration for Wilton. "I completely understand how you might feel that way, but if what you three know can help us, then Mr. Wilton's killer won't get away with these unthinkable crimes. Even if Alicia was part of it, chances are she didn't pull this off alone. We need all the help we can get to find the person or persons responsible for what happened at that cabin."

Carter nodded. "I can see that now. I think we were all just so upset that we weren't thinking clearly. I can tell you that we all firmly believe Alicia was up to something. We talked about it on several occasions. She would sneak away and stay gone for hours, then tell Mr. Wilton that she'd been home all day and was bored just so he'd take her somewhere for dinner or whatever. She's conniving like that."

"You have no idea where she went when she left the house on these occasions?" Bent pressed.

"Jose did follow her once. She drove to a small house in Park City. The next day I drove to the place, but no one was there. When I looked into it, I found out it's one of those Airbnb places. I can give you the info I found online. The discovery didn't tell me what Alicia was doing there, and I realized it was pointless to try and track down the owner. Privacy issues or whatever protect the identities of guests. But, given what's happened, that person might talk to you since you're the sheriff."

"Jose didn't see anyone else or any other vehicles?" Vera wasn't sure the follow-up would give them much of anything unless the person who rented it used their real name. If it was Alicia, the question would be why. If it was someone else, they might be the answer. The issue with these types of rental was that, in all likelihood, the owner or agency that listed the place probably never actually saw or met the person who rented it. It was all generally executed online.

"No." Carter shook her head. "Jose said it was just her car. Maybe someone came later or was already there and had parked the vehicle they used elsewhere."

Vera looked to Bent before asking the question pounding in her aching brain. "Ms. Carter, were you aware of any trouble with any business associates of Mr. Wilton's? Any professional dealings gone the wrong way?" She'd been employed by the man for eight years. If he'd ever had trouble, she may have heard the talk.

Carter's head moved firmly from side to side. "Mr. Wilton did not do bad business. No underhanded activities. No slighting the IRS. Nothing like that. He was an honest man. He didn't have to do bad business." She looked from Vera to Bent and back. "He made a huge fortune. He invested wisely and had several more big successes in recent years. He didn't need to find ways to make money. He was set. In fact, he gave away—donated—more money every year than most big businessmen make in their lifetimes. That's the worst misfortune of all in this. He was a truly good person who didn't deserve such a tragic ending."

The other two interviews went exactly the same way. Both confirmed Carter's story about Alicia's behavior and seemingly secret rendezvous. All three insisted they were at their respective homes all weekend, catching up on chores.

Once Bent let the last interviewee go and had closed the door to the office, he joined Vera on the settee.

"How're you holding up?" He searched her eyes, worry in his own.

"Well, my head hurts like hell." It was incredible that she'd suffered such a blow and there'd been no blood involved. At the moment she was grateful. The thought of washing her hair made her want to curl into the fetal position. "The nausea is mostly gone, and I don't feel dizzy—sitting down, anyway."

"You should go home now and relax. At least until tomorrow."

He was probably right, but that wasn't going to happen. Her cell vibrated. She'd silenced it for the interviews. "I have a call. I'm sure you want to check in with your deputies. Let me know if they find anything relevant."

"I assume that's my cue to exit the room."

Vera smiled. "Thank you."

He grabbed his hat and settled it into place, his eyes on her the whole time, then he walked out the door. Vera smiled, no matter that doing so hurt. The call had ended but came again almost immediately.

"This is Mina Childers," the voice on the line said. "You left a message for me to call."

Nola Childers's mother. Childers was Erwin's roommate at university and the stated reason for her making the move to the Fayetteville area. Hopefully this contact could provide some additional background information on Erwin.

"Thank you for calling me back, Mrs. Childers. I know it's been a while, but I wondered if you remembered Valeri Erwin, your daughter Nola's roommate at Lipscomb?"

The silence that followed had Vera's anticipation building.

"I do remember her, yes." A sigh whispered across the line. "She and Nola were very close. Valeri didn't have any family in the area, so she came home with Nola for holidays and sometimes just to get away from campus. Over time we came to consider her a second daughter. Such a sweet girl."

Vera recognized what came next. "When did things change, Mrs. Childers?"

"After Nola died, we never saw Valeri again. Well, other than at the funeral. Not long after that, we learned she had settled in Fayetteville, and it was a little hurtful that she was so close and never bothered to so much as call. I suppose it's understandable somehow. She had to move on. But she had made us feel as if she adored us, so it was hard to accept when she just disappeared from our lives. It was like losing two daughters."

Erwin's decision to walk away from any sort of relationship with the family wasn't very nice of her, but it wasn't a crime.

"Then you haven't heard from her in all this time?"

"No. I tried to call after I found out she had taken the job with Mr. Wilton, but she never called me back. Maybe she felt guilty because the job was to have been Nola's. She shouldn't have. Nola was gone. But my husband and I decided that might be the reason she didn't want to see or speak to us again."

The ache in Vera's head suddenly dropped off her radar, and her full attention zeroed in on the caller's words. "You're sure Nola had already accepted the position with Mr. Wilton?"

"Oh yes. She was top of her class. Mr. Wilton recruited her during the final semester of her senior year. She was so excited." Childers cleared her throat as if emotion had gotten the better of her. "Mr. Wilton paid for her funeral expenses and insisted that since Nola had already signed a contract with his company, that we were entitled to the one-million-dollar insurance policy. He was unexpectedly kind about everything."

Vera regretted the necessity of asking the woman about her daughter's death, but it would be far quicker than contacting the police involved and asking for the report. "Mrs. Childers, would you share with me how Nola died?"

"It was such a terrible heartbreak." The poor woman's voice trembled with emotion. "She was celebrating graduation and the start of her new job. It was the Friday before she was to begin work on Monday. Valeri said they went out to eat and came home to share a bottle of champagne. Later Nola ran a bubble bath in that big claw-foot tub in the house they rented." A long moment of silence, then a big breath. "Apparently she fell asleep and slipped under the water. Nola wasn't much of a drinker, so the champagne likely went straight to her head."

She took another moment to steady her composure. "When Valeri woke up the next morning, she found her in the tub. It was one of those bizarre accidents that you never expect to happen. A simple mistake that cost our sweet girl everything. I guess the good Lord just needed another angel."

Vera's instincts were screaming at her. She would be requesting a copy of that autopsy report. There had to be one. "I'm so sorry, Mrs. Childers. But I thank you for sharing the details with me."

"It's just awful about Mr. Wilton and his wife. I swear I don't know what this world is coming to."

Vera couldn't claim to know what this world was coming to, but she damned sure recognized when a tragic event that turned out to be a lucky break was a little too providential to be mere luck.

After the call ended, Vera sat for a moment and thought about what this meant. Valeri Erwin takes the job her dead friend was supposed to get. Then she pretends the family she had adopted no longer exists.

More suspicious in Vera's opinion, a girl who rarely drank suddenly drowns in the bathtub after drinking too much champagne with her roommate in the same apartment, sleeping off her own overindulgence.

Valeri Erwin had just scooted into a tie with Alicia Wilton on Vera's suspect list.

13

Wilton Residence
Giles Hollow Road, 2:15 p.m.

"Hello?"

Speak of the devil.

Vera had wandered into the kitchen for more water, suffering only two bouts of dizziness on the journey, when she heard Valeri Erwin's voice at the front door.

"Hello?" Erwin called out again.

"Kitchen." Vera winced as she turned to face the footsteps hurrying her way.

Too bad Bent was outside, going over the search results with his deputies. Vera would bet money Erwin had told the deputy standing guard out front that she was expected. Otherwise he would surely have asked Bent before allowing her to enter the house. At this point Vera wouldn't put a thing past the woman.

Erwin rushed into the huge kitchen. She made a surprised face. "I thought you'd be at home in bed. Are you holding up okay?"

Looking at the butterfly strip on the woman's forehead annoyed Vera all the more. She glanced at her shoulder bag. Exactly the right size for a brick or nice-size rock, in Vera's opinion. All she'd had to do was swing it hard enough. Vera could easily see the plan playing out. Erwin slammed Vera in the head, then took a quick look at her notes and made a hasty mess of the room. Finally, Erwin tossed the brick somehow—maybe in the shrubs around Vera's front porch—and proceeded to injure herself on a doorframe or some such thing just in time for Vera to come around. Maybe Vera was reaching, but it wasn't impossible . . . except that nothing casually tossed into her shrubs or yard near the front door had been found.

"I'm fine." Vera stretched her lips into a smile. "How are you? Any issues with balance or nausea?" Another blast of irritation soared through her. Of course not. The woman was barely nicked.

"Nothing like that." Erwin shrugged. "I guess I was lucky."

"Yes you were." Vera leaned against the counter, deciding to save her strength for more important challenges. "What brings you here? Did you remember something about this morning's intruder or about Mr. Wilton's business dealings?" Vera's gaze narrowed. "I hope you didn't talk to the reporters outside the gate."

"Of course I didn't. And no, I didn't remember anything new." Valeri shuffled over to the island and climbed onto a stool. She dumped her bag unceremoniously onto the stool next to her. "Honestly, I was just afraid." She shuddered to punctuate her statement. "After what happened, I'm terrified someone will break into my place and try to kill me." She braced her elbows on the shiny marble counter and rested her head in her hands. "This is the only place I feel safe."

Vera saw right through her explanation. Erwin needed to keep her thumb on the pulse of the investigation—even if it meant lying to get past a deputy.

"Nothing new comes to mind about Alicia or the trouble you sensed between her and Thomas?" The other staff members had basically confirmed her allegations, but that didn't prove the wife had killed her husband. It only suggested Wilton had made a bad decision when it came to his love life, or that they were merely having trouble meshing their lives, as couples sometimes do.

"I'm sure the staff told you that she was up to something. I mean, the woman was always sneaking around. You couldn't trust anything she said." She nodded to Vera. "I firmly believe Thomas had realized she was keeping secrets from him. I'm thinking that's why he set up the weekend get-together. To handle the situation. He probably intended to get to the bottom of things with the other man and then Alicia would be gone—along with her trashy friends."

It took Vera a moment to open her mouth without laughing at the idea. "When a man believes his wife is cheating, I'm thinking he might not be interested in handling the situation by getting naked with her potential lover. Personally, I believe the party was a setup of a different kind. One that included murdering Thomas Wilton."

"Please," Erwin scoffed. "I'm not sure Alicia is that smart." She sent a pointed look in Vera's direction. "I mean, she was really good at spending money and being mean to us lesser humans, but anything else . . ." She shrugged. "I can't see it."

Vera mounted a stool on her side of the expansive island with its arrangement of glossy copper pots hanging overhead. "Maybe. But whether she planned it or someone else did, my biggest issue with the scenario is that Thomas fell for it. He was a genius, right? I keep thinking that maybe the whole thing came to fruition via someone he trusted." Her gaze settled firmly on Erwin. "Someone whose loyalty he would never have questioned."

Erwin slid off her stool. "I need a cola." At the fridge, she glanced over at Vera. "You want one?"

"Sure." The sugar might do her good.

Erwin prowled in the massive fridge for a bit, then returned to the island and slid a canned soft drink across the counter to Vera. She settled on her stool once more and opened her own drink.

Vera took a long swallow of the fizzy, sugary drink. "I spoke with Nola Childers's mother this morning."

"Really? How is she doing?" Erwin hid her surprise well, but Vera spotted the slightest flicker of alarm.

"She and her husband are doing all right. She was sad that she hadn't heard from you since the funeral."

Erwin looked away for a moment. "It was just too difficult to go back. Losing Nola was the worst thing to ever happen to me. But the idea that I could have helped her if I hadn't drunk so much that I passed out on the sofa . . ." She pressed her lips together for a moment. "I just couldn't face her parents again after the funeral. I felt way too guilty."

"Why do you suppose Nola drank so much that night?" Vera sipped her cola. "Her mother said it was completely unlike her." Maybe she didn't say those exact words, but the understanding was there.

"That was my fault too. I kept pouring the champagne. Then we moved on to a second bottle." She drew in a big breath. "I never mentioned that part to her parents. I didn't want to hurt them, because the truth was that Nola drank more than they realized. She was a regular party girl. But she was careful. She didn't want anyone to know. Her folks are really religious."

How convenient. Particularly since Nola wasn't around to confirm or deny.

"How did you end up with her job?" Vera waited until the other woman's startled gaze connected with hers. "Mrs. Childers was really surprised by that as well."

Erwin shrugged. "Thomas and I had met a couple of times. I went with Nola to his house once. So . . . when she died, he called me. I guess he figured I was the next best thing. He knew we both had the same major. Both were at the top of our class. At that point I was just thankful to have a job. Anything to move beyond missing Nola."

More convenience. And not a soul left to confirm it.

"I thought you hadn't met him before the funeral." At least that was her previous statement.

Erwin blinked back what appeared to be tears. "Okay, the truth is, he found out about Nola's drinking, and he decided not to hire her. He wanted to hire me instead. I felt weird about it, so I said no. I wouldn't do that to Nola. Then after she died, it felt like all I had left."

This story just got better and better. Vera had to hand it to her, she was quick on her feet with the comebacks without missing a single beat.

A characteristic that said one of two things: She was either telling the truth or had a great deal of practice at lying. Vera was leaning toward the latter.

"Then why the celebratory champagne?" Vera couldn't wait to hear her explanation for that one.

"Nola had decided to leave Tennessee. She wanted to get away from her parents and everyone else. It was the first time in her life she'd decided to do what she really wanted to do, so we were celebrating."

Good save. But Vera wasn't buying it.

The sound of the front door opening and closing drew Vera's attention in that direction. A moment later Bent walked into the kitchen.

"Ms. Erwin." He gave her a nod, then glanced at Vera.

"Sheriff." Erwin scooted off her stool. "I was just saying how I'm really concerned for my safety at my place—especially after what happened this morning. I don't have a security system. I think it would be better if I stay here."

Vera should have seen that one coming. Not going to happen. There was no way Bent would allow her to stay in this house, considering it was easily a secondary crime scene.

When Bent would have spoken, Erwin quickly added, "I know Thomas would want me to see after things. If your search is finished, I don't see why I can't stay. I have so much to do for his business. By now people will be asking questions. Wanting to know what's going to happen moving forward. There are endless arrangements that need to be made."

"You're right," he offered, "about our search. We've been over the place, but we'll probably do it again."

The woman's expression fell.

"I'm sure you're aware," he went on, "Mr. Wilton has attorneys to take care of his estate." Then he removed his hat and ran his fingers through his hair. "But there's another issue we need to talk about, Ms. Erwin."

So he had found something. Vera perked up. One glance at Erwin warned she was braced for trouble. The woman definitely had a guilty conscience about something. Possibly a good many somethings.

"Mr. Wilton's personal attorney just called. I thought it might be important to my investigation to know the beneficiaries of Mr. Wilton's estate."

Erwin frowned. "I was under the impression most everything was going to a variety of charities. There might be a copy in the wall safe of his bedroom."

"That's true, but there are other beneficiaries as well." Bent joined them at the island, placed his hat there.

Like Erwin, Vera stared at him expectantly. She couldn't wait to hear the rest.

"Ten million dollars is slated for his wife, should she survive him. As you said, a great many charities were funded generously. So much so, in fact, they account for 90 percent of his estate. But the remainder"—Bent stared directly at Erwin then—"the other sixty million is split between the staff he trusted most: ten million to Helen Carter, ten to Renata Hernandez, ten to Jose Martinez, and the rest to you."

"How strange," Vera said since Erwin appeared to have been stunned into silence. "You get more than the man's wife."

"No." Erwin shook her head, her expression showing astonishment. "He would have told me." She got off the stool once more and backed up a step or two. "That doesn't even make sense. Why would he do that?"

Vera had to hand it to her, she had the whole "I can't believe this is happening to me" act down pat. Like she hadn't looked at the will in that safe. The woman had likely inventoried every little thing in this whole massive house. Maybe Vera was just angry about the idea that the woman was possibly the one to give her a concussion.

"I suppose," Bent offered, "because he appreciated the work all of you have done and wanted to ensure you were left well provided for." He reached for his hat, obviously done with delivering news. "As for your question about staying here, I'm afraid you and the rest of the staff will have to remain off the premises until my investigation is finished."

"But why? There are things that need to be taken care of." Erwin threw up her hands. "This is insane."

"What this is," Vera countered, "is motive. No one with that much motive can be on the property." Actually anyone not part of the official investigative team could be here.

"But who will see after everything?"

"The attorneys will handle Mr. Wilton's estate." Bent gestured to the door. "We'll let you know as soon as we have anything new on the investigation."

Vera watched in satisfaction as Bent escorted Erwin from the house. The news regarding Wilton's bequests was an unexpected turn of events, for sure. But the really unanticipated part, in Vera's opinion, was how surprised Valeri Erwin was at hearing she'd just inherited thirty million dollars.

Maybe she was a far better actress than Vera had estimated.

When Bent walked back into the kitchen, Vera had to ask, "Do you believe her? That she didn't know, I mean?"

"She does have the combination to all the safes," he offered. "It's hard to believe she hasn't taken a look at the will at some point. The trouble is, what I just learned from the attorney gives the employees closest to Wilton the most motive for killing him."

"They've all four admitted to noticing tension between Wilton and his wife," Vera put in. "They all four knew about the planned weekend."

"They all four"—Bent leveled a knowing gaze on hers—"would know how to get on the property without coming through the one and only gate. Because the security camera footage shows no one coming through that gate after Wilton's Mercedes returned just after dark on Friday."

Anticipation seared through Vera. "So what's next, Sheriff?"

"Olson is getting in touch with the previous owner of the property—not that I expect him to be much help since there was nothing but woods when Wilton bought the place. I've also got three deputies checking the fence all the way around the perimeter of the property. It'll take some time, but if there's evidence of someone coming through, hopefully they'll find it."

"What about any aerial photographs?" Wealthy landowners loved having aerial views of their property.

"Olson is checking on that too." He held up a finger. "And I've already called Carter and warned that we'll need another interview with the three of them."

"Are we meeting with them now?" As much as Vera wanted to be a part of those conversations—especially now—she really needed to check in on her sisters first.

"I didn't say when." He grinned. "Maybe tomorrow. I thought I'd let them sweat for a while."

Despite the ache pounding in the back of her head, Vera managed a laugh. "I think I'm rubbing off on you, Sheriff." His move sounded exactly like one she would make.

Bent chuckled. "Or maybe I rubbed off on you all those years ago."

A distinct possibility. Even at twenty-one, Bent had known how to heighten the tension and make a person—especially her—sweat.

Vera remembered well.

14

Carter Residence
Coldwater Creek Road, 3:30 p.m.

Helen reminded herself to breathe again. She had to keep everyone calm for however long this investigation took.

Renata shook her head, her dark curls swaying with her frustration, and warned, "I don't like this."

"It's fine," Helen assured her for the third time. "Everything went exactly as it should have. We have nothing to worry about."

This reaction was her only problem with these two. Why the hell could they not just stay calm? They were through the worst part.

"They ask a lot of questions already," Jose argued. "Now they want to talk to us again. This can't be good."

Funny how they could both speak such good English when it was only the three of them. Helen wondered sometimes if she could actually trust either of them. Everything depended upon trust. Maybe she was the fool here.

"Good Lord, Jose," Helen half shouted. "What do you expect? Thomas was brutally murdered." She glared from one to the other. "So were the others. When people get murdered, there are questions. Lots of questions. We work for Thomas. Of course the police have more questions for us. Until the investigation is over, we just have to do what we have to do."

"It's easy for you," Renata tossed back at her.

Was she really going there?

"Today was not about your immigration status!" Helen shook her head and paced the floor. "This was about a horrific tragedy that has to be investigated by the police. All you"—she sent another glacial stare at each one—"have to do is stay calm and answer the questions asked of you. It's that simple. We have nothing to worry about. Like I said, this is exactly what is supposed to happen when a tragedy like this occurs."

Valeri Erwin, the sneaky little opportunist, was the one who needed to worry. Helen knew exactly what she had been up to. Too bad her little plan had backfired. She was the reason everything had gone so wrong so quickly. This was her damned fault.

Now they were all being looked at as suspects.

"If you're sure." Renata stood, looked to Jose. "Let's go home."

"One more thing," Helen said, waylaying the two. When they looked back at her, she warned, "Don't talk to the reporters. They'll only make this worse for us."

They shared a look and then went on their way.

Helen watched as they walked out the back door. She dropped into a chair at her kitchen table.

She put her face in her hands and let the tears flow. Her shoulders shook with the sobs. She was so tired and so frustrated. Besides losing her husband all those years ago, this was the hardest thing she'd ever had to do. There was a time when Thomas Wilton had been almost like a brother to her. She drew in a ragged breath, scrubbed at the dampness on her face. But he wasn't. Friendship was all well and good, but blood was thicker than water.

Now here they were. If only she had paid better attention, she would have seen this coming. She should have known the past would never be forgotten. Some things could not be forgiven.

It was Erwin and Alicia who had ruined everything.

This could have been prevented if only . . . Too late for if-onlys now.

Deep breath. Helen scrubbed away the last of her tears. But she had to be strong. She could do what had to be done.

There was no other choice.

15

Barrett's Funeral Home
Washington Street, 4:00 p.m.

"You're sure you don't want to go home?" Bent studied Vera with blatant skepticism.

She didn't bother trying to produce a smile. She felt like hell. He was right about all the things he was no doubt thinking. Her head hurt. She felt ill. That late lunch he'd forced her to eat was on the verge of making a reappearance. But she was absolutely positive she did not want to go home and crawl into bed. She had too much to do. It was never good to allow a case to cool when so many little fires had been ignited.

Every member of Thomas Wilton's household and personal staff was feeling the heat. If a single one of them was holding back, right now was when they would be most worried. The tension and fear that worry prompted made them vulnerable.

"No." Vera dredged up a ghost of a smile. "I need to talk to Eve. She'll take me home."

Bent made one of those faces that warned he thought she was making a mistake. "Okay. Should I walk you in?"

She wasn't even going to answer that. "I'll see you later."

Her exit from his truck was less than graceful, so she didn't dare make eye contact with him once she was walking away. He would be shaking his head and thinking that she was too hardheaded for her own good.

Maybe she was, but if he didn't understand that was her way by now, he was well behind the curve and probably wouldn't ever catch up.

She pulled open the glass entrance door. Damn, when had it gotten so heavy. Lucky for her no one greeted her, which meant she could scurry on to the mortuary room without having to exchange all the usual chitchat with someone who wanted to sell her a deluxe funeral and burial package.

As she neared her destination, she couldn't decide which was worse: the fake floral odor of a funeral home or the atrocious music playing softly in the background.

She needed to remind Eve that when she died, she wanted to be cremated. She would not have half the town scrutinizing her cold, dead face and stiffly styled hair. Or talking about her infamous history over her casket, or any of the other stuff that people did during visitations.

At the mortuary room door Vera knocked, then braced herself for her sister's reaction to her arrival. Eve did not like to be interrupted when she was preparing a *visitor*. That was what she insisted on calling the dead people who ended up on her table. Vera reminded herself not to say *corpse* or *dead body*.

When Eve didn't open the door, Vera knocked again. Maybe her sister had started wearing earbuds and didn't hear the knocking. Doubtful. Eve liked conversing with her visitors. Yeah, there was that too.

But that was just Eve's way. She wasn't psychic (that they knew of), and she wasn't off her rocker. Well, not any more than Vera, anyway. They simply had their eccentricities. Didn't everyone?

"Vee, what're you doing here?"

Startled, Vera whirled around, suffering a bout of lightheadedness for her effort. "Hey." She steadied herself. The sudden movement had sent a blast of pain through her skull. A wince constricted her face before she could stop it. Then she frowned. Why was Eve dressed in a business suit? Where were her scrubs? "I thought you were working."

"I am." Eve grabbed Vera by the arm and pulled her toward the lobby. "I don't have a lot of time, so you'll have to talk while I prepare."

"Okay." The fast pace was not working well with Vera's overall physical condition, but she kept her mouth shut and allowed her sister to drag her along. What the hell was she preparing for?

Eve ushered her into a parlor and quickly closed the collapsable door that separated it from the long corridor. There were about a half dozen of these "parlors" along the corridor. At least two had those same collapsable doors between them for opening up into larger spaces for the *visitors* who had more friends and family than a single space would hold.

Vera grimaced when she noticed a casket surrounded by more of those unpleasant smelling flower arrangements on the far side of the room. Chairs and sofas lined the rest of the space. Tissue boxes sat on side tables and, of course, that sad music played softly. Eve hurried around the room, checking that all was as it should be. She was in her element—perfectly at home.

Funerals were Eve's thing. Vera just didn't get it. She frowned, making her head hurt all the more. Her sister wasn't usually a part of this aspect of the business. Her work was behind the scenes—preparing her visitors for their last hurrah.

At her questioning look, Eve said, "We're shorthanded. I have to host this visitation. Which starts in a few minutes, so talk fast."

That made sense, Vera supposed.

Eve adjusted a floral arrangement. "Luna called," she said when Vera remained mute. "Mr. Andrews came through the surgery. He's in stable condition, but they won't know how he's going to do until he wakes up. I was supposed to let you know, but I got busy."

Vera snapped out of the near coma she'd lapsed into. Good grief. The day was practically over, and she hadn't taken a moment to wonder how Luna's father-in-law was doing. "That's good news."

Eve's scurry around the room concluded at the casket. She unlocked it and then opened one half, revealing the prepared visitor inside. Hoping Eve would be still for a few minutes, Vera joined her there.

She put extra effort into not staring at the woman in the glittery pink box. When had they started adding sparkles to the paint on caskets? Just too weird.

"What's wrong with you?" Eve surveyed her from head to toe and back. "You look terrible, and you're acting like you're drunk."

Vera supposed she did. The jeans and tee weren't exactly proper attire when she wasn't working from home. But then she hadn't dressed this morning for leaving the house. "Someone popped in this morning and hit me with . . ." It hurt to recall that moment. "I don't know what. The weapon wasn't found. Anyway, the blow put me down, and now I have a concussion. I can't drive or run that marathon I had planned. Bent dropped me here so I could talk to you."

"Someone broke in at the farm? You didn't have the alarm set?" Eve stopped tidying the satin lining around the edge of the now-open casket.

"I disarmed it because I had a visitor." She frowned. "Not your kind of visitor—a person of interest in the case. We're not sure at this point if someone else came in after I unlocked the door." She shrugged, grimaced when the move affected her head. "Anyway, I wanted to talk to you about Luna."

Eve held up her hands stop-sign fashion. "First, you tell me what the hell is going on." She glanced at the corpse in the coffin as if to say, *Excuse me*. "What marathon were you planning to run?"

With all that was happening just now—Luna's mother-in-law dead at the bottom of her stairs, her father-in-law in intensive care after major heart surgery, and three dead as well as another on the verge of death, not to mention this damned concussion—the silly marathon remark is what got her sister's attention?

"There's no marathon, Eve, I was . . . anyway, I'm helping Bent with the triple homicide out at the Wilton place. One of the persons of interest stopped by the house, and while we were talking someone ambushed me or us." Sounded pretty amateurish on Vera's part to be caught off guard like that, but it was the way it happened.

A frown furrowed deeply into Eve's face. "You must have really made somebody angry."

Wow. No sympathy here. Obviously if she was conked on the head, it was her fault.

"Probably." Why argue? Besides, it was the nature of the beast in her chosen profession. "I'm not here to talk about that. I'm worried about Luna."

"She seemed okay when we talked." Eve finished tidying the liner. "She called about an hour ago and said she was heading home."

"She's driving back alone?"

Eve shot her another of those looks. "She's done it a million times. She'll be fine."

Vera looked around to ensure they were alone. They were except for the dead woman. Vera frowned again. "Is that Mrs. Ingle?" The woman had been her and Eve's art teacher back in middle school.

"Yes." Eve patted the corpse's cold, dead crossed hands. "She was such a good teacher."

Vera's frown deepened. "All I remember is the way she used those wooden paintbrush handles to smack me on the back of the hand when she caught me talking."

Eve glowered at her. "Why were you talking in class?"

"Because I was a kid. That's what kids do."

"Ignore her, Mrs. Ingle. She still has a disrespectful streak."

Vera wanted to roll her eyes, but she was certain it would be painful. "Seriously, I'm worried about Luna and what happened to Jackie."

"You think she had something to do with Jackie falling?" Eve shook her head. "Come on, Vee, we both know that's ridiculous."

Vera took a moment to clear her head of the dozens of questions and possibilities whirling there. "I know she would never set out to do anything to harm anyone. But something went down that she's not telling us. I can feel it. That cut-and-dried recap of how it happened is missing some element. I hear it in her voice and see it in her eyes every time we talk."

Eve appeared to consider her words for a time. "I trust you more than anyone on this planet outside Suri. If you say something's off, then it's off. How do we figure out what it is without getting Luna in trouble?"

"I'm not entirely certain that's possible." The thought of that damned hardware store receipt had Vera's gut twisting into knots. She should have looked into that today, but she hadn't expected to end up at the ER with head trauma. She had no time for this sort of issue cropping up. Damn it.

"Look," Eve said, drawing her thoughts away from the worry swelling inside her, "I don't have much time. The Ingle family will be here soon. What can I do to help with the Luna situation?"

Vera couldn't hold back her smile.

"Seriously? You're smiling." Eve shook her head again. "Sometimes I don't get you, Vee."

"I'm just thinking what a good sister you are and how grateful I am that you're mine."

The road for Eve hadn't always been easy. But she had found her way, and Vera was immensely proud of her.

"We need to call Bent." Eve's voice and expression were dead serious. Before Vera could ask why, she went on, "I'm afraid that bang on the noggin did something really bad, Vee."

Vera waved her off. "Just talk to Luna when the right opportunity arises. Make sure she knows she can tell us anything, and we'll figure out how to make it right—as soon as we know what *it* is."

"I will. I'll do that tonight. Jerome won't be back until tomorrow at the earliest, so I'll go over and stay with her. We'll talk and finish the final touches on the nursery."

Vera hugged her sister. "That's perfect."

Eve stiffened but did manage to hug Vera back just a little. Eve had never been much of a hugger.

"I can get Charlie Keller to give you a ride home," she offered, looking contrite now for being huffy when Vera first arrived.

"Charlie? I didn't know he worked here." The kid was younger than Luna. God, it was scary how fast time seemed to be flying lately.

"He does the pickups for Barrett's." Eve grinned. "If you want, he could drive you home in the hearse."

"No thanks. I'm going across the street to visit Mama first. If Bent isn't available when I'm ready to go, I'll let you know."

"Say hi for me," Eve called over her shoulder as she finished preparing the room for Mrs. Ingle's visitation.

Vera smiled again for her sister's sake. She could not wait to get out of this place. "Will do."

Dealing with death in this way had never been Vera's cup of tea. Give her a mutilated murder vic anytime.

Not that she enjoyed seeing someone murdered . . . oh hell. Whatever. Anyone—including God—listening to her thoughts got it, hopefully.

16

Rose Hill Cemetery
Washington Street, 4:45 p.m.

Vera and Eve had been so young when their mother died that separating from her so completely at first had been difficult. Their father had added a bench to the family plots to ensure she and Eve would have a place to sit when they visited their mother. They had done so often for those first few years. Eventually Vera had gone off to university and then work in Memphis, and things had changed. But since she'd come home, this was once again their special place where they could speak openly about whatever was on their minds.

Halfway across the cemetery, Vera hesitated. Someone was sitting on their bench. As she moved closer, her steps slower than usual after this morning's fun with the assailant, she recognized the dark hair and paisley-print dress.

Luna.

What was she doing here?

Vera smiled when her sister looked up, obviously sensing she was no longer alone.

Vera attempted to hurry her steps, but she didn't trust her balance completely just yet. Her symptoms were definitely lessening, but she still felt out of sorts.

"Hey, Vee." Luna patted the marble bench. "Sit with me."

Vera settled next to her little sister. Gave her a hug. Luna and that big old belly. It was still hard to believe their baby sister was about to be a mother. "Eve says the surgery went well."

"It did. His vitals are stable, and the doctor is hoping he'll be able to wake up and stay that way for longer periods soon. Until now he's barely opened his eyes. He struggles to speak but can't seem to form the words. Nothing comes out coherently. It's so awful seeing him like that."

"So he's still in and out." Vera held out hope that Mr. Andrews would wake up and explain what had happened to his wife. Like maybe he was the one who caused this tragedy.

Vera could hope. Not that she wished more pain on the Andrews family, but she'd rather it be anyone except Luna. Selfish as the thought might be.

"He is. But there's still hope he'll make a full recovery. Some patients just take a different path toward that result."

Good way to look at it. "I'm sorry you had to drive back alone." Vera wished she had been with her sister. She wouldn't have this damned concussion right now if she had been with Luna. The drive back would have been a good time to talk as well.

"It's fine," Luna assured her. "It gave me a chance to think." She smiled. "Jerome was so sweet. He urged me to leave right after the surgery was over, so I'd get out of Nashville before rush hour. I decided to stop here before going on home."

"Jerome is a good husband." Vera was so happy that Luna had found such an amazing husband. She hoped this misfortune wasn't going to damage their relationship. Sadly, the potential was there.

"He is." Luna's lips quivered.

Vera reached for her hand, held it tight. As they sat in silence, she noticed the fresh flowers on the graves. She looked to Luna. "Did you bring those?"

"Eve and I brought them. When Jerome had to leave after his father's heart attack, she thought it would make me feel better to do something besides sit in the house."

Smart. "Before I forget"—Vera settled her gaze on her mother's headstone—"Mama, Eve says to tell you hi. You too, Daddy." Then she felt bad for leaving Luna's mother out. "To you as well, Sheree." The memory of dragging the woman's dead weight down that staircase and then hefting her into the trailer flashed in Vera's aching head. She squeezed her eyes shut and forced the recall away. Ancient history.

"I'm glad they're here together." Luna looked to Vera. "We're all family."

"We most certainly are." Vera draped her arm around Luna's shoulders. She pressed her forehead to hers. "Anything you want to talk about, I'm always available. Even if I'm in the middle of work, I can stop."

Luna peered up at her. "I know I can always count on you, Vee. Just like Eve always could. You're a good sister to both of us, and we're very lucky to have you."

"Ditto." Vera smiled. Swiped a tear from her sister's cheek. "And this is going to be okay. It'll be a little tough for a while. But this"—she placed a hand on Luna's belly—"little baby is going to steal everyone's attention. There won't be time to worry about the past, no matter how painful."

Luna placed her hand atop Vera's and stared at them. "Do you believe a baby can hear what's happening outside their mother's body at this stage?"

"I've heard that's the case." Since she had never been pregnant or ever expected to be, Vera hadn't actually done any research on the subject, but she'd heard other knowledgeable people say as much. There was, she thought, extensive information to be found. "After they're born, babies usually recognize their parents' voices, so the idea makes sense."

Luna lapsed into silence then. They sat, staring at the headstones marking the graves of their parents. Vera wasn't sure how long they continued that way, but she wasn't moving until Luna did. It felt very much like Luna needed exactly this right now, and Vera intended to give it to her for as long as possible.

"Do you believe that sometimes people die because it's the best thing for everyone else in their lives?"

Vera relaxed her body when every muscle tried to stiffen. "I suppose that can happen. There are people with terminal illnesses who take their own lives because they feel it will be better for those around them. I don't know if that's the best decision or not. I imagine it is for some, maybe not for others."

Luna drew away. "I don't mean people who are sick. I'm referring to the ones who are so mean and so awful that everyone around them is happier—better off—when they're gone."

Vera wasn't about to confirm any such suggestion—not when it was clear Luna was searching for empathy or some level of agreement on the subject. "Do you mean like the idea of God stepping in and taking them out of the way or another person doing so?"

"Either one, I guess."

That's what Vera thought she was saying. "As far as what is presumed to be an act of God, I really can't say. There are plenty of strong believers who would say so. I've certainly known plenty of cases where people made the decision to intervene when a situation became unbearable."

Vera searched for a way to soften the concept of vigilantism. "Most folks are relieved when a serial killer or someone who hurts children is executed or ends up dead in a shoot-out with the police or a victim of an avenging loved one. But even killers generally have family. Someone who's sad to see them gone. Who's to say? I've been forced to make that decision as a cop, and it's not an easy one to make or to look back on. Taking a life, I mean."

Luna exhaled a deep sigh. "I know it sounds awful." She turned to Vera. "But you said I could tell you anything."

"Of course you can, and I'll never say a word to anyone."

"Not even Bent?" Luna's eyes searched hers, looking for further reassurance.

"If I say I won't tell anyone, that includes Bent."

"I . . ." Luna pursed her lips for a moment, and Vera held her breath. "I'm grateful she's gone. I wouldn't have wished it on her, but I'm glad Jackie is gone."

And there it was. Vera absorbed the ramifications of her words for a second or two, working diligently not to show any sort of reaction that would hurt her sister. "I can understand how you would feel that way. I'm sure there are others who do as well."

"Not Jerome or his father, of course." Luna stared at her mother's headstone. "It was better for you and Eve when she was gone, wasn't it? And I imagine you were glad."

Vera's heart lurched. "Lu, nothing about what happened with your mother was better. It just was. I wished her gone plenty of times, but I didn't want her to die." Okay that might be a lie. "Eve didn't want her to die. But it happened, and it was an accident." At her sister's look of wanting more, Vera went on with the painful story. "It's true that life was . . . *easier* in some ways afterward. But I would have endured whatever she did or said if it had been possible for her to keep living and to be a good mother to you." Maybe a bit of a stretch.

Luna's face fell. "So you're saying I shouldn't be relieved."

Shit. "No. No." Vera moved her head side to side despite the pain. "I think you would be a little strange if you weren't relieved. But Jackie was very different from your mama."

Vera stared at the headstone of the woman in question. Searched for a way to say something kind about the witch. "Sheree didn't have a proper upbringing, Luna. She was badly mistreated, and she had nothing. Coming from a home life like that, she learned to take whatever she could get by whatever means available to her. It was survival, pure and simple."

Luna blinked as if she was confused or bewildered.

Well, hell. "In other words," Vera went on, "she kind of did the best she could. Yes, she was jealous and would fight a bear to keep what she had once she got it, but that was only a self-defense mechanism. No one until Daddy had ever protected her, so she learned to protect herself. Jackie always had everything handed to her. She never wanted for anything, and she had fine parents. It's not the same situation at all. Jackie was just . . ." Vera told herself to shut up, but she couldn't. "She was a selfish bitch who loved making everyone around her miserable, and to tell you the truth, I am damned relieved for you that she's gone."

Vera clamped her mouth shut. She had definitely gone too far.

Luna smiled, her eyes still sad, no matter that her lips showed otherwise. "Thank you. I needed to hear that truth."

Vera wanted to feel good about it, but she wasn't at all sure she should. "Like I said, you can tell me anything."

Just please don't tell me you killed her.

But she had a bad, bad feeling that might be the case. Hopefully accidentally. Vera thought of the indentation in the drywall and the broken spindle. And that damned scratch on Jackie's arm. Probably not accidental, but she could hold on to her optimism. There was hope when there was nothing else. And even when the hope was gone, Vera would do everything possible to protect her sister.

"I just wish things could have been different." Luna's expression turned despondent once more.

"Eve says she's coming over tonight to help finish the nursery." Maybe the reminder would perk her up.

Luna only nodded, her lips struggling to pull off a smile again.

Vera's cell vibrated in her pocket. She fished it out with two fingers. *Bent.* News on Alicia Wilton's condition would be good. Or some evidence on the case. "Hey. What's up?"

"You still at the funeral home?"

"I'm at the cemetery with Luna." She glanced at her sister. "We're visiting the folks. You have news on the Wilton case? Or new evidence?"

"Nothing earth-shattering. We did find that one of Erwin's neighbors has a Ring doorbell camera, and Erwin's vehicle remained parked in front of her place between Saturday afternoon and Monday morning. No sign of her coming in or out—unless she used the back door and some other form of transportation."

Vera felt her forehead fold with frustration. She rubbed at it. "That's still not a solid alibi."

"It's not, but it is something to consider. Look, Collins wants to see us at the morgue. She's working on the preliminary examinations of the victims from the case. I'll pick you up."

Wow, that was fast. But then the new ME was all about impressing Bent. "I'll wait for you at the main gate."

Vera put her cell away and hugged her sister. "Bent's on the way. We have work. You going to be okay getting home and settled until Eve arrives?"

Luna patted her belly. "We'll be fine."

Vera intended to see that both her sister and her baby stayed that way.

17

Lincoln Medical Center
Medical Center Boulevard, 5:40 p.m.

The county was fortunate that a small portion of the basement level of the hospital had been designated as a temporary morgue—with a newer permanent location coming. For this region, autopsies were performed in Nashville. But since their new medical examiner had formal training in forensics, she could do the preliminaries here before shipping the bodies to Nashville.

Good for the county when there was a murder case and time was an issue.

Truth was, their previous ME had done the same thing without all the fanfare of a private little brick-and-mortar location to call his own. But then he'd had other failings. The old bastard had held the position far too long and used his vast knowledge of the townsfolk to his and his family's advantage.

But at least he hadn't been enamored with Bent.

Vera kicked aside what was nothing more than pure jealousy and prepared for listening to Jenny Collins regale the two of them with her brilliant deductions.

Bent parked at the back of the hospital. "Did you hear anything I just said?"

"What?" Vera had zoned out on the drive here. Maybe she should have taken a rest when Bent suggested it. She did feel like total roadkill. "I'm sorry, I was thinking about the case." Not really, but no need for him to hear what she'd really had on her mind. She doubted Bent had ever suffered a smidge of jealousy in his life.

Well, except maybe when her friend Eric visited last spring. There might have been a moment then.

"I was saying that Geneva stopped by the office after she got back from Nashville. She's pushing hard for an official investigation into Jackie's death."

Vera wanted to shake the woman. "You have an obligation to look into her allegations. We've discussed this already." The whole subject was becoming redundant and increasingly annoying. "What does she want? For you to set aside the triple homicide case and focus solely on what happened to Jackie?"

Of course she does, Vera Mae. Jackie was her sister. She'd likely poisoned Geneva's opinion of Luna. Made her believe Luna was some conniving little nefarious vixen who'd stolen her son. It was unbelievable what some mothers would do to keep their sons to themselves.

"I assured her we are working on it." He flashed Vera an expression that said *but.* "I didn't mention that you're involved. I'm sure that would only have made matters worse."

"Of course it would." She reached for his hand, gave it a squeeze. "Thanks, Bent. I realize this isn't easy for you either."

"Did you learn anything from Luna that might give us new insights into what, if anything, happened beyond what she's told us?"

Vera leaned her head back against the seat and closed her eyes for a moment. "She stands by her story, and I can't believe it was any different than what she says. I mean really, Bent. Why in the world would she do something like that? Jerome chose her despite his mother's disapproval. There isn't a single reason that comes to mind for her to suddenly decide to get his mother out of the way."

Then again, Luna's hormones might be raging. But the fact was pregnant women were far more often the victims of homicide than the perpetrators.

"The text messages Geneva showed me matched what was on Jackie's phone, but none gave us anything useful beyond how much the two dislike Luna." Bent leaned his head back against his seat as well, allowing a measure of his own exhaustion to show. Not something he did often and maybe only now to make Vera feel better.

"You never told me what was said in the text messages." Vera probably didn't want to know.

"I didn't see the need to make you any angrier, considering none of it provided enough evidence to initiate an official investigation. Basically she ranted about Luna not doing anything right—to her way of thinking. Accused her of being just like her mother."

Vera groaned. "That is so not true. Luna is an amazing young woman who didn't even know her mother."

"She is amazing," Bent agreed, "and she definitely is nothing like Sheree."

Bent remembered Vera's wicked stepmother as well. Anyone living in Fayetteville at the time would. Not to speak ill of the dead—oh why not—but Sheree was a conniving, controlling, self-centered . . . Vera sighed. As she told Luna, her mother was a woman who'd never had a decent chance.

Vera straightened, stared directly at Bent. "Did Jackie indicate in any way in those text messages that Luna made her feel threatened or had done anything at all to make her nervous or afraid?" The mere notion was ludicrous.

"She did not, but she did say she wished Luna was out of the picture."

Vera's jaw dropped. "Seriously?"

He sat up straighter then, too, nodded solemnly. "She did."

"Like out of the picture how? Divorced?"

"Dead. She wished Luna was dead. Geneva scolded her but not strongly."

Vera unfastened her seat belt, so angry now that her fingers fumbled. "We can't tell Luna about this. How awful would that make her feel."

"We won't have to." Bent sat up. "Geneva will find the perfect opportunity and will revel in revealing Jackie's true feelings for her daughter-in-law."

He was right. Damn it. "We might not be able to stop that, but we have to find a way to prove she's wrong about what happened."

"Depending on how the autopsy turns out, that might not be easy, Vee. You know what Collins said."

"Yeah, yeah, I know." Vera hadn't forgotten the preliminary findings. The memory of that damned hardware store receipt haunted her as well. He was right. It wouldn't be easy, but Vera knew there had to be another answer to how that trauma came about. There simply had to be.

"Collins is waiting." Bent climbed out and came around to her door before she could do the same.

"This will of Thomas Wilton's," she said as they walked toward the rear entrance, "gives Erwin the biggest motive. Not to mention that what I learned from Nola Childers's mother shows a possible tendency to take advantage of situations. Maybe even to manipulate those situations."

Bent entered the code Collins had no doubt given him and opened the rear entrance to the basement level. Vera refused to allow the woman to distract her. They had a triple homicide case to worry about . . . not to mention this ridiculous business with Geneva Fanning.

"Erwin's history is undeniably suspicious, considering what's happened," Bent agreed.

Vera had brought him up to speed on her and Erwin's conversation after the woman left the mansion in a huff because Bent refused to allow her to stay there. "I've already requested a copy of Nola Childers's autopsy, but I think we need Wilton's first wife's as well. We may be missing something big here."

"Like maybe Erwin has been eliminating all the obstacles in her path to Wilton."

"Something like that," Vera agreed. Except why eliminate the golden goose at the same time? If having Thomas Wilton all to herself was the goal, why kill him too? Unless he figured out her endgame and she had no choice. There was more, Vera understood. "We also need to see any will Wilton had before this one—assuming it changed after his first wife died, which is very likely. Or any changes he almost certainly made after he married Alicia. I'd be interested in seeing what those changes were."

Bent pulled out his cell. "I'll have Myra give the attorney a call and look into the possibility."

"Thanks."

Myra Jordan was Bent's assistant. She took care of his office and him like a military general organizing her battalions. Another someone whose good side Vera intended to stay on.

As they reached the door with its taped-on handmade sign proclaiming the space beyond as the morgue, Vera considered the lineup of suspects in the Wilton case. There was Alicia at the top because of the knife, but Erwin was right up there with her, possibly an accomplice. Seth Parson could have been an accomplice as well. For that matter there was Helen Carter, Renata Hernandez, and Jose Martinez. Ten million dollars was a hell of a lot of motive. Helen Carter intrigued Vera the most. She clearly knew Wilton better than anyone else. Knew everything about him and his home. She was a widow. No children. Maybe she wanted a better retirement plan. Definitely a close third behind Erwin and Alicia. A zing of new anticipation fired through Vera. The suspects and motives were coming into better focus now. It wouldn't be long until she and Bent had nailed this one down.

Then it was only a matter of finding the necessary evidence to prove the case in a court of law.

When Bent ended the call to his assistant, he opened the door and waited for Vera to enter before him.

Jenny Collins waited in the center of the room. She was dressed in full ME garb, sans the protective face mask, as if she were about to perform an autopsy right here in this makeshift morgue. "Thanks for coming. I've left a formal report on my desk for you, but I'm sure you want to see my findings for yourselves while you're here."

Meaning, Vera mused, the woman wanted to put on a little show. Fine. A closer look at the vics was always a good idea, especially considering the bodies had been removed from the scene by the time Vera was there.

"I appreciate this, Dr. Collins." Bent removed his hat and settled it on the table next to the file with his name on it.

Vera surveyed the good-size room. Collins had made herself a very professional setup in her little bartered space. A stainless steel exam table had been turned into a desk with a lamp and neat stacks of files and papers. A shiny new four-drawer file cabinet stood next to it. Two more stainless steel exam tables sat side by side on the other side of the floor space. But the coups de grâce were the shiny new refrigerated morgue drawers that housed the corpses she prepared for shipment to Nashville.

Bent passed Vera a pair of gloves. He'd already tugged on a pair himself. They joined the ME at the wall of nine drawers.

"Seth Parson." Collins opened the first of the drawers in the middle row. She unzipped the body bag and revealed the corpse within. "He appears to have been in reasonably good health. The lab work isn't back yet, but I can tell you that his blood alcohol level was somewhat high. The issue with that is decomp can cause the production of ethanol, which affects the BAC level, so we can't get a truly accurate count. Other test results for drugs will be a few days, as you know. The most accurate story will come with the autopsy report."

She paused, looked from Bent to Vera as if waiting for questions, then, when none were posed, turned her attention to the man in the bag. "You're aware of the stab wounds and defensive injuries. But I also found a tattoo on his hip."

Vera peered at the entwined set of hearts the ME pointed out. The initials, AT, were part of the tattoo. "Alicia Thurman." She looked to Bent. "Thurman, that's Wilton's wife's maiden name."

Bent raised his eyebrows. "This would seem to confirm Erwin's statement that Alicia knew the guy."

"I took the liberty of calling Vanderbilt," Collins said, drawing their attention. "Alicia has a tattoo in this same location. But the one that matched this one has been overlaid with a larger single red heart. The nurse who checked for me sent images—which you'll find with my report. Careful examination of those images shows a tattoo just like this one beneath the heart. The initials SP are there as well. It's faint, but you can make out the pattern."

"More than acquaintances then." Vera had to hand it to Collins. "Good catch."

Collins smiled as if she hadn't expected the compliment. "Thanks."

Vera considered Seth Parson. She was still waiting on callbacks from the New Orleans Police Department and the one brother Eric had located an address and phone number for. If Vera could reach the brother, he might be able to shed some light on the relationship between Seth and Alicia.

"I confirmed that the knife found under Alicia Wilton has a blade the right width and length for the inflicted wounds on all three victims. It also fits the missing slot in the knife block found in the kitchen. Alicia sustained a laceration to the left breast from the knife. It appears the injury was made when it was pushed under her body."

"Or when she fell and it was under her," Bent countered.

Collins tilted her head one way then the other as if the point was debatable. "That's possible, but more likely if she had fallen, the injury would have been deeper, perhaps lethal."

Vera was no medical examiner, so she didn't argue one way or the other.

Collins zipped up the bag and closed the drawer, then moved on to the next one. Vera and Bent stood on one side, Collins on the other. She lowered the zipper, revealing the still-unidentified female.

"She has the same tattoo on her hip." Collins indicated the left hip, where the initials LP were displayed amid the two hearts.

"Larry Parson." Vera looked to Bent. "He's the brother Eric located for me."

"We need to find this Larry Parson." Bent withdrew his cell and prepared to send a text. "I'll have Hastings follow up with the sheriff in his county of record."

"I called," Vera told him, "but I haven't had a callback yet."

"Who is Eric?" Collins looked to Vera for the answer.

"A colleague from my time in Memphis PD. Finding people and information is kind of his specialty."

Collins lifted an eyebrow at the news. But it was the tilt of one corner of her mouth that warned she suspected there was far more to know about Eric.

None of her business.

Collins moved on to the wounds on the unidentified female's body. The stab wounds were from the same knife or type and size knife as the others. As Vera and Bent had concluded, the one wound nicked the carotid artery.

"I did find some genetic material under the nail of this victim's long finger on the left hand. I've already sent it forward for testing. That may give you something to help with identifying your killer once you've found him."

Or her. Unless the genetic material was just part of the sex play that may have taken place during the party. That possibility couldn't be ruled out, in Vera's opinion. "Did you find scratch marks on any of the other victims?"

Collins smiled, recognizing where she was headed with the question. "Not unless it was on Wilton and it was dissolved given his extended period in the hot tub. As for this victim"—she indicated the female—"she has no other injuries or distinguishing marks other than what we've discussed."

In other words, nothing new. Well, except the material under the nail and confirmation that she likely came to the Wilton residence with Seth Parson. Unless his brother was loitering around town somewhere. Which could toss another suspect into the killer pool. Because one thing was reasonably certain: The dead folks in these three drawers had not done the killing.

Vera mentally added Larry Parson to her suspect list.

Lastly they surrounded Thomas Wilton's stainless steel drawer. Now that he was out of the water and lying in that open body bag, the deteriorated condition of his corpse was painfully obvious.

"The time in the hot tub played havoc with his epidermis."

No kidding. There were areas where the skin was red and swollen. Others where it was peeling and sloughing off. But it was one or more of the knife wounds that had killed him. The rest occurred postmortem. Lucky for him.

"He has two stab wounds in the region of the thoracic spine below a phoenix tattoo that extends across the width of the area. Numerous defensive wounds on both arms as well as significant damage to the right hand, where I suspect he grasped the knife blade. Two additional stab wounds to the upper torso near the sternum, one of which was fatal. A perfect strike between two ribs," Collins explained. "The blade no doubt slid directly into the heart with this one." She indicated the puckered wound in his chest. "His blood alcohol level was low. I would guess he'd had perhaps one drink."

"I'm sure the hot tub took care of any potential genetic evidence that didn't belong to Wilton." Bent knew the answer just as Vera did, but it was his job to confirm.

"Absolutely. Your forensics team found nothing else near any of the victims that might help?"

"Nothing so far."

Vera recognized that unless they got damned lucky, any hope of solving this puzzle anytime soon lay with the sole survivor . . . or with one of the names on Vera's suspect list. The scene and the bodies just weren't giving them a whole lot.

"By the way," Collins said, drawing Vera's attention back to her, although the woman was clearly addressing Bent, "that reporter, Nolan Baker, showed up at my house this morning. I'm sure he's well aware there is nothing I can share with him."

Oh he was aware, Vera mused, but that had never stopped Nolan before.

"I'll take care of it," Bent assured the ME.

"Well." Collins zipped the bag over Wilton's prune-puckered body. "I'll get the bodies shipped out in the morning with a request to autopsy as soon as possible. We can hope that will happen." She smiled up at Bent as she closed the drawer. "You have plans this evening, Bent?"

Vera turned to Bent, biting back a grin. "Yeah, Bent, do you have plans?"

"I think I'm preparing you dinner, Vee." His expression was as innocent as a little boy's. "After that knock on the head, you could use a good home-cooked meal."

"I definitely could use some pampering."

Collins looked to Vera. "What knock on the head?"

"No big deal." Vera would have shaken her head, but she figured it would hurt like hell. "An intruder at my farm."

"That sounds perfectly awful." Collins looked from one to the other. "Well, have a nice evening, you two."

Bent retrieved his hat, settled it into place atop that handsome head of his and grabbed the folder Collins had left for him. Vera removed her gloves, tossed them in the trash and put her hand on Bent's arm.

"You have a nice evening yourself," she called over her shoulder in pure-dee old meanness, as her mama would have said since she was the one walking out with Bent.

Sometimes it was necessary to mark your territory. The idea that Collins had just tested that boundary wasn't lost on Vera.

When they were out the rear exit of the building and headed for his truck, Vera warned, "Told you the ME had her sights set on you."

Bent opened the passenger side door. "And I told you, she's wasting her time."

Vera decided she was going to need a great deal of pampering tonight.

18

Andrews Farm
Boonshill Road, 10:30 p.m.

Luna sat in the rocking chair Jerome had bought her the very day she told him she was pregnant. He'd been eyeing this gorgeous rocker since they decided to start a family right after getting married. It had been handmade by an Amish man in Ethridge. She loved it. It was perfect.

She wished Jerome were here now. But their bed was empty. Even in the near darkness of her room, the emptiness felt profound. It expanded and ached through her. Threatened her ability to maintain her composure.

The baby moved, and that incredible sensation—one like nothing she had ever felt—seared through her. Her hands came to rest on her belly. She smiled down at the baby bump that made her so very happy.

"Don't you worry, baby," she whispered. "Everything is going to be fine. Your Aunt Vee promised."

Worry settled on Luna's shoulders like an elephant straddling her neck. Why did this have to happen?

Tears burned her eyes. She had tolerated Jackie's unkindness. She had ignored her continuous slights and remarks. Jerome often chastised his mother, but it never helped. Luna had asked him once about the way Jackie treated Leonard, and he'd said that his father had learned to ignore her hurtful remarks. Jackie had been petted and had her meanness overlooked since she was a child. According to Leonard, Jackie had cancer as a little girl, and everyone had treated her differently from that time on. No one dared to correct her, much less punish her. She got away with murder, Mr. Andrews would jest. Then two years ago the cancer came back. Luna and Jerome had only just started dating. That last time the cancer almost took her.

But it hadn't, and she'd lived on to torture Luna.

Not fair, Lu.

She sighed. Rubbed her belly. She didn't even want to consider how Jackie would have twisted this child and tried to turn the baby against Luna. That was Jackie's way. When she didn't like someone, she worked to turn others against that person. She had been slowly but surely doing this with Jerome's extended family.

The worst part was before this was over, she would have done exactly that—no matter that she was dead.

Luna stared at the bed where her sweet husband should be. This thing would turn him against her. But because of the baby, he would stay with her, just as his father had stayed with Jackie. And their life together would turn into that same sort of nightmare.

The horrible things Jackie had said that awful day before that harrowing fall echoed in Luna's mind.

You are not worthy of my son. If not for the baby, he would have forgotten you already.

I wish he'd never laid eyes on you!

Luna had stood like a guilty child, taking her punishment. But she wasn't guilty. Jerome loved her. She was a good person. A good woman and wife, and she would be a good mother. The bad things that had happened in the Boyett family's history had nothing to do with Luna. Her own mother, God rest her soul, was someone Luna hadn't even known. How could she possibly be like her?

But the trickle-down effect created by Jackie's evil tongue had started with Geneva. She had turned against Luna. Several of the ladies from church had started to snub her. Luna wasn't sure she could even bear to go to church this upcoming Sunday.

It was a nightmare. A total nightmare.

But it was done. Luna could not change what had happened. No matter how much she wanted to . . . she couldn't.

The sound of Jackie calling out to her as Luna stormed out the door would haunt her forever.

She closed her eyes and battled the flood of tears. Jerome's mother had been screaming for Luna to come back, but she had kept walking without a backward glance.

No one—not even Vera—could ever know that truth.

19

Thursday, September 4
Vanderbilt University Medical Center
1211 Medical Center Drive
Nashville, 9:30 a.m.

"I expect you to stand by your word."

Vera considered the man behind the wheel and his edict. "I always stand by my word." When had she not—at least where this man was concerned?

He wasn't someone she had expected to ever use for a ride, but there simply was no one else. Bent didn't need to be distracted from the Wilton investigation. Eve had two *visitors* to prepare for visitations this evening. No way was she asking Luna. Since Vera hadn't found time to make the kind of friends you call at the last minute asking for this sort of favor, she'd had to resort to calling in a marker.

Nolan Baker owed Vera. Really, really owed her, and today she had needed to collect.

"I won't be long," she promised as she reached for the door handle.

"Just one question."

Vera huffed a breath and turned back to him. "What now, Nolan?"

"Why are you visiting the Wilton heiress if she's in a coma?"

If the wannabe big news reporter only knew. Alicia was far from an heiress. When taking into consideration the amount of money and assets Thomas Wilton possessed, a measly ten mil was nothing. Alicia was a victim and a murder suspect currently imprisoned by a coma. Hopefully she would recover and be able to share enough of what had happened at that cabin over the weekend for Vera to piece together who did what—unless she refused to talk because she was the killer.

Then again *if* Alicia woke up, there was no guarantee she would remember a solitary thing.

"Just because she's in a coma doesn't mean she isn't aware of what's happening around her." Vera fully recognized if she didn't give him something, that diabolical mind of his would conclude the worst. He was a reporter, after all. "She has no family that we know of, so I thought I'd drop by and give her a little reassurance."

"Bullshit." He chuckled. "You just want her to wake up so you can close your case. You don't care about Alicia Wilton."

Vera shot him a look. "Like you care about the subjects of all your hit pieces."

"My allegiance is to my readers," he tossed back.

What a crock of shit. He was just like his mother. He was the spitting image of her, only in male form and twenty-odd years younger. Dark hair and eyes. Perfectly chiseled profile. He dressed like a media influencer sporting the hottest fashions. But Vera knew him. Really knew him. Beneath that trendy facade, he was not nearly as brave and altruistic as he would have folks believe.

"Assume what you will, Nolan, just stay put until I return. I'll be thirty or forty minutes, tops."

He reached into the back seat and retrieved his laptop case. "I'll just be working right here in the car," he promised with a big, fake smile. "Waiting to drive you wherever you want to go next, Ms. Daisy—I mean Vera."

She rolled her eyes. Having a concussion was the worst. She closed the door and headed for the hospital entrance. Actually she felt better this morning. The back of her head was sore as hell. But no more nausea, serious pain, or weakness. The lingering symptom that worried her was the slight lack of good balance. Her equilibrium remained a little off. As much as she would have preferred to make this trip alone, she wasn't stupid. Ending up dead in a car crash was not something she wanted to hasten. Causing someone else to be injured or worse wasn't on her agenda either. Not to mention that would leave Luna in the lurch with an insane Geneva Fanning.

Vera had too much to take care of to get herself killed right now, and driving in Nashville was a pinball game on steroids for those who rarely visited. A lovely city with much to do and see but crazy busy with constant road construction and about a million commuters. Not optimal for a driver well below the top of her game.

While she waited at the bank of elevators that would take her to the tenth floor of the Vanderbilt critical care tower, she considered all that Luna had said at the cemetery late yesterday afternoon. Something about Jackie's fall deeply distressed Luna. Obviously the fact that the woman was her husband's mother was distressing, but this was something more. Vera hoped it wasn't the worst-case scenario. *Just stop.* She was not even entertaining the idea in a serious light.

The elevator doors opened, and she cleared her head. Time to focus on the Wilton investigation. She would get back to Luna's situation later.

On the tenth floor Vera went to the main desk of the Traumatic Intensive Care Unit and waited until a nurse noticed her. "Hi, I'm Vera Boyett. Ms. Franklin is expecting me."

Nurse Bedwell, according to her name tag, smiled. "I'll let her know you're here."

Vera walked a few feet away from the desk and waited. She wanted the most up-to-date progress on Alicia Wilton. She'd learned long ago that the most detailed and latest reports came from the nurses, not the doctors.

"Ms. Boyett?"

Vera turned to meet the woman she'd spoken with by phone. Regina Franklin was mid-forties. Wore her hair in a haphazard ponytail, and a pair of reading glasses was suspended on the collar of her scrub top. She looked about as frazzled as Vera felt. Exactly her kind of people.

"Ms. Franklin, thank you for making time for me."

"Let's step into the break room."

Vera followed her down the corridor to the final door on the right just before exiting the unit. The room was small. Looked like a regular TICU hospital room without the beds. There were a couple of small tables and a half dozen chairs. A coffee maker stood next to the sink on the built-in cabinet that lined one wall, along with a small fridge. All the necessities for a comfortable break room.

"How's our patient?" Vera took a seat in the first chair she came to.

"Coffee? Water?" Franklin gestured to the counter. "There might be a soda in there too. But those usually disappear faster than anything else."

"I'm good, thank you."

Franklin gave her a nod and settled at the table. "Mrs. Wilton is doing better than expected. In case you haven't received the latest update, her MRI showed trauma to the back of the head as well as the visible injury to the front."

Vera had not heard. This changed things considerably. "Meaning she may have been struck with something that perhaps launched her forward?" That could explain her fall down those steps. Perhaps confirmed she was indeed fleeing for her life.

"Absolutely," Franklin agreed. "The resulting injury is consistent with a blow to the back of the head."

There had been no blood in her hair, Vera recalled. So, like her own head injury, Alicia's had likely been caused by some rounded object rather than something with an edge that would have penetrated the scalp.

Vera offered, "Any signs she's trying to wake up?"

"Her EEGs continue to show considerable brain activity. The most recent reading convinced her doctor that she's going to wake up and may well recover, as I said, better than expected. Everything looks really good."

"If there's considerable brain activity," Vera ventured, "what's to prevent her from just waking up?"

"That's the mystery of comas." Franklin shrugged. "Patients wake up when they wake up. We ensure their vitals stay as close to normal as possible. Treat any underlying causes. There are sensory stimulation procedures that sometimes work—we're doing those as well—but again every patient is different."

Vera understood. "Bottom line, we're looking good for a possible full recovery."

"All the signs are there, but we'll know more when she does wake up."

Vera hesitated when she would have let this final question go, but she needed to know. The patient was a suspect in a murder case. Stranger things had been attempted by suspects in the past. "Is there any chance she's faking it? I mean, pretending to still be unable to wake up?"

Franklin wrinkled her nose and turned her hands up. "It wouldn't be easy, but I suppose it could happen. That said, we watch her closely. Monitor her vitals and brain activity equally closely. Maintaining the act would be difficult at best. Even with our eyes closed or when we're sleeping, our brain reacts to sounds and changes in the environment around us."

"Thank you." Vera extended her hand across the table. "I'll pay her a visit and be on my way."

As they stood, Franklin said, "I have your cell number as well as Sheriff Benton's. I'll ensure one of you gets a call the moment she wakes up. Oh." Franklin popped her forehead with the heel of her hand. "I almost forgot. Alicia Wilton is pregnant. A test confirmed as much, and we did an ultrasound to ensure the baby was unharmed. She's approximately twelve weeks, and all appears to be well."

Now, there was an interesting development. No one had mentioned a baby on the way. Maybe no one knew. "Thank you for keeping us up to speed. Every aspect of her life is important to our investigation."

"Happy to help."

Vera followed Franklin to Wilton's room. The deputy on duty was not one of Bent's. She showed him her ID and entered the room. The wall between the room and the corridor was glass, allowing the nurses an unobstructed view of their critical patients.

Alicia Wilton looked pale. The bandage around her head a vivid reminder of her injuries. Her dark hair was in bad need of a wash. The readout on one of the many machines keeping track of her condition showed a good, strong heart rate and blood pressure. The rest was Greek to Vera.

IVs were plastered to her right arm, so Vera approached the left side of the bed. She hadn't planned what she would say. No need, really. No way to know if Wilton could hear her, but there were studies that suggested patients in comas could often hear what was happening around them.

"Mrs. Wilton, I'm Vera Boyett. I work with Sheriff Benton, and I just wanted to drop by and let you know that we're doing everything we can to sort out what happened at your cabin." Probably best not to mention that her husband was dead in case she didn't know and could actually hear and assimilate the voices around her.

"The doctor says you're doing really well, and we're optimistic that you'll be awake in no time. When you're awake and feeling well enough, I'm confident you'll be able to help us put the final pieces together." Vera reached down and wrapped her fingers around the woman's free hand. Her skin was cool. "We're doing everything we can with what we have. You needn't worry about anything. Your home is secure. We just want you to focus on getting better and waking up. We really need to hear whatever you can tell us."

Anything else? Vera was aware of all the usual stuff folks said to those in situations like this, but she didn't really feel comfortable tossing out any of those sympathetic expressions like "we'll be praying for you." Vera didn't know Alicia Wilton from Adam's house cat. The truth was she didn't pray very often. With the kind of luck she and her sisters had, maybe she should start.

"I'll check in on you again soon." Vera gave her hand a gentle squeeze. "And congratulations on the baby."

The steady beeping from the monitors abruptly grew frantic. Vera stared at the climbing number that reflected the patient's heart rate. In the bed, Alicia began to shake as if her body was seizing. Vera stepped back, started to turn for the door to summon a nurse, but Alicia's arms suddenly flew up, and Vera froze. She watched as the woman's arms hovered in front of her in a defensive maneuver even as her body continued to shudder. The moaning sound that rose from her throat stole Vera's breath. What was happening?

Two nurses appeared, landing on either side of the bed. Five seconds later Alicia Wilton was as silent and motionless as when Vera had first entered the room.

Vera pressed a hand to her chest. "Is she okay? Was my presence or my voice responsible for what just happened?"

One of the nurses shook her head. "This happens sometimes. We can't be sure if the patient is dreaming or remembering. But it's another indication that she's trying to wake up."

Vera relaxed marginally. "Thank you. I was worried it was me."

When all Alicia's vitals returned to normal, the nurses left the room, and Vera followed. She paused at the door and glanced back at the patient. Had she been trying to tell Vera something?

Feeling unsettled, Vera left the room. She acknowledged the deputy seated outside and made her way back to the elevators. Five minutes later she was in the parking lot, walking quite steadily toward Nolan's car. Her balance appeared to be moving back toward normal. Thank God. Being in need of assistance for transportation was intensely frustrating.

When she rapped on the glass of the passenger side door, Nolan looked up from his laptop. He hit the Unlock button and tugged out his earbuds.

"I can't believe it. Thirty-eight minutes."

"Did you get your story written?" Vera ignored his jab about the time and settled into the soft leather seat. She fastened her safety belt and sank more deeply into the comfort his daddy's money could buy in a luxury vehicle. Not only did Nolan have a very nice car, he had a very nice apartment, compliments of Daddy as well. She sent him a sideways glance. Nolan was a handsome guy. One of these days she might even see him anchoring some news desk.

Boggie would be so proud.

"The creative process takes time, Boyett." He put his laptop away and started the engine. "Can we go home now?"

"We sure can, Nolan." Vera closed her eyes. "Just watch those speed limits, please."

"Yeah, yeah. You sound like my mother."

Vera's eyes popped open. She sent him a glare but decided it wasn't worth the trouble of correcting him. Besides, she was still unnerved by the episode in Alicia Wilton's room. Not to mention the news that she had sustained more than one blow to her head and, even more astonishing, was pregnant. There had been nothing about an impending arrival at the Wilton home. No nursery. No baby items. Nothing.

"We need to stop for food. I'm starving." Nolan whizzed out of the parking lot.

Vera closed her eyes again. Feeling his frenzied driving maneuvers was more than enough to warn she wouldn't want to look. Besides, the passing landscape made her nauseous. She supposed that aftereffect would be with her for another day or two. Damned concussion.

"You're behind the wheel." If he wanted to eat, she would try to get something down. Otherwise Bent would give her trouble about it. "Pick a place. Just be sure wherever you stop has a drive-through. I need to get back."

She had work to do. Like finding a killer and keeping her little sister out of trouble.

Or maybe she actually had two killers to find. No matter that the murder weapon in the Wilton case had been found—with Alicia's fingerprints on it, no less—Vera wasn't so sure now that the new wife was the killer. Particularly after this latest news.

If the episode in her room was a memory, then Alicia had been trying to ward off an attacker, not to stab at unsuspecting victims.

But then, the whole thing may have been related to a dream.

Nah. Vera wasn't buying that scenario. What she'd witnessed was a woman trying to protect herself and her unborn child.

Just something else Vera had to find the necessary evidence to prove.

20

Vanderbilt University Medical Center
1211 Medical Center Drive
Nashville, 11:15 a.m.

Someone was in her room again.

Not the woman from Fayetteville who worked for the sheriff. Not one of the usual nurses. Her nurses always started talking as soon as they entered the room. Maybe to assure a patient who couldn't open her eyes to see who'd walked in. The doctor was usually with other people who were asking questions or receiving instructions. Why would anyone besides a nurse, a doctor, or someone from the sheriff's office enter her room?

A chill crept through her veins.

It wasn't the deputy on duty. He'd introduced himself when he came on shift. She remembered the sound of his boots as he entered her room.

Someone else had come into her room now. Their footfalls whisper soft . . . their silence terrifying.

More of those soft footfalls told Alicia this person was walking around the bed. Fear bloomed in her chest.

She urged her eyes to open, but they refused to obey. She prayed a nurse would come in, but that probably wouldn't happen either. It wasn't time for another vitals check.

Why would anyone else come into her room? Could just anyone stop in? Why was the deputy here if not to keep that from happening? The beeps of the machine monitoring her heart rate grew faster.

What if it was *her*?

Alicia's heart lunged into her throat.

Would she dare take this sort of risk? With a deputy right outside the door? Her heart dropped into her belly and started to pound frantically. What if the deputy had taken a break? What if . . .

If it was *her*, Alicia prayed she wouldn't poison her or harm her in some other way.

Oh God, what if she injected something into her IV? People did that in the movies.

No. Please don't let her hurt my baby.

Please let the nurse come in.

Cold fingers touched Alicia's arm.

Oh God. Oh God.

Alicia knew what that bitch had done. If she didn't wake up, no one would ever know the truth.

Please, please don't let this evil woman hurt me.

The fingers tightened. Alicia's heart felt as if it suddenly stopped dead still.

"Now don't you get upset on me, Mrs. Wilton," a voice said. "I'm just here to take you for a new MRI. You just relax and enjoy the ride."

Not *her* voice. Relief so profound Alicia almost wept flooded her. *Thank God. Thank God.* It was a lab person or a technician.

Alicia calmed. She was okay for now. Her baby was safe.

But they wouldn't really be safe until she woke up and told someone what she knew.

Thomas was dead . . . Seth . . . Sandy. They were all dead.

There was no one left to tell the truth except her.

Wake up!

21

Boyett Farm
Good Hollow Road
Fayetteville, 12:30 p.m.

Vera watched Nolan drive away. As much as she appreciated the lift, she was glad that trip was over.

She was feeling much better now. Since it had been more than twenty-four hours and she was markedly improved, she intended to drive herself to wherever Bent was and catch up on the investigation. Driving around her small hometown was vastly different from driving in Music City.

Before taking off she grabbed a bottle of water and her key fob. She would be okay as long as she drove slowly.

Once she was out of her driveway and onto the road, she relaxed a little. She hoped no one appeared in her rearview mirror. Passing was difficult on this curvy road, and she wasn't about to drive any faster. She didn't completely trust her reflexes not to fail her.

Her cell vibrated on the console, and she let it go to the car speaker. *Eve.*

Dread instantly congealed in her belly. "Eve, what's up?"

"I heard Geneva hired herself a lawyer."

Frustration immediately replaced all Vera's other emotions. "How did you hear that? Have you spoken to Bent?" Surely he would have called.

"No. Cynthia Roland from over at the Hayworth Law Firm told me. You might not remember her. We went to high school together."

Vera's eyebrows lifted as she turned onto Old Elkton Pike. "Geneva hired Hayworth?"

"She did. Cynthia couldn't tell me anything else, of course, but she wanted to warn me since the case involved Luna."

It was moments like this that reminded Vera why she'd run off and joined the circus in the big city of Memphis. "Well I guess dear old Geneva believes she needs legal representation." *Bitch.*

"Guess so."

"You didn't tell Luna, did you?"

"No. I haven't talked to her since I left her house this morning."

"Okay. Don't mention it until we have no choice. I'm running down Bent now to see if there's anything new on either investigation."

"Something else," Eve said, waylaying Vera's plan to end the call.

"What's that? Something good, I hope." She'd heard just about enough bad news.

"I don't know that it's good, but it's interesting. Last night I overheard Mrs. Ingle say that Geneva had spent most of her life chasing someone else's husband."

Vera braked too hard for the stop at the Highway 64 intersection. "Please tell me you are not talking about our dead art teacher?" Eve liked talking to her *visitors*, but when they started talking back . . .

"Her daughter," Eve groused. "She and two other ladies were talking about Jackie's death. The subject of Jackie's sister came up, and I heard Mrs. Ingle, the daughter, say Geneva was nothing but a trollop."

"Do you think that's true or just gossip?" Not that the woman's sex life had anything to do with her ability or qualifications to push for a police investigation. At best this sort of thing might make her an unreliable witness—assuming it wasn't just gossip.

But then, that was all Geneva Fanning was, wasn't it? A witness via secondhand information. She hadn't seen one damned thing with her own eyes. The rumors—if true—would certainly add to the uncertainty of her "good" word.

Vera smiled. Good to know.

"I don't know for sure," Eve said, "but it sounded like a long-running behavior."

"I'll look into it. Thanks, Eve."

"FYI, Jerome is coming home tonight as long as his father continues to remain stable, and he'll go back tomorrow. So Luna will be good for tonight."

As long as Geneva hadn't spent the day filling Jerome's head full of lies and innuendos, Luna would likely be thankful to have him home.

"I'll catch up with her today and make sure she's okay," Vera promised. Luna needed all the moral support she could get right now.

"All right. Talk to you later."

The call ended, and Vera turned onto Washington Street.

Damn. She needed to go by the hardware store. Her continued avoidance of following up on that damned receipt just showed how worried she was that it would prove Luna had done something . . . *bad.*

Impossible. Vera shook her head, and thankfully it only hurt a little.

Luna didn't do bad things.

As Vera stopped at the four-way of Washington and Franklin, her gaze settled on the historic house-turned-apartments where Erwin lived and now managed her own tenants. On second thought, Vera made a left instead of going straight and heading for Bent's office. Maybe Erwin had new tenants since she had taken over the building. Tenants meant neighbors. Just maybe those neighbors would have things to say about her. Rumors. Hearsay. Probably. But it wouldn't hurt to stir that pot. Maybe the idea that she was questioning neighbors would make Erwin nervous. The fastest way to a mistake was to get nervous.

Vera parked and climbed out of her vehicle. She followed the sidewalk around to the front entrance. There was no locked door that required being buzzed in, so she walked right on inside. A door on each side of the entry area provided access to the two downstairs apartments, Vera presumed. A narrow staircase led up to the same on the second level.

With no clue which one was Erwin's, she knocked on the door to her right.

A few knocks later, and it was clear there was no one home, or at least no one interested in answering the door. She moved to the one across the hall. The sound of children on the other side of the door gave Vera hope that someone was home. She knocked. A female voice inside urged the kids to be quiet. Then the lock turned, and the door opened. Young woman, mid- to late twenties maybe. Deep mahogany skin and even darker hair and eyes.

"Yes?"

Vera stretched out her hand. "I'm Vera Boyett with the Lincoln County Sheriff's Department. I have a few questions for you, if you have a moment."

The woman blinked, ignored Vera's hand and glanced upward toward the second-story landing. Vera instantly knew that was where Erwin lived.

"Can we talk right here? I don't want my children to hear any of this."

"Of course. Wherever you're most comfortable."

"Just a moment." The woman ducked back inside and ordered her children to sit and be quiet, or she'd turn off the television. Then she stepped into the corridor once more, closing the door behind her. She met Vera's gaze. "What has he done this time?"

Oh damn. "I'm sorry?"

"My brother. Is he in trouble again?"

"Oh no. It's not what you obviously think. I'm here about Valeri Erwin."

"What about her?" Again she glanced up to the second-story landing.

"First, may I have your name?"

The woman seemed to melt into the door behind her in an effort to put distance between her and whatever uncertainty had appeared on her doorstep. "Is that necessary?"

"Actually no. It's fine. We can keep it off the record." Vera held up her hands palms out and shook them side to side in hopes of allaying her fears. "I just wanted to confirm that Ms. Erwin was home last weekend. Monday afternoon and evening in particular."

The camera from a Ring doorbell belonging to a neighbor across the street had confirmed that Erwin's car was home during that time period, and there was no visual of her leaving via the front door. Still, it was important to confirm—if possible—with the folks who lived closest to her.

"As far as I know." Her brow lined as if she was digging deep for the memories. "My youngest was sick with a stomach bug, so I was here the whole holiday weekend. I didn't leave the apartment at all. I heard her moving around up there, so I think she must have been home."

Maybe Vera's other top suspect did have an alibi. "Did you hear any voices? I mean, how soundproof are the walls?"

"With the cartoons my kids watch, I never hear anything but that stuff. I only heard the movements I mentioned while they were sleeping." She nodded toward the door across the hall. "You might ask him. Sam Scott. He's not home now. He teaches at Motlow College, the Fayetteville Campus just outside town. But with no kids, he's more likely to hear any conversations. When I heard the moving around, there was no conversation. I can't tell you what time because the whole weekend ran together in one long nightmare of cleaning up puke."

Vera nodded her understanding. "Thanks. I appreciate your time."

The woman who didn't want to give her name hurried back into her apartment, closed and locked the door.

Vera turned for the exit, but a sound upstairs drew her attention to the landing. The door on the right cracked open, but no one came out. She started to call Erwin's name, assuming it was her, but her cell in her pocket vibrated. Vera checked the screen. *Luna.* When Vera looked up once more, the door was closed. Why would Erwin avoid her? The woman generally went out of her way to say hello. Maybe she was not in the mood today.

Vera exited the building and headed toward her SUV. The little blue car Erwin drove wasn't parked anywhere along the block. So maybe she wasn't home. Maybe she had a roommate. Vera brushed off the questions and took her sister's call. "Hey, Luna. Everything okay?"

"You need to come to the library right now, Vee. Right this second. Geneva is here."

22

Fayetteville–Lincoln County Library
306 Elk Avenue North, 1:30 p.m.

Vera drove faster than she should have, but the library wasn't far, and she didn't so much as meet another vehicle. She wheeled into the parking lot and took a slot. Nudging her door closed with her hip, she stalked toward the entrance. If Geneva Fanning had upset Luna, Vera was going to . . .

Deep breath. No need for her to make the situation worse by embarrassing Luna and herself.

Another deep breath, and she walked as calmly as possible through the entrance and to the counter. Luna passed whatever she was doing to the other woman behind the counter and jerked her head for Vera to follow her.

They met in the very back beyond the rows and rows of bookshelves near the rear exit.

"I'm parked right next to the back door. We'll talk out there, okay?"

"Sure."

Outside they slipped quickly into Luna's minivan. The minivan was new. Once she hit the end of the second trimester, she'd traded her cute little car in for a more practical vehicle for hauling children around. If Luna had her way, there would be at least three more. From the time she was five years old, she'd insisted she wanted four children.

Once the doors were closed and locked and the engine was running, cooling off the interior, Vera turned to her sister. "I didn't see Geneva. Was she hiding in the ladies' room?"

"She left like two seconds before you arrived." Luna plopped her head back against the seat, her hands rubbing her belly. "I swear she's making me crazy."

Vera moistened her lips. "What did she do or say while she was here?"

"She just walked around the library like she was looking for a book, but she didn't even pick one up. Every minute or so she would stare at me for a bit, then she'd move on. As she left, she stopped one last time in front of the counter and glared at me. Penny—the lady working with me today—asked if she could help her, but Geneva just ignored her and walked right on out."

"Sadly there's no law against being a bad-mannered old woman." Vera reached across the seat and took Luna's hand. "I wish I could fix this for you, Lu. You shouldn't have to deal with her crap right now. You should be enjoying your pregnancy and anticipating the future."

"She just wants to make my life miserable." Luna closed her eyes.

"Have you spoken to Jerome today?" Vera needed to push for more answers, but damn she hated to make this awful situation any worse. Vera and Luna had exchanged text messages last night. Jerome's father continued to be stable. He hadn't mentioned any issues related to Geneva.

"I called him once today, and he called me once." A smile tugged at her lips. "His father still can't seem to stay conscious. He keeps drifting back to sleep. The cardiologist says that sometimes patients are so traumatized by what's happened to them that they don't want to wake up. They'd rather not face what's happened. When he's stronger he'll come around, the doctor assured Jerome. His vitals are very good. There's no reason to believe he won't recover."

"That's really good news." Vera couldn't imagine how devastating it would have been for Jerome to lose both his parents at nearly the same time. "Hopefully Jerome and his father will be back home for good soon. The funeral can happen, and maybe things will settle down after that."

Vera wasn't holding her breath, but she kept that part to herself.

"Jerome is coming home tonight, as long as nothing changes for the worse. He worries I'll go into labor, and he'll miss the baby's arrival." Luna stared out the windshield at the trees lining that side of the parking area. "I should be looking forward to him coming home, but I'm not. It's so hard to have him look at me, knowing . . ."

The niggling worry that hadn't dissipated since she found Jackie at the bottom of Luna's staircase poked its way into Vera's head. "Why? Did he say something that made you feel as if he held you responsible?"

"No. He would never say anything hurtful, but I caught him watching me a couple of times." She turned to Vera. "He had this look on his face that made me worry that he was thinking that I had killed his mother." Her lips trembled, and tears streamed down her face. "No matter what happens, Vee, he will always wonder if I was somehow involved in what happened. He will never feel certain that I've told him everything that happened."

Vera wished she could assure her little sister that she needn't worry, but she was right. Jerome would always have questions. No matter how much he loved Luna and trusted her. Wanted to believe her. Deep down he would consider if his Aunt Geneva knew something he didn't.

"He might wonder for a while," Vera admitted. "But you didn't do anything wrong, so he'll move on eventually." She squeezed her sister's hand. "He loves you. You're the mother of his child. This will all be okay in time."

Luna shifted in the seat but had to power it back from the steering wheel to face Vera fully. Vera couldn't help herself. She giggled. "That baby is getting bigger all the time."

"Vee."

The fact that Luna's expression registered absolutely no sign of humor or happiness sharpened Vera's instincts to a razor edge. "What, sweetie?"

"Before . . . when you came to the house when Jackie had fallen . . . I didn't tell you the whole truth."

Holy shit. The barrage of swear words that paraded through Vera's brain just then would have made the proverbial sailor blush. "How so?" That her voice sounded so calm despite her sister's revelation stunned her.

"Jackie came over around eight like I told you." Luna cleared her throat, stared at her hands for a moment, her fingers twiddling with the fabric of her enormous tentlike top. "We put up the wallpaper. The whole time she made little snide comments about how she hated the color and design. That it was the ugliest wallpaper she had ever seen."

"Oh, honey, that's not true. It's beautiful wallpaper. The birds are perfect for a boy or a girl. And that big old tree on the focal wall is just incredible. It's amazing that Jerome could create a bookshelf shaped like a tree." Vera wanted to cry herself. How dare that hateful woman say those things.

"She brought up again that I should name the baby—if it's a boy—after her husband. She said Leonard Jerome II would be perfect." Luna's face puckered with emotion again. "But I don't want my child being called LJ, and that's what would happen. I like Leonard Ray. That way Jerome and both grandfathers are acknowledged, and we can call him Leo. I like Leo."

"This is your baby," Vera reminded her. "You can name him or her anything you want. I love Leonard Ray and Leo. Whatever you name him—or her—this is going to be the cutest, most loved kid in town."

"She just hates me." Luna stared out at the trees again. "Hated, I mean."

Vera didn't push for her to get to the scary part. Frankly she was in no hurry for that whole truth. The thought terrified her.

Luna blew out a big breath. "So we finished the wallpaper with her complaining the whole time, and I got ready to paint the trim like I told you before. Jerome really didn't want me to be in the room when the trim was painted, even though it's the paint without the odor and all the really bad chemicals. His mama had promised him she would do the painting. When I saw that I needed more paint, she went off on another tangent. She said I was stupid for not realizing we needed more, and now we'd have to waste time going to get it, and it was all my fault."

Vera gritted her teeth to hold back what she wanted to say to that. It involved wishing Jackie Andrews were still alive so she could push her down the stairs herself.

"I said I'd go get more paint, and she could stay and put furniture back in place if she wanted to. She followed me out of the room, ranting and raving like a person gone over some edge. Really, Vee, I can't even begin to tell you how bizarre it was."

Vera nodded, reached for her hand again. "I can just imagine." At the same time she braced herself for the rest of the story.

"When we were almost to the top of the stairs"—Luna moistened her lips—"she suddenly ran up behind me and pushed me."

Vera felt the blood drain from her face. The world went utterly silent. For one long moment she could only stare at her sister. "She pushed *you*." It wasn't a question. It was a confirmation of a statement so horrifying . . . so heinous that it took every ounce of strength she possessed to utter the words.

Luna nodded. "Somehow I twisted as I was going down. I grabbed at anything I could, and one thing was Jackie. We both tumbled downward and twisted again. The only thing"—she swallowed hard—"that stopped me from landing on my belly was that I was able to grab on to the railing after that second twist, and the bottom of my foot hit a spindle, slowing me down. I hung on for a second before I could move. When I got up, Jackie was about halfway down the staircase. She'd hit her head against the wall. She was wailing about how her head hurt. I was shaking so badly, I could hardly stand. All I could think was, *I'm okay. The baby's okay.*"

"Your foot hit the spindle?" A new kind of tension crashed into Vera.

"I'm convinced that's the only reason I wasn't injured beyond a bruised foot. It was like a brake—a brake that helped stop my fall." Luna scrubbed at her damp cheeks. "I swear it's a miracle the baby and I weren't hurt. I mean really hurt. It was the scariest thing . . . I can't even adequately convey just how scary."

Vera drew in a slow, deep breath. Steadied herself before speaking. "Okay. So you're telling me Jackie was alive and complaining of having hit her head."

Luna nodded, her lips pressed tightly together.

"What happened next?"

"I . . . I think I was so rattled and so . . . I don't know." She shook her head. "I couldn't think straight. It felt almost surreal. I don't know if I was in shock or denial. Maybe both. I just walked on down the stairs, right past her. I grabbed my purse and left to get the paint. It was like I couldn't look at her. Couldn't speak to her. I just had to get out of the house."

Vera ordered her heart to slow its pounding. "You're certain she was alive when you left?"

"Yes. She was calling after me, saying she was hurt and needed help."

At this point only an autopsy could determine if her head injury was sufficient to have killed her.

Look at this logically, Vee.

It was her landing at the bottom of that staircase that likely killed her. And no way was a fall from midway down the stairs sufficient to have created adequate momentum for the injuries she sustained.

"We know she got up after you left," Vera began. "Maybe she started up the stairs to go back to the nursery and reset the furniture but fell back down and that's what killed her."

Luna shook her head no. "The furniture was back in place. That proves she went back to the nursery before whatever happened . . . happened."

And there were those texts she sent to Geneva. Okay, that made sense. She was unquestionably alive when Luna left her. "You were gone for well over an hour. It's possible that it wasn't until after she'd settled all the baby furniture back into place that she grew dizzy or ill—the way I did from my concussion—and fell down the stairs. Then you found her just as she was."

Luna chewed her lip now. "But with that hardware receipt showing the wrong time, how will I ever prove I'm telling the truth?"

"We'll deal with that one if and when the time comes." Vera almost hated to ask the next question. She wouldn't be telling a soul if Luna's response was yes . . . at least not until all the potential loose ends were worked out.

"Do you have any bruises? Scrapes? Scratches?" Vera couldn't help but think of Alicia Wilton. Had she been running from the scene to protect herself as well as the child she carried? Why would she set out to murder her husband and the others, knowing she could be injured or that her baby could be? But then the other head injury suggested she had been fleeing trouble. That and the news about the baby shifted Vera's suspect list for sure.

"I have one bruise on my lower shin. I guess where my leg hit the spindle above the one that my foot hit like a brake, slowing my momentum. I can't believe the spindle didn't snap completely in two, considering I'm so huge."

"You are not huge. You're perfect." Vera prompted, "Any other injuries?"

"No. But I was really achy from the twisting and how I grabbed the railing to catch myself. My arm still feels like I nearly pulled it out of its socket."

"Did Jackie grab any part of you tightly enough to leave a mark or a scratch?"

"No." Luna's face scrunched as if she was concentrating hard. "But I think I scratched her when my hand pulled free of her arm. It was all really fast and really hard." She searched Vera's eyes. "Do you understand what I mean? There was this grabbing and pulling and slipping. It was violent, and yet I somehow survived with scarcely a mark."

And that likely explained the single scratch on Jackie.

"I do understand." Vera played the scene out in her head. "Did you check your back? Anywhere you need two mirrors to see?"

"I did when I showered later that evening. No bruises or scratches anywhere."

"Okay." Vera felt confident about Luna's story. It would have been better had she called Vera after the initial incident, but there was nothing to do about that now. "The bottom line is you didn't do anything wrong, Luna. Jackie attacked you and the child you're carrying. As you said, it's a miracle you and the baby weren't hurt."

"But I left her calling for me to help *her*."

"Anyone in your position would have done the same thing. You were traumatized. Maybe in shock. Either way, you did not do anything wrong," Vera repeated.

"What if she needed an ambulance and I ignored her?" Tears brimmed fresh in her dark eyes. "Jerome will never forgive me."

"Luna, this was not your fault. If she felt well enough to get up and do the furniture rearranging, then she was in no danger of dying from that initial fall."

"But Jerome—" Luna abruptly stopped speaking. She stared at Vera, her eyes huge. Vomit suddenly hurled out of her, spewing all over Vera's lap.

Shit! Vera gasped, her hands up like a shield.

Luna burst into sobs.

Vera grabbed a handful of napkins that were tucked into a pocket on the passenger door and helped her sister clean herself up, all the while offering soothing assurances that everything would be fine.

Except Vera's outfit.

23

Vera had no choice but to drive home to change. On the way she called Eve, which would hopefully distract her from the smell. As always her sister wasn't happy about getting a call during working hours, but after hearing the story Luna had revealed, she forgot all about being irritated at the interruption.

"What happened was self-defense!"

Eve was right—for the most part.

"If what she states happened can be proven, it would certainly be considered self-defense," Vera agreed. "The trouble lies in her leaving the scene without providing assistance."

"Is that a law?"

Vera slowed for the turn onto Good Hollow Road. "To my knowledge there is no specific law that would require her to render aid. But there are moral and ethical issues. Societal expectations. That sort of thing. The right lawyer could make something of her decision to walk out. There could be a civil suit from someone like Geneva."

"Geneva won't stop until she finds the right lawyer to do just that." Eve hissed her frustration. "I don't know if Hayworth is it, but even if he only pokes around, it won't be good for Luna."

"The upside," Vera pointed out, "is that no one else knows. For now. But as upset as Luna was while telling me, this thing is obviously weighing heavily on her conscience. She could break down and tell Jerome any minute now. If Geneva gets wind of this . . . well, that would be bad. Really bad."

"But Luna said the furniture was put back into place," Eve argued. "There was no one else in the house. Jackie must have done it, which would mean she didn't die until the second fall down the stairs, and Luna wasn't there. Obviously the woman felt well enough to tug around nursery furniture. A crib and a changing table. Even a small dresser. How much damage could the first fall have done?"

"Valid points. Still, the initial injuries may have contributed to the second fall. Adrenaline after an event like that may have given her the strength to move the furniture around." Vera shook her head. "Not to mention this is Luna's version of what happened. We can't technically confirm it. This is a slippery slope, Eve. Luna needs to keep it to herself."

Silence invaded the line between them.

"The way we did about Sheree."

That damned memory of dragging their stepmother's body down those stairs flashed in Vera's head. She glanced at the passing landscape that proclaimed she was nearly home. "Yeah. The way we did."

Even after the world around them knew what they had done and no legal charges were deemed appropriate, she and Eve had still paid the price on a level that might never go completely away. The whispers . . . the furtive looks. They would always be notorious for a mistake they'd made as kids . . . for an event that wasn't even their fault.

"What're we going to do?"

Vera wasn't sure how to answer that question. "In light of this new information, there are things I need to figure out. Like how exactly did Jackie get that fracture to her left leg if she didn't hit that spindle. Clearly it wasn't fractured before the second fall, or I wouldn't think she would have been able to move that furniture around. Unless there was a whole hell of a lot of adrenaline flowing."

"*Unless*," Eve countered, "someone else came over and helped her."

Vera stopped in the middle of the road. "Luna was gone for well over an hour, so that's a definite possibility."

"Maybe her husband came over belatedly to help, and she made the whole thing sound like Luna's fault. He could have decided it was the perfect opportunity to be rid of her," Eve harrumphed. "I don't know how the man has put up with her all those years."

Vera and Bent had already had this conversation. It was certainly possible. "The question is, Do we have a reason that suggests he would want to be rid of her?" Vera moved her foot from the brake back to the accelerator.

"I don't know. She treated him like crap their whole marriage. Maybe he was done with her. I know I would've been."

As logical as the argument was, without evidence it was nothing more than a theory.

"Luna has never mentioned her father-in-law being unhappy. From what I've seen he still bent over backward to make his wife happy even thirty-odd years into their marriage." This was the big sticking point for Vera, no matter that spouses were typically the most logical suspect.

"That's why you're the detective and I'm a mortician."

Vera laughed. "And you are a very good mortician."

"Yeah, I know."

"How is Suri enjoying her conference?" Vera felt bad for not asking about her before now. Murder was like that, always getting in the way of other things—like life.

"She's enjoying the seminars, but she's ready to come home."

Vera grinned. "She misses you."

"Yeah. Okay, I gotta go. Keep me posted. I'll check on Luna when I'm done here."

"Talk later."

Vera ended the call and made the turn into her driveway. She and Eve hadn't been this close since they were kids. Just one of the many benefits from moving back home.

The vintage Volkswagen Bus parked in her driveway was an unexpected and odd sight. Vera was reasonably sure she had never known anyone—didn't know anyone now—who owned one. Had to be someone looking specifically for a Boyett—most likely her. It wasn't like anyone just happened by the farm. It was way too far off the beaten path. But just ask anyone in the vicinity, and they were happy to give directions. It was the way of things in the country.

Then she spotted the license plate. *Louisiana.* Maybe some member of the Parson family. She'd been expecting a call from the brother. An in-person visit was all the better even if unusual, considering the geography. Though she did wonder why they hadn't gone to the sheriff's office. Maybe because the only name she'd left was her own.

Vera shut off the engine, draped the strap of her bag over her shoulder and reached for her door, phone in her free hand. She would know soon enough. The man on the porch turned to watch her come up the walk. On cue the stink of vomit rose around her like a fog.

"I'm assuming you're not lost. This would be an unlikely place to find yourself unless you're looking for someone specific."

He started down the porch steps to meet her. "I assume you're Vera Boyett."

She stopped a couple yards away from where he stood at the bottom of the steps, partly not to get too close to a stranger and in part because she stunk of puke.

"That depends on who's asking." Vera pulled up her recent call list and tapped Bent's name.

"Larry Parson." He thrust out a hand. "You left a message for me about my brother."

"Hey, Vee." Bent's voice floated from the speaker of her cell as Vera shook the stranger's hand. "I'm assuming you made it back from Nashville."

"I did. Yeah. Listen, I've got a fellow named Larry Parson at my house. He's driving a vintage, sort of orange, sort of rusty-yellow Volkswagen Bus."

"A '78. The best year for the Bus," Parson put in.

Vera ignored the comment and studied the man as Bent explained he would be there in five minutes.

Five minutes would be pushing it, but knowing Bent he might just make it happen.

"You have some ID on you, Mr. Parson?" Vera slid her phone into her bag. As if the movement had stirred it up, the odor of vomit emanated anew from her clothes. She might not have time for a shower, but she definitely had to change.

Parson fished out his wallet and displayed his driver's license, which confirmed he was who he claimed to be.

"Thank you, Mr. Parson."

"Call me Larry. So you are Vera Boyett."

"I am, and I thank you for coming. I'm going to ask you to please stay right here on the porch until the sheriff gets here. I have to go inside and change clothes." She waved her hands at her attire. Too bad she'd decided to take her work-at-home garb up a notch since she was visiting the hospital. A simple T-shirt would have been far more forgiving than this silk blouse.

"Sure. Sure. But do you mind telling me what's going on? I've been trying to reach my brother since Monday night, and he's not answering his cell."

Not surprising, since he'd likely been murdered by then. Vera would much prefer that Bent make the death notification.

Parson turned his hands up. "I mean, I'm guessing it's not good since he's out of touch. Is he in jail?"

"It would be better if you waited for the sheriff."

"Oh hell." Parson's face tightened with pain. "He's dead, isn't he?"

"Please, Mr. Parson, I really need to change. My pregnant sister threw up all over me, and if I don't get out of these clothes, I may do the same thing."

He settled onto a step as if his knees had given out on him and put his head in his hands. "I told him this was a bad idea."

As much as Vera was dying to know what Parson meant by the statement, she could not endure the smell of vomit any longer.

"I'll be right back. Please don't go anywhere, Mr. Parson."

Vera started around him, and he looked up at her. "You don't have to worry about that, lady. I'm not going anywhere until I know what happened to my brother."

"Sheriff Benton will be here soon, and I'll be back out in five minutes."

Vera unlocked the door and stepped inside. She relocked it and reset the security system. She didn't know this guy, and no matter that Bent was on his way, she wasn't taking the risk. Bent could be delayed.

She climbed the stairs and headed to the bathroom. The cute silk blouse she wore came off first and hit the floor. Her shoes, slacks, panties, and bra followed. The smell clung to her skin. To hell with it. She had to rinse off. She clipped her hair up, adjusted the spray in the shower, and while the hot water made its way through the pipes, she raced to her room and grabbed a change of clothes.

Less than ten minutes later, she was showered and dressed. She ran a brush through her hair, and her gaze snagged on the foggy mirror. It was impossible to look at a fog-covered glass of any sort without thinking of the Messenger and the notes he left on mirrors and car windshields. He was her first big case. A serial killer. One who almost got her as a young, inexperienced detective—and again not so long ago.

She shook off the memories, tossed her towel and discarded clothes into the tub and hurried back down the stairs as quickly as she dared. A glance out the window next to the door confirmed that Bent had arrived. He and Parson were propped against their respective vehicles. A man thing. Bent had surely had time to give Parson the bad news and show him a pic to make the formal identification. The body had already been shipped to Nashville, so seeing his brother in person wasn't happening until after the autopsy.

Vera went through the steps for the security system and exited the house, locking the door behind her.

"Sorry about the delay." She walked over to stand next to Bent and propped herself against his truck. Might as well act like one of the guys. She'd opted to wear her sheriff's department T-shirt she'd purchased at the county fair last year, jeans, and her favorite sneakers. It was too hot for anything more sophisticated.

Parson looked from Bent to her. "So he was murdered." He shook his head. "I knew it. I told him not to come."

"Fill us in," Vera urged, "on what your brother told you about why he was coming to Fayetteville." She glanced at Bent, hoping he hadn't already asked the same question. "We have witnesses who say they saw Seth Parson here over the past couple of weeks."

"That sounds about right." Parson nodded. "He hadn't heard from Alicia in over two years. Before that they were a serious item. Had been off and on since high school. But Alicia had big dreams, so she was forever running off to chase those dreams." He made a face. "Eventually she would come back and beg Seth to forgive her. He always did."

"But she didn't come back this time," Vera suggested. "She asked him to come to her."

"Yeah." He laughed, a knowing sound. "She'd found her a real sugar daddy this time, except she was tired of playing the good little wife."

"He told you all this." Bent didn't sound convinced, but Vera's instincts had zeroed in on the man's words.

"He did." Parson shrugged. "She wanted her husband to catch her cheating. She told Seth he'd divorce her, and she'd get a whole lot of money along with all the elaborate gifts he'd bought for her like the Bentley she claimed she drove. A shitload of jewelry. She promised that she and Seth would be set for life."

Vera and Bent exchanged another glance.

Bent was the first to respond. "Do you have any proof of what he told you?"

Excellent question. Vera wondered why Alicia hadn't mentioned to Seth that her husband would be leaving her even more money if he was dead. It wasn't such a big leap to assume she had explained the other option once Seth arrived and that the two intended to kill him for the bigger payoff. The trouble was, Seth had ended up dead too. And Alicia had almost landed in the same boat. But the biggest reason the theory no longer held merit, in Vera's opinion, was the baby. She glanced at Bent. She couldn't wait to share that news flash with him. Calling him on the drive back from Nashville with Nolan in the vehicle had been out of the question. Then she'd gotten distracted and puked on.

"I have no proof except what he told me." Parson turned his hands up. "All the text messages were on his phone, so if you found it there's your proof."

"We didn't find his phone." Bent gestured to Parson. "We'll need you to tell us whatever he said to you."

Parson nodded. "Okay. She said she couldn't make or take a call because she might be overheard. She claimed the staff watched her like a hawk, so everything was in text messages. In fact, she used a burner to communicate with Seth. She insisted using her personal cell phone would be too easy for her husband to discover. He watched her super close because his first wife cheated on him."

Whoa. The first wife cheated? Vera shared a look with Bent. Wasn't she the good wife? Vera shook off the thoughts. Hearsay. The claim would take some looking into. Besides, the whole story felt wrong to Vera. Anyone could have sent those text messages. Then again how would anyone other than Alicia know who to send them to?

"What about this woman?" Bent pushed away from his truck and showed Parson a pic of the unidentified female from the collection of crime scene photos on his phone.

"That's Sandy. Sandra Owens. Shit, is she dead too?"

"Afraid so." Bent put his phone away. "She has a tattoo with your initials on it."

Parson patted his hip. "I have a matching one. We were a couple once, but that was a while ago. We're just friends—were just friends. She and Seth too. Jesus. He must have asked her to come with him for some sort of backup. He kinda let on that he was worried it might be a setup. Maybe because Alicia wouldn't talk to him. Just kept sending those damn text messages."

If this man could be believed, the whole case might very well be solved, and the wife did it. Except no homicide investigation was ever wrapped up this easily by the sudden appearance of a stranger who seemed to have all the answers. Plus there was that bizarre reaction by the pregnant woman still in a coma and the news about the knock on the back of her head. Vera could not wait to share the whole ordeal with Bent.

Ultimately, Vera realized, instead of Larry Parson coming forward with details that clarified more aspects of the case, he'd just thrown new scenarios at them that didn't fit the narrative they already had.

"I can see that you firmly believe what you're telling us," Vera allowed, wading back into the conversation.

"Look"—Parson straightened away from his vehicle—"I know you can't just take my word for it, but what I told you is how Seth—and Sandy, too, obviously—ended up here. You do what you gotta do to convince yourself, but I ain't leaving until I find my brother's killer. If it wasn't Alicia, it was someone close to her. Had to be."

Whether the statement was a promise or a threat, Vera didn't doubt the man meant what he said.

There was always a chance he was his brother's partner. After all, the actual killer was quite possibly still at large.

Parson provided his cell number. The number she had called had been his home number. Then he left to find himself a motel in town. It wouldn't take long. There weren't that many.

Once his VW Bus had disappeared from view, Bent turned to her. "Did you learn anything at the hospital?"

Vera leaned against his truck once more, feeling the exhaustion creeping up on her again. "Sorry, I meant to call you before now. But I couldn't exactly call you during the drive back, and as soon as I got to town, I had a call from Eve telling me that Geneva Fanning had hired an attorney."

"Yeah. I heard." Bent shook his head. "That's her way of making noise. She wants us to know she's serious."

Vera bit back what she wanted to say—that she would love to punch the woman. "I was headed to your office, and I decided to stop at Erwin's place. I thought I'd talk to her neighbors and see if she actually was home last weekend. Just to confirm what the across-the-street neighbor's camera showed. Particularly considering what I learned today."

Bent didn't ask what she'd learned. Rather he suggested, "She could have slipped out the back door. That Ring doorbell camera only captured the front of her building."

"That's what I was thinking." She had this feeling about Erwin. The woman was hiding something. "While the neighbor thought she heard noise in Erwin's apartment over the weekend, she couldn't say with any certainty that Erwin was home. She suggested we talk to Sam Scott, who lives across the hall."

"I can have someone follow up."

Vera nodded. "But as I was leaving, Erwin's door opened just a crack like she was checking to see what was going on. When I glanced up that way, she quickly closed it as if she didn't want me to see. It was weird. Why wouldn't she come out to ask why I was there? We both know she's not shy at all."

"Maybe she was worried about what the neighbor would say or hear."

Vera bit her lip. "Maybe." The urge to tell him everything that Luna had spilled was nearly overwhelming. "Then I got a call from Luna and had to rush to the library. Geneva showed up and made a bit of a scene. Anyway Luna was so upset telling me what happened that she threw up all over me." She exhaled a big breath and looked directly at Bent then. She couldn't wait any longer for him to ask what she'd learned. "But that isn't the strangest thing that happened today."

"Maybe being chauffeured by Nolan Baker?" He grinned, knowing full well she wanted him to ask.

Vera rolled her eyes. "Almost. The first part of the big news is that the nurse told me Alicia Wilton's MRI showed a second blow—this one to the back of her head."

Bent nodded. "So maybe she was running from an attacker. He may have thought she was dead and decided to hide the knife under her to incriminate her."

"Part two," Vera went on, "is she's twelve weeks pregnant."

Bent's eyebrows shot up. "Well that certainly changes things—assuming the baby is her husband's and not Seth Parson's."

"Exactly. Then, while I was talking to her—you know the way they tell you to talk to people in comas—she had some sort of physical response." Vera shivered at the memory. "She started moaning. Her body shook. But the truly bizarre part was that she held her arms up as if she were trying to protect herself from something or someone."

Bent's gaze narrowed. "What did the staff have to say about what happened?"

"One of the nurses said it happens sometimes when a patient is getting closer to coming out of a coma, which is good news. The reaction I witnessed may have been related to a dream or a memory."

"You're thinking she was remembering what happened at the cabin?"

"I am." Vera was certain what she saw today was a game changer. "Of course it's just a gut feeling, and I could be way off. But it felt real. Visceral." She thought for a moment. "Whatever part Alicia played in what happened, I still feel like Erwin was involved somehow. Maybe she didn't kill anyone, but she played a part. And if someone else is the father of the child Alicia is carrying, then Thomas Wilton may have been involved, and his death was a mistake."

"We certainly can't rule either of them out until we know more." Bent reached up and tucked a lock of hair behind her ear. "I trust your instincts as well or better than I do my own."

Vera smiled. His trust meant a great deal to her. "I'm glad we're on the same page."

"Always." He hitched his head toward his truck. "I have to go back to the office to follow up on a couple of things. Want to ride with me? We can pick up your SUV later. I'm cooking again tonight."

Vera would be only too happy if the man cooked every night. "I still have one more stop I need to make. I'll meet you at your place."

He kissed her cheek. "See you then."

24

Fayetteville Hardware
1100 Winchester Highway, 4:30 p.m.

Vera wanted to get this thing done. The uncertainty was making her crazy. She almost told Bent before they parted ways, but she'd decided she needed to confirm one way or the other first.

She sat in the parking lot, stared at the dozens of sales being advertised in the hardware store's windows. She was prepared for the worst-case scenario. That was her motto: Hope for the best, prepare for the worst. Luna was counting on her to turn this situation around either way. On the drive here she had considered that perhaps she would need to have a friendly drink with the ME as an excuse to pick her brain about Jackie's injuries.

Vera knew many things about murder, killers, and all the working parts and broken pieces that went together with a homicide. But she was not a medical doctor. She did not know all the what-ifs related to the human body to make informed, accurate conclusions on the many possible scenarios associated with injuries and death. It was one thing to have experienced a situation—she always tried to learn the ins and outs of every homicide she investigated—but it was another to simply know because you'd studied and practiced the subject.

Jenny Collins might be a pain in Vera's ass where Bent was concerned, but she was the top authority on the human anatomy around these parts. Besides, Vera had been back home for more than a year. It was time to make a few friends—useful ones, anyway. A girl could never have too many handy, knowledgeable pals.

No more putting it off. Vera emerged from her SUV and headed into the hardware store. At the counter she smiled for the clerk. "Is Mr. Potter in?"

Luna had said that Clarence Potter shook the can of paint and rung her up that day. He was the owner. Vera wanted to speak directly to him. The quickest way to make the gossip grapevine was to pose a dicey question to the wrong person.

"I'm sorry, Mr. Potter is gone for the day. Can I help you with something?"

Vera didn't recognize the clerk, but she looked to be about Eve's age. Maybe someone she went to school with, assuming she was from the area. Vera committed the woman's glossy red hair and green eyes to memory. She would ask Eve later. If the cash register operation and/or maintenance became an issue, it wouldn't hurt to have an inside contact.

"Thank you, but I really need to speak with Mr. Potter. What time will he be in tomorrow?"

"He's generally here by eight and leaves at five. He had to leave a little early today." She tapped her mouth. "Dentist appointment."

Another idea occurred to Vera. "Thanks. I just need a . . ." She mentally ran down a list of items sold at a hardware store. "An extension cord."

The redhead blinked. "Sure. I'll show you where they are."

Vera followed her down an aisle, wondering what in the hell made her say *extension cord.*

"White? Brown? Black?" the cashier asked. "We have several lengths."

When she stopped in front of an array of extension cords, Vera frowned. "White. Six feet, I guess."

The cashier snagged one and passed it to Vera. "There you go."

"Thanks."

The walk back to the cash register had her stomach tying in knots. Holding her breath, Vera paid for the item.

"Anything else, hon?" The cashier tucked the receipt into the bag with the extension cord, then handed it to Vera. Before Vera could say a word, the redhead pointed a finger at her and smiled. "I know you, you're Eve's big sister, Vera."

Well that answered the question of whether Eve knew the woman. "I thought you looked familiar." What was one more lie in the grand scheme of things. Lies and fibs were simply a way of life for cops and private investigators. And Boyett sisters, apparently.

"Opal Carmichael." She gave Vera a knowing nod. "That Eve is a pure miracle worker when it comes to the dead. I can't tell you how many friends and relatives she's prepared and somehow managed to make them look so natural. Everyone brags on her work."

Vera smiled. It was good to hear nice things said about her sister. She had worked hard to earn the respect of this community. "We're very proud of Eve."

Opal leaned forward as if she were about to tell a state secret. "I reckon it's Eve's calling. She makes everyone look even better dead than they did when they were living." Her eyes got way bigger. "She really has a special gift, for sure."

"She does. Well, thank you, Opal."

"You have a good day!" Eve's former classmate called after her.

It was way too late for any part of this day to be deemed good—outside Carmichael's enthusiastic praise for Eve. Vera had endured a car ride all the way to Nashville and back with the snobby son of the woman who had made her life miserable back in high school, then she'd been puked on by her poor little pregnant sister.

This was not a good day by any measure of the definition, and she didn't expect it to get any better.

She hoped it wasn't about to get worse. Vera hurried to her SUV. When she was settled in her seat and had started the engine so the cool air would blow on her face, she dared to examine the receipt.

The digital clock on her dash read 4:52 p.m. The receipt showed 4:50 p.m.

Her heart sank. Adding the time it took her to get out of the store and into her SUV, the time was right. Which meant Luna was wrong about the time she left the hardware store.

How could that be?

Her cell vibrated on the console with an incoming call. Vera let it go to the car speaker. *Valeri Erwin.*

"Shit." She tapped the Accept Call button. "Vera Boyett."

"Vera, this is Valeri. I need to talk to you in person right now. Can you come to my place."

"Are you there?" She might have tossed too much snark into the question, but she knew Erwin had been home earlier and chose not to acknowledge Vera's presence. Plus she had just suffered through the worst possible news. Vera was in no mood to be patient or nice.

"Well, yes. That's why I asked you to come over."

"Be right there." Vera ended the call. What was it about that woman that got on her nerves so? Maybe the knowledge that she was a lying, conniving little self-serving gold digger. At least that was where the background research was pointing so far.

Open mind, Vee. Sometimes even the devil himself has an excuse.

She shoved the thought of the receipt out of her head and did what she had to do.

Erwin Residence
Washington Street, 5:15 p.m.

Vera glanced at the door to the apartment where she'd interviewed the young mother who hadn't wanted to give her name. It was all quiet in her apartment now. Same with the neighbor across the hall. Vera climbed the stairs to the second floor and knocked on Erwin's door. The one on the right side of the staircase. The downstairs tenant had said Erwin lived on that side. For all Vera knew, she could have had the whole floor. But this was the door that had opened when Vera was here.

The sound of the floor creaking on the other side of the door told Vera the woman was peeking through the security peephole. Vera resisted the urge to roll her eyes. It was a bad habit she'd developed since her return to the county. Along with worsening grammar and way more swearing.

One, then two locks released before the door opened. Erwin's face looked flushed. Her eyes were wide. "Thank you for coming."

Erwin stepped back far enough for Vera to squeeze through the door. The woman could be so strange sometimes.

"What's so important it couldn't wait until tomorrow?" Vera crossed her arms and waited. She was beyond ready to go home so she could stand in her backyard and scream at the top of her lungs for a good ten minutes or so. Or maybe take a nice long run to work off some of this tension. Except she had a concussion, and she couldn't do that.

"You want to have a seat?"

Though Erwin had a very nice apartment with lovely furnishings and well-done decor, Vera had no desire to stay a moment longer than necessary. At least not until she had a search warrant. It was time they went that route with or without compelling evidence. All they had to do was convince a judge.

"I have a meeting." Not exactly a lie. Bent was cooking dinner for her. "Can we just get to whatever it is you have to tell me?"

"Oh sure." Erwin nodded emphatically. Today she wore a baggy tee and jogging pants, and her hair looked in need of a wash—nothing at all like her usual put-together self. "So I went to the mansion this afternoon right after lunch to see if I could pick up a few files from the office." She looked heavenward with an exaggerated eye roll and shook her head to punctuate it. "Trying to take care of the business from here is nearly impossible."

This was exactly why Vera had to break the eye-roll habit. It was not a good look on anyone. Particularly when accompanied with other overdone gestures.

"I'm sure Bent can arrange to have a deputy accompany you to the house for whatever work materials you need." Was that all she had to say? For Pete's sake. Vera had no time for her theatrics. This could have been covered in a phone conversation.

"That would be great, because the deputy on duty today wouldn't let me in. But that isn't the reason I called you. As I was about to leave, a man showed up, demanding to talk to *you*."

A frown worked its way across Vera's brow, likely deepening the permanent lines time itself had inscribed there. "What man?"

"He said his name was Larry Parson, and he was looking for his brother." Her eyes got even wider, if that was possible. "You know, the one Alicia was probably fooling around with. Her ex. The one who was murdered at the cabin."

Vera held up a hand. "Okay. What time was this?"

"Around one, maybe a little after. I told him he'd have to see the sheriff. The deputy said the same thing. I didn't want to tell him where you lived."

And yet he'd found the farm anyway. "Well, I appreciate you letting me know. I'll pass it along to Bent." She had no intention of telling her they had already spoken to Larry Parson.

"That's not all." Erwin grabbed her arm. "It was him."

"Him?" Vera's gaze narrowed as she tried to read Erwin's mind. Could she not just get to the point?

"The guy who attacked us. I know it was him."

If she'd said he was the Easter bunny, Vera wouldn't have been more surprised. "How do you know? You said our attacker was wearing a ski mask."

"He was. And gloves. I remembered that too. Because after he hit me, he wrapped his arm around my neck and choked me. I guess he'd expected me to be knocked out, but I wasn't. The gloves felt rough against my skin. I thought I was a goner, for sure."

That might actually explain why Erwin had lost consciousness without a serious blow to the head. There were certain choke holds that would put a big-ass man down for several minutes.

Still, that didn't clarify how she'd recognized Parson as their attacker. Or why she didn't say before that he'd choked her.

"You never mentioned a choke hold before," Vera pointed out.

"I know. I didn't think of it until he got close to me. I guess it triggered a memory. He was exactly the right size," Erwin effused. "I remember how broad his chest was. He held me tight against him. His arm felt like a tree trunk, and my head barely reached his shoulders."

"But the size of his arms or even his height can't be used as the only means to make an official identification."

"I know. I know. I watch crime TV all the time. It was his *after-shave*," Erwin insisted, as if that was all Vera needed to know. "I recognized his aftershave. I've smelled it before. But I didn't think of it until he showed up today and I smelled him."

Admittedly, the scenario was possible. Olfactory memories could be powerful. Some folks wore a memorable scent—good or bad was subject to personal opinion. Not that Vera had noticed his aftershave, but she hadn't gotten that close to him and she was covered in the stench of puke. As for the brand of aftershave, she decided not to mention that he likely wore something easily purchased just about anywhere. Parson, the live one, didn't seem like the type to spend a lot of time or money selecting a fragrance. Very doubtful that the aftershave alone meant anything. But she couldn't ignore that between his size and the aftershave, Erwin's description was leaning toward somewhat of a coincidence, and Vera didn't believe in coincidences.

"Okay, Bent and I will question him. See what we can find out. I'm sure he can verify when he arrived in Fayetteville."

"I really believe it was him." Erwin nodded enthusiastically. "Under the circumstances I'm understandably worried about being here alone. I don't have an alarm system. What if he comes here?"

"I can ask if Bent can spare the manpower to put a detail on your place."

"Oh thank you, thank you. That would be great." She visibly sagged with relief.

"I'll let you know what he says." Vera was beyond ready to go. She was way past tired, and hunger pains were suddenly gnawing at her. When had she last eaten? Oh yeah, the burger on the way back from Nashville.

"I've been thinking." Erwin chattered on as she followed Vera to the door. "Alicia's old boyfriend being one of the victims has to mean something. If she was caught cheating by Thomas and they divorced—for any reason actually—she was set to gain a considerable settlement. Plus whatever gifts he'd given her." She made a puffing sound of disbelief. "The lovestruck man had given her plenty, trust me. I can't tell you how many deliveries came from Tiffany's and all those other fancy jewelry stores in New York. Some gifts came all the way from Paris. For that matter, look at that car she drives."

How strange, Vera mused, that Larry Parson had just gone over those same details. Coincidence or collusion? But after what Vera had learned today, it would take a lot more than hearsay or conjecture to put Alicia back at the top of the suspect list. Rather than tell Erwin as much, she opted to let her talk. She might just say more than she intended.

"But a divorce wasn't what she wanted," Erwin added quietly, as if she feared someone might overhear. "If Thomas died, she would likely get more."

If this was true, the question was, How did Erwin know this? Had she looked at the will? Obviously.

"Are you telling me now that you heard Alicia say that's what she wanted, or are you making an assumption?" Vera countered. "Assumptions don't count."

Erwin shrugged. "Any fool would see that makes the most sense. Surely a judge would."

Judges weren't fans of hearsay. "Thank you for the information, Valeri. If you think of anything relevant, let me know."

"You can count on it," she assured her.

Vera started for the door as if she intended to leave but turned back once more. She had a couple more things to go over with the chatty personal assistant. And she wanted to drop a couple little bombshells before she left, just to see the woman's reaction. "When I was here earlier today talking to your downstairs neighbor, why did you peek out this door and not say anything?"

Erwin frowned. "I have no idea what you're talking about. When were you here?"

"Around one thirty."

Erwin's mouth made an O. "That's easy, I wasn't at home. I was at the mansion, remember? That's when I saw the guy who attacked us."

Yeah, she had said around oneish. So maybe Erwin wasn't here.

"Do you have a roommate, or does anyone else have a key to your home?"

"No way. I mean Thomas did, but he's the only person. He had a key in case something happened to me and there were work papers here that he needed. I sometimes brought work home." She swallowed hard, her throat struggling with the effort. "Since he's dead . . . that means someone else was in my home." She slowly turned and surveyed the room. "They touched my things." Erwin whipped back around to glare wide-eyed at Vera. "They could come back!"

As much as she annoyed Vera, and no matter that Erwin still held a spot high on the suspect list, she could very well be right. It might not be safe for her to be here. If she wasn't the killer and the killer felt she represented a threat, then she could be in danger.

"We'll send someone over to check for prints. I'll call a locksmith for you. Your locks need to be changed today. Now."

Her eyes growing wider with Vera's every word, Erwin nodded frantically. "Okay."

"For now, stay put," Vera warned. "Keep the door locked and your phone in your hand. I'll call Bent right now and get the ball rolling on someone to keep an eye on your place. Maybe you should have a close look around and make sure nothing is missing. Like any keys you have to the Wilton property." Oh hell, that may have been the reason for the intrusion.

More nodding. "I'll check everything and call you."

Vera managed a tight smile. "Good." As much as she would really prefer that Erwin had called Bent, she let it go. Now for the bombshells.

"One more thing." Vera watched her closely. "Why didn't you tell me that Thomas Wilton's first wife cheated on him?"

Erwin drew back as if Vera had slapped her. "I . . . I." She shook her head. "Who told you such a thing?" She made a face as if she didn't understand the question. "You think Lena cheated?" Big shrug. "Why would I know something like that?"

So it was possibly true. Vera lifted a shoulder in a shrug of her own. "You and Thomas were so close, I thought perhaps he'd confided in you."

Erwin's chin came up in response to the challenge, and her entire demeanor changed. "Well, we were close, yes. And we did talk about most things. But some matters are just private and don't need to be brought up again. I honestly don't see how it's relevant at this point, anyway."

Definitely trouble with the first wife. Vera couldn't wait to see if she'd been keeping this other little secret as well. "Were you aware Alicia is pregnant?"

"What?" Erwin pressed a hand to her chest as if too startled to speak for a moment. "Is she? I mean, how do you know this? Is the baby okay after what happened?"

"The baby is fine." Vera smiled, an expression just as fake as the other woman's surprise. "You should get your stories straight, Valeri. Hiding things only makes you look guilty."

"I don't like to speak out of school," she whined. "Thomas was very private about those things."

"We have to know all the secrets if you expect us to find his killer." Vera studied her a moment. "Unless, of course, you don't want us to find him . . . or *her*."

Vera was out the door and closing it behind her before Erwin could pull together a response.

As she made her way to her SUV, she called Bent and gave him the update on Erwin. A deputy would be in place in the next fifteen minutes. Then she contacted a local locksmith—one she had used before—who would be right behind the deputy.

As tired and hungry as Vera was, going home would have to wait. She intended to have another conversation with Mr. Larry Parson.

25

Regency Inn
Huntsville Highway, 6:10 p.m.

Vera had to wait an extra ten minutes since Bent had insisted on meeting her at the motel. He didn't want her alone with this guy in his room. She would let that one go, since she was still a little weak and off kilter. The concussion symptoms were considerably better. However, the ache from the blow was far from gone but nothing she couldn't handle. No matter that the dizziness and brain fog were mostly gone, she wasn't herself just yet, and she wasn't going to pretend otherwise. Being overtaken by a guy Parson's size would be a piece of cake just now. She doubted she had it in her at the moment to kick a gnat's ass.

She was pushing the limit at this point in the evening, and her body was reminding her she needed rest. And food.

Bent reached her car door, opened it and waited for her to climb out. "You look tired."

"Thanks, Sheriff." She squared her shoulders and tried her best not to appear exhausted, even though her every muscle and bone said otherwise. "You look damned good, as always."

He shook his head and closed her door. It was true. Damn it. Gray Benton always looked amazing. He was the kind of handsome that couldn't be denied, no matter the circumstances or his condition.

Naked, clothed, clean, dirty, happy, sad, pissed off. The man simply was as sexy as hell. It was his natural state.

It just wasn't fair. Women couldn't pull that off without help.

That barely there grin of his made her heart—as tired as she was just now—react. "I didn't say you don't look amazing, Vee. Because you do. You always do. But I know when you're tired. I also know when you haven't taken time for a meal."

She shoulder-bumped him as they walked to the door of Parson's room. "Does that mean you're going to take extra-good care of me again tonight?"

He hesitated before knocking, looked directly into her eyes. "You know it."

She did. And that was the God's truth. From the moment she reappeared in her hometown, this man had not once let her down. He was her friend, her lover, and the one man she would not want to do this life without. The realization unsettled her just the tiniest bit. But it was the truth, and there was no point denying it. In fact, it was time she owned that reality in the bright light of day . . . not just in the dark or when no one was watching.

Bent knocked on the door, and Vera shooed the thought away. She was really, really exhausted.

The door opened, and Larry Parson looked from Vera to Bent and back. "Come on in, Sheriff. Ms. Boyett."

Once he'd closed the door, Bent looked to Vera since this was her episode of the ongoing drama. "Mr. Parson, we really need proof of when you left New Orleans and headed in this direction."

Parson settled his hands on his hips. "I left New Orleans about five this morning."

"Why so early?" Bent matched his stance, hands on hips. "Did you have an appointment with someone?"

Parson shook his head. "I don't know anyone here. Like I said before, I've been trying to get in touch with my brother since Monday night. Sandy wasn't answering her phone either, and I was getting damned worried. I found that message"—he directed this at Vera—"you left. I didn't even realize I had a message on that old answering machine until I was going to bed last night. It was late, so I planned to call you back this morning." He stared at the floor a moment. "Anyway, about three thirty I woke up in a cold sweat. I guess it was a combination of your message and all those unanswered calls. I tried to walk off the bad feeling, but I couldn't, so I decided to make the necessary arrangements and drive up here. I figured that was the best way to find out what the hell was going on."

"Do you have any proof?" Bent pressed. "A receipt of any sort that proves what time you left?"

Parson frowned. "I stopped for gas not long after I left, then I made a quick pass through a drive-through around noon. Let me check my Bus and see if I kept the receipts." He grabbed his keys and headed for the door.

Bent exchanged a look with Vera. She felt confident he was thinking that he was glad the guy didn't close the door so he could watch him dig around in his vintage Bus to ensure he wasn't going to drive away. Vera's overtired brain stuck on that damned hardware store receipt and how she had to figure out how the timing on the day Jackie died could be wrong—it had to be wrong. She sucked in a big breath and pushed the thought away.

Parson returned to the room with a bag from a Wendy's. He kicked the door shut. "Okay, I didn't find the gas receipt. I may not have grabbed it. I usually don't. There's generally no reason to keep it. Just something else to throw away."

He sat down on the bed and prowled through the bag. The stale odor of fries made Vera's stomach sit up and pay attention. Obviously she really did need to eat.

"Here we go." Parson thrust the receipt at Bent. "That should show what time and location I grabbed lunch. Will that work for you?"

Bent accepted the receipt and looked it over. He glanced at Vera. "It's a Huntsville location at 12:15 p.m. today." He handed the receipt back to the man. "Thanks. That tells us you were nearby today at noon, but it doesn't really confirm when you left Louisiana."

"Wait." Parson appeared to have had an epiphany. "When I left, I sent a friend of mine a pic of where I hid the key so she could come over and take care of my cat."

Vera would never have taken the guy for a cat person. "What's your cat's name?"

He opened the photo app on his cell. "Felix." He showed Vera a pic of a flowerpot containing a dead plant. "I left a key under that pot."

"The date shows it was taken this morning at 4:49," she said as Parson flashed the screen at Bent.

"I sent the pic to Rhonda in a text." He showed the next screen first to Vera then to Bent.

Rho, key is here. Thanks for this. Felix appreciates it.

His friend Rhonda had replied at 4:55.

"Do you typically text your friends at that hour?"

"Rhonda works early, so I knew she'd be up."

"You mind giving me her number?" Bent reached into his shirt pocket and retrieved the small notepad he carried with him. "We can confirm what you've told us with her."

Might have been quicker and easier if the guy had just mentioned his friend when Bent first asked for confirmation.

"Once you arrived in Fayetteville"—Vera moved on to the next question—"where did you go first?"

"I went to the Wilton house. But the deputy wouldn't tell me anything. He wouldn't even tell me how to find you." He looked to Vera. "I had to look that up myself. I googled you and found a story from a local newspaper about your farm. Something about bodies discovered in a cave."

Damn Nolan Baker. Vera kicked the little shit out of her head. "Was anyone else at the Wilton home when you stopped?"

Parson nodded. "Some chick. Short." He held his hand about shoulder level. "Dark hair. She came to the door while I was talking to the deputy, but she didn't say anything." He frowned. "Who is she?"

Vera ignored his question. "One last question, Mr. Parson. To your knowledge did Seth have any contact with Alicia prior to two or three weeks ago?"

He shook his head resolutely. "When he got that first text from her, he told me he hadn't heard from her in almost two years. I mean, he was seriously torn up about it. I can't tell you exactly what day it was—two, two and a half, maybe three weeks ago tops—but I can tell you that it turned his world upside down."

"Thank you." Vera had all she needed from him at this time. "We'll get out of your way for now."

Bent said, "I'm sure we'll have more questions."

Parson held up his hands. "Like I told you, I'm not going anywhere until I know why this happened to my brother."

Something about this man's answers—his brother's past drawing him into trouble—unsettled Vera. Maybe because she knew better than most how the past could do just that. Old ghosts were rarely laid completely to rest.

When they were outside, Vera warned Bent, "I'm following you home. I don't want to be at the farm tonight."

He shot her a heart-stopping smile across the hood of his truck. "Good."

Benton Ranch
Old Molino Road, 9:00 p.m.

Not only had Bent prepared dinner, but he'd gone to her house and picked up everything she would need for tomorrow while Vera soaked in his big old claw-foot tub. Although she kept a set of her usual toiletries and cosmetics here, she'd run out of clothes and underthings.

By the time she was out of the tub, had blown her hair dry and pulled on her favorite nightshirt (that old Bon Jovi tee he'd bought her a million years ago), he already had dinner prepared.

Now, that was a man who understood how to treat a woman.

Seated at the table, Vera poured herself another glass of wine. He kept a decent selection, no matter that he was definitely not a wine man. For guests, she supposed. She'd have to remind him to get more merlot. He also kept a bottle of Gentleman Jack on hand for those evenings that required a little more bracing. Vera was a big fan of Jack.

Bent checked his cell, then left it on the counter and rejoined Vera. "That was a text from Conover. He lifted a good many prints from Erwin's apartment and confirmed the locks did not appear to have been tampered with." He picked up his glass of tea. "You know how this goes. The chance of finding a comparison print not belonging to someone she knows in one of the databases is unlikely. More frustrating, whoever broke into Erwin's place apparently used a key and probably wore gloves."

The same way they didn't find anything useful at the farm after she and Erwin were attacked. Erwin had recalled that their attacker had worn gloves, so they were never going to. Breaking-and-entering cases were difficult to close with fingerprints alone unless there was a match in the database or an actual suspect for comparison. A suspect too stupid to wear gloves.

"You know." Vera settled her glass back on the table. She was feeling very relaxed just now. "Erwin has been at the top of my suspect list alongside Alicia Wilton all week. Particularly after I spoke with the mother of Nola Childers. That whole story of their years as roommates and friends and then Childers's sudden, bizarre death and Erwin getting her position with Wilton—it was just too much. How could she not be at the top? And after what I witnessed in Alicia's hospital room and the news about her pregnancy, she dropped below Erwin on that list."

"But you're not so sure anymore." Bent traced a trickle of sweat down his tea glass with a fingertip. "About either one. Not really."

Vera watched the move with far too much interest. She tried to push away the image of him using that finger to trace a path down her body, but it wasn't going anywhere.

Focus on the case . . . The other is for later.

"I am not. What we've learned about Erwin certainly makes her a bit on the odd side, but not necessarily a murderer—at least not in our case. Parson confirmed her story about his arrival at the Wilton house. She obviously was wrong about him being the attacker. It's not impossible that our attacker wore the same aftershave as Parson, but more likely she wants it to be him because it makes sense to her. His brother was somehow involved with Alicia and ultimately ended up a victim. Erwin wants to connect all the pieces. Her subconscious may be helping her along."

Vera exhaled a big breath. "Then we have Seth Parson, whose brother insisted he had not heard from Alicia in two years until about three weeks ago, so we can assume Seth is not the father of her child. And, if Larry Parson is telling the truth about when he arrived in Fayetteville, I don't see how either of them could be involved. Not really, considering Seth is dead. So the real question is, Who was at the cabin besides the four? Alicia was clearly running from someone."

"You said yourself," Bent countered, "that Erwin is hiding things—like the first wife's affair and the second wife's pregnancy. Maybe she was there or knows who was."

"I don't doubt she knows who was there, but that doesn't make her a killer. Frankly, I can't be positive she knew about the pregnancy, but she certainly put on a show of being surprised when I told her." Vera rubbed at her forehead where the tension was building. "She was obsessed, it seems to me, with Thomas Wilton."

"Moving Erwin down." Bent braced his crossed arms on the table. "Right next to the Parson brothers."

Vera made a face. "But the first wife did die in a bizarre accident. What if Thomas Wilton wasn't the fine, upstanding guy everyone believed he was—at least not where his wives are concerned? And maybe Erwin is hiding what she knows about that too."

"I see where you're going, but we don't have anything other than the first wife's suspicious accident to put in his guilty column, and he's dead. So who, if anyone, are we moving up?"

Vera finished off her third glass of wine, which was more than enough, it seemed, since she was feeling far too comfortable. "Okay. Okay. Let's go through this again. We can agree that Seth Parson and Sandy Owens were both lured into what happened. Everyone we've interviewed until now would have us believe Alicia is the one who invited them. So I suppose it actually makes sense—no matter what my gut tells me—to keep Alicia tied with Erwin on the list in spite of the pregnancy and all else. She may have hired someone to kill her husband, and we just haven't discovered it yet. The rest of those killed were for show—to lead us off in other directions. She was injured to deflect guilt."

"That would mean Alicia wanted the probable father of her child dead," Bent reminded her.

Vera groaned in frustration. "Maybe." Vera wasn't convinced that was the case, but it was an option they couldn't deny at this point. Another thought occurred to her. She sat up straighter. "What if it was Wilton who lured Seth here? All communications were via text before Seth and Sandy arrived—as far as we know. And Wilton did go pick the two up for the weekend at the cabin. Think about it. Given his history as a creator and a businessman, I wouldn't take him for someone who allows others to be in charge of any aspect of his life."

Bent leaned back in his chair. "Good point. Maybe in the end it all went wrong, and Seth killed him." His gaze narrowed. "After seeing what her old friend has done, Alicia kills Seth and Sandy."

Vera made a face. "But who hit her in the back of the head? Who was she running from? There absolutely had to be another person involved—assuming the blow to the back of her head was sufficient to incapacitate her."

"We haven't found even one other potential suspect," Bent reminded her. "Not a single business associate who wanted Wilton out of the way. Olson and Hastings have spoken to the entire list Erwin and the attorneys provided. As Erwin has said repeatedly, he doesn't appear to have had any enemies."

Vera propped her elbow on the table, rested her chin in one hand. God, she was tired. "That takes us back to Erwin, Carter, Hernandez, and Martinez. Those were the closest to Thomas Wilton. One of them has to know something about our fifth player."

"Each one had something to gain from Wilton's death," Bent agreed. "So maybe it was one of them."

"The probability makes too much sense to ignore." Vera stared at her wineglass, wishing it weren't empty, then she lifted her gaze to Bent's. "They worked together for Wilton, what? Five years for Erwin? Eight for the others? Why now? Why not last year or next year? What was the impetus that set this whole plan in motion after so many years of dedicated service?"

"The answer takes us back to the new wife. Alicia was the most recent change." Bent stood, picked up Vera's plate and stacked it on his own. "She's the newest factor in all their lives—that we know of. Maybe the decision came as a result of how she was changing the boss or the situation. All four complained about her."

"She is the most logical trigger." Vera felt only remotely guilty for not getting up to help with the dishes. But she was reasonably sure that moving right now would not be a good thing. "We just need to know in what way the change or changes Alicia prompted set off this chain reaction—if, in fact, that's what happened. Something that will give us the evidence we need to cross the finish line."

Bent came back for their glasses. "We'll interview all four again tomorrow. Separately this time. We might just get lucky."

"We can always hope."

This time when Bent returned to the table, he held out his hand for hers. "But first, I thought we might do that tonight."

Vera frowned, confused, then she got it. She put her hand in his, pushed back her chair and stood. "I believe getting lucky tonight can be arranged."

He put his arm around her waist and started the journey toward the bedroom. "Not to toss in a downer, but Hayworth called me."

The attorney Geneva Fanning had hired. Vera suppressed the urge to groan. "You saved that until now."

"I only thought of it now." Bent paused at the door to the place where the magic happened. "He mostly just wanted me to know that he was taking her case and thought I should be aware she planned to pursue civil action against the department if we didn't thoroughly investigate Jackie's death."

Vera gritted her teeth. She so wanted to punch Geneva Fanning. Then she rolled her eyes. But that might border on elder abuse. The need to tell Bent everything Luna had confided in her nearly overwhelmed her . . . but she couldn't. Not yet.

"I don't want to talk about work anymore." Vera draped her arms around his neck. "You?"

Bent didn't say a word, just lowered his mouth to hers.

Vera relaxed against him and put all the worries about murder and mayhem out of her mind.

26

Erwin Residence
Washington Street, 10:30 p.m.

Valeri stared at the total chaos she had caused. She had looked everywhere. On top of and under furniture, shelves, curtains—every damned place she could see or think of in her determination to ensure nothing had been taken or left behind. Her belongings were flung all over the place, including the floor. She groaned.

Someone had been in her house.

She leaned against the doorframe and surveyed her living room yet again. All those classic-looking hardcovers she had collected were stacked in columns next to the sofa. Her fondest memory was of Thomas dropping by to pick up a file and taking one of her books from its shelf and saying it was his favorite. The memory made her smile.

Didn't matter now. He was gone. And that slut was still alive . . . and *pregnant*. Valeri struggled to tamp down her emotions. No getting upset. If she got upset, bad things happened. She could not allow it.

She focused on the mess she had made once more. Magazines were tossed about. Scattered across the floor were her throw pillows and the vintage quilt she'd bought at a junk sale so she could tell anyone who visited that it was her one heirloom from her grandmother.

Valeri almost laughed out loud despite her current dilemma. Her grandmother never left her anything but all alone. Her mother hadn't done any better. As for her father, Valeri had no idea who he was. She pushed away from the door and wandered through the chaos. She had basically raised herself. Put herself through college. Made her own way without any help whatsoever.

No damned body was going to ruin this for her. Unexpected interference had almost destroyed her world as it was.

But she had that under control now.

A new level of fury abruptly twisted inside her. She had worked too hard, sacrificed too much to reach this place of contentment. No one was screwing it up.

Whoever had come into her home, Valeri was not about to let them get away with it.

Whoever? *Please.* She knew who it had been. A smirk spread across her lips. No way would she be beaten by the likes of that worthless piece of crap. No way. This wasn't exactly the ending she had hoped for, but it was workable, and no one was screwing it up worse than it already was.

Valeri prided herself on always making backup plans. When one option went awry, she had another at the ready.

The immediate problem was that the intruder had entered with a purpose. Valeri needed to know what that purpose was. Since she hadn't found anything missing or left behind, she had to assume it was a scare tactic.

Maybe she needed to do a little scaring of her own. The thought incited far too much glee. She glanced around the room again. The disarray was unsettling. She should clean up, and then she would put together a plan to have her revenge.

The books and magazines would take the longest, so she started with the other random items. The quilt she arranged once more on the back of the sofa. The throw pillows she tossed in that same direction. One landed on the coffee table with an unexpected thwack.

She frowned. What the heck? Valeri picked up the pillow and squashed it against her stomach as she kneaded its soft foam insides. The feel of something hard near the zipper had her opening the removable cover. The plain square pillow was there. A black object clattered to the floor. She stared at it for a moment.

Cell phone.

"Well, well. This isn't supposed to be here." At least now she understood what the intruder had gone to all this trouble for. And she knew exactly who the intruder was.

Valeri smiled. "Did you really think you could one-up me?"

No way.

27

Friday, September 5
Andrews Farm
Boonshill Road, 7:30 a.m.

Vera parked at Luna's house and shut off the engine. She had wanted to have those follow-up interviews with Carter, Hernandez, Martinez, and Erwin first thing this morning, but Bent had a command performance with the city's and county's top brass. She didn't envy him the task of explaining where the triple homicide investigation was in terms of closing the case. Politicians never fully understood the time required to do the job right. They would much rather have someone—anyone—arrested to reassure the community that all was well in their world.

But it was rarely that simple and never quick.

Since the next step in the Wilton case was postponed until ten or after, Vera moved on to her other problem. Luna's situation. She grabbed her bag and reached for the door.

She refused to call it a case, because it wasn't. So far there was no crime—at least not one officially proclaimed as such. If she could work swiftly enough to put the pieces together, things would stay exactly that way—at least as far as Luna was concerned. And she needed to make sure Luna understood one very important aspect of what had happened between her and Jackie. As much as Vera hated to point it out, it was necessary.

As she climbed out of her SUV, the heat consumed her. It was hot already, even at this hour. No breeze. But that was just the last of a southern summer flexing its muscle. Vera surveyed her sister's neat little farm. It was quiet, for sure. A good place to raise a family. She smiled even as her chest ached. She wanted that happy ending so badly for her little sister.

A call to Luna at seven had confirmed that Jerome was already en route to Nashville to sit at his father's side. The hope was that hearing his son's voice would bring him out of what might be self-imposed isolation.

Vera climbed the steps and headed across the porch.

Luna opened the door before Vera reached it. "Do you have news?"

Of course she would think that after Vera had called and asked if it was a good time to stop by before Luna was off to the library to begin her day. "Not really. I thought we'd catch up and go over everything one more time."

Luna's face fell. "Okay. Come on in. You need coffee or anything?"

Vera closed the door and followed her sister into the kitchen. "Water would be good. Thanks."

"How about a muffin?" Luna picked up a basket of perfectly formed muffins from the island countertop. The lovely deep-brown color was highlighted with little pieces of orange and red. "They're wheat with cranberry and orange. Very little sugar. Very healthy." She poured Vera a glass of water, then picked up one of the muffins and started to nibble.

Vera suspected that wasn't her first one. Her baby bump looked as if it had grown even more pronounced in the past twenty-four or so hours.

"Sure." Vera grabbed a muffin and took a bite. Not as bad as she'd expected. She swallowed. "How is Mr. Andrews?"

Luna set a glass of water in front of Vera. "No change. We just keep praying he will wake up."

"Hopefully that will happen soon." Vera put her muffin aside and went for the water. She cleared her throat then. "Based on what you've told me so far, I'm convinced that it's as you and I already discussed.

Jackie got up. Moved the furniture around and then either tripped down the stairs or was facilitated by someone who came to the house after you left."

"But who would do that?" Luna sipped her own water, then shook her head. "You know better than I do that killing someone is not exactly a small decision."

Vera did. Not only from her professional career but also from what had happened with all those bodies found in that damned cave on the family farm.

Don't go down that path, Vee.

Pushing the past back to its place, Vera steeled herself. She hated to do this, but it was time Luna understood what had happened for what it was. The events had played over and over in Vera's brain like a bad movie reel, and there was only one way to view Jackie's intent on that day.

"Luna, when Jackie tried to push you down the stairs, she had made exactly that decision."

Luna wilted onto a stool and sat for a moment, not speaking, not even blinking. "You really think she intended to kill me?"

For Pete's sake, did she think it was just for fun? Denial. That was the problem. "Luna, she tried to kill you. Worse, she didn't care if she killed the baby too."

Luna drew back as if Vera had dashed hot coffee in her face. "No." Her hands cradled her belly protectively. "That can't be right."

"It's an undeniable statistic. Most pregnant women who are murdered are murdered by a spouse, partner, or family member. Obviously, the baby is a victim as well."

Vera hadn't wanted to share this sad truth with Luna, but she needed her to see that Jackie was the evil one in this. The guilt Luna felt needed to be gone.

"Oh my God." Luna's horrified expression announced loudly and clearly that she now got it.

Vera regretted being the one to make her understand that awful truth. "So please, tell me every ugly rumor and/or factoid you know about the woman and her sister."

"All right." Luna heaved a big breath. "Everybody—at least a lot of people—considered Jackie a pain in the butt. We talked about that. Those who weren't close to her would say she was selfish and self-centered. Everything had to be her way, which was very true." She shifted on her stool as if uncomfortable.

Vera couldn't imagine the effort required to carry around all that extra weight, especially on Luna's petite frame.

"But the most prevalent rumor that I've heard off and on over the years," she went on, "was about Leonard. There was always this nasty little rumor that he only married her because she got pregnant with Jerome. There was talk of affairs." Luna blushed. "She was expecting before the wedding, no doubt about that. Then, as the story goes, he only stayed with her because of the cancer she had when Jerome was little."

Vera made a face. "So she had cancer three times not two?"

Luna nodded. "That's right. The last time was two years ago."

"Wow." Vera imagined the woman thought she would live forever with a record like that.

As if having a similar thought, Luna squeezed her eyes shut, maybe to block the image of Jackie lying dead at the bottom of her stairs, chin jutted out.

"Did anyone ever say who they thought Leonard was fooling around with?" It was a small town. Vera would be stunned if names weren't mentioned.

"One time I heard the ladies in the women's group who meet at the library whispering about the woman, the *old maid*, they called her, who works at the Fanning accounting firm. But later I heard that was nothing but a rumor. She used to do Leonard's and Jackie's taxes, so maybe that's how the rumor got started." Luna dusted muffin crumbs off her belly. "I've even heard that it was Geneva. But I don't think that's true.

Jackie is her sister, and their husbands are first cousins. I think Trenton, Geneva's husband—you met him at the barbecue on Sunday—would have noticed."

"I did meet him." She had heard of the Andrews and Fanning families. Fayetteville was a small town. But she'd never known them until Luna married Jerome.

As for Geneva's husband having noticed a potential affair, Vera wasn't so sure. "You would be surprised how oblivious some people can be. The idea of Geneva wanting Jackie's husband would certainly up the ante as motives go."

Luna made an unpleasant face. "I just can't see Leonard cheating on Jackie with her own sister. That's just gross."

"Sometimes it's the most unexpected that turns out to be the real story."

Luna shuddered at the idea. "I just hope for Jerome's sake that this whole nightmare is not about his father."

"Do you know where these other potential players were when the fall happened? Was Leonard home alone? And what about Geneva?" Those were questions that needed to be asked. Cell phone records for all involved, including Geneva and Leonard, had been subpoenaed and should be in any day. The communication going back and forth between Jackie and her sister that morning had prompted Bent to order Geneva's records as well.

"Geneva said she was home and that Jackie was sending her all those text messages," Luna reminded Vera. "I think Leonard was home because that's where he had his heart attack, and it wasn't so long after her fall."

"But what about Geneva's husband, Trenton?" Maybe they needed his records too.

"I suppose he was at the office. Fanning and Ferguson Accounting."

Vera knew the place. Right down the street from Barrett's. Eve probably ran into him from time to time. His alibi would be the easiest to prove or, as the case might be, disprove.

"Oh wait!"

Vera almost jumped at the startled way her sister made the announcement. "What?"

"The woman at the accounting office—the one I was telling you about—I remember now that Jackie once said something about some floozy who worked with Trenton. Geneva was furious because she thought *Trenton* was having an affair. Mila." Luna nodded. "Mila Davis. I've seen her around. Very pretty. She's like the same age as Geneva and has never been married." Luna's eyes were huge, as if she'd just gossiped about the good Lord himself.

"I'll look into Mila Davis." It might not help Luna's situation, but it couldn't hurt. "Anything else?"

"I can't think of anything." Luna sighed and took another bite of muffin.

"So what about Valeri Erwin?"

Luna was the one who looked startled now. "What about her?"

"You were going to look into what she'd been checking out at the library." Any tidbit of information could prove useful at this point.

"Oh yes." Luna nodded. "True crime books. Mostly those having to do with murders—real ones. No fiction." She made a face. "In fact, when I examined her record, I realized Valeri had never even checked out a book until a month ago, and she hasn't checked out anything since."

Interesting. This news might just push Erwin above the other members of household staff on Vera's suspect list.

"Thanks, Lu." Vera stood. "I have to go, but let me know if you think of anything else about Jackie or Geneva. Or Erwin."

"I will. Thanks for everything, Vee."

Luna didn't get up. Making those moves, Vera suspected, was getting more difficult in these final days. "Anytime, sweetie."

Vera locked the front door as she left, intentionally ignoring the staircase. As she started her SUV, she decided she had enough time before meeting Bent at the Carter property to pay a quick visit to Erwin. She had some explaining to do about those library books. On the way she called Eve. She had mentioned overhearing rumors about Geneva during visitations. Maybe Eve could do a little digging as well.

It might just take all the Boyett sisters working together to get ahead of this one.

Wilton Residence
Giles Hollow Road, 9:00 a.m.

Since Erwin hadn't been at her place, Vera had called her. She was at the Wilton house picking up files. She had insisted Bent said she could. A text to Bent confirmed as much. The deputy who had been overseeing Erwin's visit onto the property and into her dead boss's office appeared all too ready to return to his post outside when Vera arrived. She put him out of his misery and sent him on his way and assumed the supervision of Erwin.

"I'm so glad you're here." Erwin hurried from behind Wilton's desk and reached for her oversize purse where she'd left it on the floor. "I came by your house this morning, but you weren't home."

"When I'm on a case, I often have early appointments." Vera's location was none of the woman's business.

Erwin removed a plastic zipper-style bag from her purse and thrust it at Vera. "I found this in my home. It was hidden in a throw pillow." She stared at the bag as if it were a murder weapon.

Vera accepted the bag and studied its contents. *Cell phone.* "Did you touch it?"

"No way. I picked it up with a bag and put it in that one."

This time Vera was prepared for examining potential evidence. She placed the find on the desk and retrieved a pair of latex gloves from her shoulder bag. Once she'd tugged them on, she opened the bag and took out the cell phone.

"You have any idea who it belongs to?"

Erwin shook her head. "No clue."

Generic device. Vera turned on the phone, which ironically still had battery life and required no access code. No pics, no email or other apps. Just calls and text messages. There were dozens of missed calls over the past three weeks. All from the same Louisiana number. She felt confident the number would be Seth Parson's. Her suspicions were confirmed when she opened the lengthy text conversation with that same number.

The series of text messages that Larry Parson had talked about between Alicia and Seth were right here on this phone. All the way up until Seth's arrival in Fayetteville two weeks ago. Then ten days ago the messages and calls ended . . . as if he'd just stopped interacting with Alicia or learned there was a different number to use or didn't need a phone to speak with her anymore. Vera suspected this was when he'd arrived in Fayetteville. As much as Vera wanted to be pleased with this new evidence, the way it had been received only made it troubling.

She turned to Erwin. "You're certain you've never seen this phone before?"

"Never." Erwin returned to Wilton's desk and picked through a stack of files there. "I assume whoever broke into my place put it there for some reason."

Like to point suspicion in her direction. But Vera wasn't saying as much. If Erwin hadn't touched the phone, then she didn't know what it contained. If she had, she wanted Vera to give her confirmation that the contents suggested she was being set up. Vera wasn't giving her that satisfaction just yet.

"I'll get this to Bent, and we'll see what we can find."

"Anything useful on there?"

Vera slid the phone back into its bag and stuffed it into hers. "It's difficult to say."

Erwin huffed a breath, as if she knew Vera wasn't being honest with her. She waved a hand at the files. "Do you have to look at what I'm taking?"

Vera hadn't explained her reason for wanting to see her this morning. The announcement of her find had derailed all else. "It would be best if I took a quick look."

Erwin dropped into the boss's chair and gestured to the stack. "There you go."

She was clearly annoyed that her news hadn't prompted the reaction in Vera that she'd evidently hoped for.

Vera skirted the desk and began a slow, thorough perusal of the first file. She paused before moving to the next one. "You have a thing for true crime?"

Erwin's expression turned puzzled. "What? No. I hate those documentaries."

"But you check out true crime books from the library." Vera thumbed through the next file. So far, business reports. P&Ls. Letters to associates.

When Erwin didn't respond, Vera glanced at her. "You didn't think we'd have a look at what you read? The things you do in your spare time? You said yourself you watch crime TV."

"I do sometimes," she groused, "because half the time that's the only thing on television worth watching. But I don't *read* about it." Her shoulders sagged as if she'd been defeated somehow. "The truth is, I don't do a lot of reading at all. The books in my house are just for show. I don't even know the titles. I just like for people to think I'm well read."

Vera didn't doubt this. Erwin was the perfect example of a narcissist. She went to great lengths to put on a certain facade for those around her. She needed to be seen as intelligent and accomplished. Vera had already picked up on the woman's lack of empathy when the murder victims were mentioned—her story about her roommate was a perfect example. The whole sad tale was relayed with little or no emotion for the dead girl or her family. Then there was the passive-aggressive behavior. Definitely a narcissist.

"Good grief." Erwin shook her head, her expression puzzled. "I can't believe it. I didn't even think about those books, or I swear I would have told you."

Vera closed the file in her hand, placed it on the stack. "You really didn't think we'd check into your habits? Your routine?"

Erwin's head wagged side to side hard enough to rattle her brain. "No. I don't mean that. I fully expected to be looked at as a suspect. I just can't believe I didn't think about all those weird books Alicia asked me to pick up for her. Like I said, if I had remembered, I would have told you."

How handy to blame the coma woman. "You're saying Alicia asked you to check out those books."

"I swear!" Erwin held up her right hand. Then she waved both hands in the air. "Well, technically she didn't ask me. I was far too lowly a human for her to speak directly to. She left me a list when she wanted me to do something for her."

Vera hummed a note of doubt. "I don't suppose you kept any of those lists."

Erwin huffed an exasperated breath. "I did not. But if you don't believe me about the books, have Luna pull my history. I never checked out a single book until . . ." She frowned as if trying to recall something. "About a month ago. I checked out the ones you're talking about for Alicia and then no more. Those weren't for me. I'm not a reader."

"I'll look into that." Though she felt Erwin was being truthful, primarily based on Luna's confirmation, she wasn't about to let the woman off the hook so easy. Vera finished skimming the files, and none looked suspicious. Erwin held a three-ring binder and appeared to be reviewing it. "Are you planning to take that?"

"I have no idea." Erwin's eyes were huge with something like shock when she handed the binder to Vera. "I've never seen it before. It was under a couple of those files in his inbox."

Vera placed the binder on the blotter pad and opened it up. A quick skim of the cover sheet explained the contents. No wonder it was so thick. "It's an appraisal of the Wilton property." Vera flipped through a few pages. "A very detailed, in-depth appraisal." She turned to Erwin. "The entire property." The value was staggering.

Erwin's expression had shifted from shock to something like disappointment. "Why would he have an appraisal like that done?"

"For insurance purposes, maybe." Vera was aware that high-value properties like this one were under close scrutiny by insurance companies. There was a great deal to be lost in a property this size. Staying on top of any upgrades or failures to maintain any and all structures by the owner was crucial. She glanced at the file. The concept seemed completely logical.

"I should call the appraiser." Erwin reached for the binder.

Vera held it out of her reach. "Why don't we let the sheriff make that call? I'm sure the appraiser will be more forthcoming with the authorities under the circumstances."

The shock and disappointment were gone, replaced by what looked very much like hurt. "Let me know what he says, okay?"

Vera wasn't sure why it would matter to Erwin now. Her employer was dead. The estate would be passed along or sold off, whatever the will prescribed. That was something else Vera needed to know more about. They knew what their persons of interest were set to receive in terms of dollars, but what about the actual real property? The very *valuable* property.

"Come on," Vera said to the other woman, who still looked confused about the binder. "I'll walk you out."

As they left, Erwin walked slower than usual, her gaze lingering here and there. Did she think this would be her last time in this house?

Vera paused at the front door. "Did no one on staff know about the pregnancy?"

Erwin blinked, her eyes wide with something like surprise. "What?"

"Did anyone know Alicia was pregnant?"

Erwin adjusted the load of files in her arms. "I never heard anyone talk about it. I sure didn't."

She said the last as if her teeth were grinding together. Maybe Alicia and her husband had opted to keep the news to themselves. Except Vera wasn't so sure Erwin hadn't known—not after their conversation yesterday. Moving on, Vera reminded her, "Remember to call if you think of anything else useful in the investigation."

A vague nod, and Erwin was out the door. Once she was driving away and Vera was doing the same, she called the appraiser. With Wilton's murder all over the news, it only took a moment to get an answer to her question.

Thomas Wilton had gotten the property appraised because he was considering putting it on the market. He was entertaining the notion of moving to California.

Vera couldn't be sure what this meant, of course, but her instincts were jumping at the revelation. This news could very well be somehow related to the murders.

It was far too large a potential change to be ignored.

Which of their suspects would be the most upset by this sort of news?

All four, Vera would wager.

28

Carter Residence
Coldwater Creek Road, 10:15 a.m.

Vera could see right away that Helen Carter was not happy to see them. Catching an interviewee off guard was always preferable since there was no time to plan answers. But the one being asked the questions rarely appreciated this tactic.

Carter had known she would be questioned again. She just hadn't known the exact date and time.

At the moment she was in the kitchen preparing a pot of fresh coffee. Vera waited in the living room with Bent. They'd settled on the sofa to wait for Carter's return. Vera imagined Carter had wanted out of the room in order to warn her tenants, Martinez and Hernandez, that they would be summoned soon.

This second round of interviews wasn't so much about learning new information, although that would be nice. Today was about responses. It had been pretty clear during the initial interview that Helen Carter, Jose Martinez, and Renata Hernandez did not want to talk about the murders. By now that reluctance would have expanded into fear.

On the drive over, Vera had called Bent with the news about the property appraisal. He had agreed with her conclusion that Erwin's apparent surprise at finding the appraisal was a tick mark in the not-guilty column. He'd also been surprised that she'd found a possible burner phone in her place and turned it over. There was no doubt it was the one used for communications between Alicia and Seth Parson that the brother had mentioned. The question was, Did Erwin have it all along, or had someone actually planted it to make it seem as if she had?

"Sorry to make you wait." Carter breezed into the room, carrying a tray laden with a shiny silver coffee pot and lovely delicate china cups seated in saucers.

She placed the tray on the coffee table and prepared to pour. She looked to Vera. "Cream or sugar?"

"Black is fine."

When she turned to Bent, he passed on the coffee altogether.

Carter then offered a small plate loaded with scones. Had everyone decided to bake this morning?

"They look delicious, but no thanks." Vera wanted to get on with what they'd come here to do.

Carter set the plate aside and took a seat. "Renata and Jose are on their way up. I let them know you were here."

Of course she did.

"Tell us again," Bent said, kicking off the questions, "when did Renata and Jose move onto your property?"

"About three months ago. They had lived in the ranch manager's apartment in the barn until then. Alicia didn't feel comfortable with anyone else living on the property."

Vera had seen that barn. It was huge. Heated and cooled. Not your typical horse barn, for sure. The apartment was even nicer. Definitely not a hardship to live there.

"Maybe it was a newlywed thing," Vera suggested. "Alicia may have felt she and her new husband needed their privacy."

"No," Carter countered, "it was a bitch thing."

Well all right then.

"Were Jose and Renata upset with this change?" Bent glanced out the large south-facing window, where Vera had already spotted the couple walking toward the house. He slipped his phone from his pocket as his attention settled back on Carter.

"At first." Carter settled her delicate cup back into its saucer and placed both on the coffee table. "But when I invited them here, it was all okay."

"Did there appear to be any hard feelings?" Vera asked. Most anyone would feel slighted by being kicked out of their home for such a seemingly selfish reason.

"Mostly they were worried and afraid, as anyone in their position would be."

"What position is that?" Bent no doubt understood what she meant, but he wanted her to say as much.

"They don't have their proper papers yet." Helen glanced back at the kitchen, where the screen door had just whined, announcing the couple's entrance into the house. "Thomas was working on taking care of that. I'll check in with his attorney and ensure the ball hasn't been dropped, given what's happened."

"I've been wondering," Vera ventured, "with such an elaborate barn and outbuildings, why no animals?" Seemed a good lead-in to throw out a couple of questions about the first wife.

Carter took a breath. "There used to be horses as well as goats. Mostly horses. Lena loved horses. She was a dressage champion, you know." Carter looked away a moment. "After she died, Thomas couldn't bear to look at them. He sold them all. The goats too."

Understandable, given the circumstances. "Previously," Vera said, "you stated that you were home all weekend. Catching up around the house. Is there anyone who can vouch for your whereabouts?"

Carter didn't look surprised by the question. She'd given it once already in the initial interview. Her answer came without hesitation. "Renata and Jose. We were all here all weekend. Cutting grass. Doing some repairs. We don't get extended days off often. I can make you a list of all we accomplished, if you like."

Renata and Jose stepped into the room, both looking to Carter for instructions.

"Come on in. Have a seat. Coffee?" Carter glanced from one to the other. Both declined the coffee and claimed the two remaining chairs in the fairly large conversation area.

Vera's cell vibrated in her pocket. She tugged it out. A text from Bent.

Go outside w/ Renata.

Vera put her phone away and stood. "Renata, why don't you and I go out onto the porch?"

Carter looked surprised at the request but didn't question it. She wanted to, though. Vera could see it in her eyes.

As Vera and a visibly reluctant Renata started for the door, Bent asked, "Jose, did you have any reason to suspect your position with Mr. Wilton was in jeopardy? Did the two of you have any disagreements?"

Renata glanced back as they exited the door, and Vera closed it behind them. "Let's sit." She gestured to the rocking chairs. Folks in the South liked their rocking chairs. There were a couple on Vera's porch too.

Renata glanced at the door. The poor woman looked terrified.

"Don't worry," Vera urged. "I just have a couple of questions. The sheriff will ask the same questions of Jose and Helen."

Renata nodded but still appeared immensely nervous.

Vera opened the notes app on her phone. "Can you tell me the things you and Jose and Helen did around here over the weekend?"

She hesitated a long moment, tucked a stray hair behind her ear. "We clean everything up." She nodded emphatically. "Miss Helen likes her home to be well maintained."

So not only did these two pay rent, but they also did work around the place as well. Vera supposed the three had worked out some sort of negotiation.

"What kind of cleanup?" Vera tried to think how to get more specific with the question without feeding her answers. "In the yard or in the house?"

"Yes. Yes." More nodding. "We cut grass. Pull weeds. Pick up sticks and . . . trashes."

Vera listed each item in her notes. "Anything else?"

Renata pointed to the railing at an unpainted section of spindles. "Repair bad wood. We work hard. Much work. All of us very tired after working for Mr. Wilton. Time off is good to catch up here."

Vera waited for her to go on. Frankly what she'd said so far didn't sound like enough work to keep three people busy over a long weekend. The Carter property wasn't that large.

As if she suddenly understood, Renata pointed in the direction of the little cottage they occupied. "Paint in our house. New floor in bathroom."

Okay, so they were getting somewhere now.

"Anything else that you recall?"

"Cleaning." She laughed a little. "We never have time to clean our house."

They would definitely have plenty of time now. At least until they found new employment. Then again, with ten million dollars each, they might not want to go back to work for anyone else. They could start their own businesses.

"Did you or Jose go anywhere? Did you leave the house at all?"

"Hardware store. Nowhere else."

Since there was only one hardware store in this town, Vera was reminded once more of that damned receipt. She forced the thought away.

Moving on, she asked, "Did you see or talk to Mr. Wilton or his wife at all over the weekend?"

Big side to side swing of her head. "No. Just home working."

"Do you like Mrs. Wilton?" Vera sent her a pointed look. "She's your boss now."

Renata pursed her lips for a long moment. "She not nice woman. She make me clean same thing over and over." She patted her chest. "I know clean. No need for her to tell me."

So she didn't like her.

"Was Mr. Wilton nice to you and Jose?"

A smile appeared. "He was. Very much." The smile faded. "But he changed after Alicia came."

This was new. "How did he change?"

"Not friendly. Too busy to even say hello. Not care about the property so much." She shook her head again, her expression sad. "Not happy. I could see it."

"Do you have any idea what made him unhappy?"

"*She* make him unhappy." Renata glanced around as if fearing someone might eavesdrop. "Cheater. Thief. She came for his money." Her lips trembled, and emotion glistened in her eyes. "She make bad man out of him. Ruin all things."

"Did Jose have some idea of how to fix this or take care of the problem?"

"We . . ." Renata appeared to recognize the trap before going on. "No way to fix. We just live with it."

"What about Lena Wilton, the first wife? Was she nice?"

Renata smiled. "Oh very nice. An angel."

"Was she cheating on Mr. Wilton?"

Her smile faded, replaced by a frown. "No way."

"Are you sure?" Vera pressed.

The other woman hesitated . . . blinked. "I very sure."

"Why did Mr. Wilton sell all the horses and goats?"

"Oh he hate them." She blinked again, her expression startled. "I mean, after wife die he can't stand to look at them."

The reactions just kept coming. None of these questions should have startled her or had her struggling for an answer. Clearly, she was holding back.

"Did you know Alicia is pregnant?"

This time her expression was beyond startled. *Shocked* was the better description. "I did not."

"Were you and Jose aware that Mr. Wilton was planning to sell the place and move to California?"

Her expression closed, shut down like a television that had just been unplugged.

The interview, for all intents and purposes, was over. The rest of her answers were exactly the same: She didn't know.

Vera pulled a card from her shoulder bag and passed it to Renata. "Please call me if you think of anything else or if you just need to talk."

Renata took the card and studied it. She lifted her gaze to Vera's. "It was the wife. She mean, mean lady. Not love Mr. Thomas. She kill him. Probably just want baby to be sure she get all money."

Apparently she did have more to say.

"Are you sure about that?" Vera pushed, knowing full well she would only get the woman's opinion or, possibly, the answer she'd been told to give if asked.

The stare-off lasted five or so seconds, then Renata focused on putting the card in her pocket. "I just see it coming. That's all. She do bad things. Bad trouble was coming."

Bad trouble definitely came. No question about that.

A couple minutes later the door opened and Bent appeared. Helen Carter assured both Bent and Vera that they should call or come back anytime if they had more questions.

Once Vera and Bent were standing between their vehicles, he handed her two sheets of paper.

"I asked Carter and Martinez to make a list of their weekend activities."

Vera scanned first one, then the other. "This is pretty much word for word what Renata told me."

Bent glanced back at the house. "How did it go with Renata?"

"She was definitely nervous. She insisted the killer was Alicia. As for my revelations, she didn't believe the first wife cheated. She called her an angel. But it was the news about the pregnancy and the property sale that really rattled her."

Bent considered this for a moment. "Martinez was more than just nervous. He didn't want to answer any questions, but he did. He looked to Carter each time before answering. His body language spoke loud and clear—he was not happy to be questioned again. Like Renata, talk of the pregnancy and the property sale unsettled him."

"Their answers were unquestionably scripted." Anyone who'd spent any time at all conducting interviews could not have missed the telltale signs. "Carter made sure they all gave the same answers." Maybe Vera was wrong to make Carter the leader in this, but that was how it felt.

Bent looked toward the house. Like Vera, he understood they would be watching and wanted to make them even more nervous.

"Carter was as cool as a cucumber." Bent reached for Vera's door and opened it. "But the question about the property sale was the one time she hesitated with her answer. Maybe she didn't know, but I can't see that being the case. Carter was at that mansion all day, nearly every day. How would she miss appraisers tromping around, measuring and taking photos?"

"Good point. Obviously the same applies to Erwin." Vera hadn't thought of that. Still, Erwin's reaction to the news of the potential sale was obviously emotional. Whether she'd known about it or not before finding that appraisal, the idea pained her. Vera climbed into the driver's seat of her SUV. "So you think our four are hiding something significant?" She would bet money on it.

Bent leaned in close to whisper in her ear. "I don't think they're just hiding something, I think they either did the killing or know who did. Or possibly facilitated the effort. Maybe not all four were involved at the same level, but each one played some role in what happened."

Vera looked toward the house once more, dared to hope they truly were getting closer. Then she turned to Bent, nose to nose. "I believe you just might be right, Sheriff. We only have to prove how it was worth it to all three to commit cold-blooded, premeditated murder for a mere ten mil each." She gave a knowing nod. "Or maybe it was about what they stood to lose. After all, it makes sense that Wilton's will would have changed if he moved on with his life. Maybe those big asset distributions would have disappeared along with their jobs."

Bent grinned. "This is why I needed you on this one," he admitted. He closed her door, and she powered the window down. "Where you headed now?"

"I have some research to do on Luna's situation." Vera needed to close that whole scene. For both her sister's and her own sake. The look on Bent's face signaled he had something else on his mind. "Did you have something you needed me to do?"

"Wilton's attorney, Lee Kilgore, called. He has an opening for a meeting at eleven thirty this morning. After that he'll be out of town for the next few days. As much as we need to hear what he has to say, I can't be there. When Myra sent the text, she reminded me that the mayor set that press conference for eleven forty-five."

Vera made a face. She'd rather walk on broken glass than do a press conference. "You have to be at the press conference, so go. Don't worry about the other. I can do the meeting with the attorney. I have a ton of questions for him, anyway."

"Thanks." He tapped the roof of her SUV. "I'll catch up with you later."

She gave him a knowing smile. "Looking forward to it."

29

Carter Residence
Coldwater Creek Road, 11:05 a.m.

Helen watched as the sheriff and his hireling conversed with their heads close enough to kiss. What the devil were they talking about?

"She is suspicious of us," Renata announced.

"You're overreacting." Helen didn't take her eyes off the scene in front of her house until the two had driven away. Then she turned to the couple inside her house, who were making her batshit crazy. "I told you both"—she looked from one to the other—"that all we have to do is stay calm and answer their questions."

"He believes it was me," Jose argued. He jabbed a finger toward the sofa. "He sat right there and looked at me like I was the one."

Helen stepped away from the window and braced her hands on her hips. What was she going to do with them? "First off," she said to the man she trusted completely, "you are not the one." She shifted her attention to Renata. "You are not the one. I am not the one. We all know this. They need to close their case, so they're desperate to pin it on someone." She flung her arm toward the kitchen. "On the counter by the back door is today's newspaper. The top headline is about the murders at the Wilton property. If you bothered to read it, you would see that the bigwigs in town are pushing the sheriff to get this done. They want their community protected."

"You think," Renata ventured, "they are trying to trap us into saying something that makes us look guilty?"

Helen nodded. "That's exactly what I'm saying. I knew Thomas Wilton since he moved to this town. He trusted me completely. I had the run of his home. I made the food he ate . . . the coffee and tea he drank. Like I told the sheriff, if I'd wanted to kill him, I could have done it long ago and with a lot less fanfare."

Jose nodded, slowly at first, then faster as a grin claimed his face. "You did. He was not so happy when you put it to him like that."

Helen laughed. "You're right."

Then Renata laughed. "But it's true."

"Damn straight."

Finally the tension in the room returned to a bearable level.

Maybe they might just make it through this. She should have known the looming property sale would come out. It was only a matter of time.

Didn't make any difference, she decided. None of it proved one damned thing.

The big question just now for Helen was, How the hell did that little bitch hide the fact that she was pregnant?

30

Lee Kilgore Law Office
Main Avenue, 11:25 a.m.

Vera parked on the west side of the town square. She had called Myra to get the details on the visit to Kilgore. Bent's assistant had already faxed the attorney a copy of the warrant for the Wilton property. Not that the warrant specified the will, but it included the house and contents as well as the property. Hopefully Kilgore would answer her questions about the current will as well as the previous one. The man would have no idea if they had found the will and merely had questions about the asset distribution or beneficiaries. This would hopefully work to her benefit.

Kilgore was Thomas Wilton's personal attorney. Wilton also had two corporate attorneys; both had been most helpful in providing information about his business. Hopefully Kilgore would be as well about the man's personal affairs.

A call from Eve waylaid Vera's exit from her SUV. "Hey, you have something for me?" She could always hope.

"Give me a sec." Eve sounded flustered or out of breath. "Okay. Sorry. I had to run back up the hill to the funeral home."

"Where were you?" Vera reached for her bag and draped the strap over her shoulder.

"I was at the CPA's office down the street." She blew out a breath. "Down the *hill.* Mila Davis works there. She's the woman Luna told us about. The same one I heard the Busybody Buddies talking about."

Vera made a face. "The what?"

"The Busybody Buddies. That's what I call the old ladies who get together at every viewing and gossip about everyone but themselves. I swear it's basically the same women every time."

Maybe Vera didn't need any friends close enough to know her secrets. "Was this Mila Davis willing to talk about whatever rumors she was privy to?"

"She is the rumor."

"Oh." Vera remembered then that Luna had said as much. "So what did she say?"

"To give you a little background," Eve went on, "Mila is in her late fifties, and she's never been married. She was willing to talk to me because she owed me a favor."

Vera couldn't help being curious. Eve was a mortician, after all. "What kind of favor?"

"I'd just started at Barrett's when her mother died, and she was so upset, she didn't want to leave her alone that night after the visitation. She wanted to stay near her. She and her mom were really close."

Vera's eyes bulged. "You didn't let her stay overnight, did you?"

"We stayed together in the visitation room. Every hour or so—whenever she asked—I rolled Mrs. Davis out of cold storage so her daughter could see her."

"Wow. Okay. You're a really good person, Eve, and you're right—she owed you big-time." Vera would have suggested counseling to the woman, but thanks to Eve they had leverage for information. God, that sounded so cold. But it was a murder investigation, after all.

"Trenton Fanning is her boss. Has been for years. But he was also her childhood sweetheart. They were together all the way to graduation. Then when it was time to go off to college, Mila had to stay behind because her mother had a stroke. She took care of her from that point forward while Trenton met someone else and got married and had a family."

"How sad for Mila." For Trenton too, considering he was married to Geneva.

"It gets better," Eve assured her. "Two years ago Trenton was sure Geneva was having an affair. Mila let him cry on her shoulder, and the next thing she knew, *they* were having an affair. They stopped a while back, but they still talk secretly."

So the older woman at the accounting firm, Mila Davis, did have an affair—like Luna said. And the affair was with Trenton—not Leonard. Damn. This might be a small town, but these folks got around. "Did Mila have any idea who Geneva was cheating with?" The answer might not matter, but Vera was never one to let any possibility go without a look.

"Trenton was certain it was his cousin, Leonard Andrews."

So Geneva had fooled around with her sister's husband.

"That's low." Vera had an even worse opinion of the woman now, and that was saying something.

"I've heard others say Geneva was always jealous of her sister," Eve went on. "Considering Geneva got the looks in the family, obviously the jealousy was about her sister's husband."

"Makes a twisted kind of sense," Vera agreed.

"To make it worse," Eve said, the volume of her voice in and out as if she had laid the phone down and was moving about, "two years ago would have been when Jackie had cancer that third time."

"Damn. That is bottom-feeder level." Geneva was a real lowlife. "Anything else?" Vera was dying to hear the attorney's answers to her list of questions.

"Only that Mila would love to be your accountant if you haven't chosen anyone since moving to Fayetteville."

Oh, okay. Her taxes were about the furthest thing from her mind right now. "Thanks, Eve. I'll keep her in mind. Talk later."

Vera ended the call and climbed out of her SUV. The sooner she got this meeting done, the sooner she could move on to the next step for Luna.

Geneva Fanning was about to find out what happened when you messed with a Boyett sister.

The bell over the door tinkled as Vera entered the law office lobby. There was no one at the reception desk, but Kilgore himself promptly appeared from somewhere beyond the reception space.

"Hello, Mr. Kilgore. I'm Vera Boyett, a consultant with the Lincoln County Sheriff's Department. I'm here for Sheriff Benton."

"Yes, Myra called and said you were coming. Come on back to my office, Ms. Boyett."

Vera followed him inside. After she'd taken the seat he offered, she opened the notes app on her phone. "I'm not recording," she assured him. "Just taking notes."

He gave her a nod. "Frankly I'm surprised the warrant was so comprehensive. Typically the instructions are somewhat more limiting."

"We have three dead, one in a coma, and no idea what the killer or killers were after. It's a huge property with an incredible inventory of valuable goods that may have been the motive for the murders. It's difficult to specify, given the circumstances. Fortunately we had a judge who understood the gravity of the situation."

"Fortunate indeed." Kilgore braced his elbows on his desk and steepled his fingers. "So, how can I help your investigation more than I already have?"

He had been kind enough to provide a limited number of details about the will to Bent already, but Vera understood that he hadn't been happy about it then and obviously wasn't now. "The real property distribution was surprising. As you know, motive is a tremendously important aspect of solving a homicide, and these details are just full of motive."

Kilgore reached down for the file in front of him and opened it. Vera imagined it was a copy of the last will and testament of his client, Thomas Wilton.

"Then you're aware that the entire real property—the land, the house, and all other structures on said property—will go to charity. This does not include any of the contents of said structures or the automobiles and such, only the real estate itself."

"Would it be possible for you to provide a complete list of those charities along with the point of contact for each?" Seemed like a reasonable request to Vera.

"I can do that. However, I assure you that these charities are all legitimate, well-known organizations."

Vera produced a smile. "I'm confident that's the case, but the additional information would make our job so much easier." She took a breath and went for the next big question nagging at her. "The will was changed after his first wife died and then again when he married his second wife. Was that only related to his change in marital status? Any other changes that might suggest issues with staff or business partners, relatives?"

His gaze narrowed. "What exactly are you looking for, Ms. Boyett?"

"Motive, Mr. Kilgore. Like I said, it's an essential element for finding the person responsible for these heinous crimes."

He studied her for a long moment—long enough that Vera worried he wasn't going to give her what she'd asked for. But then he spoke. "The first will I prepared, the one he made about five years ago, was significantly different, yes. The real property and the majority of the monetary assets were bequeathed to a single charity: Quantum Leap."

"I'm afraid I've never heard of that one." Her instincts went on point.

"The way Thomas explained it to me was that Quantum Leap is a research facility with a singular focus devoted to helping mankind. I was surprised he didn't leave some aspect of his vast estate to research and development of national defense, since that was his specialty. But no, he wanted to do more for the people rather than the government—he said he'd done enough for the government. He insisted this was very important to his wife, Lena. Quantum Leap was her pet project—his words, not mine."

"That is a really generous gift." A damned huge motive too. "But that aspect of the will changed at some point after she died?" Vera couldn't wait to hear the details.

"Yes. It was perhaps a month after her death that he came to me and asked to prepare a new will. He wanted Quantum Leap completely removed."

Surprising, in Vera's opinion. If the project had meant so much to his wife, why cut it out completely? Unless doing so was to disavow her completely because she'd cheated. Which meant the rumor could be true. "Did he say why? Did he no longer wish to honor his wife's pet project?"

Kilgore studied Vera for a long moment. "I'm certainly not a mind reader, Ms. Boyett. But I will say that he was quite adamant. Angry even. He wanted it done ASAP."

Now Vera's instincts were on fire. If the man was angry . . . the cheating rumor was likely true. "Do you have the point of contact information for Quantum Leap?"

"I'm sure I can find it." He turned to his computer and pecked at the keyboard.

Vera's pulse was racing. Maybe this was nothing, but it sounded like a whole lot of something. She watched as he wrote something on a sticky note, then handed it to her.

"If I can help in any other way, please let me know. How is Mrs. Wilton?"

Now it was his turn to dig for info. Vera was happy to oblige. "She is stable but still in a coma. We hope she will fully recover. She's the only witness to what happened in that cabin."

"Good luck with the case, Ms. Boyett."

That was her cue to go. Vera stood. "Thank you, Mr. Kilgore. We appreciate your assistance." She stood but hesitated before leaving his office. "One last question. Were you aware Wilton intended to sell the property?"

The attorney considered the question for three or four seconds. "I was."

A new urgency nudged Vera. "Under the circumstances, was he having an updated will prepared?" Stood to logic.

Kilgore nodded. "He was."

Damn, was she going to have to pull it out of him like extracting teeth? "Any significant changes other than the real estate?"

He leaned back in his seat, eyed her cautiously. "Let's just say, he was no longer feeling quite so generous anymore. But that will was still a work in progress, so the terms are irrelevant."

Vera just couldn't leave it at that. "Not so generous to charity?"

"Not so generous to anyone." Kilgore stood. "Good day, Ms. Boyett."

Vera's heart pounded as she left the office. She had to talk to Bent. Actually, she needed to be in three places at once. Who the hell was behind Quantum Leap? She stared at the name of the LLC on the sticky note. She would have to do some digging, it seemed, to find the answer. Maybe Erwin had some idea. If not she would need to call Eric again. There was no time to beat the bushes.

This news—the dumping of Quantum Leap and the less generous new will—changed everything.

Vera climbed into her SUV and drew in a big, deep breath. Bent needed to hear this ASAP—no, that wasn't possible, since he was in that damned press conference. Vera drew in another big breath and reviewed the long list ticking off in her brain. She had to talk to the ME. That one couldn't wait.

Lincoln Medical Center
Medical Center Boulevard, 12:20 p.m.

"What an unexpected surprise." Collins pushed a refrigerated drawer closed. "If you're here about the autopsy reports on your homicide vics, I haven't heard anything yet."

Vera nodded. "There's always a wait."

"I did, however, get a look at the other autopsy reports you requested."

"Lena Wilton and Nola Childers?"

Collins nodded. "Both were fairly cut and dried. Wilton's death was caused by head trauma, specifically an epidural hematoma. The report indicated there was an undiagnosed brain hemorrhage after a horse-riding accident. It happens. Sometimes there are little or no symptoms and then suddenly it's too late to save the patient."

"An accident then," Vera confirmed.

"Sadly, yes. Unless, of course, you somehow discover that someone caused the horse to throw her off." Collins sent her a challenging look. "Oh and Lena was pregnant. Ironic, don't you think?"

Wow. Okay. Definitely, considering Wilton's current wife was in a coma and also pregnant. "Ironic for sure. What about Childers?"

"Childers's death was ruled accidental as well. Her blood alcohol level was more than four times the legal limit. There was also Xanax. Yet another sad statistic that occurs more often than most people realize. Xanax and alcohol is a very bad combination. Equally ill-advised is doing either and bathing. A recipe for disaster."

No question about that. *Xanax.* Vera would need to check with the mother about that one. "Thanks, I appreciate it. I also wanted to ask you a question about Jackie Andrews."

"Mrs. Andrews is a popular lady." Collins cocked her head and studied Vera. "You aren't the only one who's keenly interested."

"Oh really." Vera was surprised, though clearly she shouldn't have been.

"Mr. Hayworth, an attorney, is pestering the shit out of me. He claimed he was hired by Geneva Fanning to investigate the death."

Vera laughed. She couldn't help herself. "Yeah, well if it makes you feel any better, I'm sure dear old Geneva is giving him hell too."

Collins leaned against the wall of drawers and crossed her arms over her chest. "So how can I help you, Vera?"

"That tibial fracture, how else might that have happened?" Vera leaned a hip against the empty and shiny stainless steel exam table. Though her headaches had eased to primarily soreness, and she was no longer dizzy or weak from the concussion, she did tire more easily than usual. She hoped that would pass soon. "I asked Luna about that spindle, and it was already damaged. So I've been trying to figure out how Jackie's leg ended up fractured."

Collins thought about the question for a time. "The placement and type of fracture—based on the X-ray—tells me that it was caused by pressure from some sort of momentum, which is why the damaged spindle made sense. Either she hit her leg in some odd manner on the way down, or she was standing still and some sort of momentum struck her shin and did the damage—perhaps propelling her forward."

"They were moving furniture. Something could have fallen and hit her leg, is that what you mean?"

"That's possible, but bear in mind that the concentration of impact required would need to be focused in such a small spot to cause the damage I saw." She held her thumb and forefinger about an inch apart. "A very hard blow to a very specific target area. Which is why hitting that spindle on the way down seemed consistent with the injury. Beyond that scenario, my best guess would be that someone or something struck her, causing the fracture."

Considering where the fracture was . . . that would be a low blow, no pun intended. "Like a kick to the shin?"

"A really hard kick in the shin would do it. Which is why soccer players wear shin guards. A kick, particularly if the person doing the kicking wore sharp-toed or steel-toed boots, would do the trick. There was significant discoloration of the epidermis in the area, so that is quite possible."

Vera tried to picture the type of footwear she had seen Geneva wearing, but she had no memory of her feet. She was always too busy glaring at her hateful face.

"Anything else that struck you as off? Beyond the scratch on her forearm?" Vera was suddenly ready to get out of here so she could call Luna and find out if Geneva wore boots of any sort.

"Nothing I noticed. Perhaps the autopsy will give us more."

"If we're lucky." Vera straightened. "Thanks, Jenny. I appreciate your time and your insights."

The ME walked toward the door with Vera. "We should have a girls' night sometime. Share war stories."

Vera wasn't sure she was ready to share war stories with the woman, but she smiled anyway and lied. "Sounds great."

Vera exited the building and climbed into her SUV. As worrisome as the additional information about Jackie's injury was, the business with the Xanax nagged at her. She dug her phone from her bag and called Nola Childers's mother. The woman answered on the second ring. "Hey, Mrs. Childers, it's Vera Boyett again."

"Hello, Vera. I hope you're doing well."

"I am. Thank you. I hope you don't mind me asking another question about Nola."

"Not at all. I love talking about Nola."

Vera wasn't so sure she would love this part. "Did Nola ever mention needing an anxiety medication like Xanax?"

"Let me think. No, I don't think so. Wait, now." She hummed a note of uncertainty. "No, I'm wrong. Well sort of. Nola told me that she went to the doctor and asked for a Xanax prescription because Valeri was having some terrible anxiety issues and, you know, the poor girl didn't have any health insurance. So Nola got it for her."

"Thank you, Mrs. Childers. That clears up a little mystery for me." Vera hesitated but then decided to go for it. She needed to understand why the Xanax wasn't mentioned in their previous conversation. "Mrs. Childers, did you or your husband view a copy of Nola's autopsy report?"

The older woman sighed. "I suppose we should have, but the truth is neither of us could bear the idea of reading the details. We just couldn't."

"I understand, thank you again. I'll call you when I have more news."

"Looking forward to hearing from you, Vera."

Vera shook her head as she ended the call. Every instinct she had was screaming at her. Valeri Erwin killed that poor girl.

Her cell vibrated, and Vera jumped, almost dropped it. She stared at the screen. A Louisiana area code. "Vera Boyett."

"Vera, it's Larry Parson. Look, I had this weird visitor waiting for me when I got back from lunch. I think we need to talk about it if you . . . if you've got a few minutes, I mean."

"Sure. Who was this visitor?" Vera climbed into her SUV and prepared to back out of the parking slot.

"This woman. She wouldn't give me her name. I met her before but . . . look, I . . . I'm not trying to be creepy or anything, but can we do this in person? You don't have to come into my room. We can talk outside . . . you know."

Vera frowned. Had he been drinking? "Be there in five minutes."

Before leaving the town square, she shot off a text to Bent about the call from Parson. Bent was likely still in the press conference postmortem, but she had learned the hard way not to barrel into risky situations without telling anyone. It never ended well—for her.

"Been there, done that," she muttered to herself. Hell, she'd bought the T-shirt.

31

Regency Inn
Huntsville Highway, 1:00 p.m.

Vera spotted the VW Bus that belonged to Parson. She parked a couple of slots from his vehicle and got out. There were a few other cars scattered along the front of the motel but no sign of Parson, or anyone else for that matter.

Maybe he hadn't expected her to get here so fast. She pulled out her phone and called him. After the fourth ring, it went to voicemail. Vera turned all the way around. The place was quiet, other than the traffic noise from the highway. Pool area was empty.

"Damn it." She tucked her phone into the pocket of her jeans and headed toward the room. There were two floors on this end. Stairs several yards away led up to the second level. Parson was on the first.

She paused at the door, listened for a few seconds. No sound except the hum of the air conditioning. Worry started its nasty dig into her gut. "Mr. Parson," she called out as she knocked on the door. "It's Vera Boyett."

Still nothing. Vera didn't like this. His vehicle was here. She'd spoken to him just over five minutes ago. Was this his way of getting her into his room? Sweat, mostly from the damned heat, dampened her skin. She glanced around the parking lot, then reached for the doorknob. It turned without resistance. Vera pushed the door inward and scanned the dimly lit room without stepping inside. It took a moment for her vision to adjust. Bed was made but slightly rumpled. Television was on but muted.

Feet.

Near the far corner of the bed, she could see bare feet.

Pulse racing, Vera rushed across the room.

Larry Parson, fully dressed except for shoes, lay supine on the aging carpet. Next to him was a puddle of puke.

Shit!

A quick check of his pulse confirmed he wasn't breathing. Lips were blue. Skin clammy. A quick check of his eyes showed constricted pupils. She glanced around the room. Spotted a half-empty bottle of whiskey and a glass.

She called 911.

Once the emergency dispatcher had finished her spiel, Vera said, "This is Vera Boyett. I'm at the Regency Inn, room 121. I'm looking at a middle-aged male I think has possibly overdosed on an unknown substance. No pulse. I'm starting CPR. Please send EMS and call Sheriff Benton for me."

Vera put her phone on speaker and placed it to the floor next to her so she could start chest compressions. She answered whatever questions the dispatcher had while keeping the necessary rhythm.

"Come on, Larry, breathe!"

By the time EMS arrived, Vera was exhausted, and the man still wasn't breathing. The paramedics took over, and she grabbed her phone and moved out of their way.

Struggling to slow her pounding heart, she walked over to the other side of the bed and checked the nightstand. Since she was once again without gloves, she didn't touch the pint of whiskey or the glass next to it. The top drawer was partially opened. She could see a Bible, and on top of it was an open packet of cocaine.

She glanced over at the paramedics. "There's cocaine in the nightstand. It may have been laced with something." Which would explain Parson dying on the floor across the room.

What the ever-loving hell? Anger fired through her. Was anyone even remotely related to this case going to survive the investigation?

She watched as the paramedic administered NARCAN.

Vera closed her eyes and shook her head. She took that moment and then she pulled herself together. This could be a crime scene. Maybe not, considering the coke. Could be an accidental overdose. But he'd called Vera, concerned about a visitor he'd had. The only reason to call her was if it somehow related to the case.

"Vee?" Bent was suddenly next to her.

She hadn't heard him come in.

"Hey." She exhaled a big breath. "Parson called me and said he wanted to talk. He sounded rattled. Said he'd had a strange visitor. He was supposed to be waiting for me in the parking lot." She gestured to the scene across the room. "But I found him in here like this." She shook her head. "I swear, Bent, I was here five minutes after that call."

A glance in Parson's direction showed the paramedics preparing to use the defibrillator.

"I'll call Conover." He glanced at the nightstand. "You didn't touch anything?"

"No. I didn't have any gloves."

He jerked his head toward the door. "We can wait outside until they're done, if you like."

She nodded, defeat tugging at her. "Let's do that."

As hot as it was outside, it was still better than being in that room.

Bent made the call to Conover, then propped himself against the passenger door of her SUV. She was already braced there, too frustrated and exhausted to hold herself upright.

"So he said he'd had a strange visitor?"

"I think the word was *weird.* Someone he'd met before." She made a face. "Now that I think about it, he sort of sounded high when we talked. You know, like he'd had a toke or two or a drink or three. But not sloppy. Not really slurring. Just different than when he talked before."

"Okay. I guess we'll know more when the toxicology report comes back." Bent glanced toward the room. "I have a feeling this guy is not coming back from whatever he ingested."

Bent was right. The paramedics left without the body since Bent wanted the ME to have a look first. A few minutes later Collins arrived—all within about half an hour from when Vera had made that initial call to 911. Then again the hospital was only five minutes away.

Conover had arrived, too, and started his thing. Vera followed Bent back into the room. She might as well watch the show.

The lock on the motel room door hadn't been tampered with in any obvious manner. Small window in the bathroom was painted shut. Whoever had come in was allowed in by the deceased or was damned good at bypassing cheap locks. Possibly his weird visitor. The motel had no security cameras, and the manager hadn't seen one damned thing. He'd been working on reports in his office behind the counter. Bent had deputies interviewing any guests available within view of the room.

Collins estimated time of death about forty-five minutes ago—basically five minutes after Vera's phone conversation with the man.

"Vee." Bent jerked his head, drawing her to the small closet. He gestured with a gloved hand to the baseball bat in the corner. Vera crouched down and studied the barrel without touching it. She shook her head and pointed to a blond hair.

"I'm calling it." She stood. "The bat and what is likely my hair. We both know both were planted. The man wasn't even in Fayetteville at the time Erwin and I were attacked." Apparently whoever had put the bat here didn't know that. Vera was fairly certain they had not mentioned this to Erwin.

Bent chuckled. "Unless he came on Monday and went back after he did the killing at the cabin. Then your message brought him back."

Vera held her hands up in exasperation. "Why would he kill his own brother? Or his ex-girlfriend?" This made no sense. Nothing about this entire week made sense!

"Maybe because of the ex-girlfriend," Bent suggested. "She was partying with his little brother—or so it seems. Maybe the two got together while Larry was in prison. When he finds out about the business up here, he takes his opportunity for revenge."

Vera blew out a big breath. Bent was right. It might be a long shot, but it was possible. She wasn't thinking clearly.

"We need solid proof," Bent added, "about when the guy left New Orleans to be absolutely certain he wasn't involved with the murders or with your attacker."

Vera exhaled a big breath. "I get that. But my gut says this is just another red herring in our wild and crazy case." She peered deeper into the closet. "Oh and there's the ski mask and the gloves." She shook her head. "My only question is, What the hell was Parson doing while our unknown perp was planting these items?"

"Maybe he went into the bathroom while his visitor was here?"

"No, wait." Vera replayed the brief phone conversation with Parson in her head. "He said it was a woman—one he'd met before—and she was waiting for him when he got back from lunch, so she may have broken into his room and then he came back and she was caught, so she had to pretend to want to talk to him."

"Yeah," Bent granted. "I can buy that."

This close to the bathroom, Vera peeked inside to have a look at the guy's toiletries. A bottle of Brut aftershave sat on the toilet tank. An oldie, for sure. Even if that was the one Erwin had recognized, Vera still wasn't buying this too-pat scenario. She turned back to the room and the cast of characters, including the ME prowling through every inch.

"Bent. Vera." Conover, who had worked his way to the three-drawer cabinet beneath the television, motioned for them to join him.

Vera could just imagine what this would be. A signed confession?

"Have a look," Conover suggested.

In the middle drawer was a pair of skimpy panties and a bra. Along with a bottle of perfume. Vera studied the labels. Aubade lingerie and a bottle of Miss Dior. Big bucks.

"What do you want to bet"—Vera turned to Bent—"these belong to Alicia Wilton?"

"Since I don't like to lose, I'll pass." He turned to Conover. "I need something, Conover. Anything that proves someone else was in this room recently."

"Besides the housekeeper and the hundreds of other guests who've stayed here before and left DNA," Vera muttered.

But she got it. This no-doubt-planted evidence was supposed to prove prior contact and that Parson had been here before the big killer weekend. And that maybe Alicia Wilton was playing both brothers.

Except it just didn't work for Vera.

"Blame it on crime TV," Collins said as her assistant prepared to bag Parson. "Now they all know how to cover their tracks and steer guilt where they choose."

Valeri Erwin watched crime TV, Vera mused. Maybe Erwin should be nudged back up to the top suspect spot. Vera thought of the news about the Xanax in Nola Childers's autopsy report. And now this. A shiver worked its way through her. She would bet money that whatever was in that coke killed Larry Parson. Coincidence? Highly doubtful.

"All I can say," Vera tossed back to the ME, "is we better close this case fast, or there's not going to be anyone left to arrest."

"By the way"—Collins looked Vera up and down—"you were careful what you touched, right? Even him?"

Vera nodded. "I only did the chest compressions." Worry trickled through her. "I did check his carotid pulse and his pupils, but that's it."

"Good. Because if this is fentanyl poisoning as I suspect," Collins went on, "you could have ended up in a body bag too."

An even colder shiver raced through Vera. "Yeah. Thanks." Maybe that was exactly what whoever did this wanted. Anyone involved with the case would expect that Vera and/or Bent would come to the scene. The idea sat like a block of ice in her gut.

Bent's voice drew her attention toward the door. He'd gotten a call. Vera joined him there and hoped this was something useful and not more trouble.

When the call ended, he said, "We need to get back to the office."

Vera's shoulders sagged. "What now?"

"The sister of our vic, Sandy Owens, is here to see me."

"Seriously?" Vera shook her head. "Under any other circumstances I would be surprised, but somehow I'm not." Vera followed him out the door.

This case was sounding more and more like a family reunion, except everyone in attendance ended up dead.

32

Vanderbilt University Medical Center
1211 Medical Center Drive
Nashville, 2:00 p.m.

Alicia felt her fingers move.

Her breath caught. She tried to open her eyes . . . to see. But her lids still would not open. Damn it! She had to wake up! She had to get out of here!

Deep breath. She focused on wiggling the fingers of her right hand. They worked! She felt the movement.

She tried the other hand. Those fingers moved too! Her heart beat faster. The monitor keeping track of her heart rate beeped more quickly.

Okay, if she could move her fingers, why couldn't she open her eyes?

Focus, Ali.

Her heart ached worse than her head. Seth had called her Ali, and now he was dead. And it was somehow her fault. She had to work harder to wake up . . . for the baby.

A deputy, a woman, came in several times a day and spoke to her. She frequently assured Alicia that they were doing everything possible to figure out what had happened at the cabin. Alicia wanted to tell her. She tried so hard to open her eyes or to speak, but she couldn't.

You can do it!

Focus. She had to focus. To concentrate on opening her eyelids.

She had to wake up and tell them.

A new kind of pain welled so quickly inside her that she couldn't breathe.

Thomas was dead . . . They all were.

33

Lincoln County Sheriff's Department
Thornton Taylor Parkway, 3:45 p.m.

Vera would have known this woman was related to Sandy Owens even without the introduction. The two looked so much alike.

Rebecca, Becky, Owens Lancaster was a year older than her sister Sandy. She, too, lived in the New Orleans area but well outside the city. She had been trying to get in touch with her sister and was worried sick. Sounded familiar. When she got the message from Bent's office, she made arrangements for someone to look after her kids and headed here.

"When was the last time you heard from your sister?" Bent threw out the first question. He was the one behind the desk and with the title sheriff, so it made the most sense.

Vera sat in the chair next to the one Lancaster had claimed in front of his desk. The woman was tall, thin, with brown hair and a deep tan. She was a single mom with two kids and a full-time job to juggle.

"I spoke to her on Sunday afternoon, but I haven't been able to reach her since." Lancaster shook her head. "Look, I'll be the first to say that Sandy is a little on the wild side. She hops from one guy to the next. Never keeps a job for long. But she is—was a good person." She swiped at a tear that slipped past her hold.

"She was involved with Larry Parson frequently," Vera suggested.

Lancaster smiled, sadness clouding the expression. "Those two never seemed to be able to get over each other. They would break up for a while and then end up back together. I always called him her addiction. She couldn't resist him." She turned to Vera. "That's when I first realized something really was wrong. Yesterday afternoon I went to see Larry. It took me some time. I didn't have his number or know where he was living since he got out of prison. Anyway, his friend Rhonda was there feeding his cat. She said he'd left for Tennessee because there was trouble with his brother. I knew then that Sandy was likely in trouble too."

"When did Rhonda say he left for Tennessee?"

"Like at four in the morning or something."

"Yesterday? Thursday." Vera figured this would confirm Parson's statement about when he left and arrived.

"Yeah." Sandy nodded.

"Myra spoke with Rhonda Moore a little while ago, and Moore corroborated Parson's departure time," Bent said to Vera.

So it was official. Parson could not have attacked her and Erwin. He had nothing to do with any of this bad business. The man had merely been worried about his brother. His death only made the evolving circumstances more sinister.

Unless, she reminded herself, like Bent said, he came on Monday, did the killing and went back to wait for a call about his dead brother and ex-girlfriend. Vera just didn't feel that one. But it was a viable scenario. Except . . . why would he leave Alicia alive? Maybe the two of them had plotted the whole nightmare. Nah. Vera wasn't buying that one either.

"When you spoke with your sister"—Vera turned to the woman seated next to her—"did she talk about how things were going here? Or why she and Seth came in the first place?"

Lancaster made a sound that wasn't a laugh but something on that order. "She said plenty. Seth had gotten all these text messages from Alicia—the two of them were a couple off and on for years. Talk about addictions, now those two were really addicted to each other. But it had been like two years or something since he'd heard from her the last time."

Bent leaned forward and braced his elbows on his desk. "Did he have any idea where she was?"

"He knew she was somewhere in Tennessee and that she'd found this mega-rich guy to marry." Lancaster did laugh then. "Poor guy. He probably had no idea she would never stay. I mean, Alicia's a gorgeous girl, for sure, and she's pretty nice for the most part. But she could never stay away from Seth. At least until this last time, and who knows how much longer that would have lasted. I guess that's why he fell for whatever kind of setup this was."

"Setup?"

Bent beat Vera to that one. She couldn't wait to hear the answer.

"Sorry, I'm skipping around on you. So, about two and a half or three weeks ago, he started getting these text messages from Alicia saying that he had to come. She needed to see him. She couldn't take this fake marriage any longer. Would he please come and rescue her because this guy was never gonna let her go. Sandy said she was even using a burner because her husband was watching every move she made."

The story was a close match to Parson's. Vera asked, "Did they do more than text? Did they actually have a phone call? Did they meet somewhere away from Fayetteville?"

Lancaster shook her head. "I don't think so because if they had, none of this would have gone down."

"How can you be sure it wouldn't have?" Bent asked.

"Because when I talked to Sandy, she said the whole thing was effed up. Alicia claimed she had not sent any text messages. She insisted she had no idea why Seth was here. Sandy said she pretty much believed her because she seemed truly shocked and really upset that Seth had come. She was like tripping all over herself to explain to her husband what was going on. I guess on account of all that stuff in the text messages, Seth was worried that Alicia was just afraid of her husband and was pretending she hadn't sent those messages. Seth wouldn't leave until he was sure. But Sandy believed Alicia was telling the truth. She said Alicia even offered Seth big money to leave. Like a hundred thousand dollars."

"But he wouldn't go," Bent guessed.

"He wouldn't. Sandy said he was really worried about her and wanted to hang around for a while to see what was what. I guess Alicia's husband was suspicious and decided the best way to figure out who these strangers were was to have a weekend alone together. I guess he didn't believe Alicia when she said Seth and Sandy were just old friends of hers."

"You're saying," Vera reiterated, "that Thomas Wilton set up the weekend at his cabin and he invited Seth and Sandy."

"Yes. Alicia was horrified. She begged Sandy to talk some sense into Seth and leave, but he wouldn't do it, so Sandy was going along with him to hopefully keep things from exploding. Didn't help, I guess." She dabbed at more tears.

"You're certain"—Vera decided to go at the question from a different angle—"that Seth wouldn't have wanted to try blackmailing Alicia. That he wouldn't use his prior relationships with her in that way."

"No way. He wouldn't even have known where exactly to find her if not for the text messages."

Though they had the burner, the chance of tracing it to a buyer was pretty much a big fat zero.

"We haven't been able to locate next of kin for Alicia," Vera said. "Do you know if she has any family?" Maybe they could check that one off their list.

Lancaster shook her head. "Her parents died when she was a little kid. She was raised in foster homes. If she had anybody other than Seth, I never heard about it."

"Thank you." Bent passed a business card across his desk. "Please call if you think of anything else that might be helpful. I'm sorry for your loss, and I'm sure you understand your sister's body won't be released for a while yet. Leave your contact information with my assistant Myra, and we'll let you know as soon as we can about that and about the case."

Lancaster shook her head. "I can't believe she's dead. This is wrong, Sheriff. Really wrong. Whatever happened in that cabin, my sister was an innocent victim. I hope you find who did this. None of them deserved to be murdered. Seth and Larry were good people too."

"Yes, ma'am. We'll do all we can."

Bent walked the woman out and introduced her to Myra. When he came back into his office, Vera was ready to go.

"We need to talk to Erwin. I have a lot more questions about what we just learned and the info Kilgore gave me." At Bent's questioning look, Vera groaned. "After what happened at the Regency, I forgot to give you the details from my meeting with Kilgore." She would love to blame her inability to keep up on the concussion, but at this point she wasn't so sure. The truth was she was a little overwhelmed.

Bent pulled her into a hug. "It's okay."

Vera relaxed against his chest. God, she was tired. After a bit he drew back. "Tell me what you learned from Kilgore."

Vera squared her shoulders and exited the little pity-party session. "The Wilton property—every single acre, the house, and every other structure—was all bequeathed to a charity research organization called Quantum Leap. Until," she emphasized, "a month after his first wife died. Kilgore said Wilton was not happy—angry, even—when he came in to sign the new will, taking Quantum Leap out."

"What the hell is Quantum Leap?"

"I'm hoping Erwin can help us with that. Whatever it was, it was his wife's project. I feel like if he loved his wife and she loved the project, why take everything away?"

"Kilgore didn't know more?" Bent grabbed his key fob.

"If he did, he wasn't saying." Vera followed him from his office and waited while he gave Myra an update on the rest of his afternoon. Once they were headed out of the building, Vera went on. "But the real kicker was the new will in progress—the one that didn't get signed because Wilton was murdered."

Bent paused on the sidewalk and waited for her to reveal this game changer.

"The new will—this is Kilgore's exact words—was 'not so generous to *anyone*.' And that," Vera went on, "is big-time motive for all our suspects."

Bent nodded. "You did good, kid. And you're right, that gives our top four huge motive for wanting Wilton dead."

"And if it was Erwin who showed up at Parson's motel," Vera added, "she's working hard to shift guilt."

"If we're lucky, we're about to find out. You riding with me or meeting me there?"

"I'll take my SUV. I may go home after we talk to Erwin."

Bent opened the driver's side door of her vehicle. "You should be resting more. That kind of concussion takes time to recover from. Even if you're feeling better, that doesn't mean you shouldn't take care of yourself."

"You're right." No point in arguing with him. He was absolutely right. "See you at Erwin's apartment."

She didn't want to think that her inability to bounce back was about age. She wasn't that old.

But she felt as old as hell today.

34

Andrews Farm
Boonshill Road, 4:20 p.m.

Luna stared at her cell phone long after the call with Jerome had ended. He planned to start home by five. He had sounded so tired. So miserable.

No matter what Vee said, this was partly Luna's fault. She had known that Jackie hated her. She should have helped her after what happened on the stairs, no matter the horrible woman's intent. What good was going to church every Sunday if she wasn't going to be a good person?

Only a bad person walked away from someone calling out for help.

Luna rubbed her belly and cried. She wanted to be a good mother. A good wife. A good person. But what if that hardware receipt wasn't wrong and she was somehow confused?

No, she was certain of what happened. The account she told Vee was true. Jackie had tried to push her down the stairs.

And Vee was right about that too. Jackie hadn't only tried to push her down the stairs; she had tried to kill Luna and the baby.

Anger lit inside her. She needed to tell Jerome what had happened. All of it. But what if he didn't believe her? Jackie was his mother. Was he going to believe such a horrible thing about his own mother?

But it was true. No matter what anyone said, it was true.

The only problem was that hardware store receipt.

Luna got to her feet. She couldn't take this anymore. She had to know if there was an issue with the time she'd checked out at the hardware store or something else she had forgotten. Maybe she had made another stop and couldn't remember. She may have driven around . . . God, she just wasn't sure anymore.

She grabbed her phone and her fob and walked out of her beautiful home. The one her sweet husband had built for her and their family.

Luna couldn't sit back and let anyone ruin their lives.

35

Erwin Residence
Washington Street, 4:30 p.m.

"Quantum Leap?" Erwin sat on the sofa in her eclectic living area and seemed to contemplate the question. "I recall hearing Lena talk about it, but I can't tell you a whole lot about the organization. I know it's focused on like the betterment of mankind. What does that mean? I have no idea. It was Lena who got involved, and Thomas bankrolled whatever his wife wanted. That's all I can tell you."

Bent had apparently gotten a text, since he was doing something on his phone. So Vera moved on with the questions.

"But the donations stopped, and Quantum Leap was taken out of the will after Lena died."

Erwin stared blankly at her as if she didn't see any reason to respond.

Vera gave it another go. "If this particular group was so important to the woman he loved—so good for mankind—why did Thomas suddenly end support?"

"Like I said," Erwin stated flatly, "Lena was the one who started it. She never talked to me about it directly."

"Started it? Who else was involved?"

A half-hearted shrug lifted one shoulder. "I can't remember his name. Some guy."

Vera took a chance. "Is this the man Thomas suspected was having an affair with his wife?"

Erwin's eyes flared to saucers. "I . . . I don't know."

"But she was having an affair? You should know," Vera pressed. "You seemed to know a good deal about Alicia's indiscretions."

Erwin sat up straighter and looked directly at Vera then. "Yeah, okay. It was a shock to everyone, but yeah, Lena was having an affair. Thomas was devastated. They fought—privately. I don't think anyone outside the house ever knew. He found out, and then the next thing we knew, she had that terrible accident." She made a *whatever* face. "It was sad, but you'd think if she was such a big-deal champion, she could have stayed in the saddle."

That was the thing about a narcissist—they could never help themselves when it came to belittling others. "Meaning what?"

"Just that when she took her crazy-expensive horse for a ride that last time, she got thrown."

This part was in the autopsy. "Had this happened before?"

Erwin shook her head. "Don't think so."

Vera wasn't schooled in horseback riding, but she did understand that a well-trained horse didn't just throw off its rider for no reason. "Did anyone figure out what caused the animal to throw her off?"

Erwin squinted as if trying to remember. "Something about saddle panels. I guess she wasn't keeping her gear properly maintained."

Or, Vera countered, someone wanted it to look that way. "Was anyone on staff having trouble with Lena?"

Erwin laughed. "Are you kidding? Everyone loved Lena." She rolled her eyes. "She was a saint."

"To everyone except you, obviously."

Erwin seemed to catch herself. "Well, she was cheating, and Thomas was devastated. But he would have forgiven her anything." She shrugged. "Then she ended up dead."

Vera glanced at Bent, who was still on the phone. "During the autopsy, it was discovered that she was pregnant."

"Yeah." Erwin studied her cuticles. "He was really torn up about that."

"How strange," Vera suggested, "that now his second wife is seriously injured, and she's pregnant. I would almost be worried about his desire to have children, except he's dead."

Erwin stared at Vera as if she didn't see her point, then she blinked. "Did you find out about the property appraisal?"

Oh yes, there was definitely far more to learn about this woman's interest in the wives of her employer. Vera decided to turn Erwin's question around on her. "When we looked at the property appraisal, you said you had no idea why Mr. Wilton would have requested an appraisal. Have you given more thought to this and come up with any ideas?"

Erwin kept her face blank now. "Well, I did do some thinking about that, and I recall once or twice overhearing Alicia say that life on the West Coast would be so much better. I really think she wanted to make that happen." She made a squinched face. "I may have heard Thomas discussing a sale on a phone call about three weeks ago. Of course I'm sure everyone saw the surveyors and the others tramping around all over the place. We all suspected something was going on."

Of course they did. "Any idea who he was talking to?"

She shook her head. "Sorry no."

Okay, so Wilton was undeniably on the precipice of selling.

"How did you and the other members of his staff feel about the potential move?"

Erwin shrugged. "I have no idea how the others felt or if they even knew about it. I mean I assume they did, since they had to have seen what I saw. We haven't ever really interacted beyond what was necessary."

"You didn't say how *you* felt?" Vera wasn't letting her off the hook.

"I expected I would be going with him. He would need a personal assistant wherever he was."

Just another revelation that didn't surprise Vera one bit. This case seemed to have more cropping up every day. Too bad none got them closer to nailing down the actual killer.

"Larry Parson was found dead in his room at the Regency Inn." As Vera made this announcement, Bent rejoined the conversation.

"Oh my God." Erwin adopted a look of horror. "He's the one I think attacked us." She looked to Vera. "I remember the aftershave."

"Brut," Vera told her. "I checked."

"That's it! My college counselor wore it. I hated it. He kept it in his desk. Green bottle, right?" She shuddered. "I swear that man was a closet porn addict."

"Brut aftershave comes in a green bottle, yes." Vera didn't bother explaining to the woman that Larry Parson could not have attacked them because he hadn't even arrived in Tennessee when the event occurred. At least that was the theory she was sticking with for now.

"Did you find anything else? I'm certain he's the one who attacked us."

Her anticipation was palpable. "What makes you think there was anything else to find?" Bent settled next to Vera on the small sofa. "Surely a smart perp would dispose of whatever he used while committing a crime."

Erwin looked entirely deflated. "Guess so."

"Someone visited him at the motel just before I found him," Vera told her. "He called me about his visitor."

Something along the order of fear flashed in Erwin's eyes and on her face before she could school the reaction.

Vera gritted her teeth to hold back an accusation. Too soon. She couldn't be sure. "He was poisoned, we think. But I got to his room just before he died." Might as well give her something to sweat about, as Bent would say.

Erwin shook her head. "That's too bad. But you know the old saying: 'Live by the sword, die by the sword.'"

Vera clenched her jaw to hold back a snarky retort. Then she thought about her call with Mrs. Childers. "Have you ever taken anxiety medication? Like Xanax?"

Erwin made a face. "No way. That stuff is for people who can't deal with real life. That is not me." Her mouth suddenly formed an O, and she made a sound of surprise. "But you know, my roommate, Nola, took Xanax. She had way more problems than anyone knew. Really, really sad story."

Yeah, and Vera was looking at the poor girl's biggest one.

"If we have more questions, I'll let you know," Bent announced as he stood.

Vera followed suit. Evidently his call was something that wouldn't wait. Didn't matter. She wanted Erwin to stew for a while. "Thanks for your time, Valeri."

As they left the building, the woman in the downstairs apartment with the children was coming in.

"Nice to see you again." Vera smiled at the children, who quickly lined up against their mother's legs.

The woman offered a hesitant smile that wasn't much of a smile at all.

Vera gestured to the man at her side. "This is Sheriff Gray Benton."

Bent gave her a nod. "Nice to meet you, Ms. . . . ?"

"Johnson," the woman said finally. "Kayla Johnson."

The two little boys hiding behind their mother peeked out, and Bent smiled at them.

"I'm sorry I wasn't much help the other day." Johnson looked from her children to Vera. "I had just lost my grandmother, and I was having a really bad day."

Vera nodded. "I understand. I'm very sorry for your loss."

Johnson thanked her, then herded her children into her apartment. Vera was glad to know it wasn't just her less-than-award-winning personality that had made their previous meeting so uncomfortable.

As they exited the building, Vera remembered another thread she needed to follow up on. "Did we learn anything from the other downstairs neighbor? Sam Scott?"

"He was out of town all weekend." Bent glanced at her. "Sorry, I thought I told you."

"No problem. It's been that kind of week." It was hard to believe tomorrow was Saturday, and they were no closer to nailing down their killer or killers. Damn, it had been a long four days.

"I have another meeting at the office." Bent paused at Vera's SUV. "The mayor and the chief of police want to go over the case again."

Damn, and they'd just had a press conference. But that was the way of things at the top. They wanted results. Fast. No matter the situation. The trouble was, closing a homicide case was rarely fast.

"I'm going home," Vera admitted. "Where are we tonight?" She hesitated on the sidewalk next to him. "Did I ask you this already?" Her brain just wasn't keeping up today.

"My place." He gave her a quick hug. "I'll cook."

A grin stretched across her face. "I'm in. See you later." She hesitated. "Wait, I forgot to ask how that press conference went?"

He gave his head a little shake. "About like you'd expect, considering we still don't have anything to offer as progress. Nolan Baker was front and center. He wanted to know why you weren't there."

She made a face. "Sorry. I'm sure that was unpleasant."

"Most press conferences are."

"Look, I think I'll call Eric for help on getting more information on Quantum Leap, since Erwin didn't give us anything. I did some googling after I spoke with the attorney, but I got basically nothing. We could waste a lot more hours searching and still find nothing. He has the resources to find what we need far more quickly."

"You're right." Bent nodded. "Do it."

Vera glanced back at the second floor of the building Thomas Wilton had bought for his assistant. The curtains on the living room window moved. She'd been watching.

"I can't get past the idea," she said to Bent, "that Erwin is hiding something, maybe a lot of somethings."

"She's back on top of my list," he agreed. "How about yours?"

"Right next to Carter, Hernandez, and Martinez," Vera admitted. "It's a damned four-way tie."

"By the way," he said, "that rental—the Airbnb in Park City that Carter mentioned—was a bust. It took Myra about a dozen calls to track down the owner, and he sent her to a service who handles the rentals. The service refuses to give out any information without a warrant. They did say there were no cameras in or around the property. With what we know now, I'm not so sure it's worth the hassle."

"Don't bother," Vera agreed. "I think we can pretty much rule out Alicia based on the statements from Parson and Lancaster. The knife being found under her was clearly a setup. As for the others, I can't think of one reason to rule even one of them out. They all have motive. They all had means and opportunity. The only trouble is proving it."

"All four disliked Alicia," Bent reminded her. "All four felt she made things worse. Their boss. Their working environment. Their lives."

Vera nodded. "True. Maybe Erwin not so much. She just announced she expected to go with Wilton if he moved to California. But I can't get the story about the first wife she just told me out of my head. There's something there too."

"Could be," Bent admitted. "What we need is for one of them to break."

"Right." Vera doubted Erwin would be the one to break. More likely Martinez or Hernandez. Analyzing people was her specialty, but she was a little off her game this week.

Bent cocked his head. "I say we play a little game with our top four."

Vera grinned. "I like the sound of that."

"We'll bring all four in and put them in a room together and let them stew for a while, then we'll question them—together."

"Erwin and Carter will go head-to-head." Vera was sure of it. "Sparks will fly."

"Maybe accusations will be thrown, and we'll learn something we don't already know."

"Good plan."

He gave her a little two-fingered salute. "See you at home."

She waved, then wandered to her SUV. *Home.* Where exactly was home now? She watched him drive past. With Bent, she decided. Wherever he was . . . was home.

As Vera pulled onto the street, she made the call to her old friend. Eric promised to have something as quickly as possible for her on Quantum Leap. She thanked him and ended the call. Another call immediately buzzed in. *Luna.* Her face flashed on the dashboard screen of Vera's SUV.

She steeled herself and accepted the call. "Hey, Luna. Everything okay?"

"I'm sitting in the parking lot at the hardware store."

The news sent a new shot of adrenaline through Vera's chest. "Luna, you—"

"I can't live with this anymore. I need to tell Jerome, and I just can't until I talk to Mr. Potter. That receipt has to be wrong."

"Give me time to get there, and I'll go in with you." Vera pressed harder on the accelerator. "Please, Luna, don't do anything until I get there. I'm on my way."

She hoped like hell there was some sort of explanation for Luna's timeline that morning . . . otherwise this situation was going to hell in a hurry.

36

Fayetteville Hardware
1100 Winchester Highway, 5:00 p.m.

Vera parked and hurried to catch her sister before she reached the entrance to the hardware store.

"Are you certain you want to do this now?" Vera needed her to be certain. She really did. She wanted to be certain as well. But the truth was she felt utterly terrified after making her own purchase and finding the time stamp correct. Her heart pounded, and ice slipped through her veins.

"Vee." Luna's expression was more confident than Vera had seen it in days. "I know you're worried about this, but I'm not. I know about what time I came over here and about what time I left. It's true that pregnancy brain is a real thing and that I am more forgetful these days, but there has to be an explanation."

Vera blinked back the damn emotion that burned in her eyes. "You're right. I'm sorry for doubting you." She inhaled a deep breath. "Let's do this."

With that she walked side by side with her little sister to the entrance and prayed with every step that since it was past five o'clock, Clarence Potter would have gone home already. Because deep down Vera was so not ready to do this.

The bell over the door jangled, drawing the attention of the two customers perusing the nuts-and-bolts aisle. The customer service counter was in the center of the main floor area, so she and Luna headed in that direction.

"Welcome to Fayetteville Hardware." The guy behind the counter wearing a yellow vest looked from Vera to Luna. "Hey, Lu, how are you doing?"

Now that Vera thought about it, the man looked to be about Luna's age. Her sister spent far longer than necessary telling him about the baby and the nursery and how excited she and Jerome were, and then the big gut punch came.

"I sure was sorry to hear about Jerome's mama."

Luna's smile faded, of course, and she nodded. "It's just awful. Really awful."

Vera needed this over. She couldn't take the tension any longer. "Is Mr. Potter in?"

"He said a minute ago he was leaving, let me check." Yellow Vest Guy rushed over past a couple of tool aisles and disappeared through a door marked "Office."

"You okay?"

Vera blinked. Realized her sister was asking the question she should have been asking. "Sure. You okay?"

Luna nodded. "I will be in a minute, hopefully."

Hopefully.

The door opened once more, and Yellow Vest Guy hustled out with Mr. Potter on his heels.

Vera groaned inwardly. Oh well, at least now they would know.

Mr. Potter joined them in front of the counter. "How can I help you ladies?" When his gaze settled on Luna, his pleasant expression slipped. "We're all so very sorry to hear about Jackie and Leonard. We hope you and Jerome are holding up all right."

"This has been a difficult time. We're taking it day by day."

Luna was like a little angel. So sweet and so perfect. She would never ever, ever push her wicked mother-in-law down the stairs. Never. Flashbacks of Vera and Eve dragging their stepmother's dead body down the stairs at the farm made her stomach twist up into a pretzel.

Good thing Luna was nothing like them.

Potter looked to Vera then. "Is there something I can do for you today?"

"Mr. Potter," Luna spoke up, "I was here on Tuesday morning to pick up that paint, remember?"

He nodded. "I sure do. I was shorthanded that day. Some folks"—he shot a look at Yellow Vest Guy—"were laid up with after Labor Day hangovers."

If this moment had not been so grave, Vera would have laughed out loud, or maybe she just needed to break her own tension.

"I'm worried about the receipt," Luna explained. "It says that I paid for the paint at nine forty-five, but that can't be right because I didn't get home until after eleven. Unless I got lost and don't remember it." She laughed, the sound showing her nervousness now.

"Good gracious." Potter shook his head. "I'm so sorry, Luna. That other cash register refused to maintain the proper time. And it was new. Every time I had it adjusted, it lost anywhere from an hour to two within the next twenty-four hours. It just wouldn't keep the correct time. They brought me a new one yesterday morning."

Vera wilted with relief. Thank God.

"Would you like me to make you a new handwritten receipt?" He glanced at the receipt. "So your receipt should have read ten forty-five or later. I am so sorry for the confusion."

"That's not necessary," Luna said. "I was just worried that I'd lost my mind."

Potter patted her on the shoulder. "You're fine. It was the register. Anyone who doubts that need only ask me."

"Why don't you go ahead and make that new receipt for us?" Vera sent a smile at Luna, hoping she would go along. "It's important for the baby book. You know every little event has to be documented these days, if not in a baby book then on social media."

Vera had no idea where that ridiculous explanation came from, but it worked. Potter was only too happy to write a note regarding the old register's inability to keep time.

It wasn't until they were outside that Vera could breathe again.

"See." Luna beamed a smile at her. "I told you."

"You sure did." Vera hugged her hard. She had never felt so relieved in her life. Even her knees felt weak. Thank God! Now they could all relax. "You hang on to that letter. Put that old receipt with it. Now." Vera gave her a firm look. "Go home and relax. Focus on yourself and your husband. I will take care of the other. You weren't even in the house when Jackie died. This was not your fault."

Luna hugged her tight, or as tight as she dared with that enormous baby bump in the way. "Love you, Vee."

"Love you too."

Once Luna had driven away, Vera loaded herself into her SUV. She was so ready for this day to be over.

Her phone vibrated on the console. Bent's handsome face flashed on the screen. "Hey. Your meeting over already?" If so, that was a record.

"It's ongoing, but I thought you'd want to know. I got those cell phone records for Luna and the others. Luna's phone was at her house all morning like she said because she forgot it when she went to the hardware store."

Vera held her breath.

"Geneva Fanning's was pinging off the same cell tower as Luna's from 9:50 until 10:55. At 11:20 it pinged off the same tower as Leonard Andrews's phone. Leonard's was at home all morning. Jerome's was pinging off the tower near his workplace."

"Oh. My. God." Vera's mouth gaped. "So Geneva was at Luna's at the time of Jackie's death, and she rushed to Leonard's house after that. It had to be Geneva, Bent."

"We can place her at the scene, for sure," Bent reminded her, "but we can't prove she pushed her sister down those stairs."

They needed evidence . . . or a confession.

"You're right," Vera admitted reluctantly. "Thanks for the news. See you later."

Vera made a quick call to Luna to fill her in, then tossed her phone onto the passenger seat. Damn it! Then she smiled. Maybe dear old Geneva needed a little prompt. But first there was one thing Vera had to do.

Fanning Residence
Lincoln Avenue, 6:40 p.m.

Vera parked on the street in front of Geneva Fanning's historic home. It wasn't one of the grand ones like on Mulberry, but it was a lovely home nestled among numerous others on one of Fayetteville's nicest streets.

At the front door Vera pressed the antique buzzer, but it really wasn't necessary because Geneva had been watching her ever since she emerged from her SUV. But rather than come to the door, her husband, Trenton, opened it.

"Ms. Boyett." Trenton studied her cautiously, as if she were there to pinch the family's valuables. "What a surprise."

A surprise for certain. Her sister was being considered for legal action by the man's wife. Typically anyone involved or related to the potential defendant stayed clear of the plaintiff.

But there was nothing typical about the way Vera did things.

"I hope I'm not interrupting your dinner." Vera smiled pleasantly.

"No." He shook his head, seemingly confused by her statement. "We haven't . . . No, we were just catching the news."

"Great." Vera stepped forward, and he instinctively stepped back, which put her over the threshold. "I felt it was really important that I speak with you and Mrs. Fanning personally before this situation develops further."

He backed up another step, and Vera closed the door. Geneva appeared from the room on the left, where she'd obviously been eavesdropping.

"What do you want?"

The woman's demand echoed down the elegant entry hall.

Vera ignored it and continued her conversation with Mr. Trenton. "I thought you might want to know that the medical examiner has confirmed time of death for poor Jackie, and Luna has documentation that she was not at home during that time frame, just as she stated previously. Mr. Potter at the hardware store waited on her personally and has signed a statement as to the time she departed the store."

"That's a lie. She was right there in that new house her husband built her." Geneva glared at Vera like a wild animal and stabbed a finger in her direction. "She pushed my sister down those stairs. Jackie told me how Luna had been badgering and threatening her that morning."

"Whatever your sister told you," Vera said so calmly that it shocked even her, "she lied. In case Jackie didn't tell you, she pushed Luna down the stairs, and it was a flat-out miracle she caught herself, saving not only her life but that of her and Jerome's baby. Jackie tried to kill my sister, and I will prove it if it's the last thing I do."

Okay, so she hadn't meant to say that last part.

"My sister called me." Geneva snatched the phone out of her pocket and tapped on the screen until it revealed whatever she planned to show Vera. "See that." She stuck the screen in front of Vera. "My sister called me at ten minutes after nine that morning and left a voicemail telling me Luna had tried to—to kill her. When she got back from that hardware store, she finished the job." She drew the phone away and slid it into her pocket, her expression daring Vera to top that one.

"And what did you do, Geneva?"

Wife and husband stared at Vera as if she'd asked if they wanted to have dinner now . . . with her.

"I mean," Vera went on when they both just kept staring, "did you rush over to see her? To offer moral support?" Vera shrugged. "To make sure that petite, seven-and-a-half-months-pregnant Luna didn't come back and throw five-foot-eight, one-hundred-and-eighty-pounds Jackie down the stairs?"

Physical characteristics were all in the preliminary report Collins had worked up and sent along with the body. Giving Jackie credit, she'd carried the weight well.

"Get out of my house," Geneva snarled.

Vera held her ground. There was more she intended to say before she was strong-armed out the door. "Before I came here this evening, I drove from the hardware store to Luna's house, then back. It takes exactly twenty-eight minutes to drive from Luna's house to the hardware store. She paid for the paint at 10:45. So if we go backward, I think we can safely estimate that Luna would have been in the store for about thirty minutes to pick out the paint, have it shaken, and then pay for it. So that takes the time clock back to 10:15. Subtract twenty-eight minutes from that, and we can assume Luna left her house no later than about 9:45 or 9:46."

"I'm not listening to any more of this." Geneva glared at her husband as if she expected him to do something.

"Your attorney may have told you this already," Vera went on when Trenton did nothing but stare at her, waiting for the next shoe to drop. "The sheriff subpoenaed the records for Jackie's phone, Luna's, and yours, Geneva. Thankfully those records just came in." Vera smiled. "Before I give you that news, let me remind you that the ME has put Jackie's death between ten and eleven. And guess what? You—at least your phone—was at Luna's home from 9:50—right after Luna left on Tuesday morning—until 10:50. Luna didn't leave the hardware store until 10:45, which means she didn't get home until approximately 11:13 or so. Which means she just missed you. But when she walked into the house, what she did find was Jackie at the bottom of the stairs."

Every speck of color drained from the woman's face.

"Oh and another thing." Vera almost forgot this part, and it was the very best part. "When you left Luna's house, why did you go to Leonard Andrews's house? Were you there when he had his heart attack?"

"What are you trying to say?" the husband asked, his voice thin.

"I'm saying that Luna did not push Jackie anywhere. She wasn't even at the house when it happened. Both she and Jackie got up and walked away from Jackie's attempt to heave Luna down those stairs. But what happened after that was someone else's doing. Someone who came to Luna's house"—she stared at Geneva as she said this—"and pushed Jackie down those stairs."

"How . . . how do you know she didn't just fall? She may have had some sort of medical event after the argument or whatever it was with Luna?"

Even as the husband asked this second question, the wife stood mute. She knew damned well she was caught.

"Well, Mr. Fanning, unfortunately that isn't possible because Jackie sustained a fracture to her left tibia. The sort of fracture the medical examiner found suggests Jackie was hit in the leg with something or maybe kicked by someone wearing boots, perhaps. This is likely why she fell down the stairs that last time."

The gasp that slipped from Geneva Fanning then was the final nail in her coffin, as far as Vera was concerned.

"Not to mention that her position at the bottom of the stairs suggested not just a fall but a hard push. Someone wanted to make sure she wasn't getting back up. Then, barely an hour after Luna found poor Jackie, she and Jerome get the news that his father has had a heart attack. Maybe Leonard did push her and then rushed back home, but his poor heart couldn't bear what he'd done. Except we know that isn't the case because I guess I forgot to mention that both Jerome's and his father's cell phone records were subpoenaed as well, and Leonard was at home the whole time—at least his phone was."

Trenton Fanning glared at his wife. "You were at his house when he had the heart attack? Did you call the ambulance for Leonard?"

Geneva shook her head, still unable or unwilling to find her voice.

"I swear if the two of you have started back up . . ." Trenton was the one pointing a finger now—at his wife. "I won't let it go so easily. I did last time because of Jackie's cancer. I didn't want her to know what you had been doing with her husband. But there is nothing to stop me now."

"I'm calling my attorney," Geneva wailed.

Vera was enjoying the show far more than she should have. Now might be a good time for Bent to show up.

Her cell vibrated, and as if the thought had summoned him, it was Bent. "Hey, I—"

"We have to get to Nashville, Vee," he interrupted. "Alicia Wilton just woke up."

Hope fired through Vera. "You still at the office?"

"I'm walking out the door."

"I'll pick you up."

Since the Fannings were still shouting, Vera let herself out and hurried to her SUV. This was good news. She wouldn't get her hopes too high until they knew how well Alicia had recovered, but this could be a big step in getting to the whole truth about what had happened at that cabin.

37

Vanderbilt University Medical Center
1211 Medical Center Drive
Nashville, 8:20 p.m.

Bent had spent far too much of this week eyeball deep in dead bodies and forensic reports. Every top honcho in Fayetteville politics was breathing down his neck. They seriously needed a break in this case. He hoped like hell Alicia Wilton was it.

As they waited for the elevator to the Traumatic Intensive Care Unit, he studied Vera. She had come to pick him up, but she'd insisted that he drive. Made sense. It hadn't been that long since her concussion. She'd been on fire with the news about the hardware receipt, which she apparently had forgotten to tell him about, and the visit with the Fannings.

He loved watching her when she got like this. She was so animated and . . . beautiful.

Twenty miles into the trip, and she'd crashed. She'd slept the better part of the drive.

When they loaded alone into the elevator, both choosing to lean against the back wall, she sent a glare in his direction. "I still don't understand why you let me sleep almost the whole way."

"You were tired." He held back a grin. That would only piss her off. Instead he turned his head and looked directly at that gorgeous profile. "Besides, you're going to need that rest for when I get you home."

She rolled her eyes. He loved it when she did that, but it annoyed the hell out of her. Vera did not like anyone seeing what she was thinking, and right now she was working hard to be irritated at him, but she couldn't work it up.

"You should be thinking about this case." She folded her arms over her chest. "Not about *that*."

"I firmly believe that you are doing enough thinking on the subject for both of us."

The doors opened onto the tenth floor, saving him from whatever she intended to blast him with next.

At the nurses' station, Bent removed his hat and explained that the doctor had called about Alicia Wilton. He and Vera were immediately buzzed into the unit. The nurse in charge was waiting for them.

"I'm Selma Panter. I'm the nurse practitioner who works with Dr. Holden. He had to leave before you arrived, but he wanted me to fill you in."

"Thanks, we appreciate it." Bent was way beyond ready to hear from their one witness.

"Mrs. Wilton is doing really well for someone who sustained the degree of head trauma she did and remained in a coma for the better part of five days. Physically she is doing very well. Cognitively her recovery is remarkable. She speaks perfectly and reacts without hesitation. That said, she's been through a lot. Her body is weak from fighting for survival, so we would prefer that you limit your time with her to about twenty minutes. We don't want her to feel overwhelmed."

"Does she recall the events that brought her here?" Vera asked.

"She knows her husband is dead and that she was attacked. We didn't press for any other details."

That was actually more than Bent had hoped for.

"So if you're ready, you can go in now."

"Thank you." Bent turned to Vera and waited for her to go first.

Panter entered the room with them. "Alicia, do you remember me?"

Alicia moistened her lips. "Yes." She looked to Vera and then to Bent. Her eyes instantly welled with tears. "Can you tell me who did this, Sheriff?"

Bent was grateful she recognized him. Though they weren't acquainted personally, the fact that she knew the sheriff in the county where she lived was a good sign.

Bent approached the bed, Vera next to him. "Mrs. Wilton, we're working on that. You can help by telling us what you remember about that day."

She fiddled with the edge of the sheet folded at her waist. "We all went to the cabin on Friday. I was not happy about it, let me tell you."

"What part were you not happy about?" Vera asked. She smiled, and Bent's heart reacted, no matter that the smile wasn't for him. "I'm Vera Boyett. I work with the sheriff's office on cases like this."

Alicia gave a small nod. "I recognize you."

"You were saying that you weren't happy about going to the cabin," Vera prompted.

"Yes." Alicia sighed. "Seth was an old boyfriend of mine. I hadn't seen him or Sandy—the woman he brought with him—in ages. Anyway, he came up here claiming I asked him to come. That was a total lie, but he just wouldn't leave. He kept saying he was afraid for me. That someone was setting him up and me too."

"Do you know of any reason someone would want to set you up?"

"No. That's the weird thing. I mean, I've done some things in the past I'm not proud of. Like cheat on my boyfriend or whatever. But I've been a different person for a while now. And after I met Thomas, I knew I was never going back to my old life."

"How did the four of you end up at the cabin for the weekend?" That part puzzled Bent the most in light of what she'd just said, as well as what Sandy Owens had shared with her sister.

"When I told Thomas what was happening, he was worried too. He felt doing this weekend thing would maybe help bring out the truth. He wasn't worried about it being me who'd done something wrong, if that's what you're asking. He knew I was telling the truth. You may not know this, but we're having a baby. We weren't thinking about anything else.

The truth is, once we really talked it all over, we both actually believed Seth's story about being lured to Fayetteville by a person he thought was me. Thomas wasn't quite as certain as I was, but he trusted my judgment. The weekend at the cabin was his idea. He insisted on seeing how the weekend went down, just to be sure."

"If you started to believe Seth," Vera ventured, "who did you feel might be responsible for what was happening?"

She gave a dry laugh. "Take your pick. They all hate me. Valeri, Helen, Renata, and Jose. I don't know what I did, but I couldn't trust them with anything. Whatever I said or did, they twisted it around and tried to make me look like I was somehow mistreating them. They even went to Thomas about it. It was just crazy."

Bent and Vera exchanged a look, and she asked, "Is there one you felt was the ringleader?"

"Valeri, for sure," Alicia insisted without hesitation. "She did not like me from the beginning. She preferred having Thomas all to herself."

Bent could see the possibility. "When did the trouble start at the cabin?" At her pained look, he added, "Take your time."

"By Monday we pretty much had everything worked out. Thomas was confident someone else was behind the situation, even if he wasn't ready to believe it was one of his dedicated employees. He planned to hire a private detective to figure it out. So we all relaxed. Sandy and I were talking about what we should make for dinner and baby names. It was a perfect day. I tire easily, so I decided to take a nap that afternoon while the others prepared dinner."

She fell silent for a while, but Bent didn't push. This was difficult enough.

"Something woke me up. A loud noise of some sort. I got up and came downstairs . . . The first thing I saw was Seth on the floor by the sofa." She pressed a hand to her chest. "I ran to him, but he was dead. Then I saw Sandy, and my heart almost stopped."

She shuddered. "All I could think was that I had to find Thomas. I rushed onto the deck." Tears spilled down her cheeks. "He was floating face down in the hot tub. I reached for him, and that's when I heard someone behind me. I glanced back, and there was this black figure—clothes, mask, all black. I ran, but something hit my head." She touched the bandages there. "I remember falling. I was face down, and he was on top of me. He kept banging my head into the wooden step. His hand was twisted in my hair, and he banged and banged and then . . . I don't remember anything else."

"You're certain it was a man?" Bent asked.

"I can't be sure," she said, "but the person in black was very tall and broad shouldered. Really strong."

"Did you notice eye color?" Bent asked. "Did you see any part of his skin that could tell if he was white or otherwise?"

"It happened so fast . . ." She drew in a big breath. "I honestly can't say. I just remember the black . . . ensemble, I suppose, is the best way to put it."

"Did you notice how he smelled?" Vera asked. "Did he say anything?"

"He didn't say anything, and I don't recall any smells. I think I was too terrified for my baby. The next thing I knew, I was here. I could hear things, but I couldn't wake up until now."

After a moment, Vera asked the next question. "Would you tell us why you and your husband as well as your guests were naked?"

Alicia looked confused. "What?"

"When we arrived at the cabin," Vera explained, "all of you were naked."

"How is that possible? We all had on clothes. Sandy and I had on shorts and tops. Thomas and Seth were wearing shorts and T-shirts—at least when I went to our room to take a nap. Seth and Sandy had clothes on when I found them." She hesitated, as if trying to recall. "Thomas had taken off his tee, but I don't know about his shorts."

"Had everyone been drinking?" Bent held up a hand. "I'm not asking because I want to use the information against you or anyone else, Mrs. Wilton. I'm trying to gauge the situation in terms of how everyone reacted to the attack."

"Thomas had been careful about how much he drank up until then. Of course I wasn't drinking at all. But after we figured out that someone had set us all up, everyone kind of let loose, so they may have all gotten pretty buzzed while I was napping."

"But you're certain you were all clothed?" He didn't like pressing the issue, but he needed to know she was certain.

"We were. Yes. No one walked around naked that weekend." She made a face that revealed exactly how awful she considered the idea. "No one."

"What about drugs?" Vera asked. "Cocaine was found. There was weed."

Bent could see that being part of the setup as well.

"No way. Thomas is strictly antidrug, as am I. We've both dabbled in the past, but not anymore. I never knew Seth to use drugs either. I can't say about Sandy, but I can tell you none were brought into the cabin. Thomas searched their things. He wanted everything on the up-and-up."

"Did Sandy bring clothes and a handbag with her?" Bent asked.

Alicia frowned. "She did. Sure."

He and Vera shared a look. Someone had taken those items to slow down the investigation. Not surprising. That same someone had gone to great lengths to convey a certain perception of the weekend.

"Thank you, Mrs. Wilton." Bent glanced at Vera. "We appreciate you answering our questions. If you think of anything else, just let the deputy outside your door know you need to speak with me."

"One more thing," Vera said. "Were you and your husband arguing in the weeks or days before your weekend at the cabin?"

A new sadness settled over her face. "No. Not at all. I suppose we were both feeling the tension of Seth's sudden appearance and the other decisions in front of us."

"What sort of decisions?" Bent nudged.

"We were planning to sell the property and move. Thomas thought we needed a fresh start. With the baby coming and after all he'd been through." She sighed. "It just felt like the right thing to do. We were moving to Southern California. He and his parents vacationed there when he was a child. He always loved it, he said." She frowned then. "Did someone say we were arguing?"

"It was mentioned, yes." Bent opted not to say by whom.

"Maybe we had a tense discussion or two. He wanted Valeri to come too." She shrugged. "To continue being his assistant."

"But you didn't want her to come," Vera suggested. "Because you felt she wanted Thomas all to herself."

Alicia smiled, but it wasn't pleasant. "Valeri is very good at her job, which Thomas truly appreciated and respected. But there's something off with her. She finds a sore spot and rubs it until it bleeds. I mean, she loves to create trouble. Thomas told me she's the one who warned him that Lena was cheating—which turned out to be true, but she flat-out lied about me. She's the one who told him about seeing me with Seth." She moved her head side to side, anger darkening her face. "I swear, I will always believe she's the one who sent Seth all those messages." Alicia looked from Bent to Vera. "If you really want to know what I think—the woman is a psychopath. Capable of anything."

"She gossips," Vera said. "She likes making trouble. Was there something more you saw? Something that scared you?"

"Perfect example," Alicia explained, "she had Helen and the others believing I talked about them all the time. She would tell them how I wanted something done again or differently. She wanted them to hate me, and she succeeded. Once when I was out for a walk, I ventured into the barn. Jose was there, and he told me I'd better watch out or I'd end up like the other wife. Whether it was all Valeri's doing or not, they all hate me."

Vera looked to Bent then, and Bent asked, "Do you have any idea what he meant by that?"

"Well, I can't be sure, but Thomas had told me that he would never understand how Lena failed to notice the problem with her saddle. It just didn't make sense. He chalked it up to her being too distracted by her lover."

"Did he ever say who she was involved with?" Vera asked. "He might be able to tell us his thoughts on her accident."

"I don't know who he was, and Thomas never said, but I can guarantee you Valeri knows. She knows everything. And if it doesn't suit her purpose, she changes it."

"Can you think of anything else that may have been bothering Thomas?" Vera asked.

"He wasn't sure how Helen and the others were going to take the move." She looked directly at Vera then. "But we had both decided we weren't living our lives for anyone else a minute longer. We were going to live our lives for us and our child."

"Was he concerned," Vera asked then, "about their reactions to changes he intended to make to his will?"

Alicia made a sad face. "I'm sorry, but he never discussed the will with me. I know he was preparing changes, but he didn't mention the details, and I didn't ask."

Just then the door opened, and Panter stuck her head in and suggested it was time to wrap up the visit.

Bent thanked Mrs. Wilton again and assured her once more that they would find the person responsible for this terrible tragedy.

He hoped like hell they could sooner rather than later.

Back in the elevator, Vera turned to him as they approached the lobby level. "Do you believe her? I noticed you didn't ask about the knife."

"I do. For now, anyway."

Vera shook her head. "I knew Valeri Erwin was hiding something. Alicia Wilton is right: Erwin is a damned psychopath. Their stories are totally opposite."

"One of them is lying. That's for sure." Bent's money was on Erwin with that one.

"They're all lying." Vera looked up at him. "Erwin, Carter, Hernandez, and Martinez. You heard what she said about Martinez. He basically threatened her in that barn." She shook her head. "All those loyal employees."

"Loyalty sometimes only lasts for as long as it's beneficial to one party or the other." Bent had learned that during his military days.

"Another thing," Vera pointed out. "The killer wanted Alicia to look guilty. Like she set the whole thing up and there would be no one to confirm she was telling the truth when she said otherwise—assuming she survived. Christ, and the way he banged her head on that step. I don't think he expected her to be around to tell anything." She shook her head. "The way I see it, one or all had to know about the will and the move. That has to be the reason this whole thing was set in motion."

"We know it wasn't a burglary," Bent agreed. "Not one thing appeared to be taken. Not the Rolex lying on the bureau in the bedroom or the wallet filled with cash next to it. That leaves the will and the move, like you said. Those with the most to lose had to act before it was too late."

"The burner phone and the innuendos from the staff would leave Alicia—dead or alive—looking like the killer," Vera said almost to herself. "A jury would believe it, too, considering she's the only one who didn't get stabbed. The drugs and the lack of clothing would all serve to confirm it was a wild sex party—just as we assumed. It has to be Erwin and the others."

And like always, Vera was on the money with her conclusions.

Benton Ranch
Old Molino Road, 11:50 p.m.

Bent collapsed onto the mattress. He was spent. "That was . . . well . . ." He laughed. "Damn, I can't find the right word."

Vera rolled to her side to face him. "I think the one you're looking for is *out of this world*."

"That's four words."

"Whatever." She flopped onto her back and appeared to admire the authentic historic beams he'd added to this room's cathedral-style ceiling. "You know, I really do love this house. I know I've told you this before, but your mother would be so proud of you."

He rolled toward her, a smile stretched across his lips. "I can say the same about you and your mother."

Bent was grateful he had known Vera's mom. She had been a very special woman. She had helped him when he had no one else. He wished Vera could have known his mother, too, but she died when he was just a little boy. They had both lost someone very important to them, and somehow they made it anyway.

"You absolutely can." Vera smiled, traced a fingertip down his jaw. "I love looking at your face."

Her words did things to him that made him want to . . . but they'd already done that a couple of times since getting back from Nashville. First in the shower and then just now. "You know if you love this place so much, you should just move in. Let Eve and Suri move to the farm."

Vera made a face. "What makes you think Eve or Suri wants to live on the farm?"

"Because they love it. Remember last Christmas when you hosted dinner. It was all they talked about."

More frowning. "You're right. They love the grandfather clock. The fireplaces. Eve should have just said so."

"She would never say anything to make you feel like you had to accommodate her."

"You might be right." Vera rubbed at her forehead.

"Your head hurting?" He wanted to kill the guy—or woman—who'd hurt her. But first he had to confirm their damned identity.

"No. It's just too full of case notes and faces and scenarios."

He leaned over and kissed her forehead. "Stop thinking about the case. We talked out all the scenarios and details we know on the drive back from Nashville."

"You're right," Vera agreed.

"We're not talking about work anymore." He tugged at a strand of her silky hair. "Do you want to move in here with me?"

She studied him again in the dim light the bedside lamp managed to cast across the bed. "You really want that, don't you?"

"Don't you?"

"Just say that you do," she tossed back at him, "and then I'll say."

"You do realize how immature that sounds?"

"I do, but I stand by the demand."

"Yes." He stared into her eyes. "I want you to live here with me. I want you to be with me for the rest of our lives. I love you, Vera Mae Boyett. I have loved you since I was sixteen years old and saw you for the first time at the store with your daddy."

She laughed. "You have not."

"Yes, I have. But I knew you were out of my league. Then when I was helping your mother, I was finished. I understood there would never be anyone else."

"I won't remind you that you left me after that."

"I did, and it was the only thing I could give you at the time. Your freedom to become the amazing crime analyst you are so you could come back here all these years later and help me keep the people in this county safe."

She laughed, and he laughed with her. God, he loved this woman so much.

"You're getting sappy, you know."

"If that's what it takes to get the point across, I'll be sappy."

"Well." She sniffed. "Just so we're clear, I love you, too, Sheriff. Now let's get some sleep so we can get the bad guys in the morning."

"So you're moving in?" He held his breath.

"Damn straight, and you're stuck with me even if you regret it."

He sat up and reached for his phone on the bedside table.

"What're you doing?"

"I have to call Eve. She made me swear to call if you said yes."

"You two are awful." Vera started to laugh, and Bent was pretty sure he would never be happier than he was at that moment.

38

Saturday, September 6
Benton Ranch
Old Molino Road, 7:30 a.m.

"It's Eric." Vera set her coffee mug down and picked up her cell from the countertop. "Good morning."

Bent joined her at the kitchen island, propped a hip against it and continued drinking his coffee.

"I'm putting you on speaker so Bent can hear," she said, tapping the screen.

"Morning, Bent. I think I might have found what you need to close your case."

"That would be the best news I've heard this week." Bent held up crossed fingers for Vera.

He was certainly in a good mood this morning. Vera was glad. Getting past major decisions could do that. Vera was feeling loads lighter herself. Between the decision to move in with him and clarifying that hardware store receipt, Vera felt immensely relieved. She smiled to herself. The whole truth was that she had been in love with Bent since she was seventeen. She could not imagine her life with anyone else, and God knew she'd tried. But this—she studied his profile as he and Eric chatted—was the man she would spend the rest of her days with. She almost laughed out loud at the memory of Bent giving Eve the news. It warmed her heart to know how happy Eve was for her. Luna would be as well. Vera didn't have to wonder.

But what she did have to do was help Bent solve this damned case. The thing with Jackie was basically behind her, but this one was glaring at her face-to-face.

"This Quantum Leap organization," Eric was saying, "is currently under investigation by the FBI."

Vera shared a surprised look with Bent. "So it's a scam."

"A long-running one," Eric confirmed. "The start-up happened about six years ago, and it continued to amass incredible sums of money until two years ago. But there's little to nothing to find in terms of accomplishing its stated goals for the betterment of mankind. You already know the primary donor."

"Thomas Wilton." One of the most brilliant, wealthiest men in the world had been scammed for nearly a decade. Wow. Vera was astonished. But then even a genius was only human.

"That's the one. However, those donations stopped just under two years ago. Shortly after the Wilton donations ceased, Quantum Leap donated all remaining funds to various other charities and then closed up shop."

"Closed?" Bent glanced at Vera. "If it's been closed for almost two years, what brought the company's attention to the FBI?"

"An anonymous tip," Eric explained. "About a month ago the tip came in, and now an investigation has begun in earnest."

"Wow. Do you have any other details on the founder?" Vera wanted to talk to this person as soon as possible.

"The founder is a Gill Jamison III. His office is in his home in Hazel Green, Alabama. I'll text you the details."

"Did you find any other source of income for Jamison beyond the organization he started and then closed?" Bent asked.

"He's a trust-fund baby. He inherited millions from his father."

Vera shook her head. "Thank you so much, Eric."

"Thanks, man," Bent agreed. "We owe you one."

Vera ended the call and grabbed her mug to finish off her coffee. "I'll never understand how a man with Wilton's assets could be fooled so completely. Especially by a guy who's never even had a real job."

"Pretty sad," Bent agreed. "Six years puts the organization setup not all that long after Wilton moved to the area. But he didn't pick up on the scam until what, four years later?"

"About the same time his wife died," Vera noted. "She wasn't employed. Lots of women in her position choose a charitable cause to support. She may have been the one who was fooled. After her death, Wilton figured it out and cut ties."

"Why wait almost two years to turn them in?"

Vera didn't get that one either. "Unless it wasn't Wilton who did it."

"If we're lucky"—Bent took his mug to the sink—"we're about to find out."

Jamison Residence
Mitchell Drive
Hazel Green, Alabama, 9:15 a.m.

Based on the county tax assessor's website, Jamison had purchased this fifty-acre wooded property five years ago for a cool half million dollars.

Given the high brick wall around what could only be called a compound that Vera was looking at, the man had invested a whole lot more in the property.

Bent pressed the button for the intercom at the towering iron gates.

"Yes?" Female voice.

"Sheriff Benton here to see Gill Jamison."

A long pause. Vera and Bent shared a look. She'd scanned the info Eric emailed her. Jamison was thirty-five. Single. Never married. No children. No religious preference. Lived in the area his whole life. Had degrees in software engineering and information technology. The photo included with his details showed a handsome man with a charming smile. Gill's grandfather had been a NASA pioneer, and the company he'd created had expanded further under the guidance of his father. But then Gill was on the board in name only. Likely never lived up to Daddy's expectations.

"Mr. Jamison had to run an errand, but he'll be back shortly. I'm opening the gate now, Sheriff. Please drive up to the house, and you may wait for Mr. Jamison if you wish."

"I'll do that. Thank you."

The gate opened, and Bent rolled through.

"So he has the massive compound"—Vera visually followed the hand-laid cobblestone driveway winding through the woods—"but he doesn't have a security guard, and his staff doesn't ask for ID before allowing a stranger onto the property."

Bent sent her a humorous look. "The more people around him, the more opportunities for his secrets to get out."

"Good point." The more people breathing who know your secrets, the less likely they are to stay secret. But, in the end, there were some secrets that just couldn't be kept. "But there was a camera and screen in that box back there. She could have asked for ID."

Bent shot her a grin. "Maybe I have a trustworthy face."

Vera couldn't deny this.

As promised, a woman, middle age, trim looking with a helmet of gray hair, waited on the veranda of the enormous home.

"Good Lord," Vera whispered.

Bent reached for his door. "Vee, I don't think the good Lord had a single thing to do with this."

The man was just full of smart-alecky comebacks this morning.

Vera produced a smile as they crossed the cobblestone veranda. "Ma'am, good morning. I'm Vera Boyett. I work with Sheriff Benton."

"Ingrid Deaton." She nodded. "This way, please. Mr. Jamison should be arriving within the next few minutes, if it suits you to wait."

"Suits us just fine," Bent confirmed.

Inside, the mansion was just as stately as it was outside. Towering ceilings, awe-inspiring decor. Vera was no decorator, but it looked very Asian to her. Soft colors. Very modern and organic.

"Would you like coffee or water?" Deaton continued along the entry hall until they reached a grand great room complete with a concert-size baby grand piano. Wow.

"No thank you." Vera surveyed the room. Floor-to-ceiling windows. Sleek polished wood floors. The walls and trim were painted in a soft beige while every single piece of furniture was a sleek black.

"What about you, Sheriff?"

"No thanks."

"Very well. I'll alert you when Mr. Jamison arrives." With that she closed the massive doors and left them alone in the enormous room.

Vera wandered over to the wall of glass. Floor to ceiling, the entire width of the room. The view showed off a beautifully manicured lawn, but beyond that was mostly woods. She glanced back to Bent, who was roaming the room, pretending to study the artwork. It was likely best not to talk since the owner could have cameras or, at the very least, listening devices.

She drifted to the broad section of bookshelves tucked behind another grouping of furniture designed to promote conversation and interaction near the wall of glass. Lots and lots of books. A few photos of Jamison at various locations where he had presumably made donations. Many more photos of him receiving awards. Vera leaned closer to one and studied the people in the photo. Then she smiled. He'd photoshopped the same group repeatedly, adding them to different locations to make it appear like different award ceremonies. She wasn't surprised at all. The man was obviously very good at the business of putting on a good show.

Bent was at the piano now. Studying the framed photographs stationed there. Vera moved to the fireplace, where a good many more framed photos were scattered about the mantel. Most were of Mr. Jamison hunting. The man appeared to really like hunting. Oh and there was boating, except the boat looked more like a yacht. Another showed him in one of those mini helicopters. Vera gritted her teeth. What a piece of utter crap.

But it was the photographs right in the middle of all the others that made Vera's morning.

The first one to capture her attention was of Gill Jamison and a woman he evidently held in high regard since she was hugged tightly to him in the photo. They were smiling widely at the barbecue that had been held right here in that neatly manicured backyard of his. The woman was perhaps eight or so years his senior. Gorgeous dark hair. Lovely pale skin. Gill's embrace was not simply loving, but possessive. The woman in his arms was Lena Wilton. But Thomas Wilton was nowhere to be seen in the photo. So maybe this was the other man in the first wife's life. Explained her decision to take on his LLC as a pet project. As if to confirm Vera's assessment, there were numerous other photos of Gill with Lena. It appeared the couple had spent a good deal of time together.

Another shot caught Vera's eye. This one was taken around Christmas in front of a nicely decorated tree. But this time the woman Jamison's arm was draped around was not the first Mrs. Wilton. This woman was Helen Carter. Vera recognized the room as Carter's living room.

"Well, well now," Vera murmured. "What do we have here?"

Bent appeared at her side. "See anything interesting."

Vera gave him the answer with a glance at the photograph. "See for yourself."

The doors opened, and Deaton appeared once more. "I'm so sorry," she said as she moved toward them, "but Mr. Jamison has been delayed. He can't be sure how long he will be, so it wouldn't be wise to wait."

Bent shot Vera a sideways look. "Somehow I'm not surprised."

Vera held back a smirk. Sounded like there had been a miscommunication about allowing them inside. "Ms. Deaton, could you answer a question for me?"

She presented Vera with an agreeable expression. "I can certainly try."

"Who is this woman in the photo with Mr. Jamison?"

She hurried over to the fireplace and studied the photograph. "Why that's Mr. Jamison's Aunt Helen. She raised him after his mother died. His father was far too busy to see after a child. Helen took care of him until he was off to university. He actually thinks of her as his mother."

And what would a mother do to protect her son?

Vera had never been a mother, but she had a feeling she knew the answer. This was the piece of the puzzle they had been looking for—the one that might just push them over the finish line.

Bent gave the lady one of his cards and urged her to have Jamison call as soon as possible.

With Bent navigating the drive back to the gate, Vera asked, "Are we going to interview Helen Carter again?"

"No." He glanced at Vera. "We're going to arrest Helen Carter and her accomplices." He braked at the gate to wait for it to open fully. "At least we're going to make them think that's what's happening."

Vera chuckled. "That should get a reaction."

The three would be questioned until properly agitated, then they would turn on one another and the truth would rise to the top—just like churning butter. Vera couldn't wait to watch the show. It was one of the most satisfying parts of police work—seeing all your hard work push the whole story into the open.

Bent made the call to Deputy Hastings. She and a team of four other deputies were to go to the Carter property and wait for the sheriff.

Talk about a Saturday surprise. Vera stared out the window at the passing landscape. She thought of all that had happened this week. The lives that were lost . . . the ugly secrets uncovered. Sometimes she wondered if it was better to live your life never knowing these things. As a detective and then a crime analyst for so many years, she had seen just about everything imaginable. She wondered now how much that had changed her life view. She'd always assumed it hadn't. Her work was just that—work. But maybe her work was the reason she'd avoided full-on commitment all this time.

She glanced at Bent. That, she decided then and there, was going to change.

Bent's cell phone sounded off with another call. "What's up, Olson?" He listened for what felt like forever before he ended the call. He turned to Vera then. "They found no other gates or forms of entry in that twelve-foot fence surrounding the Wilton property."

Vera dropped her head against the seat. "Maybe our killer or killers climbed over the fence." The easiest way would have been to shut off the cameras and go through the main gate, but that would have been a huge red flag right off the bat.

"Or flew in." Bent glanced at her. "Olson found a small clearing in the woods less than half a mile from the cabin. Nothing large enough for a helicopter—"

"But maybe perfect for one of those mini helicopters," Vera offered. "And guess who has access to one?"

"Tell me there was a photo." He sent her a hopeful look.

Vera nodded. "In that same grouping with the photo of his dear Aunt Helen."

Bent smiled. "Maybe dear Aunt Helen can help us put this all together."

Vera had a feeling the rest of the morning was going to be even more interesting. That said, this latest development potentially changed up everything. It was possible—based on his relationship with Wilton's first wife—that Gill Jamison was their killer. But why wait two years for his revenge? If he believed Lena's death was murder, why not go to the police or confront Thomas Wilton before now? And why had Wilton waited almost the same to report Quantum Leap as a scam? There had to be something more. Something else they were missing.

A frown worked its way across Vera's forehead. The suspects with the most immediate motive were Erwin, Helen, and the others. Those four stood to lose now. Unlike Jamison, they didn't have trust funds to fall back on.

In the end, however, was money a strong enough motive to turn someone like Helen Carter into a cold-blooded killer? Or any of the other three, for that matter. Well, except Erwin. Vera wouldn't put anything past that one.

The sound of her cell phone ringing deep inside her handbag had Vera reaching for it. She instantly recognized the number. *Erwin.*

"Vera Boyett."

Bent glanced at her with a questioning look.

"I need to talk to you. It's important."

Vera tried to read the inflection in the other woman's voice. Worried. Frightened. Something on that order. "I'm a little busy right now, Valeri." She thought of the interview with Helen Carter. Vera really wanted to be a part of that. "Can this wait?"

"No. Please, can you come now?" Her voice had dropped to a whisper. "There are things you need to know. This can't wait. Please."

"I'm on my way. Maybe fifteen minutes before I can get there."

Erwin thanked her, and Vera ended the call. As much as she wanted to ignore the woman, her instincts warned that wasn't the smart move.

"That was Erwin. Evidently she's worked up about something. She sounded a little terrified. Can you drop me there?" Vera made a face. "As much as I hate to miss the fun with Helen Carter and friends, we can't ignore Erwin. She's in this deeper than we know, I suspect."

"I'll have Hastings pick me up there so you can keep my truck. I don't want to leave you stranded." He sent a worried look her way. "Maybe Hastings should stay with you."

"Give me a break," Vera tossed back, "I can handle Erwin."

39

Erwin Residence
Washington Street, 10:15 a.m.

Vera watched Bent leave with Hastings before heading up the steps to the entrance of Erwin's building. The curtains in the first-floor apartment belonging to Kayla Johnson fluttered, and Vera waved. She hoped this meeting with Erwin wasn't a waste of time, considering the Carter et al. gathering would likely be far more exciting.

Since she was here, there were a number of pointed questions Vera intended to ask Erwin, and she better be ready to answer without ducking and dodging or flat-out lying. After all, this meeting was her idea, and they were way past all the foreplay. Vera knew far too much and suspected even more about Erwin. The time for games was over.

Maybe Erwin would throw the others under the bus to save herself.

As Vera climbed the stairs to the second floor, she considered they should have invited Erwin to Carter's place and interviewed them all together the way she and Bent had discussed. But Vera had a feeling that Carter and Erwin were involved with these murders in completely different ways and with totally different motives and ideas on how this should end.

At the door she knocked and waited. The least Erwin could have done was watch for her arrival—if what she had to say was so all-fired important.

No answer. Well, hell. Vera knocked harder. "Valeri, you need to open this door."

Muffled sounds of movement inside were followed by the releasing of locks. The door opened just enough for Valeri to stick her head out. "Hi, Vera. Did you need something?"

What the hell? The woman called, begging for a meeting, and now she acted as if she wasn't expecting Vera. A burst of outrage tore through her. "I'm coming in." Vera bullied her way through that narrow opening, and Erwin had no choice but to back up. Vera went toe to toe with her. "What's going on, Valeri?"

The door slammed, and Vera whirled around.

"Hello, Ms. Boyett."

Fear throttled through her. Then she recognized the face staring at her. As if he'd stepped out of one of the photos at his luxurious mansion, Gill Jamison leaned against the closed door. The weapon he held wasn't the typical .38 or even a .9 millimeter. No, it was a Swiss-made SIG Sauer with a walnut grip. Very nice. Vera might not be an authority on home decor, but she knew her weapons. She also recognized this was bad. For her, at any rate.

"I see you got our message." Years of cop instincts overtook all else, and Vera braced for whatever move he made next. "That's good, because we need to talk."

He rubbed his jaw with the weapon's gleaming stainless steel barrel. "We do indeed."

There were times when Vera carried a weapon. Not so much since she'd left Memphis PD. And definitely not today. Too bad. She could use one just now. But she had her wits, and that would just have to do. She ordered her heart to calm. Slowed her breathing and focused her full attention on the six-foot-plus male in front of her.

"Why don't you start?" Vera suggested. "After all, this is your party." She needed him to let his guard down. To relax. So she did the same, relaxing her posture, angling her head as if she couldn't wait to hear what he had to say.

"I'm sorry," Erwin whispered in her direction. "He just showed up, and I didn't know what to do."

Vera forced a smile for her. "I'm confident you had nothing to do with this, Valeri."

Jamison scoffed. "Of course she did. Valeri is a regular little troublemaker." His glare was murderous. "In fact, she's the one who turned this into something far bigger than it should have been, aren't you, Val?"

"I don't know what you're talking about." Erwin edged behind Vera.

Jamison pushed away from the wall and took a step in their direction. Vera held still, as if she had no reason to fear him coming closer. No matter what her brain said, her pulse reacted to his nearness.

Calm, stay calm. All you need is one moment of distraction.

"Since you're here, you need to understand," he said to Vera. "Lena and I were in love. She was carrying *my* child."

"You can't be sure," Erwin snarled, peeking around Vera's shoulder.

Vera wondered the same. "How can you be sure the baby was yours? After all, she shared a bed with her husband night after night."

Jamison laughed. He was more relaxed than she would have expected, under the circumstances. Arrogant, she decided. Overconfident. The rich boy who never had to worry about a thing. Worked for her.

"The obstetrician said the sonogram showed she was exactly ten weeks. That put the conception date during Wilton's trip to DC and New York. He was gone for two weeks. You remember," he taunted Erwin. "You went with him." Then he looked back to Vera. "Trust me. We were certain."

"You're angry," Vera offered. "I get it. But what did he do, other than cut off your funding after his wife died?" She spread her feet a little wider apart and prepared to make a move.

Jamison laughed. "Lena didn't just die. She was a world champion. She would never have allowed an issue with her saddle to go unnoticed."

"People make mistakes." Vera shrugged. She watched his left arm relax at his side, the weapon in his right hand tilted slightly downward. "Are you suggesting her death was no accident?"

"It was no accident," he snarled, fury flashing in his eyes. "The bastard killed her. I know he did."

"No he didn't." Erwin was standing next to Vera now. "*I* know he didn't."

Vera glanced at her. What the hell was she doing? Might as well play to her move. "Are you sure about that, Valeri? Thomas was pretty angry when he learned about Lena's affair with Gill."

Valeri shot her a confused look.

"Lena warned you'd be sorry for telling him," Jamison growled at Erwin, leaning into her. "This whole situation is your fault."

So Erwin set off the chain reaction. Vera was not surprised at all.

"Really, Gill," Vera argued, hoping to pull his attention back to her, "you must know that what happened was as much your fault as anyone's. After all, you fucked the man's wife."

Gill forgot all about Erwin and grabbed Vera by the hair with his free hand. He jerked her close, nose to nose, the muzzle of his weapon shoved against her temple. "You don't know anything about what we had!"

Heart pounding once more in spite of her best efforts, Vera stared him straight in the eyes. "Why don't you explain it to me."

His mouth twisted with anger. "You wouldn't understand. We had a plan."

"You loved her." Vera readied to jam his right forearm upward and twist away.

"I knew it. That's why I told Thomas the truth," Erwin shouted. "Lena was lying to him about everything."

What the hell! Would Erwin not shut up!

Dragging Vera with him, his fingers still tangled in her hair, Jamison closed in on Erwin. He shifted the muzzle of his weapon to her forehead.

If the damn woman would just stay out of this, Vera might be able to make a move. As it was, Erwin was going to get them both killed.

"I didn't want her to keep hurting him," Erwin shouted. "But he wouldn't listen. He wanted to forgive her for the baby's sake, and he couldn't even be sure it was his." Her face was red with fury now. "I had to do something."

Vera wanted to kick her. She had to shut up, or this guy was going to lose it.

Jamison laughed again, long and loud. "Fuck's sake. I should have realized it wasn't him, it was you who set her *accident* in motion."

Erwin stumbled back a step, but his weapon remained trained on her.

"I didn't do anything," she wailed, the burst of anger gone now. "It was Jose. He was supposed to see that the repairs were done to her saddle. It's not my fault he didn't."

Vera kept her gaze fixed on Jamison. She had to get this situation under control. Right now. "So what are we doing here, Gill? You're already in trouble with the FBI, do you really want to add kidnapping or murder to that?" Although she was fairly confident it was a little late for him to worry about the latter.

"The FBI can't touch me. That money was for our life together. Lena set up the whole thing to keep the bastard from leaving her with nothing. The FBI won't find shit."

"You killed him and the others," Erwin accused, making things worse again. "I know it was you. I heard Helen on the phone, telling you to just stay calm, and she would fix it."

Well, hell. Vera wanted to shake Erwin. It damned sure would have been nice to know this like three days ago. Then all of this could have been prevented.

"Whatever you did," Vera offered, "you still have time to go." She gestured to the door. "You can disappear, and no one will ever find you. You have the means. Just do it."

He smiled, but it held no humor. "That was the idea, Ms. Boyett. I planned everything down to the last detail. And it all went perfectly. Even with Alicia surviving, there was nothing that pointed to me. I was golden. But then a little note I received this morning"—he sneered at Erwin—"reminded me I had one last loose end to tie up before I disappeared."

"You could still go," Vera urged. She had a feeling this was hers and Erwin's last shot.

The man's fury settled on her. "I could have, but then you showed up."

40

Carter Residence
Coldwater Creek Road, 10:30 a.m.

Carter had already started packing when Bent and his backup arrived.

Myra was at the judge's house, getting the warrant to search the property.

"What's going on, Sheriff?" Carter looked for all the world as if she had no idea why they had shown up.

She might have pulled off the whole innocent act if it hadn't been for the two suitcases lined up next to the door.

"Looks like I arrived just in time." He glanced at the suitcases. "Why don't we have Jose and Renata join us?"

Carter pulled out her cell phone to make the call to her tenants. Bent's cell vibrated with an incoming text. Myra was on the way with the search warrant.

When Carter ended her call, Bent said, "The warrant is en route. Do we need to wait for it to arrive to get started with our search of your property?"

"No." Carter shook her head. "Don't bother. It was me."

Bent studied her a moment. "It was you what?"

"I killed them. I was angry that they were moving away, and I killed them."

Bent held up a hand. Anticipation of a confession had his instincts on point, but this was a little too easy. This was way off somehow. "Why don't we back up a moment—"

"Just read me my rights, Sheriff," she shouted, tears streaming down her cheeks.

That was about the fastest confession Bent had ever gotten. The trouble was, he was pretty positive she was lying.

His cell vibrated again. "Shepherd," he said to the nearest deputy, who hustled over to Bent. "Read Ms. Carter her rights, and take her in. Same goes for Ms. Hernandez and Mr. Martinez."

Bent stepped onto the porch and took the call. He didn't recognize the number. "Sheriff Benton."

"Sheriff, this is Kayla Johnson. I live in Valeri Erwin's building."

Bent remembered. "Yes, ma'am. What can I do for you?" He was a little busy at the moment, but she was in the building where he'd left Vee, so he'd give her a minute.

"I saw Ms. Boyett go into Valeri's apartment a little while ago, and well, about fifteen minutes before she got here, a man went to Valeri's door as well. He banged on the door really hard. That's what made me peek out my door. Anyway, when Valeri answered, he was very rude. He shoved her back into her apartment and went in and closed the door. I thought when Ms. Boyett arrived, she'd come to take care of the trouble, but now I'm getting worried. I heard someone shouting and then it got like too quiet. I don't know what's happening, but it doesn't feel right, Sheriff. My kids are here, so I can't do anything."

"One second, Ms. Johnson." Shepherd had just escorted a handcuffed Carter out the door. Bent raised a hand for his deputy to hold up, uncertainty pulsing in his veins. He had to get to Vee. "I need your cruiser keys."

Shepherd looked at Carter and then back to Bent. "I thought—"

"Now!" The uncertainty had morphed into outright fear. Vee was in trouble.

Shepherd gave him the keys, and Bent bounded toward the cruiser. As he climbed in, he asked, "Ms. Johnson, can you describe the man to me?"

"Ah . . . he's, I don't know, mid-thirties. Tall. Good-looking white fellow. Dark hair. Dressed well."

A quick mental run-through of all involved in this case, and the image of Gill Jamison stood out. No way to be certain, but given their visit to his place this morning, he was the most likely. "Did you see a weapon, Ms. Johnson?"

"No . . . I didn't. But I can't be sure he didn't have one under his coat."

"Don't worry. I'm on the way. You stay in your apartment. No matter what you hear, you and your children stay put. Keep a watch out the window, and if you see them leave, pay attention to the vehicle and the direction they go."

"I got you, Sheriff."

The minutes that followed dragged by like molasses. No matter that Bent drove like a bat out of hell, it still took him way too long to get to Washington Street. He'd called for backup, but he didn't want his deputies to arrive before him. Too risky.

His phone vibrated. It wasn't until then that he realized it was still clutched in his hand. "Sheriff Benton."

"Sheriff," Johnson whispered, "they're leaving the building."

"Don't let them see you looking out the window."

"Okay, but I saw a gun . . . He's got a gun."

A new blast of terror lit inside Bent. "I'm almost there."

He tossed his phone aside as he zoomed through the intersection of Washington and Elk. On the next block, Vera, Erwin, and the man with the weapon were on the sidewalk. Even without the sirens and lights, they heard the roar of the cruiser's engine and looked in his direction.

Bent waited until the last minute to hit the brakes, sliding into the sidewalk.

The man jerked back, yanking Vera with him. Erwin hit the ground.

Weapon in hand, Bent barreled out of the cruiser.

The other man's weapon leveled on Bent.

Bent kept charging forward.

Vera's left arm flew out, knocking the man's arm upward as she twisted and kicked his legs out from under him. They went down in a heap. The weapon slid across the sidewalk.

Bent was on top of the bastard with a boot ground into his chest before he could make a move to get up. *Gill Jamison.* Bent pressed the muzzle of his weapon against the man's forehead. "Don't move, asshole."

41

Lincoln County Sheriff's Department
Thornton Taylor Parkway, 1:00 p.m.

Vera settled into a chair on Bent's side of the table as he readied to interview Gill Jamison. In a surprise move, Jamison had waived his right to counsel.

They had already interviewed the others. Hernandez and Martinez did not have visas, and Carter had threatened to turn them in and even to lie and say they had stolen from her if they didn't help with her plan. Alternatively, she'd promised to give them every dime she had in savings if they cooperated. They didn't have to kill anyone. The goal was to distract the police investigation from what her nephew had done. To shift blame to the Parson brothers and to Alicia.

For the most part the two reluctant participants only had to say what Carter told them to say. Martinez confessed to attacking Vera and Erwin. It was the one illegal demand Carter had made of him, besides making false statements to the police. Hernandez had used Thomas Wilton's key to sneak into Erwin's place and leave the burner phone—her one illegal step. Both unknowingly giving Carter even more control.

Carter claimed that Erwin had planted the phone in Alicia's room just before they all left the mansion on Thursday evening, but Carter had retrieved it. Carter also admitted to having personally broken into Larry Parson's motel room—she insisted it was easy. The door lock had shimmied open with the use of a credit card. She did this while he was out to lunch. She left the bat and other items in the closet, as well as Alicia's personal things in a drawer, to help frame him. But she denied having anything to do with his death. She insisted she was out of the room and gone before he returned.

Conover had confirmed that a deadly level of fentanyl residue was found in the whiskey glass on the nightstand next to the bed, which, according to toxicology, was the culprit in Parson's death. It would take some time and some doing to prove Carter was the one to plant that as well. Might even be impossible, but so far she was spilling her guts about everything else.

Vera hadn't actually expected Carter to cop to Parson's murder. She had a theory about that one as well as the "weird" visitor Parson had called her about. To that end she had asked Conover to go to the Regency and check Parson's room again for a certain item. She should be hearing back from him any minute now.

But the coup de grâce of the day no doubt would be Gill Jamison's confession. Vera studied him as he surveyed the interview room. He didn't appear the slightest bit nervous or angry or resigned. He just sat there, looking around.

Vera couldn't wait to hear the whole story—assuming he decided to give it.

Once Bent had switched on the recorder and identified all in the room, he started with a direction question. "Mr. Jamison, why don't you begin by telling us about your day on Monday, September 1, from the moment you arrived on the Wilton property."

Gill relaxed in his chair. He looked from Bent to Vera and back. "I landed my Mosquito—my mini helicopter—in a clearing just over a quarter of a mile from the cabin. From there I hiked to my destination. I lingered in the woods, watching and listening until I was ready to go in."

Vera was surprised that a rich guy like him was just throwing it all away.

"Did anyone provide details about the occupants of the cabin or their plans to you?"

"No. My aunt—"

"Would you identify your aunt," Bent interrupted.

"Helen Carter, my aunt, wouldn't tell me anything that was happening on the property because she had figured out I intended to do Thomas Wilton harm." He shrugged. "I ran into Valeri Erwin on Thursday. She complained about having to shop for the big party at the cabin that weekend. So I went to the cabin and planted a few bugs. I basically knew what was going on inside from the moment the two couples arrived on Friday evening. While I was there, I selected my weapon. Took it with me for when I came back."

"Why did you want to harm Mr. Wilton?" Vera asked.

"Because he killed the woman I loved. Lena Wilton. She was pregnant with my child, and we were planning a life together."

Bent glanced at Vera, and she asked, "I realize we talked about this before, but for the purpose of the recording, can you tell me again how you knew she was carrying your child and not Thomas Wilton's?"

"The obstetrician helped us narrow down the conception date to a period when her husband was out of town for an extended time." His jaw pulsed with anger now, even knowing what he was facing by telling this story. "I restrained myself for two long years. Thomas Wilton killed Lena, and I wanted more than my next breath to make him feel what I felt. I wanted him to recognize that he was about to lose everything, and there was nothing he could do. But to do that, I had to wait until he married again, and his new wife was pregnant. That was the only way he would ever know the agony I suffered."

"How did you know she was pregnant?" Bent asked. "Alicia didn't tell anyone."

Vera wouldn't put it past Erwin having told the guy. She loved causing chaos.

"I monitored her credit and debit cards," Jamison explained. "I knew when she bought her first pregnancy test and then when she visited an obstetrician."

Clever man. But then it was easy to be clever when he had every imaginable resource. Vera wondered if he had a clue what prison life was going to be like. Then again, those with the money could often make the situation more tolerable.

From there, he explained how he'd slaughtered Seth Parson and Sandy Owens, no matter that they were just in the wrong place at the wrong time. He carefully cut their clothes from their bodies so the cops would assume exactly what they did. He took great pleasure in recounting how he killed Wilton, stripped him and dumped him in the hot tub. The latter had been necessary since they struggled, and he didn't want any of his DNA left on the guy. He carefully cleaned up his tracks and removed the bugs he had planted and the clothes he'd cut off the victims. To hinder the police investigation, he took Sandy's personal belongings.

But he failed to recognize his one mistake until later, when he was back home in the shower and felt the injury on his neck where Owens had grabbed at his mask. Owens had scratched him. But it was too late to rectify the oversight.

"I was in such a frenzy after killing Wilton," he went on with the telling of his murder spree, "it took me a moment to realize I still had one more player to take out." He shook his head. "It was like playing a video game. Winning was my singular focus. I was just about to go back inside, looking for Alicia, when she rushed out onto the deck. In a moment of inspiration, I decided she would be my scapegoat. I made it appear as if she'd been leaving the scene and fell, hitting her head. I put the knife I'd used under her and then I left."

He made a sound, not quite a laugh but something on that order. "It all went almost exactly as I'd planned. A few glitches notwithstanding." He exhaled a big breath, looked to Vera. "Even so, you didn't have my DNA and no way to get it without a court order based on evidence, which you didn't have." His face tightened with anger. "I shouldn't have underestimated Valeri Erwin's need for her own revenge. She left me that fucking note, and I foolishly reacted. Then you showed up." He shook his head. "I was so close to walking away unscathed."

Vera opted not to mention that close only counted in a game of horseshoes. But there was one little part she was unclear on.

"You mentioned a note from Erwin. When did you receive this note?"

"She left a note at my gate early this morning. *I know it was you.*" He shook his head. "Not exactly original, but it got the point across. She didn't sign it, but apparently she didn't care that I knew she was the one who left it, since she smiled for the camera at the gate."

Why was Vera not surprised? The woman truly was a piece of work.

A couple minutes later Jamison was escorted away in handcuffs. Vera and Bent stood in the corridor outside the interview room and watched him be led away. She stretched her neck and rolled her left shoulder. Her back and shoulder were killing her from hitting the ground with the bastard. She hadn't pulled a move like the one she'd used to take Jamison down in years. God, she was out of shape.

"You just wait," Bent said, "when all that cockiness vanishes after a few nights in a cell, he'll be trying to plead an insanity defense."

Vera turned to Bent. "Until then, I guess that closes your case. Well except for Larry Parson's murder."

He removed his hat and ran his fingers through his hair. "I have this top-notch crime analyst." He smiled at her as he replaced that beloved hat. "I was hoping she'd help me figure that one out."

Vera laughed. "I think I may already have a lead on it."

"You want a final shot at Erwin?" Bent grinned, understanding exactly what she meant. "She's in the lobby, waiting for word on how this is going to shake down."

Vera gave him a nod. "I would love it."

"Give me a minute to settle her in my office. You can talk to her there."

"Works for me." This was going to be epic. She could feel it.

Bent hesitated. "Thanks, Vee. You make my job easy."

"Yeah, well, it's definitely a joint effort." Her cell vibrated in her back pocket. She slipped it out and checked the screen. "It's Luna." Her heart stumbled. She hoped this wasn't more bad news. "Hey, Lu, everything okay?"

"Jerome's father is conscious, and he's good, Vee. Really good. They may even release him tomorrow or the next day if his condition remains stable."

"That's wonderful news, Luna. Jerome's father is awake and doing great," she said to Bent. He'd hung back when she'd told him it was Luna calling.

"Vee, put me on speaker," Luna urged. "Bent needs to hear this next part."

"Let's go to my office," Bent suggested. "I'll get Erwin when we're done."

"Hold on," Vera told her sister. "We're going to Bent's office." Vera couldn't wait to hear the rest. Had to be related to Jackie's death, since Luna wanted Bent to hear, too, and she sounded upbeat, excited even. Thank God.

Once they were settled in his office, Vera told her little sister to let loose.

"It was Geneva," Luna explained. "Jackie called her and told her that she and I had argued and that we fell down the stairs. She just didn't mention that she was the one who pushed me. Anyway, we know Geneva went over to my house while I was at the hardware store because, like you said, the phone records showed she did. After that she went to Jackie and Leonard's house and told Leonard that Jackie was dead. She even said that now the two of them could be together. Can you believe that?"

Vera smiled. She could, actually. And Luna was right. "The phone records show that Geneva left your house and drove to Leonard's house, arriving in that area around 11:20. If she told Leonard that Jackie was dead, how did she know that? I hadn't even arrived at your house at that point."

"That's the thing," Luna cried, her voice quavering. "She could not have known unless she was the one who killed her!"

"Luna," Bent said, "did Leonard say anything else about Geneva's visit to him?"

"He kept saying he couldn't believe Geneva just left him there after he started having chest pains. She used his phone to call 911 and thrust it at him, then took off like she didn't want anyone to know she had been there."

Vera shook her head. What a heartless bitch. "Maybe she thought if he survived, he wouldn't remember her even being there."

"Maybe so," Luna agreed.

"Vee and I will finish this for you, Lu," Bent promised. "You and Jerome focus on his father."

As soon as the call ended, Bent invited Erwin into his office and went back to the business of arrest reports with Myra. Like Vera, he understood that Erwin would open up more to Vera without him in the room.

Vera settled behind Bent's desk so she could face the woman.

"Is it over?" Erwin dropped into a chair. "I've been waiting forever to hear something."

"Mostly," Vera confirmed. "You were right about the aftershave. It was Brut, but our attacker wasn't Larry Parson. It was Jose Martinez." Conover had found a bottle in the bathroom at the house he and Hernandez rented from Carter.

"Are you serious?" Her face scrunched in concentration. "Maybe I had smelled that aftershave on him before, but I don't remember." She hugged herself as if the memory disturbed her. "I don't usually get that close to him. He always scared me. I guess that's why I don't recall it." She stared at Vera then. "Why would he do that?"

Vera decided that was her cue. "I can tell you everything I know if you tell me what you know."

Erwin's gaze narrowed. "That sounds like blackmail."

"No." Vera shook her head, reminding herself to be patient. The woman was exasperating. "It's a negotiation."

Erwin shrugged. "Okay. What is it you want to know?"

"Based on our encounter with Jamison in your apartment, you're the one who told Thomas that his first wife was cheating on him. Is that correct?"

Erwin hesitated a moment. "I felt it was my obligation as his friend and his assistant."

Vera supposed that was a reasonable assertion. "Did you have anything to do with her accident?"

Erwin's guard went up then. "Of course not. Why would I do anything like that?"

That was the question. "But you said Jose Martinez was supposed to have fixed the problem with the saddle. How did you know that?"

She shrugged. "Because Lena said Jose should take care of it for her. He always did things like that for her."

Vera had a feeling she knew where the ball had been dropped. "Who told Jose to take care of it?"

Erwin blinked. "What?"

"Did Lena tell him, or were you supposed to tell him?"

A frown furrowed its way across her brow. "I don't know. I ordered the parts she told me to order."

Vera's instincts were right. "But when the parts came in, you didn't mention this to Jose, did you?"

Erwin pouted. "I don't remember. Thomas kept me very busy. I didn't have time to deal with Lena's needs. She should have taken care of it herself. Besides, it wasn't my fault she didn't check or that she was thrown off and injured. Or," she ground out, "that she didn't go to the doctor when she should have because she was too proud to admit to anyone that she'd fallen off her stupid horse."

Vera nodded. Maybe not exactly murder. But exactly what a psychopath would do. "There's something else you've been hiding all this time. I want to know what it is."

"You're supposed to tell me something," she tossed back at Vera. "Tit for tat, Ms. Boyett."

Vera gave her a nod. "Gill Jamison confessed to killing Thomas, Seth Parson, and Sandy Owens."

Erwin scoffed. "No surprise there."

"Why did you leave that note? Weren't you afraid he would come after you?"

She turned her hands up. "It was looking more and more like he was going to get away with it, and I couldn't prove what I believed. I needed him to make a move you"—she glared at Vera—"would notice."

"We certainly appreciate your help, but you could have just told me." It was obvious to Vera that Erwin couldn't stand knowing what she knew and believing that no one else did.

Erwin shrugged. "I guess I didn't really think it through."

"But there's more, right? More secrets you've been keeping that we didn't figure out." Vera needed her talking. Bragging. Showing off all that she knew and Vera didn't. Playing to her ego was the fastest way to make that happen.

Erwin puffed out a breath. "Fine. I guess it doesn't matter now, anyway. I was in love with him. Thomas. I thought after Lena died, he would want me. I did everything for him. He told me over and over that he didn't know what he would do without me, and then he didn't want me. Not for a wife. I think the others—Helen and Renata for sure—knew how I felt. I figured they would try to use it against me. When I found that phone, I knew they were trying to frame me."

Vera nodded. "You did use that phone to lure Seth Parson up here in hopes of breaking up Thomas and Alicia's marriage, didn't you?"

"You can't prove that," she countered, her expression cocky.

"Probably not." Vera cleared her throat. "How about I give you one more thing and then you give me one more?"

Erwin shrugged as if she suddenly found the whole game boring. "Why not?"

"Alicia said Thomas wanted to take you with them to California."

Something like glee filled her eyes, and she smiled. "I knew he wouldn't leave me."

Vera opted not to mention that Alicia had changed his mind. The point was moot now. "Tell me the rest of the story about Nola Childers."

Confusion lined her face. "I already told you everything."

"It feels like you're holding something back, Valeri," Vera argued.

Erwin held up her hands, surrender-style. "Fine. Fine. Everything happened just like I said, and FYI, she took Xanax that night too. Really stupid, and everyone thought she was so smart."

Vera rolled her hand in a gesture of keep going.

Big sigh. "I told you I passed out, but I didn't. When she was in the bath so long, I went to check on her and she was under the water. I started to pull her out, but then I didn't."

No matter that she had suspected as much, Vera was still startled by the woman's coldness. "Was she dead already?"

Erwin made a face. "I don't know. I just walked out and closed the door."

"You didn't try to help her. You didn't even check?"

"No." She stared at her hands clasped in her lap. "I dream about her sometimes," she said softly, as if suddenly feeling bad about what happened. "I see her under that water."

There was a lot Vera would like to have said to her just then, but none of it would matter or change her way of seeing things. Instead she decided there was a far more important secret to prod out of her. Yet another depraved act she couldn't prove, but her gut said she was right. "You went into Larry Parson's motel room, didn't you?"

Erwin's guard was back up again. "I don't know what you're talking about."

"Sure you do. Helen Carter said she noticed your car there when she was leaving after planting that baseball bat and other stuff in his motel room." This was a total lie, but Erwin couldn't be sure.

Vera's phone vibrated with an incoming text. She read the news from Conover and smiled. She looked to Erwin once more. "No point lying to me, Valeri."

"Okay. Yes, I went to his room. I knew he was the one who attacked us, or at least I thought so. But it's not like I broke in or anything." Another of those big huffy exhales. "The truth is, I followed Helen there. I knew she was up to something. I watched her break into his room. She had barely gotten into her car before he was driving back into the lot." She laughed. "Old Helen almost got herself caught. Anyway, I was curious about why she'd gone in there, so I knocked on his door. He invited me in, and I demanded that he tell me the truth about what he'd done. But he just kept saying he had no idea what I was talking about. He said he was just here to find out what happened to his brother. I didn't really believe him, though."

"He offered you a drink." Again Vera was following her gut here.

Erwin's gaze narrowed. "So what. I'm over twenty-one. If a guy offers me a drink, I can take it."

How cavalier she sounded. She clearly felt absolutely no regret for her actions. Vera had encountered her fair share of psychopaths, but Valeri Erwin was one of the coldest, and yet she gave the appearance of being harmless.

"Sure," Vera agreed, "but you left him a little something in his glass, didn't you? Something to go with his whiskey."

For about two seconds a challenge sparked in Erwin's eyes. She wanted Vera to know what she had done and gotten away with. But she caught herself just in time.

"I have no idea what you're talking about." She folded her arms over her chest. "You should talk to Helen. If something bad was put in his glass, she had to have done it."

"But you did have a drink with him?" Vera pressed.

"Sure, what of it?"

"Where's the glass you used?"

That deer-caught-in-the-headlights look kicked aside her smug expression.

"You see, our forensics guy checked, and the other glass—there are two to a room—is missing from Larry Parson's room. Did you take it with you? Like a souvenir?"

She shrugged again. "Maybe. I don't remember. What's the big deal?"

"Why did you steal the glass? If you only had a drink, what did it matter if you left your prints in the room on that glass?"

"I was just being careful," she argued, feeling cocky again. "Besides, whoever put something in his glass, no one made him drink it."

"He's dead, Valeri," Vera pointed out.

"I didn't kill him. He killed himself. Like I said, talk to Helen. She was the one who broke into his room."

"We'll need your statement regarding your visit to him. Don't leave anything out, Valeri. Word for word, all that you just told me. I'll tell Bent if you forget anything."

Erwin rolled her eyes. "Fine. And what do I get for that?"

Three to fifteen years, Vera suspected. She rounded up a notepad and a pen and placed both in front of Erwin. "We'll see how thorough your statement is, then I'll let you know if I still owe you something."

Anticipation lit Erwin's face as she picked up the pen and started to write. Vera doubted whatever came out in her statement would prove she'd murdered Larry Parson. But one of them—Erwin or Carter—had poisoned him. All they had to do was find where the fentanyl came from.

A needle in a haystack . . . but if they kept digging, they would find it eventually.

One way or another, Valeri Erwin was going down.

42

Fanning Residence
Lincoln Avenue, 5:30 p.m.

As Vera and Bent approached the door to the Fanning home, four other deputies had surrounded the property, ensuring no one left before the sheriff was finished.

Trenton Fanning opened the door before they rang the bell. "Sheriff." He looked to Vera. "Ms. Boyett."

"We need to speak with Mrs. Fanning," Bent said.

"Come on in. We've been waiting for you."

Vera glanced at Bent. They had been waiting for them? Then again, her husband was on the county council. He likely had a contact in the sheriff's department.

"Geneva is in the parlor. This way."

Trenton led the way into the room on the left. His wife, dressed to the nines and makeup just so, sat on the elegant sofa. Bent removed his hat and, like Vera, waited for the show to begin.

"It was an accident."

Vera wanted to hold up a hand and ask what kind of charade this was, but she figured it might be best to let the woman talk.

"Ma'am," Bent interrupted.

Vera wanted to punch him, but she got it. He had to do this right.

"It might be best if you called your attorney for this," he suggested.

Vera barely resisted rolling her eyes.

"I do not want my attorney," she announced. "I waive my rights. Now listen, I don't want to have to say this twice."

Her husband stood behind her. Vera wondered if he was already planning his new life with the lady from his accounting firm.

"I rushed over to the house after Jackie called. She was upstairs, putting the furniture back in place in the nursery. She told me what she'd done." She glanced at Vera. "She almost killed poor Luna."

Vera almost gagged at her fake sympathy.

"I don't want to think what would have happened to the baby." She drew in a big breath. "Anyway, I was telling her how awful what she'd done was. We finished up in the nursery and were walking toward the stairs when she lit into me like she was possessed by a demon." She batted her fake eyelashes. "Why, Sheriff, I had to defend myself. We struggled, and I was swatting and kicking at her." She gave Vera the side-eye. "I was wearing my favorite boots. You'll find them in my closet. Anyway, the next thing I knew she was flying down the stairs, and I barely—I mean barely—kept from falling myself." She let go of another breath. "She died instantly. There was nothing I could do. I suppose I was in shock, because all I could think to do was rush over and tell Leonard."

Vera kept her mouth shut when what she wanted to do was say, *Well that was some story. When are we going to hear the truth?* But at least this removed any doubt whatsoever from Luna. Vera would take it.

"Ma'am, you understand there will have to be an official investigation, and if Mrs. Andrews's death is ruled a homicide, you'll be charged with manslaughter, maybe even murder."

Her lips trembled, and one eye twitched. "I do."

"All right then," Bent said. "I'll need you to go to the station with Deputy Hastings and write up your statement, and we'll go from there."

Vera felt almost let down. She'd anticipated a big showdown, and instead they got a prettied-up confession. Well, at least it was over. The Boyett sisters could breathe easy again . . . at least for a little while.

There were no other secrets that Vera was aware of. And the homicide case was mostly done. She and Bent were due a break.

Benton Ranch
Old Molino Road, 9:00 p.m.

Vera ended the call. She released a sigh and reached for her wineglass.

"Everything okay with Luna?"

Bent dried another plate from the dinner they had shared. They'd had Chinese delivered. Who wanted to cook after the day they'd survived?

"She and Jerome are okay. It'll take time to put this behind them, but at least he knows the truth. And his father will probably get to come home on Monday."

"Good news." Bent put the plate away and tossed the towel on the counter. "While you were in the shower, Alicia Wilton called me."

Vera drew back. "Why didn't you tell me before now?"

"Because the food arrived, and I didn't want it to get cold." That slow, easy smile that always made her smile right back no matter the situation spread across his lips. "Besides, it was all good news. She'll be coming home next week as well. She wanted to thank us for all we did to bring her husband's and friends' murderer to justice."

Vera studied the wine in her glass. "I wonder what her plan for the future is?"

"She mentioned that she plans to move forward with the sale so she can relocate to that Southern California town her husband loved so much." He shrugged. "Their child should be raised there, she said."

"Wow. That's a good plan." Vera sipped her wine. There was so much she wanted to say to him right now. After all she'd heard and seen the past few days. The ugliest side of relationships . . . the most hurtful aspect of human nature. The up-close look at unexpected loss like the murder of a husband just when there was so much to look forward to. The death of a mother, who should have been looking forward to her first grandchild rather than trying to destroy lives. Not that she hadn't seen this sort of thing before, but this was fresh . . . new. Life was so very short and sometimes uncertain.

Even amid all the tragedy, she had also seen determination and survival. That was the part that reminded her there was still time . . .

"Bent."

He picked up his beer and took a swig. "Yeah?"

"I want us to make a plan."

He set the beer aside, studied her a moment. "What sort of plan?"

"Our plan." Her nerves were suddenly jangling, and she figured she had better set her glass down before she dropped it. She placed it on the counter next to his beer. "Our future. I want *this* to be *our* home like we talked about. Not just where we've chosen to live together but our home. Our special forever place. And not at some point but now. Right now."

The spark of happiness in his eyes made her heart skip. What in the world had she been waiting for? It was time—past time. She couldn't wait to see what came next for them.

Bent leaned down, kissed her cheek. "I would love that. I love you, and this is where I want to be—with you, always."

Vera was beyond ready to get on with the rest of her life, and she wanted to share the news with her sisters. It was about damned time the Boyett sisters—all three of them—had their happily ever afters.

Hers and Bent's started right here, right now.

ACKNOWLEDGMENTS

Thanks to all the folks who live in Lincoln County, especially Fayetteville, who have overlooked my embellishments and creative license when writing these stories. It is a joy to live in this lovely community.

ABOUT THE AUTHOR

Photo © 2019 Jenni M Photography LLC

Debra Webb is a *USA Today* bestselling author of more than 170 novels. She is the recipient of the prestigious *Romantic Times* Career Achievement Award for Romantic Suspense, as well as numerous Reviewers' Choice Awards. In 2012, Webb was honored as the first recipient of the esteemed L. A. Banks Warrior Woman Award for her courage, strength, and grace in the face of adversity. After publishing her hundredth novel, she also received the distinguished Centennial Award. The author has sold more than ten million books in numerous languages and countries.

Debra's love of storytelling goes back to her childhood, when her mother bought her an old typewriter at a tag sale. Born in Alabama, she grew up on a farm and spent every available hour exploring the world around her and creating stories. To learn more about the author and her work, visit her website at https://debrawebb.com.